MAGDALENA
THE SINNER

MAGDALENA
THE SINNER

a novel

LILIAN FASCHINGER

Translated by Edna McCown

HarperCollins*Publishers*

HarperCollins books may be purchased for educational, business, or sales promotional use. For information please write: Special Markets Department, HarperCollins Publishers, Inc., 10 East 53rd Street, New York, NY 10022.

FIRST EDITION

Designed by Elina D. Nudelman

Library of Congress Cataloging-in-Publication Data

Faschinger, Lilian, 1950–
   [Magdalena Sünderin. English]
   Magdalena the sinner : a novel / by Lilian Faschinger.
      p.   cm.
   ISBN 0-06-018653-4
   I. Title.
PT2666.A76M3413   1997
833'.914—dc21   97-7297

97 98 99 00 01 ❖/HC 10 9 8 7 6 5 4 3 2 1

For my friends

It's vague, life and death.

—SAMUEL BECKETT, *MALONE DIES*

MAGDALENA
THE SINNER

"Hear me now, Reverend. *Listen with your* ear, your Catholic priestly ear, finely tuned as it is to the nuances of both grave and venial sins, an ear you have turned in compassion to so many. You will not have the choice of closing your fine Catholic ears, with their dark blond hairs sprouting from the outer auditory canal. It is impossible to cover your ears when your hands are bound. Nor shall you have the opportunity to drown out what I will tell you with prayer formulas and liturgical song, or to summon your organist to help you by drowning out with pedal notes what I say. Your organist, with his organ and his pedal notes, is far away. It is impossible to call for help with a gag in your mouth, just as it is impossible to proclaim prayer formulas or intone liturgical song with a gag in your mouth. You are helpless, Reverend. Like apples pelted against a windshield by spiteful children, my words, my sentences will beat down on your eardrums such that the membranes will begin to vibrate horribly as the sound waves emitted from my mouth are swiftly conveyed to your hammer, anvil, and stirrup. Your stirrup will hasten them along to your inner ear by way of your *fenestra ovalis*. The sonic pressure, magnified one hundred and eighty times, will penetrate your oscillatory cochlea like a metal ball speeding along the spiral path of a pinball machine on its way to your tympanic cavity. The nerve impulses will hurry across your auditory nerve to your cerebral cortex, which ultimately will be responsible for seeing to it that you hear me. The little bulbs in your brain will flash red, green, blue, and yellow like a lighting console rhythmically connected to the music of my words, and finally, you shall hear me."

So began the sinner, after she had sat me down under an acacia in the high grass of early summer and forced my back against the trunk, where my hands could feel the warm cracks in the bark despite the fact that they gradually were beginning to lose all feeling because of the faded rope they were tied with. As she tightened the knot of the green nylon clothesline that bound my ankles, she continued talking.

"It's an odd thing, Reverend," she said, "but even now that you're in my hands, totally in my hands, all the way down to your alb, dalmatic, and stole, even now I fear that one of those saints you summon up with such alarming frequency and for such various reasons could come to your aid and with one gesture of his hands, tapered by countless woodcutters making countless cuts, render me motionless, as motionless as you are now, could strike me dumb with one single glance from those martyr's eyes, painted and repainted by countless fresco painters, as dumb as you are now. It calls for every scrap of my Alpine reason, every particle of what remains of my once highly developed Austrian sense of reality, to deflect my fear of such a miracle, the fear, for example, that St. Sebastian, wasted and pierced with arrows, could step out of the underbrush into this clearing with his oddly springy gait, pull out an arrow, and send it through my heart, which longs to confess, before I have poured it out to you. The fear that St. Catherine could glide down from the crown of this acacia, amazingly fresh and unscathed after her death on the wheel, and, with a single word from her holy lips, undo the knots in the nylon clothesline and faded rope that took such effort to tie, take you in her arms, and disappear again into the crown of the acacia. The fear that at your intercession St. George could gallop up on a bay sorrel, lift you onto the saddle with him, and carry you off, not, however, before slicing off my head with one swift stroke of his sword. I must banish such images, such absolutely unfounded fantasies, for it is I who have just carried you off from the small parish you so carefully tend, from the church with the pretty little burgundy dome, in which you were celebrating the Pentecostal mass."

Having uttered these words the sinner shook her long, strawberry blond hair, sat down in front of me in the grass, and paused for a moment to squint up at the sun. I felt the hairs stand up on my forearms at the memory of the event that so abruptly had changed my life.

"It was much more difficult than I had imagined," she said then. "Though I've been watching you for days, and had become familiar with your priestly routine. Perhaps I should have chosen another situation, a situation in which you would have been alone. I should have stuck the barrel of my Smith & Wesson in your back as you were softly droning on about the Holy Spirit, arranging the red and white Pentecostal roses in the vases, and changing the candles on the altar, having already covered it with the red Pentecostal cloth. I should have surprised you in the sacristy as you were polishing the requisites for mass, the baptismal bowl, the Communion cup, the ciborium; I should have lain in wait for you evenings in the cemetery that surrounds your church and put my black motorcycle glove over your mouth as you were making your way from the church to the parsonage. Perhaps that's what I should have done, it would have been much easier. What made me choose the Pentecostal mass as the stage for my action was my proclivity for the spectacle, my inclination toward the sensational, my love of the public.

"I need a public, Reverend, a need you as a priest undoubtedly will understand. The public is the eyewitness, without a public every act is meaningless from the outset, an attentive public is proof of an active existence. You must admit that my action was a noteworthy public event, which must have elicited a strong feeling of solidarity, a sense of the primary brotherhood of man. As we sit here now under this acacia tree, in this remote place, the ripple effect of my Pentecostal public action, my successful church happening, is growing. People from your parish, mortal enemies who have been shifting the border stones marking their property lines back and forth secretly at night for decades now, are approaching each other to ask: Any news of our priest? Has the chapter put up ransom money?

"So, Reverend, the two of us made a great team in setting in motion an event that finally will restore to the collective its finest feelings of solidarity. You went along with me instinctively, proof of your sense of the dramatic. For that I congratulate you. The look you gave me as you turned at the sound of my heavy motorcycle boots in the midst of the transubstantiation was quite expressive and will remain forever in the minds of your congregation. Your eyes wide, your body frozen, your hand as it let go of the Communion cup as I marched up to you, the visor of my motorcycle helmet hiding my face: You're a natural, Reverend, a born actor. Restraint, economy of movement coupled with intense expression—you appear to have the gift. Your altar boy, unfortunately, didn't exhibit the same theatrical quality, which probably can be attributed to his youth. The way he childishly lost his head and gave those sharp little cries as he began to swing the censer back and forth when he saw that I was threatening you rent the translucent theatricality of my act; on the other hand, the clouds of smoke he created allowed me to abscond with you, the victim of my abduction. But it might also be said that your altar boy's lack of feeling for the finer degrees of dramatic nuance was compensated for by the tremendous spontaneity of his performance.

"The congregation behaved beautifully: Rising from their seats, they followed with apprehension and amazement the individual stages of the scene I had set into motion, a response most directors could only dream of. From their expressions it could be surmised that they soon would experience an inner catharsis, be gripped by fear and sympathy as soon as I exited the nave with you. And it is this catharsis that gives my admittedly drastic act its humanitarian justification, and it should fill you with pride, Reverend, that you contributed to this purification of the human heart. There was something magnificent, something even nuptial about the two of us walking down the aisle toward the Roman portal, flanked by the faithful standing in respectful silence. With your instinctive flair for the dramatic you immediately grasped the possibilities inherent in this little scene, keeping your eyes straight ahead despite, or because of, the pressure of my Smith & Wesson against your back, your priestly head raised and showing not the least irritation that your organist up on the balcony, cued by the cries of your altar boy, long since had broken off his playing to look down in horror and call out: Reverend, stay! Your congregation needs you! Yes, there was definitely something of a wedding about it: I, the bridegroom, leading you from the church and into a new life following the nuptials, you, the bride, obeying the one you had been chosen by with respect and humility. A success, I thought to myself, once I had escorted you to the sidecar of my Puch, seated you in it, and driven away with you. Superb adherence to the unity of time, place, and action, the model of ideal theater."

The sinner stopped talking to pluck a few blades of grass from the earth, and then a clover leaf.

"Not a four-leaf clover," she said. "I've looked for a four-leaf clover my entire life. Not one single time have I ever found one. That has not been granted me. Others stroll through the landscape and as soon as they look down they spot a four-leaf clover. They go home with entire bouquets of four-leaf red clover, white clover, crimson clover, alsike clover. They shower them on friends and relatives who place the clover leaves in books and then stack other, bigger books on top of them. They have whole towers of books piled up in their apartments, pillars of the *Brockhaus* encyclopedia, atlases, the *Encyclopaedia Britannica*, and in every single book at the bottom of the pile, a paperback edition of Burton's *Anatomy of Melancholy*, say, or the letters of Maria Theresa to her daughter, Marie Antoinette, or an earmarked copy of Frost, in every bottom book there is a long-since dried-up four-leaf clover. These friends and relatives scarcely know how to protect themselves from the well-meaning gifts of those destined to find four-leaf clovers, they permit four-leaf clovers to be pressed upon them, one after the other, with the result that they find it increasingly difficult to move around their aesthetically furnished old apartments, forced as they are to make their way through towers of books, each of which houses a barely, or halfway, or totally pressed four-leaf clover.

"I, however, find nothing," she said, twirling the stem of a little three-leaf crimson clover in her fingers, "nothing is what I find. My life being as unencumbered as it is, I have plenty of opportunity to wander about, park my Puch side-car motorcycle next to some hazel bush, follow some meadow path, and let my eyes wander through grass shot through with clover. I make a beeline for clover leaves, thinking, this time a four-leaf clover. It is not a four-leaf clover, however, but an ordinary *Trifolium hybridum*, an ordinary *Trifolium incarnatum*, a truly ordinary *Trifolium pratense*. You're deep in thought, Reverend. Perhaps you're asking yourself whether I'm nearsighted, whether it's due to a hereditary or acquired nearsightedness that I have never found a four-leaf clover. I assure you that it is not, I have extraordinarily sharp eyes, sharp eyes are a legacy of my father's side of the family, my father's side of the family is equipped with extraordinarily sharp eyesight. On top of which, spotting four-leaf clovers has nothing to do with having sharp eyes, something I have learned over the course of time. It has to do with intuition, Reverend, with intuition pure and simple. Someone who has the gift of clover will go into a field of clover, of white clover, say, or purple clover, in which there are no more than two four-leaf clovers, stop for a moment to sniff the air, the four-leaf clover air, and then, without hesitation, walk over to a certain spot in the meadow, bend down, stand up again holding one of the two four-leaf clovers in his right hand, turn, walk out of the meadow, and present this four-leaf clover to his companion.

"I seem to remember reading in an American scientific journal that at Yale, or, to be precise, around Yale they conducted an experiment with a representational cross-section of people who are sensitive to four-leaf clovers and people who are not, the sensitive and the nonsensitive being chosen from various age groups, various races, various social classes, various sexes, and various religious confessions, and then sent out into the clover fields of Connecticut. The results, apparently, were bewildering. The most ungifted of the sensitive nevertheless found 25.8 percent more four-leaf clovers on average than the most gifted of the nonsensitive. The difficulty in establishing quasi-ideal conditions for these experiments consisted less in coming up with a representative number of the sensitive and nonsensitive than, as you might imagine, in taking a complete pre-experiment inventory of four-leaf clovers in the clover fields of Connecticut, chosen for these experiments with the understanding of their owners.

"That I do not number among the exclusive group of finders of four-leaf clovers is a fact I must live with. It is a gift that life has withheld from me, as much as I would like to claim otherwise. We are not talking about an ability that one might acquire through practice. You can stand for hours each day in fields rich in clover: If you are not gifted you will find catchfly, buttercups, and yarrow, adderwort and annual bluegrass even, but no four-leaf clover. One simply must accept this, just as one accepts all the other adversities, disappointments, absurdity, and disenchantment that life offers. And you must also see the positive side of this nongiftedness:

It prevents even more towers of books from springing up in aesthetically furnished old apartments, towers that would take up even more space and further limit the movement of the aesthetes who occupy these aesthetically furnished old apartments. This thought has always been a comfort to me."

The sinner smiled at me. She had a forehead so high and so perfectly formed, rounding upward and slightly outward, that it frightened me a little, with translucent little veins in her temples and a thicker vein running down the middle of her forehead that seemed to swell or contract in direct proportion to the urgency of her speech. An obstinate chin, cool blue eyes that could darken to blue-black, also depending on the degree of passion with which she spoke, a small round mole roughly eight-tenths of an inch above the right corner of her mouth. All of this in a baroque frame of strawberry blond hair that fell far below her shoulders. Her smile deepened.

"What are you looking at, Reverend? No, don't lower your eyes, look at me. Look at me. Take in everything your eyes can hold, let them roam over me at will, let them, accustomed to privation as they are, feast."

She continued in this vein, stretching her upper body in her black leather jumpsuit and sitting in the grass like some malevolent mermaid washed up onto shore. Then she reached up to her neck and unzipped the long silver zipper an inch or two, revealing a shimmering triangle of skin that gently rose and fell, creating a play of light and shadow on the skin's surface, the sight of which suddenly made me so uncomfortable that I turned my eyes upward to contemplate the leafy foliage our Maker had created in such lush abundance, not without first involuntarily watching as the sinner raised her arms to run her long white fingers through her strawberry blond curls, loosing a fireworks of yellow and red reflections of light. While I, stimulated by the early summer foliage, kept my eyes turned to heaven and tried to lose myself in a lengthy contemplation of the infinite variety of divine nature, she continued to talk, her husky voice, which I was forced to listen to because of my limited potential for movement, nipping my meditation in the bud.

"Priests never look you in the face, except in cases of extreme emergency," she said. "They either lower their eyes, because, I would suppose, of the demands of Catholic humility, or raise them to heaven, to praise God, I assume. The effort they make to avoid looking at the average person has always irritated me, their eyes are almost always focused exclusively on the extreme forms of humanity, either on those crawling along the ground or those ascending to heaven, neither of which I myself personally feel drawn to. But sometimes a priest's eyes dart quickly to one side, quick as a chameleon's tongue, to size up the average person in a fraction of a second before returning to heaven or earth. Why don't you look me in the face, Reverend? What have you got to hide? What are you afraid of? It's clear that these and any other questions that follow are purely rhetorical on my part. I hope you will forgive my insistence on this rhetorical form. To tell the truth, I am not the least bit interested in your answers, as the black gag I have stuffed in your mouth surely makes clear, a gag that I created, incidentally, by twisting up a black Kashiyama bodysuit, ideal for this purpose because of its elasticity. Prior to your abduction I practiced a bit of gagging and tying, so as not to leave anything to chance. I am someone who does not like leaving things to chance. The knots binding your wrists are a clove hitch, whereas those at your ankles are a cow hitch. It's completely up to you whether I will have to tie a double sheet bend or not. Surely you're aware that knots that are tied correctly get tighter the more you strain against them, for which reason I will discourage you from making any sudden movements.

"It's a matter of you listening quietly without interrupting me—I who have been constantly interrupted—and without cutting me off—I who have constantly been cut off. Were you to cut me off, were you to interrupt me, it would put you in great danger, greater danger than you already find yourself in. Having so often been interrupted, so often been cut off, I am hypersensitive, irritable in the extreme when it comes to the flow of my thoughts or my words, respectively, being arrested. If you're constantly interrupted you never get past the babble stage, a frustrating condition that results in terrible anxiety, making the one who is thinking or talking, respectively, highly unpredictable. There are those who specialize in systematically sabotaging the even flow of other people's thought, diverters, interrupters, breakers-in, disconcerters, know-it-alls, interveners, hecklers, whisperers, and so on, among whom, of course, must be counted one's parents and blood relatives, followed by entire professions, at the apex of which stand teachers from the elementary and middle schools, from vocational schools, high schools, and universities, as well as all types of psychologists, psychiatrists, psychoanalysts, psychotherapists, and other so-called ministers to the spirit. As you belong to the last, I have taken precautions so that our conversation might proceed unimpeded, at the end of which, more than likely, I shall remove the Kashiyama bodysuit, put it on again under my leather jumpsuit, and ask you to utter one sentence only: *Ego te absolvo.*"

A bit surprised by these words I diverted my eyes from the

crown of the acacia and directed them at the face of the sinner, as she pensively stroked with her right index finger the
dark brown mole above her lip, without, however, pausing in
her speech.

"I want to make a confession, Reverend, that's all. For
decades now I have tried to create the right conditions for
making a confession, but as yet I have not succeeded. It
began with my parents. Any attempt to confide in my mother
or my father failed. My mother interrupted me each time I
reached my second sentence, usually saying: Don't talk such
nonsense, and then she would go in the kitchen and put on
some water for tea. My father would mutter something or
other about my being a complicated child, and slam the door
of his study—at which I was standing in order to unburden
myself—in my face. My teachers would listen to me with
expressions of displeasure until roughly the beginning of my
fourth sentence, usually during recess, standing in the hall
that echoed with the noise of the other students. I could feel
their impatience and would stutter, and my fourth sentence
would dissolve in a slow fade, at which the teachers would
clamp our corrected and uncorrected homework notebooks
under their arms and say: We'll have the opportunity to
speak about this later in greater detail. But right now I'm in a
hurry, I've got a test to give sixth period. Reverend, you can
see what a devastating effect such rebuffs would have on a
little girl's innocent eagerness to confess. Dedicated to the
Christian principle of *agape* as you are, you will surely understand that the little girl with the high forehead, standing at
the kitchen door, the study door, the classroom door,
defenseless in the face all of these huge wooden doors, would
be compelled to pile up all of these unarticulated thoughts,
these undelivered speeches inside her, like crates of dynamite

in a secret underground depot. You will be able to imagine how the little girl with the strawberry blond hair would go back and forth between her disappointing house and her disappointing school, how her path would become more and more wearisome, the dynamite cases increasing in number and weight. The university changed none of this. Following a passionate classroom session devoted to Erasmus of Rotterdam and European humanism delivered by a young lecturer in a loden jacket, the girl with the dark brown mole above the right corner of her mouth, who had grown in the meantime, went up to him, full of hope, and began opening one of her cases of dynamite. The young lecturer shivered, pulled his loden jacket to his narrow chest, and took two steps backward. Come by during my office hours, he interrupted in the midst of her third sentence, after which he cleared his throat and covered his mouth with the hand bearing a signet ring on the little finger. As he canceled his next three office hours, the girl, who had grown in the meantime and whose hair now fell far below her shoulders, went to see a psychologist, who interrupted her first sentence to ask her to take a multiple-choice test, during which, he said, she should remain silent. A half-hour later he snatched the test away and shoved her out the door with the comment: You are not alone! I ask you, Reverend, would anyone be surprised that after all of this I arrived at the dangerous idea of setting a slow fuse to the dynamite in my underground depot and blowing it sky-high, simply in order finally to unburden myself? Had I arrived at the idea of forcing someone to hear me out sooner, perhaps I would not have become a murderess and killed seven men."

The sinner looked at me.

"You look at me as if to say: Why didn't you go to a Catholic confessional, one of the many in this land and the countries that surround it? Is that what you mean to ask with your inquisitive expression, your hazel eyes opened wide? I will not keep you waiting for an answer to your silent question: Reverend, despite my aversion to that narrow, three-chambered booth I was thoroughly willing to enter one and convey my confession to an understanding and benevolent priest who would listen through the rhomboid grille. Despite the fact that the wooden benches in the confessional booth are hard and that the little window grille makes me think of jail, of high-security prisons, I was prepared to sit myself down and unburden myself to some kindly priest with a round face and a ruddy complexion. Once I had given up my sedentary life in favor of a nomadic one—for reasons I will get to later—my path often took me past a diverse variety of Catholic churches, Romanesque churches, Gothic churches, cathedrals, chapels, oratories, pastorates, cloisters, pilgrimage churches, and baptisteries. As soon as I sold all of my movable and immovable possessions I bought a Puch sidecar motorcycle, in which I was always pulling up to Catholic churches.

"Despite my aversion to the smell of incense, which permeates churches like the smell of fish a fish store, like the smell of medicine an apothecary, I would take heart and pass through the Roman or early Gothic or late Gothic or high Baroque portals to stop before richly carved confessionals. I would sit myself down before priests from Burgundy, Burgenland, Bavaria, Sicily, and Wales, and begin my confession in German, French, Italian, or English, attempting, of course, to say what I had to say in an understandable, cogent, and interesting manner. My experiences were various and surprising, but never, not in one single case, was I able to give a full confession and receive absolution.

"Once, in an idyllic little church in Oxfordshire, the priest even fell asleep. I didn't notice, however, until roughly half an hour into my exhausting confession, that he was in a deep, sound, and relaxing slumber. I was confused, for I didn't know exactly when he had fallen asleep and how much of my confession he actually had heard. After all, I had related a murder to him in detail and feared it had all been in vain. I stuck my hand through the grille and poked his chest with my index finger to wake him up, at which he started with a scream, fixed me with a stare, crossed himself, and stammered something in Latin. Then he jumped up, pulled me out of the confession booth and over to the holy water font, and gave me a generous sprinkling of that strange liquid. Then he pushed me outside through the portal and I heard the gate close behind me with a dull thud. Looking for an explanation of his behavior I decided he must have had some terrible Catholic nightmare while seated in the confessional box. Annoyed, I mounted my Puch sidecar motorcycle and rode off through the autumnal forests of England, in the direction of Ascot-under-Wychwood.

"As disturbing as this episode was to me, it got even more unpleasant: Along the way, after the arduous experience of driving through the Furka Pass, I decided to attempt another confession in Oberwallis. The uncommon ugliness of the Swiss priest there has impressed itself upon my brain, his dirty hair long and sparse, his skull visible underneath, his continually smiling, thin-lipped mouth with its bad, yellow teeth, his receding chin, and the wart in the middle of his forehead. Just as I, intentionally disregarding the true sequence of events, was beginning a factual account of my third murder, his smile got even bigger and he stuck his arms through the rhomboid grille, his bony hands grabbing for my breasts, concealed as they were both by the black leather of my motorcycle jumpsuit and my Kashiyama bodysuit, and latching on to them with his long fingers. It took practically all the strength I could muster to escape those fingers, for the priest demonstrated a tenacity and body strength that was in direct contrast to his physiognomy. His priestly fingers attached themselves like a magnet to the leather. Only when I dug my long nails into the liver-spotted backs of his hands did he loosen his grip, allowing me the opportunity to give his slender thumb a good strong bite. He screamed, instantly pulled his fingers back through the grille, lurched out of the confession booth, and disappeared down a stone stairway into the crypt. I left the church quickly, not before casting an eye on the noticeably well-preserved frescoes in the vestibule. On the way to my motorcycle I considered how differently I would have reacted had the father confessor been a good-looking young priest, which caused me to recall another unsuccessful confession in one of the many Baroque churches of Syracuse. This memory was so pleasant that it kept me occupied all the way to Unterwallis.

"Once there, I sat patiently on the hard wooden bench of the Baroque confessional booth, waiting for a priest. When the little door was shoved open I looked up and right into the black-ringed amber retina of a Sicilian, who could not have been a priest for long. He smiled at me and bade me speak. I noticed that his young face, framed as it was by tawny hair, his strong throat, and his prominent Adam's apple all engaged my fantasy. Never have I told my story so vividly, so colorfully, so enthusiastically, and, at the same time, so convincingly and conclusively. The young priest listened attentively, giving an occasional nod at the elegant and insightful parts, and at other points casting down his eyes, with their long lashes. His cheeks began to flush, the delicate brown nostrils began to tremble almost imperceptibly. I first related an event from my early youth, a rather venial sin that nevertheless had caused me deep shame, and that I truly believed I regretted. Strangely enough, in relating the actual and extensive details of this embarrassing event I began to get a warm feeling, a physiological shift that appeared to affect the young priest as well, for he began fanning himself with his missal, though without turning his benevolent attention from me. The delicate and yet masculine gesture with which his powerful fingers moved the missal back and forth fired my imagination, which in turn heightened his willingness to hear me, evidenced by the burning look he was giving me.

"The heat rising from my side of the confessional booth was mixing at the grate with that emitted by his amber-colored Sicilian eyes. I suddenly noticed that I could no longer sustain the intensity of my tale, that the stress and tempo with which I was telling it had subsided, and I experienced a strangely weak feeling that crept up from the soles of my motorcycle boots through my calves and thighs, and then higher. On the other side of the grating the young Catholic priest briefly licked his lips, then pulled his tongue back into his mouth in shock and cleared his throat huskily. Because of my sudden weakness I lost the thread of my story and no longer knew what I was saying, so I simply stopped talking. Apparently overcome by a similar weakness, the priest briefly leaned his Botticelli-like head against the grate. At the same time I rested my overheated forehead against the cool bars and suddenly his tawny and my strawberry blond curls were entwining each other and the latticework grille. You will forgive me, Reverend, but at this point my memory of this event, which has always been clear as day to me, gets a

bit dim. With my inner eye I can see an image of hair and fingers intertwined, crisscrossed by the thin but solid grid bars.
What happened then, Reverend, what happened then? Did
we stand up and exit the confessional? Did each of us push
the wine red velvet curtain to one side? Did we proceed
without a word to the steps of the empty church that led up
to the organ gallery? Was it I who followed him? Was it he
who followed me, his priestly hands exploring the leather
about my waist? Reverend, the image blurs. And once in the
gallery, what happened there? The organ pipes that we
leaned against, the powerful labial and lingual pipes, were
cool at least. I remember a humming in my ears, a note you
have never heard your organist play. But there was no
organist in the gallery of the Baroque church in Syracuse,
the church was empty except for the young priest and me.
Did the heat between us create air currents, vortexes that
caused the pipes to sound, did we ourselves create the air
that crossed the wind chest into the pipe work to bring forth
these sounds, these unbelievable sounds that engulfed us, the
intensity of which forced us down onto the organ pipes?"

The sinner broke off her story, closed her eyes, and sank
into the high grass, so that I could no longer see the face that
had been turned toward me. The recounting of her Sicilian
confession had so captivated me, against my will, that I had
completely forgotten the unpleasant situation I found myself
in, which once again became clear to me. On the one hand I
was drawn to her beauty and vivacity, on the other I felt cast
aside by her and considered her totally unpredictable. A
woman who has the effrontery to kidnap a Catholic priest
from a crowded mass surely has turned away from God. She
had also mentioned in passing two murders she had committed, and I asked myself whether she was telling the truth or

whether she had only invented these monstrous acts to scare me, to torment me. It was scarcely imaginable that this charming female had killed two men. Her lifestyle was very unusual, of course, and many of her views were in blatant contrast to those of average women her age. I thought of my dear sister, Maria, who kept house for me and who by now was surely wandering about the parsonage consumed with worry about me. I hoped they were looking for me, that our clearing soon would be surrounded by police, that heavily armed members of the antiterrorist squad would emerge at any minute from the forest shadows and a megaphone voice would admonish my kidnapper to give herself up, assuring her that we were surrounded and that any resistance was futile, telling her to raise her hands above her head. I thought about the many things I had to do. The letter to the congregation must be prepared, I had to write my next sermon and issue an invitation to the string quartet for the next church concert. Who would baptize the children, perform the marriage and funeral ceremonies? I knew that during my absence my sister, Maria, would be able to represent me only inadequately.

In contrast to the sinner, my sister, five years older than I, had followed the right path. I would never forget that decisive moment in her life when she had chosen to place herself in my service, and therefore in the service of the faithful and of God. She had been very pretty as a young girl, and in purely superficial terms there was perhaps even a certain resemblance to the sinner, though her beauty, of course, in contrast to that of the latter, mirrored the purity of her soul. I remember how she used to comb her hair in the bedroom we shared in our youth: She sat before the mirror in her high-necked, white linen nightgown, and the light from the lamp on the nearby chest of drawers made the curves of her young body slightly visible. I watched from my bed as she undid her long braids, and then she would pass the brush through her wavy chestnut brown hair repeatedly, from top to bottom, a motion that never ceased to delight me. Even today, when she removes the black hairpins from her bun and combs her long gray hair in a motion that is a bit wearier, but still very graceful, I often think of the time when we were half-grown, and of the old gold-framed mirror over the chest of drawers that reflected the image of her innocent face. My absence would pain her, I knew that, for we had become quite accustomed to each other over the years.

The thought of my sister worrying began to worry me, and in order to distract myself I thought about the rosary beads she had given me as a present during a trip we took to the Holy Land, fingering them in my imagination with hands that the sinner had bound with rope behind my back. One imaginary Ave Maria bead after another, one invisible Our Father bead after another passed through my fingers, many small and a few large beads, a painful rosary. Silently I uttered one Our Father, one Ave Maria after another under the acacia, my mouth firmly bound with this blasphemous piece of clothing. At my thirty-fourth Ave Maria the strawberry blond head of the sinner emerged from the grass.

"You won't believe it," she said, "but talking makes me hungry, especially talking about memories connected to intense emotions."

She stood and went over to her motorcycle, parked a few yards away in the shade of a spruce tree, and began rummaging around in the tin tool kits. She returned with a large tomato and a piece of cake, sat down in the grass in front of me, and bit into the cake. Watching her eat, observing the good manners with which her slender right hand elegantly guided the piece of cake to her mouth, which she opened just wide enough to take a delicate bite without also opening her eyes wide in the process, the way she chewed with her mouth closed without screwing up her face, and swallowed without sticking out her chin, one could scarcely believe she had committed a transgression of the flesh with a consecrated priest in an organ gallery in Sicily. For though her tale had become somewhat vague toward the end, and though she had not wished to fill in many of the gaps in her memory, I had no doubt that that is exactly what happened. I have always felt that women, with the exception of my sister, are mysterious and unfathomable, even demonic creatures, have always, with the exception of my sister, avoided them when I could, and now my early intuitive judgment had been confirmed to a most emphatic degree. Even more so than before I now understood the theses that medieval theologians had directed against the female sex, theses that at first glance appeared hostile, such as their assertions that women were lovely to look at from the front, but were devoured by snakes, spiders, and scorpions from behind. I understood the urgent warnings that pious monks issued before these vessels of sin, with whom one must not enter into relations unless one wished to be plunged into ruination and forfeit eternal life. Women, my sister Maria excepted, dragged you down with them to a stinking swamp you would sink into, forced you into unnatural acts, the memory of which made the blood rise to your cheeks, confounded your spirit with their forked-tongue talk, their devious whispers, and sucked you dry like a giant tarantula, leaving nothing behind but an empty shell. The woman seated eating before me was a typical example: beautiful form, diabolical content.

"Glazed apple cake," the woman said curtly and shoved the rest of it into her mouth. "Glazed apple cake with cinnamon. Basically, I returned to Austria only for the pastry. The pastry and you. With the exception of its pastry Austria has nothing that would make it worth returning to, nothing one longs to return to once one has finally left its borders behind. But I missed the pastry. The Austrian pastry I missed ruined the most beautiful places abroad for me. I sat above the Gulf of Salerno, a slice of moon above me sharp as a knife, a bottle of San Pellegrino bitters before me, and looked down at the dark sea and almost wept, because for half a year I had not had a piece of *Rosinenpotize*. As I was breakfasting with a devoted lover in Paris's Fifth Arrondissement, in a small kitchen with sloping walls and a view of the Pantheon, the thought of a *Spritzstraube* plunged me into such despair that my devoted lover up and left me. Simple *Spritzstrauben* squeezed from a star-shaped dough bag into hot oil, browned until golden on both sides. Laurent just didn't understand.

"The worst was in England. It was Devon, Exeter. A bakery in Exeter. It began with a fight with the saleswoman because there was nothing in her display case that even remotely resembled *Dukatenbuchteln*, *Ribiselschaumschnitten*, or the fluted shape of a *Germgugelhupf*. Even in Exeter one should be able to look forward to some version of *Germgugelhupf*, some variety of red currant *Ribiselschaumschnitten*. One might anticipate that the *Germgugelhupf* would lack grated lemon peel, might tolerate the fact that the stems of the red currants used for the *Ribiselschaumschnitten* may not have been removed with the greatest of care. But nothing at all? I left Devon and took the ferry to Calais. Austria's pastry either keeps you in the country or draws you back. I could cite countless examples. Austrian pastry has brought many a successful career abroad to a premature end, for the Austrian careerists could not make it abroad without Austrian pastry. It has caused people to return to Austria even though they knew the police here were looking for them. Which do you prefer, Reverend, family cake, locksmith boys, or lady's fingers? I can't say that this country means anything at all to me. On the contrary, when I return — for the pastry — I always think: This is a disagreeable country and one would do well to treat the great majority of its population with the greatest of caution, the greatest reserve, if one wishes to avoid irreparable damage. Were it not for the pastry I would not have set foot on Austrian soil for years. People who choose an unencumbered lifestyle, those who move from place to place such as myself, are always in danger in Austria. Austria doesn't like such people, particularly when those people are women. One is happy when those people leave, and distressed when they return. A nomadic existence is suspect in Austria, in Austria sedentariness is highly valued. The sedentary are familiar. Each change of address arouses distrust, each trip skepticism. A person who tends toward the nonsedentary has no place in Austria. A nonsedentary woman such as myself gets away as quickly as possible. Only because of the pastry, only because of that am I here."

She then took a small and decorous bite out of the plump tomato without its red juice spurting between the slight gap in her two front teeth, without it running down the sides of her mouth and over her chin, to drip on the smooth black leather of her jumpsuit.

"I have chosen an Austrian priest to hear my general confession because it is clear to me that only an Austrian priest is in the position to fully understand this general confession. Only an Austrian priest will be entirely able to put himself into the twists and turns of an Austrian brain, the cerebral convolutions of which, of course, are arranged differently from the convolutions of those who live in other countries, only he will be able to penetrate deeply into an Austrian's gray and white matter. Only an Austrian priest will be able to forge ahead to the left and to the right auricle of the Austrian heart, only he will not lose his composure on beholding what the chambers of such a heart contain. His blood will not freeze in his veins when he sees what beasts, what monsters are housed there, because in all probability he is not unfamiliar with the conditions under which such monsters have stolen into the chambers of the Austrian heart. Had I been truly precise I would have kidnapped a priest from Carinthia, from the north shore of Lake Ossiach, a priest from the village where I was born. Such a priest would be familiar with the historical, social, cultural, and linguistic prerequisites for the creation of these fiendish Austrian heart chambers, these heart sac horrors. But as I am not truly precise, I shall make my confession to you, East Tyrolean and non-Carinthian that you are, for because of the geographical proximity of East Tyrol to Carinthia you nevertheless will doubtless be able to understand the dreadful, abominable, frightening things that are harbored in the chambers of the average Carinthian heart. A confession by Magdalena Leitner will not unduly shock you."

The sinner stood up, stretched her arms, and twirled for a while in circles, her long hair spinning like a carousel with all its seats empty. Then she stood straight as a post with her legs together and touched the ground in front of her feet with the palms of her hands, her hair flowing down like a light orange waterfall. She repeated this exercise some twenty times, then went over to her sidecar motorcycle, bent down on her right knee, and leaned her elbow on the black leather seat.

"I should have bought this machine sooner," she said. "Just as I should have decided to kidnap you much sooner. A lot of things would have gone differently, things that followed a quite complicated course would have been abbreviated. Since the time I disposed of my movable and immovable effects in order to lead a nomad's life, I feel much relieved. There wasn't much, of course. My entire immovable effects consisted of one boggy meadow of four hundred square meters that bordered on the property owned by my parents. This meadow, bisected by a small brook and covered in soft cotton grass and high sharp tussock, was presented to me by my parents with the preposterous suggestion that I build a small house there, next door to them. Totally preposterous, Reverend, do you understand? On that swampy morass, totally preposterous. One could perhaps construct some sort of lake dwelling, some unorthodox little lake dwelling like they built in the Hallstatt period of prehistory, something like that, perhaps, but you have to realize that the little brook cut through the property at a diagonal. To live so close to a brook, even, so to speak, on or over a brook, is life-threatening.

"Any even halfway gifted dowser can tell you what it means to live on or over a brook. It's comparable to suicide, if not physical, then mental suicide. Aside from the various incurable physical ailments that such a capillary can produce, direct proximity to water can drive you crazy. Living by, on, or over such arteries, you soon totally lose your mind, and only death can pull you out of it. Water makes you crazy, Reverend, it's a scientifically proven fact. I would have moved into my little lake dwelling near my parents, and within a few months I would have gone totally nuts, a few months and my mental state would have been totally beyond repair. Out of maternal and paternal love, my mother and father would not have taken me to a psychiatric clinic, even had they been advised to do so. So I would have remained in my lake dwelling, my hair becoming more snarled with every day that passed, my eyes and cheeks more hollow, my skin grayer. With time, I would have become so unpredictable that my parents would have become afraid of me, refusing to bring food to me themselves, but rather having a special hinged door built into my lake dwelling so that they could shove my food through it. Other than my parents, no one would have dared get near me. That's where the crazy woman lives, schoolchildren would have whispered on their way to school, pointing at my lake dwelling. When her mother wanted to bring her food, she bit off her little finger, they would have said to each other. Her mother now has a prosthesis for a finger, a synthetic finger. And they would have been telling the truth.

"At night I would have looked out the window of my lake dwelling and talked in a secret language to the full moon hanging over the silver lake. Sometimes I would have left the house in a bloodred kimono with black blossoms to stroke the cotton grass blossoms and read the future from them, a future of misfortune to the area. I would have dipped my hands in the water of the brook and perceived much in the little waves I created. My parents, in the meantime, would have enclosed the property in barbed wire, for reasons of safety. My madness would have become more pronounced, as would my gift of prophecy, occasioned and fostered by my madness. When my mother or father would bring me food I would say amazing things to them. News of that would have gotten around, and one day my parents would have allowed the first person to come to me who wanted his future foretold. The number would have increased, my parents would have removed the barbed wire, and I would have become famous far beyond the borders of my own land, people would have arrived with their interpreters from Slovenia, Friuli, and Venezia. Because of this fulfilling prophetic activity I would have become more peaceful and ceased biting people. My parents would have collected the income from my prophecies, which would have been steady. I myself would have had no use for it. And so, for no small amount, I would have sold the small meadow property to a bank clerk from Mödling, who would have wished to install a fish pond there. That was one possible future scenario, which became impossible when I sold my land.

"Sometimes, Reverend, sometimes I think that madness is not the worst of all possible future scenarios, madness paired with prophecy, an oft-occurring combination. Perhaps I could have made my fortune as a madwoman. The chances of making one's fortune in this world are quite limited, Reverend, you must constantly apply all your gifts to approach the goal. And the gift of madness is not a gift to be underestimated, as numerous examples from history attest. The mad are the wise of this world, Reverend, that much is clear, I am not telling you, a man of the Church, anything new with this; the history of the Catholic Church and its saints is a history of madness that not always, but sometimes, was wisdom. The history of the Catholic saints is the history of a long series of the obviously, though not always truly inventive, mad. I have always had a great deal of respect for the mad, an attitude I can recommend to you as well. But I scarcely need to express this, for as a man of the Church you surely respect the mad.

"When one lives life such as I do one often comes in contact with the mad, frequent encounters with the mad are unavoidable in an inconstant lifestyle such as my own. Even if I wanted to I couldn't avoid the mad, they're to be found at every street corner. I'm always happy to see them, they're easy to recognize once you know how. Has it ever occurred to you that their number is on the increase? Officially they're not saints, of course, at least not any longer, they're the secret saints of our day. The Church would never be able to keep up with the canonizations, at the rate at which crazy people are multiplying, but, then, conferring sainthood on today's mad is not necessary, it's enough to recognize and respect them. In a certain way the mad guarantee that our world will continue to function, for because of their gift of prophecy, their prophetic foresight, they can always be found where things are most dangerous. Their sixth sense places them in dangerous—the most dangerous—situations, which they then disarm. That is the invaluable service of the crazy—who knows how many fires, explosions, serial murders, acts of terrorism, and plane crashes have been avoided because a crazy person was at the right time in a place that threatened to become the focus of catastrophe. Their intuition leads the crazy to ominous places, above which disaster gathers like a huge black storm cloud, places at which the timed fuse of calamity ticks louder by the minute. The mad arrive like sleepwalkers and quickly defuse the bomb. That's why I welcome the sight of them. I smile at them and thank them with my smile for the fact that their presence probably has saved me from some misfortune. Contrary to popular opinion the mad are good luck, just like black cats.

"Madness as a calling, as a talent placed at the disposal of humanity—an interesting topic. These spontaneous assertions on my part almost make me regret that I didn't stay with my parents and become a prophetic madwoman. I robbed myself of this eventuality with the sale of my movable and immovable effects. Standing at a crossroads, I rejected this possibility and chose a nonsedentary life, a momentous decision that excluded madness as a lifestyle and ushered in my development as a seven-fold mass murderess of men. These were the two paths that fate offered. Others stand at different crossroads and are offered, for example, the possibility of an intact marriage with four children, or of remaining single and entering into a long series of exciting or, respectively, less exciting love affairs. They can choose between an existence selling hardware and software for the Apple Macintosh, or an existence as second violin in a radio orchestra. Madwoman or murderess, those were my two choices. More was not offered me.

"Basically I am not dissatisfied with the path I took, chosen with the sale of my movable and immovable effects, for there is something to be said for the alternative of mass murderess of men, primarily that a life lived as a murderess is infinitely more active than that of a madwoman. The mad are creative but largely introspective people. Murderesses are better oriented to the outside world; they act, whereas the existence of a madwoman is an internal, an introverted life. Murderesses are active people of a sanguine or choleric nature, who deal decisively with their surroundings, changing them powerfully at their own discretion. Madwomen are grumblers whose fluids mark them as melancholic or phlegmatic. It may be assumed that murderesses, for the most part, are day people who like to get up early and who are tired by nine in the evening, whereas madwomen, in contrast, are night people who pace their rooms at three in the morning and are still in bed at ten. It's all a question of temperament. In my case the sanguine-choleric side triumphed: Someone in whom the melancholic-phlegmatic side dominated would scarcely have disposed so lightly of her immovable effects.

"Concerning my movable effects, I sat amid my furniture, my dishes, my curtains, rugs, and pictures, my books and clothing, and tried to imagine what it would be like to live without these things. I sat on my sofa, which I had dragged into the middle of the room, sat there despondent with my elbows propped on my knees, my chin in my hands, surrounded by piles of books, open and sealed boxes and crates, rolled-up rugs. I had taken my pictures from the walls and was now looking at the square patches where they had hung, somewhat lighter than the rest of the walls. How would I live without the sofa on which I had lain, sat, knelt, and stood, on which I had eaten, drunk, read, written, thought, which I pulled out into a bed each evening, to sleep alone or not alone, to breakfast alone or not alone. This wide and solid sofa with its comfortable arms and light gray cover represented my innermost life, my true living space, it absorbed my aura like a sponge. To leave it behind, to give it up, to sell it meant to be without a home, to be without a homeland in the extreme. At the same time, this piece of furniture hindered my freedom of movement, it was like a massive ship, so big that you notice only too late that you have begun to sink and would drown if you didn't abandon it in time.

"Reverend, I didn't know how difficult it is to leave a sinking ship, I didn't know that I would feel guilty later, as if I had been the captain and it was my duty to go down with it. But I wasn't the captain, I was merely a completely ordinary sailor who had signed on for nine months. Once I had made this clear to myself I called a junk dealer, who was willing to take the sofa off my hands and would pick it up right away. As I was waiting for his truck I took a look around at the rest of my furniture. I ran my hand over the veneer of the bookcases, opened the empty drawers of the desk and closed them again, and with my finger drew a spiral in the dusty glass of my round-top table. Then I unscrewed the light bulbs from the lamps and sat in my four armchairs, one after the other. When the doorbell rang I got up, and when I reached the door I turned and looked back into the room. You will hardly be surprised, Reverend, when I say to you that the room was flooded with water, that the light furniture and books were bobbing on its surface, with only a corner of the sofa visible above water level. As a man of the Church you undoubtedly are familiar with the phenomenon of visions; many Catholic saints passed their entire lives in such visions. My vision, of course, was only an insignificant, a totally trivial vision. My vision of a flooded living room is, of course, not to be compared to those visions of the Catholic saints that superseded time and space, it is scarcely worth mention. And by the time I returned with the two young furniture movers the water had already disappeared, and the sofa was standing there as if it never had been totally submerged except for one small corner sticking up out of the water.

"As the two young furniture movers in sleeveless white T-shirts were agreeing on which grips they should use to carry the cumbersome pieces of furniture down the stairs, I had the opportunity to observe the muscles bulging under the taut skin of their upper and lower arms. The play of their muscles, the tendons protruding from the inside of the upper arms, the throat, and neck captured my total attention for a while, as did the bracing odor that had entered the room with them, and in order to devote myself to these sensations for just a while longer, once they had carried the sofa to their truck I offered them a beer. The young men accepted the open bottles dotted with little beads of water, holding them in their large fists and raising them to their lips. The movement of their Adam's apples as they drank equally held my attention, which is why I then served them both a second bottle, an offer they did not refuse."

Having said this the sinner shifted her eyes—focused until then on a point at some indeterminable distance—to my face, where they dwelt for a while before slowly moving to my throat and then downward.

"I ask myself," she said softly, "I ask myself what sort of muscles, what sort of tendons are concealed under your alb. Do you have on a sleeveless T-shirt, Reverend? What kind of underwear are you wearing? Do you even wear underwear? And if so, where do you buy it? Are there rules governing the underwear of Catholic priests? Do the color and fabric change as do the color and fabric of your robes, according to the Sabbaths and holidays of the Church calendar? I would be interested in knowing that. For reasons that are obvious, a priest's underwear surely should not fit too tightly. Is that so, Reverend, is that so?"

Magdalena, who had wandered from the path of God, smiled at me.

"I'm tempted to remove my Kashiyama bodysuit before I begin my actual confession, if only to hear your answer to these questions. But I won't give in to that temptation. There are other ways of informing myself of such things."

And with that she came closer and grabbed the hem of my dalmatic and then that of my alb, and lifted them both a bit.

"Dark gray socks," she said. "Worsted. I didn't notice them when I tied the rope around your ankles."

The sinner's touch was highly unpleasant to me, and to distract myself I tried to imagine my sister, Maria, still dressed in her nightgown when, the morning before, she had laid out these socks and everything else on the valet, as she did every day. Try as I might, my sister's features remained strangely indistinct, I couldn't even imagine her long gray hair, of which I was so fond. When I felt the hands of the sinner on the bare skin above the tops of my socks the familiar figure in her pastel-colored nightgown vanished into thin air. I saw instead the face of my abductress, quite near my own, the mole, the curve of her upper lip, the bluish vein that ran down the middle of her forehead. Her eyes were half-closed, probably in order to better explore the section of skin in question with her undoubtedly well-developed sense of touch.

"Relax," she said, "just relax. It's pleasantly dry, your skin. The hair is softer than I would have thought. Asthenic type, weak-muscled, thin-boned. Interesting. A small scar on your shinbone. Delicate ankles, just as I imagined. Ankle joint, heel bone, Achilles tendon. But you're trembling," she said, and finally withdrew her hand. "I've obviously touched a sore spot. Forgive my curiosity, Reverend, I'll give you the chance to get to know me a little better before satisfying it further. It is not my intention to offend your priestly sense of shame. Even if you are at my mercy, that doesn't mean that I am without understanding of your order's qualms about women. An attitude quite different from, say, your average furniture mover. As my two furniture movers were on their third beer it suddenly became clear to me that I was not to retain any of my movable effects, that I must free myself of all of my personal possessions, of my books and my clothing. It was a kind of epiphany, a vision, which you as a Catholic priest are not unfamiliar with, a sudden inspiration, which in my case was oddly connected to the up and down movement of the Adam's apples of my furniture movers.

"I discussed my epiphany with them, which they immediately understood, suggesting that they cart away the rest of my furniture for adequate recompense. The shorter of the two said he could use the desk, the taller one said he could use the bookshelves, the table, and the accompanying chairs. They knew others who would be interested in the lamps, the rugs, and the pictures. At that I unrolled my rugs, and the furniture movers proved well-versed in terms of placing their origin in time and space, and of the pattern and knitting and knotting techniques involved. The shorter of the two recognized immediately that the largest of my four rugs, with its fine French knot stitching, had come from an area near Kerman in the Iranian salt desert, and that the most beautiful of them had been executed in the Gordian knot technique popular in the area around Tashkent. But the taller mover also manifested an impressive knowledge, which was not limited merely to the history of Turkish kilims, but extended as well to the famous wall hangings of Bayeux, to the Gobelins of the Cluny Museum with their representation of the mysterious lady and the unicorn, as well as to the production of carpets dating back to the Spanish rug makers of thirteenth-century Alcarez, southwest of Albacete. After they had inspected my rugs I offered them a fourth beer, which they did not refuse, and then turned around the pictures, which had been facing the wall. It happened that they also knew something about painting. The taller of the furniture movers dated my small English hunting scene almost exactly, and this was followed by a brief conversation on British landscape painting of the nineteenth century in general and on William Turner in particular, above all on his representation of light, which was then adopted and further developed by the French Impressionists. After the shorter of the two men had correctly assessed the value of a Japanese ink drawing, we had a brief discussion on the Sinboku technique developed in the fifteenth century under the influence of Zen Buddhism, as well as on the Japanese color woodcut, during which we discovered a mutual admiration of Utamaro. Before I began searching the piles of books in the room for a volume of woodcuts by Hokusai, in order to show the shorter mover one of my favorites, *Loving Women*, I opened two more bottles of beer.

"Actually, I was not so surprised at the knowledge exhibited by the two furniture movers, for I often have experienced that so-called simple people in reality possess a great knowledge of art and a highly developed sensibility, whereas the so-called educated are almost always the dumbest. I have never been so deadly bored as among the so-called educated, I have never had to endure more simpleminded conversation than as a guest at the aesthetically furnished apartments of the so-called aesthetes. I have endured torment at their tables, their aesthetically prepared meals before me, in vain I have sought excuses to flee rooms filled to the rafters with the sounds of their aesthetic musical selections.

"There is scarcely anything more soporific than the conversation of the so-called educated classes, scarcely anything more deadening to the spirit than the surroundings they have created for themselves. If you've seen one aesthetically furnished apartment, you've seen them all. If you've choked down one aesthetically prepared meal, you've choked them all down. The conversations of aesthetes consist of prefab standard parts, any original word that is interjected completely throws them from their conversational path and is disturbing to them in the extreme. Academics, of course, are the worst. And when it comes to the art of deadening the spirit, cosmopolitan academics are the furthest along, the Francophile, Italophile, Anglophile academics with their endless number of cultural vacations, from which they return bearing cookbooks and spices. If one is so careless as to find oneself at their table, one is forced to eat dishes that, according to them, are prepared only in the northeast of Madagascar, and there only by an Indian-Christian minority, or dishes prepared only in the immediate vicinity of Bogota, and limited then to the festivities of the Jewish-Indian minority.

"I was greatly indebted to the two furniture movers, for in helping me get rid of my movable property they relieved me of the decision concerning a nomadic lifestyle and therefore of my leave-taking from the so-called educated. Not that the so-called educated, the so-called cultured, would allow me to go so easily. They had become accustomed to seeing me seated on their sofas covered in batik fabric from Sumatra, they enjoyed my conversations with their dull-witted children, whose dull-wittedness blossomed in the company of even duller-witted aesthetic children in the various painting, ballet, and flute lessons offered by dull-witted aesthetes. Based on my inherent good-naturedness, an instilled tractability and compliance, I was no longer capable of freeing myself from this dangerous environment. I had fallen into bad company, and only decisive action could liberate me. And it was high time, for the leaden apathy, the paralyzing boredom of the cosmopolitan academics had already taken over, threatening to render me completely incapable of movement.

"You must try this dish we discovered in South Burundi,

the academic cosmopolitans would say, you must hear these songs, sung only in a small mountain village in the Sardinian interior by three ninety-year-old women during Easter week, and which we were fortunate enough to have made available to us through the tireless efforts of a Viennese ethnomusicologist. You must put on this mask carved of two-hundred-year-old sequoia wood at the end of the nineteenth century by a direct descendant of Tecumseh, the Shawnee Indian chief. And the masks: If you've ever accepted an invitation to the home of cultured academics, you've found yourself constantly positioned under or next to fright-producing statues and masks from all over the globe, which the academically cultured have brought with them from their cultural vacations to hang in their elegant homes on the outskirts of the city, the walls of which were painted white by undocumented workers from the East, or to place on their parquet floors polished to a shine by cleaning women from Indochina. For you must know, Reverend, that the educated love anything primitive. The more educated the educated, the more primitive the primitive he loves. I had nightmares after each visit I paid to the educated; their masks and their statues pursued me into my dreams.

"Once I recognized the growing psychological danger posed by the cosmopolitan educated, particularly by the high percentage of psychologists, psychoanalysts, psychiatrists, and psychotherapists of the various schools among them, I considered how best I could escape them. In my inherent goodheartedness and my instilled tractability and compliance I had allowed these psychotherapists, psychologists, psychiatrists, and psychoanalysts to get to me, to knock me over the head with their fright-producing masks, their terrifying pictures. You have to be on guard against psychologists, psy-

chotherapists, psychiatrists, and psychoanalysts, just as a
Catholic must guard against the temptations of the flesh;
they'll work at persuading you of your own spiritual inepti-
tude for so long that you'll start believing them, start letting
them help you, letting these mechanics of the soul work you
over with their oil-smeared fingers, a step many have regretted taking. For in letting them help you you're not helping
yourself, of course, you're only helping the psychiatrists,
psychologists, psychoanalysts, and psychotherapists of the
various schools. That these psychiatrists, psychoanalysts,
psychologists, and psychotherapists are in desperate need of
help themselves is clear to anyone who has observed them,
either briefly or at length. Reverend, I, who have been
blessed with uncommonly sharp eyes inherited from my
father's side of the family, have never encountered such serious, truly serious behavioral problems, crass peculiarities in
terms of expression and gestures, and other human oddities
and idiosyncrasies to the degree I did among psychotherapists, psychiatrists, psychologists, and psychoanalysts, have
never anywhere else felt with such unfailing certainty that I
was dealing with people who were so absolutely unfit for life.
Unfortunately, the cunning of the species becomes apparent
only when one falls into the trap of one of their number. And
once a harmless person has fallen into their trap they mani-
fest an amazing tenacity in holding on to their prey, the
harmless person, which becomes understandable when one
realizes that each harmless person who falls into their trap
represents a means to their own cure. And once that person
has been taken in, once they finally have him in their care
and he lies totally in their power, defenseless on their couch,
they want to keep him, of course, and begin with him their
own healing process.

"By the time this unsuspecting person recognizes the methods of the psychologists, psychotherapists, psychoanalysts, and psychiatrists it is often too late, for the psychiatrist, psychologist, psychotherapist, or psychoanalyst is sitting across from him in a session, pleasantly observing him like a spider observing a plump housefly. We're dealing here with a so-called vicious cycle, Reverend, for even if this harmless person, who scarcely has any money left at all after paying the average fee charged by these psychoanalysts, psychotherapists, psychiatrists, and psychologists, should succeed in escaping, the next one is lying in wait for him and what little remains of his cash.

"This group of psychiatrists, psychotherapists, psychologists, and psychoanalysts played a central role in my plan to flee the cultured educated, as I knew that they, above all others, would offer the most vehement objection to any outbreak on my part. The first thing was to render the educated cultured harmless as a whole. I decided to defeat them with their own weapons: Years ago an acquaintance of mine, a dilettante sculptor, had created a crude bust of me in wood, and had presented it to me as a gift. I didn't dare throw it away, and so for years it had been standing in my closet. When a cosmopolitan academic invited me to his home I took the bust out of the closet, pulled a number of rusty nails out of an old board, hammered them into the wooden head, and presented it as the nail bust of a Mali shaman. I used the lively interest and general excitement that ensued to disappear.

"As I left the house I noticed that two of the psychoanalysts, psychiatrists, psychotherapists, and psychologists were following me. I had reckoned with such a possibility, and stopped at the next street corner and let them catch up. Then

I threw out to them—a roughly forty-year-old psychiatrist of the Lacanian school and an elderly woman who was an orthodox Freudian—a few catchwords to start a professional discussion. As the two were busy attacking each other I boarded the next number 7 streetcar. I sat down at a window seat, and before the streetcar turned onto Bahnhofstrasse I looked back at the two of them, who stood gesticulating by the side of the road. Not long ago I heard that the two had married and are spending their honeymoon in Heidelberg, where they are studying the documents of the so-called art of the insane, assembled there in the famous Prinzhorn collection. You can see, Reverend, that even though I gave them the slip they have found new ways to vigorously pursue their healing process, at the cost of those who have no choice of escape, either because they're dead or because they're locked up in clinics."

After these remarks, which, convincing as they sounded, nevertheless seemed to counter traditional Western logic, Magdalena paused briefly. I was a little dazed, and surmised that her intonation, the hypnotic ebb and flow of her melodious voice, had caused my stupefaction.

"You see," she then said, "you see how difficult the attempt to leave one's homeland can be. Only once you decide to leave does it become clear how many people have profited from your presence, and therefore do not wish to see you go. After the two likable young furniture movers, into whose hands I quickly pressed two bottles of beer on leaving, had driven away with my furniture, I decided to donate the rest of my household belongings, my books as well as my clothing, to various charitable organizations, and made a few calls toward this end, at which a number of charitable organization workers appeared, happy to receive my possessions—

among them my Alessi lemon press, my edition of Schwitters, and the little black sequined cocktail dress that a young Viennese designer had created for me—in order to distribute them to those diverse regions of the world visited by floods, war, famine, earthquakes, volcanic eruptions, and revolutions.

"You, as a Catholic duty-bound to *agape*, doubtless have already given the disadvantaged of this world a portion of what you own. Do you ever think about those present owners? I often ask myself who in Rwanda is now wearing my little black sequined cocktail dress, and to what affair, and hope that she is a pretty woman. I think about who in Somalia will have occasion to pull on my scarcely worn Bruno Magli fur-lined boots, and imagine a Bosnian woman setting out, bullets flying around her, to get the lemons to squeeze in my Alessi lemon press. And my edition of Schwitters? I see it impaled on the bayonet of a Central American counterrevolutionary who has come across it while pillaging the home of some poor peasant.

"Have you ever thought about the flood victim in Bangladesh who is now wearing your discarded alb? Or whether the gray combed-cotton socks your housekeeper darned for you with such care disappeared into some crack in the earth created by an unexpected aftershock in southern California? As someone trained by your religion to be familiar with the more metaphysical dimensions of existence you surely have thought about the mysterious connection that binds you to the Icelandic fisherman sitting in one of your somewhat threadbare soutanes in a barracks hastily constructed following the most recent devastating eruption of the Hekla volcano. Such questions quickly lead to dizzyingly hypothetical areas, and no doubt could be compared to those issues faced by a scholar of the High Middle Ages, don't you agree? It's not at all difficult to imagine that the pretty Rwandan woman wearing my little black sequined cocktail dress was shot and that my little black cocktail dress is now ruined, perforated by bullets from Russian, French, or American machine guns; that my Schwitters edition has been incinerated along with the poor peasant's farmstead in Central America, torched by the counterrevolutionaries; that my Alessi lemon press is still functioning, but lies hidden under the corpses buried in the rubble of a Bosnian apartment building. It is also easy to imagine that the Bangladesh flood victim gave your alb to his cousin, who used it as a nightshirt, stained with blood on the night three months later when he appeared at a police station in it at two in the morning with a knife in one hand, to announce that he had stabbed his wife in their wedding bed; that the daughter of the Icelandic fisherman used her Singer sewing machine to turn your soutane into a very short if high-necked little black cocktail dress, the attractive brevity of which caused the driver who picked up the daughter of the Icelandic fisherman one night on the road between Borgarnes and Stykkisholmur to rape her, an event that brought your authentic Austrian soutane in contact with Icelandic sperm. All of which lies within the realm of possibility, don't you think? Mysterious are the links between human fates, or, as you would say, God moves in mysterious ways. You've scrunched down, Reverend, here, let me set you upright again."

Magdalena stood, grabbed me by the shoulders, pulled me upright, and pressed me against the trunk of the tree. It was true, her thoughts concerning my clothing had depressed me a little, and this decline in mood had caused me to slide down the trunk of the acacia a bit.

"Such considerations must be considered," she continued, "such thoughts must be thought, even if they aren't especially pleasant considerations or especially cheerful thoughts. The indirect consequences of charitable acts are sometimes amazing. After the charitable organization workers had stocked up on my household belongings, my books, and my clothing, I counted the money I had made from the sale of my movable and immovable effects as I stood on the parquet floor of my empty apartment, which I already had given notice on. It wasn't much, but it would be enough to buy a Puch sidecar motorcycle."

The sinner threw a loving glance in the direction of the motorcycle parked in the shade of the spruce tree.

"You know, with the purchase of my motorcycle I fulfilled a childhood dream. When I was a little girl my great-uncle Karl, who owned one of these, would often put me in the sidecar and take me for a ride. I sat in the open Felber sidecar, the wind blowing through my hair. The memory of those excursions in the Felber sidecar is the loveliest memory I have."

With this she pulled a serrated photograph from the breast pocket of her leather jumpsuit and held it in front of my face. It showed a roughly sixty-year-old man with a bushy mustache, seated on such a motorcycle, dressed in a leather coat with wide lapels and a wide belt, a leather cap on his head, and wearing goggles.

"That is my great-uncle Karl," Magdalena said. "He almost drowned once when, under the influence, he drove into Lake Ossiach. He had three wrecks in which he suffered injuries: a concussion, a crushed kidney, and a cerebral contusion. He didn't survive the fourth. Broke his neck."

She stuck the photo back in her breast pocket.

"The Puch 800 with the Felber sidecar hasn't been built for decades now, by the way. And they only manufactured it for a few years as it was. It's the most powerful Puch. Four-cylinder four-stroke engine. What makes it special—besides its extremely powerful eight hundred cc capacity and four-cylinder four-stroke engine—is that the ports open to only one hundred sixty degrees instead of one hundred eighty. The reason for this is uncertain today, but perhaps has something to do with the handling without the sidecar. A suspension so good you can hardly believe it. Pressed steel forks with hand-adjustable shock absorbers. Great mileage. You hardly see these machines anymore.

"Around the time I was considering leaving my homeland there was an old man—he was about seventy—who lived in my parents' town and had a Puch 800 parked in his shed, a Puch he had not driven for years and only seldom before that, so it was almost like new. I had spoken to him over the garden wall a few times, as he was in the process of adding shin guards he had seen advertised in a motorcycle magazine. At first he was a bit distrustful of a woman who expressed interest in his motorcycle, but when he realized I was familiar with the model and talked about it just as passionately as he did, he became friendlier and opened the garden gate to show me the details of the machine. Finally, he let me climb into the sidecar, just as Great-Uncle Karl once had, to drive me around town. You can imagine my excitement. Just picture someone letting you hold an anklebone of St. Faustina mounted in ivory and set with rubies and sapphires. Or a diamond-encrusted Baroque monstrance. Or a page from a 1486 first edition incunabulum of *La Danse Macabre*, printed in Paris by Guy Marchant. Or imagine that the Pope invites you to tea to honor your service to the East Tyrolean

Catholic Church. That will give you some idea of how excited I felt. I visited the man often after that, we had technical discussions and talked about the advantages of the Veigel dial tachometer over the old tachometer, the protective action of the shock absorbers, the expert construction of the internal expansion clutch. The man trusted me, and after some time went by I had the feeling he would sell me the machine if I asked him to. When I articulated my wish he gave me a hard look up and down, and replied that such a machine could not be had for money. But I persisted. After two further visits we came to an agreement and he named me an acceptable price.

"After I had sold my four hundred square meters of land to the bank clerk from Mödling and turned over my household belongings, my clothes, and my books to the two likable furniture movers and the charitable organization workers, after I was rid of the cultured educated, particularly the psychoanalysts, psychologists, psychiatrists, and psychotherapists among them, and became the owner of the Puch sidecar motorcycle, I packed a few essentials in the tin tool kits stamped with the Puch name, among them a 1905 G.C. Sansoni edition of the *Divina Commedia* by Dante Alighieri, published in Florence; a German paperback edition of Artemidor of Ephesus's interpretation of dreams; Lingen's *Large Illustrated World Atlas*; my Swiss army knife; my pink Sony Walkman; a two-cassette recording of Johann Sebastian Bach's *Well-Tempered Clavier*; and a habit from the Order of the Shoeless Carmelites, given to me by the younger of my two older sisters after she had abandoned the Order without taking her vows, having served for a year as a novice. I assumed there would be no further obstacles to my departure, at least not from my parents, who had turned away from me in disappointment once I had disposed of the four-hundred-square-meter property, but not before holding up to me as glowing examples my two older sisters, both of whom lived in the near vicinity.

"My departure was made easier by the fact that my parents had turned away from me in disappointment. Had my mother, especially, not turned away from me in disappointment she might not have hesitated to employ the arsenal she had at her disposal to keep me there, the arsenal of her cooking. Come by for lunch before you leave, she might have said in passing. You shouldn't travel on an empty stomach. And in the naiveté with which I always underestimated my mother I happily would have accepted, Reverend; I could—and in all probability shall—relate to you all sorts of human tragedies, dire dramas that all can be traced back solely to the imprudent underestimation of mothers. The underestimation of mothers is one of the biggest oversights, one of the greatest frivolities one can ever commit.

"In my bottomless frivolity and oversight I would have appeared punctually at the home of my parents, and my mother cheerfully would have led me to the table covered with the lovely white batiste tablecloth with bright flowers, which she embroidered herself, and set with the matching napkins in the old silver napkin rings, the crystal goblets of Bohemian glass and the porcelain service she inherited from her own mother, and first would have served a sliced-spleen soup. She would have sat next to me, leaning her arms on the table, and watched happily as I spooned up my soup. She then would have ladled me another bowlful and continued to watch as I ate her deep-fried sliced rolls, covered with a delicious spread of grated spleen, minced onions, bread crumbs, salt, pepper, nutmeg, and finely chopped parsley. Then I would have leaned back, my stomach pleasantly filled, as she, humming, served pike perch à la Budapest. A bit over-heated by the double serving of spleen soup I would have begun eating the perch from what would have been the head end, had she not already cut off the perch's head. I would have worked my way to what would have been the tail end, had she not already cut off the tail, taking plentiful helpings of the sauce of fish broth, thinly sliced mushrooms, onions, sweet paprika, and sour cream, and the potatoes with pars-ley. Slightly benumbed by the Italian Riesling she served, I would only with effort have prevented her from filling my empty plate again. Smiling, she would have removed the fish and meat plate, only to appear two minutes later with roasted ox lungs, Viennese style. She would have set it before me, with its aromatic blend of root vegetables, bacon, and garlic, and, slightly exhausted from the work of devouring the head-less and tailless perch, I would have continued to eat. The well-cut, larded lungs would almost have melted in my mouth, and despite the fact that I would soon have been full, I would have been able to stop only after I had cleaned my plate. Too exhausted to protest, I would have allowed my mother to serve me two more slices of meat, and would have eaten these two slices, as well as the rest of the caper sauce, to my mother's happy cooing.

"As I would scarcely have been able to move, my mother would have set the Bohemian crystal goblet of heavy red burgundy to my lips and made me drink, such that the wine would have run down the sides of my mouth. As soon as my mother disappeared into the kitchen with the meat platter, my head would have fallen to the embroidered batiste table-cloth and would only have been raised when she lifted me by my hair, after which she would have served dessert. As if through a veil I would have perceived that I was dealing with rice Trauttmansdorff. My mother, supporting the back of my head with one hand and holding a silver fork in the other, would have shoved the sweet rice with whipped cream and sour cherries into my mouth. Unable to protest with my mouth full, I would have thrown up part of the rice and cherries on the embroidered tablecloth, at which my mother quickly would have lifted me up under my arms and dragged me over to the living room sofa, onto which I would have sunk, deathly pale.

"Whistling softly, my mother would have hurried back to the kitchen and returned with a crystal bowl full of Linzer drops, which she would have placed on a low table next to me. As soon as she pinched my nose to make me open my mouth so that she could shove one Linzer drop after another into it, to then pour coffee down my throat, I would have lost consciousness. And while unconscious I had a dream.

"I dreamed that I got up from the sofa, with one motion sweeping the Linzer drops and the coffeepot inherited from my grandmother to the floor, and ran to the front door, my mother in pursuit. With the last of my strength I pushed aside the slab of bacon that barricaded the door. Running across the lawn, I slipped several times on the Pischinger, Sacher and Dobos tortes hidden in the grass. Just before my mother caught up with me I threw myself into one of the ditches that surrounded the property and were filled with various sauces. I looked back and saw my mother standing on the bank of the sauce ditch, wringing her hands. Once I had swum laboriously through the sauce rings, the Bordelaise ring, the béchamel ring, the cumberland ring, and the vinaigrette ring to reach the other side, I faced my last hurdle, a mountain of curried rice. I slowly ate my way through the mountain, always in danger of being crushed by the weight of the rice. But finally I reached the other side. I was free. And then, Reverend, I would have awoken."

Magdalena gave an audible sigh, obviously a bit affected by the effort involved in telling her story. I opened my eyes, which I had closed during her account, and was strangely happy to see her sitting there before me.

"But that is all speculation, Reverend," she continued, "idle speculation and insignificant dreams, evoked by the conjecture, which does not correspond to reality, that I might not have sold the marshy piece of land that once belonged to my parents, and that they, in turn, would not have turned away from me in disappointment.

"The reality of the situation is that one Friday in April I started my Puch 800 and headed south, toward the mountain chain that divides Austria and Italy. There wasn't a cloud in the sky, it was unusually warm for that time of year. I was listening to the *Well-Tempered Clavier* by Johann Sebastian Bach through the headphones of my Sony Walkman and humming along with it. I was so carefree, so lost in the music and in the sight of the daffodil-dotted countryside in spring, that only as I began the serpentine ascent through the pass leading to the Italian border did I notice that my sisters were following me in the Audi of the elder of the two. I should have known, Reverend. I should have known that my sisters would be opposed to my decision to leave the family. In the rearview mirror, which the former owner had mounted on the steering rod, I saw the Audi coming closer. In terms of speed, of course, a Puch 800 can't compete with the newest, most expensive model of Audi. There are individual cases in which the machine and sidecar have reached a speed of one hundred ten kilometers an hour, but these are exceptions. I couldn't do better than eighty an hour on the steep and curving road leading up to the pass. In the rearview mirror I saw the younger of my two older sisters stick her arm out the open window on the passenger side of the car and signal me to stop.

"My situation was becoming increasingly precarious. Only one more serpentine curve lay between me and my sisters, and I knew they wouldn't hesitate to pass me and force me off the road. In the excitement my pink headphones slipped down around my neck and I could hear the cries of the elder of my two older sisters, who was sticking her head out the window as she drove. Unreliable one! she called. Have you forgotten that you're an aunt, that you have four nieces and three nephews, two of whom are also your godchildren, four nieces and three nephews to whom you owe your auntly munificence, your auntly interest, your auntly favor? One aunt is not enough for seven nieces and nephews all told! How is your sister to bear all auntly responsibility alone, to go alone with four nieces and three nephews to the amusement park, to remember the birthdays of four nieces and three nephews, to praise the essays and drawings and pastime projects of seven nieces and nephews, all told! Neglecter of duty, leaving your sister in the lurch with seven nephews and nieces, all told! Even the most devoted aunt could not bear such a burden. Come back! Accept the duties delegated to you by nature, do not shirk them! Your three nieces and four nephews, two of them your godchildren, are waiting! Do not disappoint them as you have already disappointed our parents, embrace your auntship!

"She must have had her foot on the gas pedal the whole time she was yelling all of this, for the Audi was so close that I could also clearly hear the voice of the younger of my two

older sisters, which by nature is softer than that of the elder
of my two sisters: And that's not all! she cried. That's not all!
Who now will don the habit of the Order of the Shoeless
Carmelites? It fit you as if you had been poured into it, you
looked wonderful in it when I gave it to you after I broke off
my novitiate. I had such hopes for you, not only as an aunt,
but as a future Shoeless Carmelite. Aunt and Carmelite, you
were so well-suited to both. How can you throw over a full
life as an aunt, a happy life as a Shoeless Carmelite, in favor
of a vagabond life, an uncertain future with no permanent
residence, a homeless, gypsy existence? You're a defenseless
woman, who will protect you from thieves, robbers, murder-
ers, rapists, from wind and weather, who will save you from
hunger and thirst? We, your two older sisters, understand
you as little as do your, and my, seven nephews and nieces.
Turn back before it's too late, choose a happy, bright, carefree existence as a seven-fold aunt and member of a greatly
respected Order of the Catholic Church. Don't foolishly
expose yourself to a dangerous life on the road, stop! Your
and my nieces and nephews, as well as your future sisters of
the Order, await you!

"In the meantime my sisters had come within thirty feet of
me, for their pleading had not been in vain and had moved me
to take my foot off the gas. No sooner did I make the decision
to pull over to the side of the road, stop, and repentantly take
my sisters in my arms, than, suddenly, the Mediterranean
appeared before my inner eye. Reverend, you, as a fellow
countryman, know what the sea means to those who are landlocked. This unexpected slice of the Mediterranean that
appeared before my inner eye—a stretch of ocher-colored
rocky coast, a pine towering against the pale blue sky, silver-
topped waves, and a pinkly shimmering beach—allowed me

to push aside the thoughts my sisters had aroused in me, and with a jump that would have done a cross-country cyclist proud, I vaulted the low wooden fence that ran along the narrow mountain road and began slaloming down between the tall trees of a pine forest. Before I entered the dark woods I saw my sisters get out of the Audi and try to climb over the wood fence in their tight skirts. There was not the slightest chance they would ever catch me."

Magdalena wrapped her arms around her knees, looked up at the sky, and sighed.

"*Ach*, my sisters," she said, "if you had a sister you would know what I'm talking about, you would know how ambivalent one can feel about one's sisters."

I thought of Maria, who in the meantime was probably close to total despair, with a strange detachment. Perhaps the sinner's remark was true, perhaps one's feelings toward sisters were ambivalent. The care she showed me, which doubtless was well-intentioned, had become a bit of a burden of late, and mornings, when she pushed to one side the curtain that separated us, I no longer found her hair as appealing in the morning light as I used to, her features had taken on a careworn look and certainly were not as vivacious, for example, as the face framed by strawberry blond curls that the sinner now turned toward me.

"On the one hand I am devoted to my two older sisters," Magdalena continued, "and on the other I felt very happy as I jumped the fence and left them behind. Not for nothing did military and police employ this Puch model in its time in the most remote, most mountainous regions of Austria. Because of the hand-controlled shock absorbers and the particularly smooth differential suspension in the pressed steel shaft, the Puch 800 is an extremely good machine for cross-country use, which proved an advantage during my flight from my sisters. So I drove on the soft, needle-covered ground among the pines, which, luckily for me, were spaced fairly far apart, deeper into the forest, and there I rested briefly. Three hours later the Po Valley spread out before me, and the next day I reached the Mediterranean. I was finally in foreign territory.

"Far away on the other side of the mountains was Austria, the homeland in which I had never felt at home. Do you feel at home in your homeland, Reverend? Even if you don't feel at home in Austria, our mutual homeland, that can't be much of a problem for you, for any country, for Austria, can only be a substitute homeland for you anyway, a makeshift homeland, a surrogate homeland for the simple reason that your true homeland, of course, is the community of believers, the Catholic Church. A Catholic's homeland is in the lap of the Church, a Catholic is never without a homeland. I am not a Catholic, I am, so to speak, a paradoxical woman. If I find myself in my Austrian homeland I often feel quite foreign, sometimes not even here. Nowhere else do people look at me on the street, if people look at me on the street at all, with more amazement than here in Austria. Most of the time they look right through me. But when they do look at me there is such amazement, such surprise in their eyes that I hurry home and stand in front of the mirror to see if I've grown a second head, to see if a third eye has appeared in my forehead, if my left cheek is sprouting some flaming mark. I examine my limbs and check whether I've suddenly grown a humpback or a clubfoot, and I'm relieved to see, to feel, that I haven't changed. Sometimes when my fellow countrymen look right through me I look in the mirror expecting to see nothing at all. And I'm encouraged each time I find my reflection there, a reflection I can concur with.

"I have a similar kind of experience when I address my fellow countrymen on the street in our native language. As soon as I formulate my first sentence my fellow countrymen stare at me, dumbfounded. In these cases, too, I have to reassure myself, have to go home and speak a few sentences into the little microphone that goes with my pink Sony Walkman. Has my vocal apparatus brought forth nothing but grunts in place of sounds signaling communication, instead of understandable words and phrases? Is my glottis not functioning, are my vocal cords too long, too short? I press PLAY and heave a sigh of relief each time I hear myself speaking in a pleasant-sounding voice, uttering something cogent and coherent, occasionally even something sharp-witted and spirited. A series of such puzzling encounters soon led to my not feeling at home in my homeland. But each time I left Austria's borders for foreign soil I felt I was at home. Even when I was stammering incomplete sentences in a language I was largely unfamiliar with, people nodded and understood me. Even when I didn't know the language at all and fell completely silent, or when I tried to make myself understood through gestures and mime, there was not the least problem with communicating. I never needed a mirror in a foreign country, because no one looked through me, causing me to doubt my own existence, because no one tried to suggest with empty and uncomprehending eyes that I was abnormal, a curiosity, a monstrosity. Foreigners, for me, were friendly mirrors."

Here Magdalena fell into a brief silence, and stroked a tuft of grass with her left hand, lost in thought. As I observed her relaxed features, her slightly open mouth, the little gap between her front teeth, the lock of curly hair that concealed her right eye, her lowered left eyelid, the lashes of which threw a soft shadow on her cheek, I tried to imagine that someone could look through her, could manage not to see her. How could this woman fade into thin air, how was it possible that the aura of light she emitted would not penetrate the cornea of the passerby, move through the lens and vitreous body to be received by the retina and then carried by the optical nerve to the brain? It would be unthinkable that Magdalena's image as outlined by the dioptrical mechanism would not be transformed by the retina into nerve impulses, that the color-sensitive cones would not reflect the light orange color of her curls, the blue of her eyes, the white of her perfectly formed teeth, that the chiaroscuro-sensitive rods would not register her curvaceous body, encased in her black motorcycle jumpsuit, the charming line of her throat. Otherwise, what good was that person's macula lutea, his roughly 125 million optical cells?

"So I was traveling along the coast of the Gulf of Genoa," Magdalena said, interrupting my reflections concerning the obviously oft-lacking optical apparatus of the average Austrian passerby. "And right after Lerici I saw from afar a cliff towering far above the sea and crowned by a church. Though at that moment, a moment preceding my first homicide, I felt no particular need to confess, I decided to ride up the twisting road to the church, drawn by the beauty of the view. The view of the sea was breathtaking. I parked the Puch 800 on the cobblestone courtyard of the church and went to the gate, above which stood the words: Abbazia di San Michele Arcangelo.

"Do you like fairy tales, Reverend?" Magdalena asked abruptly, looking at me. "But of course you like fairy tales, as a priest you are familiar, through your readings of the Old and New Testaments, with a great number of such tales and their tellers. The Old Testament prophets and the New Testament evangelists doubtless number among the most gifted of storytellers, just as the Old and New Testaments count among the most lovely collections of fairy tales, bringing together the most colorful array of exciting and moving stories of magic, wonder, farce, animals, horror, fate, and formula. And because you like fairy tales, as a Catholic priest must, is almost even forced to, you will also, as a Catholic priest, like what I now will tell you.

"Abbazia di San Michele Arcangelo stood over the gate, which was closed. As I turned to leave, a toothless little manikin with a bunch of keys stepped out of a side door and said that surely I wanted to see the coffins. Before I could answer he took me by the hand and pulled me along behind him into the interior of the old abbey, through the nave, past a shining silver statue of the Archangel Michael swinging his sword, and down a stone stairway. Taking out a rusty iron key, the little man opened a lovely wrought-iron gate and we entered a huge room, which was filled to the ceiling with shelves packed with ancient books. The toothless little man patted the yellowing leather spines with their faded gold lettering.

"'Secrets,' he giggled, 'many secrets. No one reads the books, no one learns the secrets.'

"The little man moved on, down a second set of stone steps to the depths of the church, and over to a statue of Christ, bleeding from countless wounds, that was standing under a transparent nylon awning.

"'Our Christ,' the little man explained. 'For the processions. Our processions are the longest. People come from great distances to see our processions.'

"The little man led me to a small round window.

"'Look,' he said. 'Look at the sea. There lies the sea.'

"The abbey was perched on the cliff directly above the sea, and you looked out the windows as if out of the porthole of a huge ship. The sea spread out below, an infinite plane of gray pasteboard waves. The hazy outline of an island could be seen in the distance.

"'My beauty,' the little man giggled, looking up at me, 'my lovely.' And he lifted his right hand to stroke my shoulder and pinch my cheek. 'Oh, my little one, what all you have yet to endure. There,' he said, taking his hand from my hip, where it had landed, and pointing into the semidark of the corridor. 'Go. There are the steps.'

"And with that the little man turned and departed with his clanging bunch of keys. I slowly made my way along the winding corridor and down a short spiral staircase, until I was standing before a broad iron door. I pressed the large and cold door handle and the door opened. I found myself in a kind of chapel, a subterranean church, in a room lit by weak candlelight, with two rows of wooden benches, some of which had cracked seats. I walked between the rows to an altar covered with a crimson-colored cloth, before which stood four small, gilded coffins, like children's coffins, two to each side. The lids of the coffins, which also were covered in crimson-colored cloth, were pushed to one side, and the coffins were empty. There were four human skulls standing on the altar, in an order that intimated that a fifth skull was missing. I stood before the altar and looked at the red and gold coffins, the skulls shimmering whitely, and the faded fresco on the dirty altar wall of a pink pelican feeding its young with its own blood. When I perceived a long dark shadow behind the altar table to the right, I took a few steps in that direction. The outline of a larger coffin came into view. In this coffin a man was stretched out, the fifth skull on his chest. I leaned over him and he opened his eyes, looked at me, took the skull in both hands, and sat up.

"'An extraordinary abbey,' he said in English. 'Have you met its strange curator?'

"I stared at the skull in his hands.

"'Oh,' he said. 'I merely wanted to take the opportunity, you know. One doesn't often have the chance during one's lifetime to lie in a coffin. A strange sensation. New sensations are always interesting, don't you think?'

"The man stood and stepped out of the coffin. He was about six feet tall and extremely thin.

"'Hold this,' he said, and pressed the skull into my hands. Then he dusted off his black Diesel jeans and his black denim shirt.

"And that, Reverend, is how I came to know the Frisian."

Magdalena stood and took a few steps over to the brook, partially concealed by tufts of grass and patches of moss, which flowed at the edge of the clearing, clasped her hands behind her, and stared into the water. I was hot, the sun was shining directly in my face and blinding me.

"That's how it began. Beginnings are always the nicest, don't you agree, Reverend? Beginnings like the one with the Frisian. After the beginning, which is also the high point, begins the decline: a slippery slope, a plunge over a cliff, a downward corkscrew, like a feather in the air or an oak leaf in the fall, the steep drop into a valley, with or without a helmet, a vertical drop in an elevator, a stumbling down a spiral staircase. It's always a descent."

She bent down. Something in the grass beside the brook had caught her attention.

"I've always loved beginnings," she said. "I ask myself in

all seriousness whether one of the things that turned me into
a seven-fold murderess of men was the brevity of the descent
and, therefore, the accelerated initiation of a new beginning.
I ask myself in all seriousness. The descent must be cut short.
If you can't totally eliminate the descent, there are always
measures you can take, various machinations that reduce
them to a minimum.

"A strange creature," she then said, bending down further.
"Highly strange. As I said, the most important thing is to
reduce these descents to as little time as possible. There's no
way to eliminate them, to get rid of them completely, because
of the laws of Western logic. Once a beginning has been
defined as such and nothing follows, then it wasn't a beginning. And beginnings must, under all circumstances, be
retained.

"Some sort of grasshopper," she murmured, pushing a tuft
of grass to one side, "a mantis. Hard to find. All beginnings
are breathtaking, exciting, intoxicating, and magical, yet no
two are alike. You're traveling along the autobahn one foggy
November day when suddenly you skid, flip over twice, lose
consciousness, come to in an ambulance, gaze up into the
green eyes of an ambulance attendant, and you're lost, just as
the ambulance attendant is. You fall down the steps of an
escalator in a department store, pulling a thirty-year-old dec-
orator down with you and feel, even as you fall, the enormous physical attraction between the two of you. You trash
your apartment in a fit of rage and beat your wife and child
so badly they have to be hospitalized, and as they put you in
a straitjacket to take you to the nearest psychiatric ward you
spot a deathly pale student sitting on a bench in the same
ambulance, and the sight of her makes your heart leap into
your throat. You go to formally declare the bankruptcy of

your small business, and as the somewhat full-faced official is explaining more than you ever wanted to know concerning the minimal existence you will be leading from this point on, it becomes clear to you that you have finally found your purpose in life. You're arranging your father's funeral and you fall in love at first sight with the no-longer-quite-young clerk of the flower shop where you order the funeral wreath. You're in a Laundromat and open the safety catch of the washing machine to remove your tangled bedsheets to discover that everything has been faded a light blue because the person before you has left a dark blue wool sock in the machine. You yell at this person, who now is removing his wash from the dryer in order to fold it, and as you're yelling at him you notice in yourself all the symptoms of incipient passion.

"At such beginnings the sleeping car of your existence is derailed, the freight cars of fate jump track, the bogie flatcar of being rolls down the slope, the express train of life leaves the rails. After such beginnings you're no longer the same person you were before such beginnings. Beginnings are the best.

"Truly, it's a praying mantis," Magdalena said, shaking her curls back and forth. She reached down carefully into the grass, then stood and came toward me with a light step to stretch out her hand in my direction. On her palm sat a strange creature I had never seen before, a delicate, light green insect roughly seven centimeters long, with a narrow head, overly long front legs, wings that folded upon its back, and a triangular head with a broad forehead.

"*Mantis religiosa*, the praying mantis," the sinner explained. "So named because it lies in wait for its victims with its front legs raised, as if in prayer. This is the second praying mantis

I've encountered in my lifetime. I discovered the first on the Kaiserstuhl in Baden. Judging from the size of this one, we're dealing with a female. The females, by the way, devour the male after they successfully mate."

The sinner set the insect on my left knee and took a step back.

"Hold still, Reverend," she said, "I'll be right back." She ran over to her Puch sidecar motorcycles and got an empty marmalade jar from her tool kit. She held up the jar. "One of my mother's marmalade jars. Raspberry, 1990. Long since eaten. I love raspberry marmalade." She approached cautiously. "An unusual catch," she said, slipping the jar over the praying mantis sitting on my left knee, then turning the glass over to screw on the lid. "We couldn't just let it fly away, now could we, Reverend? Such a rare insect." She held the marmalade jar up before her eyes. "We'll watch her. We'll study her. Such an interesting insect. Eats the male. Insect cannibalism. Keep your eyes open, Reverend. Keep your eyes open for a male. It's not unlikely that there's a male in the vicinity." She placed the marmalade jar down on the ground beside me. Then she continued her story.

"When I saw the Frisian it was instantly clear that this was one of those new beginnings. I recognized in him a male archetype that often appears in my dreams, in the form of a roughly six-foot skeleton that pursues me as I try to escape. In the subterranean church of the Abbazia di San Michele this skeleton finally caught up with me. From the look the Frisian gave me it could be assumed that I, too, embodied his dream woman. Had we not heard the shuffling footsteps and clanging keys of the little man, we would have slipped right into the coffin together, overjoyed at the surprise of this unhoped-for encounter. Instead, we put the fifth skull back in its place on the altar and gave the little man a tip. He took the bill and bowed to us several times.

"'*Cari, carissimi,*' he said. 'Ah, the lovers. What all you must yet endure. Ah, you lovers.'

"He positioned himself between us, took my right hand and the Frisian's left, lay them on top of each other, and giggled.

"'Go,' he said. 'Go and take pleasure in each other.'

"We left the abbey, and it was understood that the Frisian would get into the Felber sidecar and go with me. He left his bicycle with the curator's plump daughter, who was hanging the wash on the small terrace near the abbey, overlooking the sea.

"We decided to take the ferry from the next harbor town and go over to the island we had seen from the Abbazia. During the trip I stole frequent sidelong glances at the Frisian, who was staring in silence at the sea, smoking one cigarette after another. He was an ugly man, of a sort of ugliness that was very attractive to me. His arms and legs were thin and overly long, as were his fingers; he hunched slightly, and his head was small in relation to his body, his eyes deepset, his skin covered with old acne scars that had healed poorly; his teeth were bad and nicotine had turned his fingertips a yellowish-brown. He had a large mouth with wide, protruding lips that stuck out and turned down at the corners, like the mouth of a fish, and which were enclosed in the parentheses of deep lines both left and right. He held his cigarette in his right hand and constantly pulled at the skin of his lower jaw with his left. He laughed often and his shrill laughter, which came in fits and starts, startled me. My companion's unfortunate appearance was underscored by his burning, fixed stare. Yet all of these repulsive physical attribules combined to make him irresistible. His ugliness was so unadulterated that in the end it transformed itself to become a new, darkly shining beauty, made even more fascinating by the fact that it bore all the sensuality of ugliness.

"Beauty is always concealed in ugliness, and ugliness in beauty. I have always been interested in apparent ugliness, because beneath the appearance of ugliness is beauty, passion, and sensuality. It is important to view apparent beauty with skepticism, for under the layer of apparent beauty it is highly probable that true, and not apparent, ugliness lies, ugliness, coldness, and boredom. Are you, like the rest of the world, hung up on the good, the true, and the beautiful? Just like the rest of the world you are of course hung up on the good, the true, and the beautiful. If you gave it some thought, Reverend, you would become a follower of the apparently evil, untrue, and ugly, as I did, and in doing so would transform yourself and the world around you.

"It was the sensuality that I sensed beneath the Frisian's ugliness and the passion I attributed to this man who resembled, on the one hand, a daddy long-legs, and on the other a carp, a perch, which led me to look so forward to visiting the island, the features of which were becoming more and more visible as we stood on the deck, leaning our arms on the railing.

"An island is a place of longing, Reverend, it is paradise regained after long wanderings. The knowledge that a sojourn to a place of longing is finite, that one will be driven not only from original paradise, but sooner or later from paradise regained as well, should not diminish the joy at arriving in such a paradise, but it does.

"Our island was a mirage of bluish contours in a shining sea, a utopia of bays and overhanging cliffs, wrapped in the scent of lemon and orange blossoms, an acoustic illusion of softly lapping waves and the prolonged signal tones of passing ships.

"We rented a little blue house that stood alone in the midst of a lemon grove above a cliff that dropped down to the sea. I would have preferred an apartment closer to the small fishing village at the south end of the island, but the Frisian was of the opinion that you couldn't trust people, you had to distance yourself, keep as much space between you and them as possible. That should have made me stop and think, that and the fact that when I met him he was lying in a coffin with a skull on his chest. But at the time nothing made me stop and think, absolutely nothing. At the time I wasn't thinking at all, I was concentrating solely on the nights to come that I would spend with the Frisian in the little blue house, and once they arrived I concentrated on enjoying them. My intimations concerning the sensuality and passion concealed by the Frisian's ugliness had not proved wrong.

"They were long nights, during which the Frisian, whose body seemed to consist of nothing but skin and bone, demonstrated amazing tenderness, sensitivity, and devotion. We often spent these nights outdoors in some sheltered place. There was a narrow and steeply winding path behind the house that led down to the sea through yellow blooms of thorny broom bushes. Once darkness fell the Frisian would give me a look, take my hand, and motion with his head toward the door. He would give me just enough time to grab the sleeping bag and a bottle of wine, and then he would pull me out of the house and down the narrow moonlit path to the edge of the cliff. There we would spread the sleeping bag out on a stone plateau washed smooth by the sea. The waves broke on the rocks, shooting white plumes into the air around us, spraying us with a fine coat of water that made our bodies glisten green-white in the moonlight. We couldn't hear our own stammering sounds, the roar of the crashing waves drowned out everything. The shadows of the bats that lived in the small grottoes that dotted the shore cut lines through the night that were darker than the dark. An occasional ship would pass by, bright with lights.

"During the day we walked around the island, often pestered by the hunting dogs who fetched the birds shot for sport by the island's inhabitants, and we took pleasure in the yellow lemons and the blue aromatic artichoke blossoms. We fed the two cats that hung around our blue cottage and stepped gingerly through our door. One cat was skinny and wild and had one blind eye, and the other was soft and elegant, with a gray coat and the blue eyes of a Siamese. We didn't know if they belonged to anyone. The one-eyed cat always ran over to the Frisian, the other liked to sit on my lap and cautiously touch my face with drawn-in claws. The Frisian told me nothing at all about himself or the life he had come from, nor did I ask. He talked very little at all, but our nights together made up for his taciturn nature. He would sit for hours on the stone bench behind the house and stare at the sea. If I tried to stroke his high forehead he would push my hand aside. After a while I would catch him talking quietly to himself. I couldn't understand what he was saying, for he talked rapidly and almost silently, in a hissing voice that frightened me. He would gesture broadly as he talked, and during his monologues his eyes would be opened wide. I tried to get him to go down to the harbor and the small market with me, to have more contact with people, but, uncommunicative from the beginning, he would withdraw even more, pressing himself against the walls of the houses and avoiding people, so that we soon were greeted with suspicion and mistrust, which disturbed him even more and caused us to return to our little blue house even sooner than before. When I went to town alone, people would ask me if my husband were ill.

"I tried to ignore the Frisian's strange condition, but I noticed that his melancholic state was gradually beginning to affect me, and that I, too, was becoming monosyllabic. And our financial worries were oppressing me as well. It was I alone who paid the rent and bought our daily groceries, as the Frisian had next to no money at all. I was constantly trying to think up ways to get money. Once, when for the fun of it I donned my brown Carmelite costume and accompanying white mantle and wore it to the lemon grove to march up and down in it for the Frisian, an idea came to me: I would take the ferry into the harbor town on the mainland, change into the habit of the Shoeless Carmelites, and try to obtain some money through petty theft. I was convinced that a nun's habit would make stealing a great deal easier. Scarcely anyone would suspect a nun of being a thief, particularly in Italy. Would you imagine that a Carmelite could be a thief? Unaware of my money worries as he was, I would tell the Frisian nothing, let him believe I had access to limitless amounts of cash. He seemed not in the least perturbed by the fact that I was supporting him, we never spoke of money, any more than we spoke of anything of a personal nature, of our past, our families, our education. He seemed to be satisfied to live with me and eat what I set before him. And as long as he gave me those long looks in the evening and took me by the hand to lead me out of the house and down to the cliff above the sea, I would ask no questions, and see to it that he got enough sleep and enough good food so that he would be well-disposed to continue these more than satisfactory evenings.

"On top of which, he found me so exciting and desirable in my Carmelite habit that, ignoring the possibility of our being discovered by some bird hunter or one of his dogs wandering through, he would take my clothes off in the middle of the lemon grove, first the white mantle, then the robe, spread out my clothing on the grass beneath the lemon trees, smooth it out, and lay me down on it."

As if she were reliving this in her memory, the sinner stroked the grass with her lovely slender hand and sighed. I must admit that I was infuriated by this sacrilege, related so casually, by this profaning of a sacred item of clothing, by the flagrant purpose of its removal and the offense committed against a group that struggled to live a life pleasing to God. But despite my anger I found it difficult to banish the image, invoked by the sinner's words, of the two young people lying on the white Carmelite mantle in the lemon grove.

"To tell the truth," the sinner said, continuing her blasphemous tale, "I find your lily-white alb quite attractive as well, such a pure, unsullied white." She slid her lovely, slender hand under my dalmatic and devoted herself to fingering the white material that covered my knee, immediately triggering my knee reflex and sending my legs, bound at the ankles as they were by the green nylon clothesline, up into the air.

"Nice knee," she murmured, "smooth and round." Then her hand made its way to the hollow of my knee, at which I jumped again, as I'm quite sensitive there. "Oh, and the hollow of your knee, so soft," she murmured again, and withdrew her hand slowly, not before trailing her long nails gently along my shin. "To tell the truth, I find the sight of men in women's clothing extremely seductive. Unfortunately that opportunity seldom arises, only during Church services and in specialty shops do I get my money's worth in that department. But then, I always found the nightshirts my father wore to be quite fetching.

"At any rate, the Frisian would pull the Carmelite habit with its white mantle over my head, just as I could pull your dalmatic with its stola over your head if I wished, and your alb and your pluvial, if you wore one. I could pull your robe over your head, however, only if I removed the faded rope that binds your hands. And as I probably wouldn't be willing to do that, I would just pull up your alb, dalmatic, and stola, and you'd be sitting there with your robe over your head, unable to move and blind to boot. I find the idea appealing, I must admit. A priest with his robe thrown over his head, an ascetic priest's body missing the head that goes with it, a body that surely has been strengthened over the course of time by strict religious practices, sexual abstinence, fasting, perhaps even by self-flagellation, a body bound and totally at my mercy, marked perhaps by scars from the flagellation, there's an exciting idea, I must admit. To gently stroke those scars with the tips of my fingers, scars no one has ever touched, is an enticing thought."

As she said this, the sinner's eyes gleamed, and for the first time I was seriously aware of the situation in which I found myself. This woman sitting before me and talking without cease was mentally deranged, an unpredictable crazy person who would not hesitate to act out of her own spontaneous, crazed impulses, who would violate a man of the cloth, a body no woman had violated, with the exception of my sister Maria's occasional harmless gestures of tenderness. In my mind's eye I saw myself sitting there in a state of extreme indignity, the clothing of my Order up around my ears, prey to the fingers of this woman capable of anything, her slender young fingers, which tapered down to the nails, had already begun their reconnaissance, their exploration, their shameless ferreting. I was in the most extreme danger.

"But Reverend, there are drops of sweat on your brow," the sinner said, interrupting my desperate thoughts. "Wait." She came nearer and, pulling a white lace handkerchief from one of the many secret, zippered pockets of her jumpsuit, wiped the sweat from my forehead with gentle fingers.

"Hold still," she said, "don't flinch. The beginning of June, and already it's so hot. Your face is directly in the sun. Wait a minute." She took a few steps back, opened the zipper of one of the deep pockets of her jumpsuit, and finally found what she was seeking—a pair of sunglasses of classic design and very dark glass. She approached me holding the ear pieces with both hands, and pushed them onto my face.

"So," she said, "that you don't hurt your eyes, Reverend. Nothing is further from my mind that treating you with disrespect. They don't look bad on you, the Ray-Bans, they're a souvenir of Jonathan Alistair, incidentally, whom I have yet to tell you about. After it was all over, I took them with me.

"As our financial situation was becoming increasingly dire, I did in fact pack the habit of the Shoeless Carmelites into a big plastic bag and take the vaporetto to the harbor town on the mainland. Once there, I went to the women's rest room at the train station to change. I left the plastic bag containing my jeans and T-shirt in a locker. Then I got on a bus on the busiest route.

"'Come, Sister, come,' a well-dressed lady said, helping me up the two steps into the overcrowded bus. A young man immediately stood and offered me his seat, an offer I declined with thanks, as I needed to stand in a thick crowd of people in order to carry out my plan. What should I say, Reverend, it was simpler than I had imagined. First I removed the soft calfskin billfold from the elegant handbag with the shoulder strap and magnetic clasp of the lady who had helped me onto the bus, it was child's play. After I had concealed the calfskin billfold in the folds of my habit she smiled at me and said, 'Awfully crowded, isn't it, Sister? But as one can't find a taxi at this hour, the bus is your only choice.'

"The bus stopped, and as the young man who had offered me his seat passed me on his way to the door I carefully lifted the small wallet from his back pocket. As the bus started up I saw him standing at the bus stop, reaching into his back pocket and then waving his arms in the air. I was pushed further toward the back by passengers getting on, and found myself standing next to a harmless-looking elderly little man with a bald head and a black briefcase. As he was looking out the window it was not difficult to steal his wallet either, flat and clearly outlined by the cloth of his pants as it was. I got out at the next stop. I hurried along the city streets and turned into a side alley to check the contents of the three wallets. Surprisingly, the young man had the most cash on him, whereas the calfskin billfold of the well-dressed woman held only a few coins, a pocket calendar, and a photograph of a little girl. I took the money from the two men's wallets and threw them away, keeping the calfskin one with the pocket calendar, coins, and picture of the little girl. I walked a little further and then sat down on a park bench next to a young woman whose child was playing in a sandbox.

"'This heat,' the woman said. 'But my child wanted to come to the playground. Aren't you warm in your habit?'

"We talked for a while, and then she jumped up to run after her child, who had climbed out of the sandbox and on all fours was crawling with amazing speed toward the exit of the little park. I took the opportunity to unzip the small side pocket of the mother's violet plastic backpack lying on the bench, remove her Turkish cloth wallet, and close the zipper again. My curiosity was so great that I took a quick look inside, where I saw a credit card. When the mother returned with her child in her arms I joked a bit with the ugly little girl and then said that I had to go, my fellow sisters were expecting me for common prayer. I departed with the words: God's blessings on you and your child! Then I went to a large department store nearby and bought clothes and groceries for me and the Frisian, as well as a large bag I could carry everything in. I was treated with the greatest consideration, people opened doors for me and believed it when I said that my mother superior had instructed me to buy food and clothing for a family whose house had burned to the ground and, therefore, had nothing.

"'Oh, how good you are, you and your fellow sisters,' the saleswoman said. 'Never thinking of yourselves, always of others. There's a place reserved for you in heaven.'

"That evening I took the plastic bag from the locker at the train station, changed clothes in the rest room, and took the vaporetto back to the island. The Frisian was sitting on the bench at the back of the house, deep in conversation with himself, and barely acknowledged my return. When I unpacked the bag and showed him what I had bought, he expressed neither joy nor surprise. Nevertheless, that night he pulled me out of the house and down to the cliff, which he hadn't done in two weeks. For the final decline had begun, Reverend. His behavior grew stranger by the day. I suffered from the change in him, and his depression, which got worse by the day, weighed heavily upon my soul. Even his body, which to my great delight had been so agile in the beginning, appeared to have gotten heavier, and to almost crush me during the increasingly infrequent nights at the edge of the sea.

"One day when I came home from the market he was standing on a chair in the middle of the room, his neck in a noose that he had attached to a hook in the ceiling. When he saw the horrified expression on my face he smiled sadly, removed the noose, and climbed down from the chair. When I asked what he was doing he said that he was always in search of new sensations, like the time at the Abbazia when he lay down with the skull in the coffin. He was addicted to new sensations, it was in his nature, and if some new sensation didn't turn up on its own he felt compelled to create one himself. He had experimented during his lifetime with a great many sensations, he said, had created and tried out almost all the sensations one possibly could. Evenings, when he took me by the hand and led me down the steep path to the sea, well, that was also about experiencing a new sensation. And what he experienced during the many nights we spent on the smooth rocks of the cliff by the water was, in a certain sense, new to him. Unfortunately, however, it recently had occurred to him that the new sensations he experienced were beginning to repeat themselves, and therefore weren't so new. This was the reason for his depression, his weariness. He was always pushing himself to discover new sensations, and these sensations were always wearing themselves out, he said. Didn't I understand that he was a Sisyphus of sensations, pushing his sensation boulder up a steep mountain, only to watch it roll back down to the valley, and therefore be forced to begin anew? He no longer knew what to do, so the only thing remaining was the sensation of death, that was the only thing yet unfamiliar to him.

"Reverend, after this admission I tried everything possible to awaken new sensations in the Frisian, an attempt doomed from the outset, for he was interested only in the sensation of death. No other sensation was intense enough. I cooked dishes for him I had never cooked before, I played music I had never played before, I made love to him in ways I had never made love before, I put the one-eyed cat in his lap— nothing worked. He seemed to have retreated into a world I had no entry to, and I noticed what a burden he was becoming. His thoughts, circling exclusively around death as they did, hung in the air like heavy black velvet curtains that I was constantly having to raise or push to one side. Each time I left the house I dreaded my return, dreaded the state I would find him in.

"I tolerated the situation, intolerable as it was, for a long time, but once he no longer made the effort to take me by the hand in the evening and pull me out of the house I began to avoid him, to wish that he would experience the sensation of death without limit, once and for all. But he lacked resolve. If he decided to try out the sensation of gassing himself, stuffing all the cracks in the doors and windows and turning on the gas, then fifteen minutes after he stuck his head in the oven the gas company employees would go on the strike they had been threatening for ages, and I would come home from my shopping to find him lying in front of the oven, unconscious but very much alive. When he felt it was time to try out the new sensation of a lengthy free-fall followed by a bounce off a flat surface, and jumped off the cliff behind the house that dropped off to the sea, then nine feet into the fall he got snagged on a pine branch and had to be rescued by the local fire department, which set me back a good deal financially and forced me once again to pack my Carmelite habit in a plastic bag and journey to the mainland. When he decided to experience fully the sensation of slicing open his veins, he bungled it so badly that he passed out, and I had to come up with the money to clean the bathroom rug. When he wanted the experience of a fatal overdose, he took too little of the drug and had to be transported by vaporetto to the harbor town on the mainland to have his stomach pumped, a good deed that once again did not come cheap. Once, when he wanted to experience a bullet through the head, the one-eyed cat jumped up on him at the very moment he fired the pistol he had found in the toolshed, with the result that he singed his hair and a little of the skin on the top of his head, but this at least involved only the cost of a bandage.

"You will understand, Reverend, that following this and other similar events the Frisian began to repulse me to the same degree he once had attracted me. And you surely will agree when I say that inconsequentiality, if not one of the seven deadly sins, nevertheless does not number among the positive character traits, and therefore it is totally under-standable that a woman whose lover has, over a long period of time, demonstrated such indecisiveness, indifference, and lack of determination as did the Frisian, would lose respect for him and finally turn away from him entirely. Had the Frisian at least proved capable of regularly continuing our nocturnal outings to the sea, I gladly would have tolerated his other escapades in search of new sensations, and borne all the costs incurred without a murmur. These nocturnal outings would have been compensation enough for his eccentricities in the area of new sensations. But unfortu-nately these outings became ever more infrequent, and finally ceased altogether.

"To the degree to which the frequency of our outings

decreased, my wish increased that the Frisian would finally attain his desired goal, the as-yet-unexperienced, last possible sensation. When after three weeks he had made no attempt to take me by the hand and pull me from the house, I made my decision: I would create for him the sensation of drowning. Of all the death experiences, drowning would for him be the most interesting, the most unusual, for the element of water was, for him, the most alien.

"Often, when our nights at the edge of the sea got me too heated up, I would swim out into the water, into the black sea at the new moon and into the silver sea at the full moon, to enjoy the quiet, the soft splashing of my strokes, the cool water. At first the Frisian would call out to me, concerned that I wasn't strong enough to make it back to shore. But when he saw how well I swam, he expressed his admiration. He himself was a nonswimmer, which was reason enough for me to feel sorry for him. As someone who had grown up on an Austrian lake, someone who had come to know the water at an early age, I of course pitied anyone who did not have a close connection to water. Anyone who so loves the water from the beginning that her mother has to make her come in from the lake because she would never come in of her own free will, is naturally contemptuous of those who shun the water. Someone like that can't comprehend why everyone doesn't rush right into any large body of water as she does, can't understand that there are people who, as soon as they stick their big toe into liquid, immediately take it out again and get as far away as possible, who do not twist and turn in the water like fish, who don't know the different strokes— breaststroke, crawl, backstroke, butterfly—and who take no joy in diving from a thirty-foot board down to the bottom of a lake and back up again.

"Once I realized the degree to which the Frisian disliked water, and yet how much he was drawn to it at the same time, I cautiously tried to introduce him to this element. First I got him to sit at the edge of the rocks and trail his feet in the water. The next step was to slowly go out into the sea with him, first up to his calves, then up to his knees, then up to his stomach, until finally he was up to his neck in it. Then I talked him into briefly putting his head in the water. After he became a little familiar with the water I began to teach him to swim, to help him coordinate his arm and leg movements. He learned slowly, but after a few weeks he was swimming a few yards out into the sea cautiously and holding his head out of the water. But he still was rather uncertain in his movements.

"Believe me, Reverend, the decision to drown the Frisian was not an easy one. I am not a born murderess, am not a murderess by nature. No one can say of me that on foggy Saturday evenings in November I would stick a thin transparent nylon rope or a knife under my trench coat and stand on some street corner to lie in wait for innocent men to emerge from late-night movies, the sound of their footsteps echoing in the still night betraying their approach. I would never wander the woods in search of lone males with skinny necks who were gathering mushrooms, and it would never occur to me to stalk with murderous intent some youth at night in the long, tiled corridors of the last subway stop. It does not suit my nature to lure men into my apartment under false pretenses, to then chop them up in pieces and store them in the freezer until some later date. To the contrary, Reverend, look at me: My body was put here to be embraced by a man's, my skin is here to be stroked by him, my mouth here for his to kiss, my hair to be tousled by his hands. Nor did I desire anything else from the Frisian but to be embraced, stroked, and kissed by moonlight at the edge of the sea. I became a murderess involuntarily, the inalterable change for the worse that the Frisian caused in me made me one. I acted in self-defense, Reverend, I decided upon this dire measure because otherwise it would have been I who died.

"After a while I too manifested the same grave symptoms of melancholy the Frisian suffered from. I had nightmares, began talking to myself, would bubble over with joy one minute and be profoundly sad the next, began to stutter when talking to the island's inhabitants, and would press myself against the sides of houses, as unsociable as he. My pulse slowed, my eyes sunk deeper into my head, and when I went out I was afraid an airplane would fall on me. I began to believe that the two cats were bewitched, that in reality they were my two elder sisters, whose tight skirts may have kept them from climbing over the wood fence I jumped with my Puch 800, but who nevertheless had pursued me across the borders of Austria, in feline form. When I gazed into the tall Venetian mirror in the foyer of our blue house I saw a woman slightly bent over, with thin, overly long arms and legs and an empty, burning look in her eyes, a woman with a relatively small head, a large mouth with wide lips that stuck out and turned down at the corners like that of a fish, deep creases to the right and left like parentheses.

"Reverend, I had begun to resemble the Frisian in an uncanny manner, a phenomenon that frightened me and made me consider for the first time his eventual violent demise. This thought, at first only a vague idea, took on con-crete form after I found myself standing at the edge of the high cliff and staring down at the sea, or in the toolshed dreamily fingering a noose, or absentmindedly making tiny cuts in my wrists with a razor blade. But the final decision came only after it had been three weeks since the Frisian had taken me by the hand and pulled me to edge of the sea at night.

"To the right of the cliff we no longer frequented there was a small but deep grotto, entered by swimming through a narrow entryway and from the ceiling of which hung a large number of bats, who flew out in the evenings through a crack in the rocks that let in a little light. Sometimes I swam into the grotto and then turned to watch as the clear water of the waves rolled in to almost flood the entrance. I touched the wet walls of rock that formed the grotto and that were crawling with little crabs, and on which coral-red seaweed grew. Surrounded by the semidarkness of the shimmering rock walls I loved to look down into the blue-green depths below me. I wanted to lure the Frisian into this grotto, which he had never entered before. It wouldn't be easy. I waited for a time when he was in a good mood, which at that point was only after a dinner during which he had imbibed a great deal. I bought expensive sweet wines from the south of Italy, and prepared delicious meals.

"One evening when the full moon had risen like a golden discus in the night sky and he had retired after dinner to the little terrace behind the house, to lean back and drunkenly sing his Frisian seafaring songs, I went over to him, took his hand, and pulled him upright. Now it was I who headed down the steep path to the sea, and the Frisian who let me pull him along, lulled by the wine into a state somewhere between apathy and arousal. Once we reached the cliff I put my arms around him, described how beautiful the grotto was, and suggested he swim the short distance there with me. He agreed and swam slowly along behind me through the high, narrow entrance to the grotto. It was dark inside except for a single moonbeam shining through a thin slit in the rock. I turned to the Frisian, of whom I could see only a dark outline of head and shoulders against the entrance to the cave. The alcohol and the new surroundings appeared to make him amorous, and for the first time in weeks he approached and began touching me under water. But it was too late. I grabbed him by his narrow shoulders and pushed him beneath the surface with all my strength. He immediately grasped that this was a matter of life and death and began to defend himself. I would never have gotten into a struggle with him had I not known that the Frisian was physically weaker than I, a fact clearly demonstrated during our long nights together on the cliff. His light and delicate body was just as weak as it appeared to be.

"But now the Frisian was fighting for his life, and the survival instinct gave him a strength he had never before had. I kept pushing him under the water and he kept wriggling out of my grasp and shooting up again, his mouth open wide. He tried clinging to the wet grotto walls with his spidery fingers, but each time he slipped back down again. He thrashed about him, pulling my hair, but soon tired, as I had just taught him how to swim and he wasn't used to treading water for any length of time. He was coming up for air less often and fighting back with diminishing strength. I myself am a strong woman, my ancestors are Austrian peasants and craftsmen. I didn't slow my efforts, quite the contrary, I wrapped my legs around the Frisian's so he couldn't move. Half-unconscious, he stopped fighting back. It was at this moment that I was tempted to stop, even to tow him ashore and lay him on our flat rock smoothed by the sea. But that would have changed nothing, he simply would have slipped back into his melancholic state and pulled me down with him until, in the end, we would have been cringing together like identical twins at the bottom of a black hole. When I became conscious of the hopelessness of the situation, I summoned all of my strength and pushed the Frisian under the surface for as long as I could. He struggled one last time under water and then stopped moving. I carefully loosed my grip, but didn't let go of his body. When he no longer showed any sign of life I grabbed him under the arms and pulled him to shore. There I lay him on his back on our rocky shelf. There was no point in waiting for him to open his eyes."

The sinner fell silent. Obviously she was overwhelmed by the memory of the Frisian lying dead on the shore; her face took on a painful grimace and she closed her eyes and massaged her forehead. I stared at her. Had she told the truth? Had she really lured a man into a trap and murdered him in cold blood? I felt the hair of my arms stand on end, and had the feeling that the hair on my head was doing the same.

"It was no problem to present the Frisian's death to the police as a swimming accident. Police in general are of a near unsurpassable stupidity, and in Italy they appear dumber than elsewhere, just as the inhabitants of primarily Catholic countries are in general dumber than the inhabitants of other countries. This does not apply directly to you, Reverend, the dignitaries of the Catholic Church are, of course, exempted from this judgment. Dignitaries of the Catholic Church are, of course, anything but dumb. In order to keep such a large number of people dumb for thousands of years, the dignitaries of the Catholic Church, that is to say those who determine the policy of the Catholic Church, are obviously very intelligent, above all those higher-ranking dignitaries. Which is not to say that lower-ranking dignitaries are among the dumbest, either. But to call them smart wouldn't be the truth; terms such as *clever, cunning, sly,* would be more appropriate, as most lower dignitaries are—must be—in general, to sail along in the lee of higher dignitaries, as anyone who sails along in someone else's lee must be clever, cunning, and sly. It is not left to true believers of the Catholic Church, whose shepherd, Jesus Christ, so appropriately refers to them as His sheep, to think for themselves, any more than it is left to those who live under a dictatorship, or to psychologists, psychiatrists, psychotherapists, and psychoanalysts. Perhaps they are convinced that they think for themselves, that their freedom of thought is unrestricted, but the majority of the material of which their thinking consists has been dictated to them, so they don't, of course, inhabit their own bold abodes of intellect but, instead, modest prefab Catholic housing, no architectural marvel in itself, but merely standardized prefab Catholic intellectual housing. This design of the prefab housing of the Catholic intellect is reflected in general in their outward appearance, which is well-suited to the metaphor I just mentioned, the one involving a shepherd.

"Several days later the Frisian's mother—who, like most Frisians, is not a Catholic and therefore not a prefab thinker—arrived from Uithuizermeeden in northeastern Holland. Unlike the Catholic police of the island she was not convinced right off the bat that it was a swimming accident, but gave me a sidelong glance and asked a good many questions involving the relationship between me and her son. She remained skeptical even after I had answered all of her questions satisfactorily. I wanted to say: What do you want? Be glad I spared your son a long and melancholic life! Be glad I cut it short, that you don't have to spend the rest of your life in Uithuizermeeden in northeastern Holland taking care of your son, who would never have found the way out of his labyrinth of melancholy, but would have wandered more deeply into it, be glad that you don't have to quiet his nightmares, talk him down from his hallucinations, that you aren't forced to go walking with him in the marshes, to fight the salty sea wind with him, to accompany him on his increasingly morbid expeditions in search of new sensations! Thank me, I would like to have said, thank me for accelerating the end of your son's life, for speeding his demise! But I didn't, for it was to be expected that his mother, who had traveled all the way from Uithuizermeeden, wouldn't agree with my argument, which wouldn't necessarily have spoken against its plausibility but against a Frisian mother's ideas concerning death, which, though not Catholic, were traditional nevertheless. The mother departed with the plain coffin in which her son found his final rest, but not before throwing one last skeptical look my way from the deck of the ferry. I continued to live in the blue house for a while after that, feeding the cats and spending an occasional night alone at the edge of the sea."

The sinner looked at her watch. "And now, Reverend, we shall listen to the news," she said, walking over to the Puch sidecar motorcycle and taking her Walkman from one of the tool pockets, then swinging onto the seat and putting on her headphones. "Five more minutes," she said. "Five more minutes until the news. I would be very surprised if they've picked up our trail. That truly would surprise me. How could they be on our trail, since I didn't ask for a ransom. It's not about money, as you know, it's not about ideology, as it is for other kidnappers, it's not about freeing one's like-minded comrades. That's not what it could be about for me, I don't have any like-minded comrades, a fact that occasionally makes me sad, though only occasionally—for the most part it's an advantage not to have like-minded comrades. If you have like-minded comrades you find yourself dangerously close to the shepherd Jesus' aforementioned sheep. On top of which, like-minded comrades seldom prove loyal, for the most part they betray you over the long haul, for betrayal is an essential quality of like-minded comrades.

"Because I'm a woman, it was important for me to seek out like-minded female comrades, an undertaking most surely doomed to failure. If like-minded comrades are undependable, then like-minded female comrades are undependable to the highest degree. My experience with so-called like-minded female comrades could not have been more devastating, for, following brief periods of apparent solidarity, my so-called like-minded female comrades have turned against me each and every time up until this point, they have, in most treacherous fashion, betrayed, abandoned, denounced, and doubted me, blackened my name and reproached me, a situation that caused me to put distance not only between my like-minded male comrades and myself, but foremost between my like-minded female comrades and myself, avoiding them like the plague. Reverend, the most disappointing aspect of my life so far was the betrayal of my like-minded female comrades, the insidiousness, maliciousness, hatefulness, envy, and malevolence on the part of my own sex. It began with my mother and sisters. Nothing gave my mother, my sisters, more covert joy than to exploit my guilelessness, to abuse my openness. When no one was watching, one of my sisters took pleasure in giving me a swift kick in the shins, while the other contentedly hit me over the head with her doll, and my mother delighted in pulling my hair. The hidden sadism of my so-called like-minded female comrades toward their so-called like-minded female comrades went much further than the open sadism of their like-minded male comrades.

"Austrian like-minded female comrades are the worst, because they are the most unhappy. Fueled by hate, they will pursue beyond the bounds of their homeland and across the decades any like-minded female comrade who succeeds in breaking the vicious circle of Austrian women's misfortune. Should an Austrian woman dare to not accept the misfortune of the Austrian woman's fate, should an Austrian woman find it natural to strenuously reject the misfortune of women as dictated to her by Catholic Austria and strive for a woman's happiness that she considers natural, then she takes upon herself not only the opposition of Austrian men, who have profited from the misfortune of Austrian women for centuries, but, above all, the irreconcilable enmity, the vengeful bitterness of all unhappy Austrian women, a number which more or less covers the total female population of Austria. They hate it when an Austrian woman does not willingly join them in their suffering. Should it occur to an Austrian woman to lift her voice in song, she will find not only an infinite number of Austrian men's hands, but an infinite number of Austrian women's hands around her throat, cutting off her air, and an infinite number of Austrian women's voices will attempt to drown out her song with their woeful cries. Should an Austrian woman take a few hesitant dance steps, not only will innumerable clumsy Austrian men's feet block her path, but innumerable Austrian women's feet will try to trip her up. Should an Austrian woman break out in spontaneous laughter, she will find her mouth covered not only by a large number of coarse Austrian men's fingers, but also a large number of Austrian women's fingers, which intend to strangle this laughter from the outset. The majority of male and female Austrians hate nothing more than a singing, dancing woman; the majority of Austrian Catholic men and women are of the opinion that a woman should accept the suffering, the foreordained unhappiness that nature has allotted her, with masochistic joy, that she should wallow in it. Should women who want to sing and dance remain in Catholic Austria they probably will end in the madhouse, in prison, or in suicide. For women who want to sing and dance, Catholic Austria is the most unsuitable country on earth.

"The news, Reverend, the news is on," the sinner interrupted herself in her lovely voice and listened awhile, her head cocked to one side and her hands covering the pink headphones. "They're looking everywhere for us," she said, "but they have no idea where we are. They won't find us, they can't comb all the forests of East Tyrol, not to mention all the forests of Austria, the entire wooded region of Austria, which, after all, makes up half of Austria's land surface. On top of which, when it comes to stupidity the Austrian police have nothing over the Italians. We need not be worried, Reverend."

She continued to listen. "The cardinal is speaking," she said. "The cardinal is speaking of abominable outrage, he's calling me a fiend, a monster, a deplorable product of humankind. He's talking about tradition and mores, of lines which should not be crossed but which have been crossed. They're holding a special mass, Reverend, a special mass at St. Stephan's, a special national mass in your honor, a special mass to be broadcast over radio and television, with a moment of silence." She listened again. "The community of believers is with you in spirit, the cardinal is saying. The community of believers is calling upon you not to be weak in your hour of affliction, to find strength in the thought of the martyrdom of the saints of the Catholic Church, to stand fast in the face of the temptations of this devil who has dared to kidnap a man of God."

She giggled. "Naturally, they believe the kidnapper is male. The cardinal says the Pope has been informed of this monstrous event, of course. The Pope will appear on television tonight with a special message to the Austrian people, particularly to East Tyroleans."

After listening attentively for a few minutes more the sinner removed her headphones, turned off the Walkman, and shook her abundant hair.

"The end of paradise," she said softly, after a short pause. "The end of the island paradise. First quiet, peace, and happiness, then unavoidable entanglement in sin and shame. Entanglement in sin and shame cannot be avoided. Perhaps for you, Reverend, a priest gets less entangled in sin and shame than we nonpriests, a priest surely knows how to avoid the pitfalls of sin and shame better than we nonpriests. A priest in his alb can nimbly jump over pitfalls. Such evasion is impossible for us nonpriests, we nonpriests get entangled in sin and shame until we don't know which way is up."

The sinner is right, I thought to myself, and suddenly I felt sympathy for her. With the help of my sister, Maria, I had succeeded thus far in keeping my distance from sin and shame; my sister, Maria, warned me each time I was in danger of inviting sin and shame upon myself. Such lapses would have been absolutely conceivable before my ordination, one wanders from the path most easily in one's youth, in one's youth one is vulnerable to all sorts of temptation, in particular, of course, to the temptations of the flesh. Before my ordination females of the sinner's variety would approach me now and then with the intention of luring me into the

abyss of sin and shame, which, because of my youthful innocence and the fact that I was concentrating on my theological
studies, I often did not recognize as such. Without the constant vigilance of my five-years-older sister, Maria, without
her ability to immediately see through such seductive maneu-
vers, I might never have reached ordination, I would have
remained a nonpriest, caught in the snare of one of these
female creatures.

"You look as if my rope is too tight for you," the sinner
said, sliding from the seat of her motorcycle. "Are my ropes
cutting into your flesh? Just a moment, I'll loosen them a bit.
We don't want to cut off your circulation, a venous hyper-
emia won't do anyone any good at this point."

Skillfully, she began to loosen the knots of my bonds,
without giving me the least chance to defend myself.

"Practical, this cross knot," she said. "Very practical."

She stepped back. "Better?" she asked. "You feel better, I
can see that. I want you to feel comfortable in my company.
If you don't feel comfortable you can't listen well."

She sat back down in front of me and picked a daisy.

"He loves me, he loves me not," she murmured as she
plucked the white petals from the flower. "Or, as Igor said in
his bad French, '*Je t'aime / un peu / beaucoup / passionnément / à
la folie / pas du tout.*' That was in Paris. We were sitting in a
meadow of the Bois de Vincennes and Igor was plucking the
petals from a daisy. I slowly got used to his Ukrainian or,
rather, his Ruthenian accent. Igor refused to shed his
Ukrainian or, rather, his Ruthenian accent, though his
French was hard to understand because of it, with the result
that we were exposed to countless petty and less petty
ridicule from one part of the Parisian population. Ukrainian
or, rather, Ruthenian was always being exposed to ridicule,

Igor said, in the Russian empire it was denigrated as the 'little Russian dialect of the great Russian language,' at times it was forbidden to print or publish books in Ukrainian or Ruthenian. To criticize his accent was to criticize his mother tongue, Ukrainian or, rather, Ruthenian, which, following all these years of suppression, truly did not deserve any more criticism. Learning French had been a considerable concession for him. He saw the necessity of being understood in the language of the country one found oneself in, but he neither wished to nor could he renounce his accent.

"Igor tore the last petal from the daisy. *Pas du tout!* he screamed, startling the many Parisians sitting or lying in the meadow because of the warm weather, and leaped up in shock. *Pas du tout!* I knew you didn't love me! I knew it from the beginning! He grabbed my hand, pulled me up, and pushed me toward the next métro station. A Parisian youth started to intervene but I waved him away. I was used to such scenes, Igor had attracted people's attention with such scenes in every arrondissement in Paris, and in a good part of the Banlieue to boot. For weeks I had been cursing the day I got to know him.

"After my isolated island life I felt a desire for a big city, so I went to Paris. Paris, another much-desired place, not an island paradise, to be sure, but much-desired. One has so many pictures of Paris running through one's head, pictures of the City of Love, of couples kissing on the banks of the Seine, kissing in cafés, kissing in front of the Hôtel de Ville, pictures of fragile women singing chansons in bars, their voices hoarse, singing their hearts out, their fragility in need of protection from lovers much younger than they. On every street corner one sees artists, writers, sculptors; they're running around everywhere, they're gifted, they're painting, writing, and sculpting without letup, constantly creating, drinking to excess and dying young, and therefore instantly transfigured. Just as the idea of paradise includes being driven from paradise, the word *desire* includes the nonfulfillment of desire. The most important thing about Paris is not its lovers, its fragile chanteuses, its painters, sculptors, and writers, the most important thing about Paris is a parking place. Once you arrive in much-desired Paris, your only desire is to find a parking place.

"At the advice of a passerby I parked my Puch sidecar motorcycle near the Glacière métro station, under the aboveground subway tracks there. The passerby, himself a Parisian, said there were too few free parking places in the center of the city; if I were lucky I would find a free parking place under the aboveground subway tracks at the Glacière métro station, the parking places there were the best. In order to be able to intervene in any attempts to steal my cycle I took a room in a cheap hotel near the Ste. Anne mental hospital, on the rue de la Santé to be precise, with a view of my Puch 800. The hotel was called the Hôtel d'Avenir. I carried my bags up to the room, took a shower, and lay down for a short while on the sagging bed before I decided to get something to eat in a small bistro nearby, called Odessa, as I had not stopped even once on the road from Dijon to Paris and was hungry. As there was no free table the friendly waiter seated me with a man whose face was hidden behind a large newspaper printed in the Cyrillic alphabet. A candle was burning on the table and each time the man turned a page I would stop eating my blinis as the corner of the page passed perilously close to the flame. I was too shy to warn the man. To distract myself I looked out of the open window my table was positioned under, onto the street, and when I turned back to the man sitting across from me reading his Cyrillic script, the newspaper was on fire. The man looked dumbfounded at the burning paper and didn't move. I grabbed my half-full glass of beer and poured it on the flames. At this the man came to life and he, too, tried to put out the fire, with a pitcher of water from the table. But the paper continued to burn. Quickly I decided to grab the newspaper from his hands and throw it out the window onto the sidewalk. I stuck my right middle finger, which I had burned the tip of, in my mouth as an elderly woman wearing a good deal of makeup and carrying a white poodle in her arms appeared at the open window.

"'What in the world are you doing?' the lady yelled, 'throwing a burning piece of paper onto the street! You could have hurt my dog!' The woman stomped on what was left of the burning paper until the last flame was extinguished. 'Unbelievable,' she said, throwing one last look through the window before she departed. The man and I looked at each other and began to laugh. 'A beer and a vodka,' called out Igor from Odessa, and when my beer arrived I dipped my middle finger into it.

"Somewhat later I drove Igor home in my sidecar. He made us tea in the adorable samovar his grandmother from Yalta had given him, and which he had brought to Paris and still heated with charcoal. He lived on the rue d'Odessa, in a tiny back building that consisted of a single large room, near the Montparnasse Cemetery. When he had come to Paris, Igor said, he had felt a great homesickness for Odessa, and when he came across the street sign while taking a walk one day he decided to stay in the city. On top of which, he was in the direct vicinity of the grave of Alexander Alekhin, for many years a world champion in chess, who was buried at the cemetery in Montparnasse. He himself was a reasonably good chess player, he said, had participated in tournaments as a child and teenager, and was a great fan of Alexander Alekhin. When he was overcome by his emotions he would visit Alekhin's grave, with its marble chessboard and half-relief of the master, which the international chess association had donated in 1946, ten years after Alekhin's death.

"I didn't quite understand what Igor meant when he said he was overcome by his emotions, but when I asked him about it he replied only that chess was a gift of God, it cooled the hot blood typical of Ukrainians. When the *Kiev Evening Edition* had caught on fire, he added somewhat out of context, he had been reading a report on a tragedy that had taken place a few days earlier in Dnepropetrovsk, according to which a forty-three-year-old excavator driver had buried his forty-six-year-old wife and her twenty-eight-year-old lover under a mound of rocks he dumped on them, the contents of his digging bucket. He couldn't tell me whether they had survived or not, as the end of the story had burned right out from under him. 'Do you play chess?' he asked. I told him that my former Upper Austrian fiancé had taught me the game, but that I played very badly. He got out his chessboard, with its beautiful walnut pieces that a cousin of his grandmother from Yalta had carved, and we played a bit. He didn't seem to be concentrating very much and was always asking me questions about my former Upper Austrian fiancé.

"Suddenly he swept the chess figures from the board, shouting that he would erase the memory of my Upper Austrian fiancé from my mind once and for all, lifted me up out of the comfortable if worn armchair I was sitting in, and carried me up the five steps leading to the large brass bed that stood on a kind of landing and laid me down on a mattress filled with Ukrainian goose down. Reverend, it was a night I shall never forget. As tender, as sensitive and considerate as the Frisian had been, the Ruthenian was equally passionate, wild, and hot-blooded. We made love on the goose down mattress in the large brass bed dating from the former century, bought at the Porte de Vanves flea market, until the sun came up.

"Not only was Igor as satisfactory a lover as the Frisian, he was also nearly as penniless. It's true that he earned a few sous tearing tickets at a small cinema near the Jardin du Luxembourg, but that wasn't enough to support a reasonably carefree life. So I donned my Carmelite's habit, bought a monthly pass with which I could travel the entire métro system, and took to the subways at rush hours. Unfortunately, because of their laic tradition, Parisians did not exhibit the same deference, the same respect for Shoeless Carmelites as had the ultra-Catholic bus drivers in the Italian seaport, a circumstance that forced me to improve my nimble-fingeredness if I didn't want to get caught.

"Toward this end Igor, who knew of my activity and at first had nothing against it, introduced me to a friend of his, a White Russian from Minsk, a skilled pickpocket by the name of Sergei, who offered to teach me something of his art. Sergei was not only quite accomplished in his profession, he drew from a wealth of experience, and I considered myself fortunate to be his student. I made rapid progress. Unfortunately, my lessons with Sergei, who lived in the Nineteenth Arrondissement with his Senegalese girlfriend and their five children, came to an abrupt end when Igor surprised us one day in my room at the Hôtel d'Avenir, which I had rented because of the free parking place and the view of it, and where we usually held our lessons in order not to be disturbed by Igor's Senegalese girlfriend and their five children.

"Sergei, who was in the process of demonstrating how one relieved a lady in a crowd of her pearl necklace without her noticing, was standing behind me to this end, brushing my hair to one side, as it was in the way. At this moment Igor came through the door, and what he saw caused him to draw a false conclusion. First he accused Sergei of being a traitor, a common rake, and a homewrecker, and then he proceeded to the tragic history of the Ukraine, oppressed for centuries by the Russians and therefore by him, Sergei, as well. He only need bring up the partition of 1667, the Nordic War, and Masepa, as well as the year 1796 and the annexation of the regions east of the Dnieper and Volhynia following the second and third Polish partitions, not to mention the revocation of Zaporogian Cossack autonomy in 1675. Taking Sergei by the lapels of his jacket, he then shoved him out the door and threw him down the stairs, calling out that he was sorry the hotel didn't have 192 steps, like the 192 Potemkin Steps of the Nikolai Promenade, built between 1837 and 1841 in his hometown of Odessa on the Black Sea.

"When the Spanish dancing teacher who lived next to me opened his door and demanded an explanation for the racket, Igor called him a pomaded gigolo, accused him of having an eye for me as well, and forbade him ever to speak to me again. He then closed the door to my room, called me a whore, slapped me a few times, and threw me down on the narrow bed. What can I say, Reverend, it was a night I'll never forget.

"Igor's jealousy, as vehement as it was unfounded, and which I had suspected in him from the very first evening when he asked me all those strange questions about my former Upper Austrian fiancé, had erupted for the first time.

Though it surfaced ever more frequently over time I was unable to leave him as long as our nights remained what they were—an explosive fireworks of love. In contrast to the Frisian, whose sexual interest was in direct inverse proportion to his growing melancholy, Igor's sexual drive was not in the least impaired by his jealousy; to the contrary, the more he lost his head, the more he raged, the more impressive were his displays as a lover, at least at first. I found myself getting more and more deeply involved in a dilemma that eventually proved unresolvable.

"My erotic dilemma was soon joined by my financial dilemma, once Igor saw me stealing on a car of the number 4 line of the métro that ran between Porte d'Orléans and Porte de Clignancourt. I myself had invited him along, suggesting that he gain an idea of my professional activity in this way. When he saw me lift the wallet out of the back pants pocket of a tall young black man he jumped up and began making a scene right in the middle of my work, which, of course, requires the greatest concentration. Had the métro not entered the St. Sulpice station at this point we wouldn't have been able to get away; the métro passengers, in a fury over me and my costume, doubtlessly would have nabbed me and turned me in to the police. Igor was screaming at me even as we ran through the subway passages and up the steps to the exit. What kind of profession was that, he yelled, out of breath, what sort of occupation was that for a woman, that entailed coming in constant and intimate contact with men's rear ends, he wouldn't tolerate the fact that I was constantly coming in intimate contact with men's rear ends, the money he earned as a ticket-taker was enough for us both.

"As we were hurrying across the square in front of St. Sulpice he wrung his hands and shouted that the only way to keep me from practicing this horrible occupation further was to marry me, which he would do just as soon as I agreed to a Russian Orthodox ceremony. At any rate, it was time for me to move to rue d'Odessa and keep house for him. When I objected to this suggestion on principle he became so angry that he dragged me over to the fountain in the middle of the square in front of the church and dunked my head in the water, an act that attracted the attention of the quarter's inhabitants, who never before had been confronted with the sight of a Shoeless Carmelite having her head dunked in the fountain of St. Sulpice. Another Ukrainian exile, in whose restaurant Igor had worked briefly, happened to be passing by and was able to bring him to his senses by alluding to his responsibilities as a Ukrainian patriot. My cowl dripping, I followed Igor to the house in the back courtyard on rue d'Odessa and into the big brass bed.

"The ban that Igor imposed on my activities as a métro thief caused our finances to shrink to the point that I was constantly forced to think up new ways to get money, and finally I approached Igor with a suggestion: What did he think of my continuing my activities in the movie theater where he was working? The fact that the theater was dark during screenings would make my work that much easier, and at the same time I would be under his control, which would lessen his feelings of jealousy.

"Igor considered my suggestion for a while and finally agreed to it, on the condition that I limit my prey to women, a condition I had nothing against, as it would be impossible to lift wallets from the back pockets of men who were sitting down instead of standing in the subway. It was not difficult for him to get me free movie tickets. The first film that gave me an opportunity to practice my skills was *Rear Window*, with James Stewart and Grace Kelly. I left my nun's habit behind in the hotel, as in the dark of my new milieu it was unnecessary to disguise myself. Before entering the movie house I would look over the women waiting in line, hoping that the sharp vision I had inherited from my father's side of the family would help me to recognize the more affluent among them. I made a note of where these women sat down, in order to relieve them during the screening of their jewelry and, often, of their handbags or, specifically, the wallets inside them, which they heedlessly hung on the seat in front of them or put down on the seat beside them.

"The change in the sphere of my activity proved totally advantageous, and within a short time we had resolved our financial difficulties. The fact that Igor continually had me in his sights alleviated his jealousy as well, though occasionally I was forced to defend myself against accusations of using the cover of darkness to squeeze past the knees and thighs of male moviegoers more closely than was absolutely necessary, or, alternatively, of bringing them to their feet with my polite request to pass by, which gave me an opportunity to come into contact not only with their knees and thighs, but with their entire bodies.

"Usually I was successful in calming his suspicions, but I couldn't prevent the fact that there were times when he would sit in our tiny house in the rear courtyard and silently brood and drink vodka, then curse me in the coarsest of terms, sometimes in French, sometimes in Ukrainian, sometimes in Ruthenian, once in a while attacking me physically. Each time, he would apologize the following day for what he had said or done, beg me for forgiveness, and then flee to the grave of Alexander Alekhin, former world champion in chess, to hold a silent conversation with the spirit of the deceased and play a game of chess with him in his head. He would return from the cemetery refreshed, and tell me there was nothing more calming to his specifically Ukrainian emotions than a game of chess.

"My life with Igor might have continued along its relatively satisfactory path, we might have continued to be useful to each other at his workplace, had I not been gripped by the so-called film mania. As I was going about my business in the dark my lips began to silently mouth the dialogue, which, as the Hitchcock festival had been running for quite some time, I more or less knew from memory by then. More and more often I would throw a sidelong glance at the screen, at what was going on there. Had Igor's movie theater, located close to the Jardin du Luxembourg, not been showing Hitchcock films but French love stories, Czech animation, or Oscar-nominated, wide-screen American epics, I would never have lost my concentration, never have been tempted to turn my attention from the act of stealing to the screen. But Hitchcock's films put a spell on me. It wasn't just the suspense and the believable depictions of the characters' psychological depth that caused me to sneak a look at the screen, it was, above all, Cary Grant and James Stewart, whose good looks enchanted me and drew my eyes like a magnet.

"Reverend, I gladly assume the lion's share of the guilt for the spectacular demise of my career as a movie thief. But it was contributed to by Igor's sick jealousy, which kept me from even the most harmless contact with men. Igor's sick jealousy prevented even the most innocent observation of another male in his presence, a condition that led me to satisfy my innocent need in the dark of a movie theater, where no one could control where I looked, a need that in its innocence became ever more uncontrollable, and ended in the owner of the movie theater throwing me out, instead, I am happy to say, of having me arrested.

"As a result of my frequent sidelong glances at the screen, namely, I began to fumble, to miss the chance for a quick grab, and it wasn't long before a woman furiously snatched out of my hands the purse that I had not nabbed quickly enough. I murmured something about having confused it for my own, an excuse that the woman eventually accepted. But my next lapse of concentration resulted in a robust American woman in her mid-fifties grabbing my hand as it was sliding into her purse, clasping it in her iron grip, and dragging me past a horrified Igor out of the screening room to the owner, who, only because he knew of my relationship with Igor, didn't turn me over to the police, but nevertheless the next day told Igor to look for a new job.

"Our mutual unemployment led Igor to become ever more irritable and to increase his control over me. In my despair I took my neighbor, the Spanish dance teacher, into my confidence, and he offered me the understanding I was so in need of. During a hushed and hasty conversation on our landing I noticed that he had an interesting profile and a sympathetic smile. Igor's unpredictable nature made even the most superficial contact with the dance teacher highly dangerous, therefore my contact with him became even more erotically charged, and in my dreams the profile of Cary Grant was soon transferred to that of the Spaniard from Santiago de Compostela, who had been living in Paris for five years.

"Reverend, I had missed the fact that the inexorable decline long since had set in. Igor drank more and more and one evening, as the waiter in the Odessa Bistro wished me *bon appetit* and gave me a friendly smile as he was serving my borscht, Igor hauled off and knocked the bowl out of his hands, an impulsive reaction that caused us both to be banned from the restaurant, so infuriating Igor that he punched me in the ribs on the way home, at which I fell down and broke my middle finger. I went to the outpatient clinic of the Pitié Hospital, where they already knew me, and had my finger put in a splint. The next day Igor appeared at the Hôtel d'Avenir, repentant and meek, a bouquet of daisies in his hand—the result of a conversation and chess game with Alexander Alekhin—and we spent passionate hours in the narrow hotel bed, hours that lost some of their unforgettable quality because the Spanish dance teacher was practicing a few new flamenco steps at the same time, which took its toll on my attentive devotion, as the staccato of his high-heeled dancing shoes clearly could be heard in our room.

"Toward evening I walked Igor down to the hotel entrance, and as we passed by the porter, our arms wrapped around each other, the latter called out to me and handed me a letter from the Frisian's mother from Uithuizermeeden in northeastern Holland, which had been forwarded to me and in which she inquired about her son's silver cigarette case. The silver cigarette case, which her son had inherited from his father, her husband, who had died of a tick bite on a trip to Austria eight years, nine months, and thirteen days before, should have been in her son's belongings but wasn't. The fact that Igor didn't recognize the sender of the letter, whose first name was abbreviated, and that the letter was in a language foreign to him led to the outbreak of another jealous fit in the hotel lobby, in the presence of the porter and three paying guests from Guernsey, who stayed there during their business trips to Paris. The objections these three guests raised against Igor's behavior had serious consequences: As I entered the hotel the next day, following another brief stay at the outpatient clinic of the Pitié Hospital, my arm—Igor had dislocated it on the street after this unpleasant scene—in a sling, the porter waved me over and in a soft voice said that Paris was full of hotels in the Hôtel d'Avenir's price range, and that surely it would not be difficult for me to find a new room.

"I was now unemployed and without a roof over my head, so there was nothing for me to do but move in with Igor on the rue d'Odessa. He interpreted my express refusal to marry him, on principle, as my desire to reserve for myself a certain erotic freedom, and his distrust of me grew immeasurably. At first he still allowed me to don my Carmelite robes and go to the library of St. Genoveva, near the Pantheon, to the Library of the British Council, or to the huge library of the Centre Beaubourg in search of new financial sources. Readers were always getting up from their seats to fetch or return a book or to ask a question of the staff, and this gave me the opportunity to quickly go through the billfolds they left there.

"This didn't bring in much, as most of the readers were poor students, but at least I didn't feel totally dependent on Igor. I had left my Puch 800 parked near the Glacière station, and when I went there, roughly two weeks after I moved out of the Hôtel d'Avenir, to move it to a spot in front of Igor's tiny rear courtyard dwelling, I found a half-wilted bouquet of carnations in the sidecar, and a letter from the Spanish dance teacher in which he asked me to contact him. He had grown accustomed to seeing me at the Hôtel d'Avenir, he said, and missed me greatly. The thought that I was at the mercy of my brutal boyfriend was causing him sleepless nights, and since I had left he couldn't stop seeing my face before him, my cool blue eyes, high forehead, and the small round mole roughly two centimeters above the corner of my mouth.

"Reverend, I read this letter with trembling hands, for I, too, in spirit had often gently traced his face with my fingers. I drove the Puch 800 to the rue d'Odessa and parked it in front of the tiny rear building. Unable to throw the wilted carnations away, I took them out of the sidecar and put them in a vase, at which Igor, seated in front of a half-empty bottle of vodka, became immediately suspicious and began tormenting me with questions about the bouquet's origin. He assumed that a student from one of the three libraries I frequented had become enamored of me and made me a gift of the flowers. In a fury he smashed a full glass of vodka against the wall above the big brass bed, then pushed me down it and, consequently, onto the vodka-soaked goose down mattress. It was not a night I'll never forget. For some time now Igor's skill as a lover had suffered from his overconsumption of alcohol, insofar as he kept falling asleep in the middle of our lovemaking."

Magdalena interrupted herself and sliced the air with a sudden motion. "A fly," she said. "I've caught a fly. We've got to feed the praying mantis. If we don't feed her she'll die on us." She picked up the marmalade glass, unscrewed the lid, threw in the fly, and immediately screwed the top back on. She then watched the praying mantis devour the fly. It was slowly getting dark and I was having trouble making out my immediate surroundings because of the dark sunglasses I was wearing.

"There were fewer and fewer fireworks to speak of," the sinner continued. "Had the heavens of our nights continued to include bright missiles and exploding orange palms, lavender stars, and green cones of fire I never would have decided, following an unprofitable afternoon in my Carmelite habit in the library of St. Genoveva, to drive my Puch 800 to the Hôtel d'Avenir and visit the Spanish dance teacher. I nodded briefly to the hotel porter, who didn't recognize me and because of a certain respect for the Order didn't ask me whom I wished to visit. As I stood at Pablo's door my heart began beating like mad. I knocked, he opened the door and, without a word, without a question concerning my unusual choice of clothing, took me in his arms, then slowly removed my habit, one layer after the other. First he took off the white scapular, then he loosened the belt, then he pulled the tunic over my head, and finally he led me to his bed, over which hung a color reproduction of a still from Carlos Saura's film of *Carmen*. The hours that followed made up for Igor's growing incompetence as a lover.

"It's getting dark," Magdalena said then. "I'll take off your sunglasses. You don't need them any longer. Forgive me for not having thought of it sooner." She got up, came over to me, and removed the sunglasses from my nose. Then she stretched and yawned. "Twilight makes me tired," she said. "I'd really like to lie down and sleep, but you probably want to know how the story with Igor went, don't you?"

I opened my eyes wide and nodded, to indicate that I was interested in how this episode ended. In the meantime I had recovered from the small shock of her report of the Frisian's death. There was no excuse for her actions, of course, but it couldn't really be said that her relationship with the Frisian had brought her much happiness. Providence didn't seem to have very much positive in mind for her, for her relationship with Igor from Odessa also apparently was taking an unpleasant turn. Mixed in with my fear of this woman, my horror at what she had done, I felt a trace of sympathy for her.

"Though Pablo implored me not to return to Igor, as he sensed that something terrible would happen, I put my nun's habit back on as darkness was falling and drove my Puch 800 to the rue d'Odessa, where Igor was already drunk and waiting for me. Reverend, it would have been better had I followed Pablo's advice, yet despite all the scenes, despite all of Igor's abuse, I felt some remnant of loyalty to him. And I also hoped that our nights would return to what they had been, an exploding fireworks of love, I hadn't totally given up hope, an illusion that became clear to me once and for all when I saw Igor sitting at the table, dead drunk. When he saw me he stood up slowly, supporting himself with both hands. Slurring his words he then took me to task, again called me a whore and accused me of having betrayed him with the student who had given me the carnations. His attempt to hit me in the face misfired because of his drunkenness; his fist merely brushed my left ear. One last spark of hope rose in me as he pulled me over to the bed and threw me down on it, but a minute later he was lying on top of me, heavy and snoring.

"Reverend, as I was lying there, his inert body on top of me, his face, swollen with vodka, next to mine, something happened to me inside, something totally disengaged from my conscious will. It was as if I had a double. One part of me still lay under Igor, apathetic, without hope, totally broken, while another part of me slipped out of Igor's grasp without his noticing, and went over to the table on which stood one empty and one almost full bottle of vodka, along with a burning candle. The candle was one of many devotional candles that Igor's grandmother from Yalta sent to Paris now and then, and which came from a small Russian Orthodox chapel in which she prayed for the salvation of her grandson, living as he was far from the Ukraine. They were tall white wax candles and they were supposed to protect Igor from bewitchment and lightning, as well as from death by fire or water.

"The vodka had come from a cousin of his grandmother, the cousin who had carved the chess pieces. Every month a case of vodka arrived, carefully packed. The alcohol content of this vodka, which the cousin distilled illegally on his farm located on a bend of the Dnieper River, was eighty proof, and I often had used it to flambé the rice Trauttmansdorff I served Igor now and then to spoil him. The part of me that had freed myself from Igor's heavy body took from the table the almost full bottle of vodka and the burning candle and walked back over to Igor with the jerky mechanical motions of a robot. Then this human machine poured the vodka over the bed and over Igor, who even in his sleep opened his mouth to receive a drink, and touched the candle flame to the fringe of the bedspread we had so often made love on, and which was one hundred percent acrylic.

"Before my Frankenstein-half turned in her mechanical way to leave the tiny house in the rear courtyard, she looked on as the bedspread on which Igor and her other, impassive, and despairing half lay caught fire. My Frankenstein-half then took the key from the lock and closed and locked the door behind her. She mounted the sidecar motorcycle, looked in the window, which formed a red square in the darkness, started the machine, and drove in the direction of the Hôtel d'Avenir. At the end of the boulevard, large and round and orange, was the full moon."

Magdalena fell silent. She sat before me in the darkness; I could see only her outline, which reminded me of a squatting Indian. The end of her tale had shaken me and again aroused my fear of this woman and her frightening divided nature. Examples of this kind of loss of consciousness were not unknown to me, it wasn't unlike the rapture of the saints, the ecstatic trances that many nuns experienced in the late Middle Ages—though I could not think of a case that ended in the same horrible way, with the exception of rare cases of religiously motivated self-immolation, in which, however, perpetrator and victim were identical. When I thought of Igor and his behavior I fleetingly asked myself whether he indeed had been an innocent victim, and then brushed this question aside, crossing myself in my thoughts.

"Pablo was happy to see me arrive. Without being conscious of it I had brought the rest of the bottle of vodka with me, as well as the half-burned devotional candle, and we toasted our happiness by candlelight."

It was so dark by now that I could hear Magdalena's voice, but could barely see her.

"I don't intend to justify my act," her voice said after a long pause. "I don't intend to justify myself, Reverend, but I have never sought anything but love. If you're looking for love and you get something you think in the beginning is love, and which truly is love in the beginning, but which nevertheless changes inexorably into something that has nothing in the least to do with love, then the result is disappointment. If the face of someone you think is your salvation, your ideal, becomes slowly distorted, your disappointment is so great that you begin to hate this face. If you expect understanding and are faced with a lack of understanding, then disappointment turns to vengeance. In the beginning is the search for love, in the end is the wish for the destruction of the former object of love, now an object of hate. There is nothing more dangerous than a woman whose desire for love has consistently been disappointed, such a woman is to be feared more than a brainwashed terrorist, a religious fanatic, is to feared, if you understand what I mean. There is a great deal yet to be said on this topic, Reverend, one could talk for hours on this topic. But now I'm tired, and we'll get some sleep."

I saw her shadow move over to the Puch sidecar motorcycle and return with a large object. It was very quiet, the babble of the small brook and the chirring of the grasshoppers were the only sounds. Occasionally the little green light of a glowworm blinked in the dark. Something that felt like a blanket was spread across my legs. I heard a rustling sound and saw her shadow stretch out on the ground beside me. Suddenly a bird flew up with a cry from the crown of the acacia as a head pressed itself against my hip. I would have liked to lay my hand on her reddish-blond curls.

I awoke in the middle of the night, startled out of a terrible dream. I was sitting in the sidecar and looked up at Magdalena, who was driving the motorcycle dressed in the habit of a Shoeless Carmelite. We were in a barren mountainous landscape on a steeply ascending road. To our left were craggy rocks, protected against rock slides by fine netting, to our right a deep abyss opened up right at the edge of the road, with no guardrail for protection. A torrential mountain stream rushed through the ravine far below. Magdalena was wearing her pink Walkman and singly loudly and off-key to the music of the *Well-Tempered Clavier*. She was driving very fast, her nun's veil flapping in the wind, and when she took a curve I felt dizzy. She sometimes interrupted her discordant song to laugh out loud, a laugh that echoed in the mountainscape and each time caused me to flinch in my sidecar. Her features changed from minute to minute, they became ever more contorted, uglier, increasingly mirroring the madness, the destructiveness within her. I was very afraid and called out: You're going too fast, you should slow down if you don't want to have a wreck. But she didn't listen, the pink headphones seemed to grow larger, and I, too, could hear the music of Bach's *Well-Tempered Clavier* droning through the barren mountain landscape. Suddenly I saw Magdalena's right hand fooling with the cable between the motorcycle and the sidecar. No! I screamed, and watched as the sidecar rolled away from the motorcycle and toward the abyss. Then I awoke, her terrible laughter and the droning music of Bach in my ears.

I took a deep breath and slowly calmed myself in the quiet, starry, early-summer night. Next to me I heard the steady breathing of the sinner. I didn't know exactly what time it was, perhaps three or four o'clock. It was cool, but the blanket over my legs protected me from the night chill. I tried to move my hands, which were tied behind my back. As Magdalena had loosened the faded rope somewhat, they had regained feeling, but my entire body ached because of the uncomfortable position I was sitting in. I tried to pray, I implored God to show me the way out of my hopeless situation. But God, who until then had been more or less reliable in terms of hearing my prayers, remained silent as a clam. I noted that my respect for Him was waning, and that His silence was beginning to irritate me. Help me, will you, I heard myself say to Him despite my gag, it's your obligation, after all. As a priest I come directly under your protection, I'm closer to you than the others and therefore count on certain privileges, on preferential treatment from your side. What about those lightning bolts you punish your enemies with? Brew up an early summer storm and toss down a lightning bolt at the sinner, who holds your servant through force. As soon as I expressed this wish I immediately took it back, for if one looked at it rationally one could assume that a lightning strike would kill not only Magdalena, but me as well, right next to her as I was with her head resting against my hip.

I had other suggestions for ways in which God could save me, but He didn't take them, maintaining, it seemed to me, an awkward if not helpless silence. I sat in the dark, the stars glittering above me, and felt the rough bark of the acacia tree at my back The rough bark! Perhaps that was a possibility. I began to move my hands a little, back and forth against the bark in the hope that the faded rope would begin to fray and finally break. I had to be careful, for the curly head of the sinner rested against my hip. I rubbed and rubbed the rope against the acacia bark, an activity that was very tiring. I couldn't give up, couldn't fall asleep, for breaking the rope was my only chance. A narrow band of red appeared on the horizon, a bird began to sing. The world slowly emerged from the darkness and took shape. I could see the plaid checks that covered my knees, and Magdalena asleep next to me in a sleeping bag. She sighed softly, moved a little closer to me, and laid her head on my groin, throwing an arm across my thighs. The nearness of her, the weight of her head, the warmth of her hand, which I could feel through my dalmatic, through my alb, rattled me a little, aroused in me feelings of a sensuous nature unbecoming to a priest. Disturbed by these signs of abominable animal behavior I began to rub my bound hands against the trunk of the acacia so strenuously that the sinner sat straight up from her sleep, rubbed her eyes, and instantly comprehended what I was in the process of doing.

"Well, look at you," she said. "Reverend dares an escape.

But that is not nice of Reverend. That is not nice at all. Wanting to flee before the end of my confession. I'm a long way from the end of my confession. I would have thought my confession would be of interest to you, Reverend. Your expressions seemed to me to indicate an inner engagement on your part. Actually, it is of no importance whether you find my confession interesting or not, whether you have an inner engagement or not, interest and engagement do not play a role here. As a Catholic priest it is your responsibility, your duty, and your obligation to hear me. The father confessor from Oxfordshire, whom I mentioned before, tried to evade my confession by falling asleep, and now you are thinking of escape. That's not nice. Let's see how your attempt to free yourself is going."

The sinner stood up and took a look at the faded rope. "Truly, had you not awakened me you soon would have done it. Most regretful, that, most regretful for you. You will understand that I must intensify the conditions under which I am holding you here. Every prisoner is subjected to intensified conditions following a failed escape attempt. And I had planned to ease these conditions. The attention and engagement your expressions implied, the obvious interest with which you were following my confession, had already made me decide to remove your gag and give you the opportunity to comment on what I was saying. But now that circumstances have taken such a sad turn your gag will not be removed, on the contrary,"—and with this she secured the black Kashiyama bodysuit even more tightly, such that my head was jerked back—"on the contrary, the planned removal of the gag will become a securing of the gag. And the loosening of the knots I decided upon yesterday will become a tightening of the knots."

With these words Magdalena went over to the Puch side-car motorcycle, took a green ball from one of the tool kits, and returned with it. "I still have a few yards of nylon clothesline. Nylon clothesline is much more reliable for binding than rope." She unrolled the ball, wrapped the line around me and the acacia at the same time, and then walked around the trunk several times with the line in her hand, so that in the end I was tightly bound to the tree. She knotted the line and cut off the end with a small pliers she carried in one of the many pockets of her jumpsuit. She stood before me with the rest of the line in her hand, placed it playfully around my neck, and pulled until I could hardly breathe. Then she loosened it, removed the line from my neck, and rolled it up again.

"Perhaps I'll have to tie a double sheet bend after all," she said, as if to herself. Then she turned to me again. "Whether I shall have to resort to more radical measures will depend totally on you and how you behave in the future. Any further attempts at escape could force me to use this little ball, which I will return to the tool kit for now, in the manner I have just demonstrated. I would prefer to avoid taking such a step, but would not hesitate to do so should the occasion arise."

She packed the ball back in the tool pocket and returned with a pear and another piece of apple pie. She took a big bite out of the pear.

"Good Luisa," she said, "an old variety, one of the best pears there is. My grandmother had a tree of Good Luisas in her orchard. You don't find this variety very often these days. When I was traveling through the Lesach Valley a few days ago on my way to East Tyrol, I came across a farmer's boy who was standing by the side of the road with a sack of Good Luisas, so I bought a pound of them, for sentimental reasons, so to speak, in memory of my grandmother and her orchard."

She ate the pear down to the seeds, tossed away the stem, and held the apple pie under my nose. I was quite hungry and the cinnamon aroma had my mouth watering.

"I probably should split this with you," she said. "For breakfast I most likely would have given you half of this slice of covered apple pie. But as things now stand, I won't do that, anyone would understand that under the circumstances it would be dumb to split this piece of covered apple pie with you. A poem, this apple pie," she said and quickly swallowed it down.

"Incidentally, I've noticed that from the side you resemble Pablo. Your profile is not unlike Pablo's. You don't perhaps have a bit of Spanish blood, do you? Don't look so surprised, it might just be possible. One could imagine, for instance, that one of your forebears made a pilgrimage to Santiago de Compostela — all of Europe, the entire Catholic world at one time made their way to Santiago de Compostela, as you doubtless know. Why might not this pious East Tyrolean forebear have met a pretty Spanish girl on his pilgrimage, around Santander, say, or near Oviedo, and decided to start a family with her in St. Jakob in Defereggen? That, or something similar, could explain the resemblance of your profile to that of Pablo.

"Pablo told me a great deal about Santiago de Compostela and about the bones of Jacob the Elder, said to have been found there around A.D. 830. His favorite food was Coquille St. Jacques, a scallop dish served in the so-called Jacob's shell, the emblem of those pilgrims who once set off for Santiago de Compostela. On the second day of our new-found happiness I went to the market that was held three times a week on the Place Monge, bought two such shells, and prepared them on the hot plate that Pablo had smuggled into his room at the Hôtel d'Avenir. In lieu of a tablecloth I spread out my white Carmelite mantle over the small round table to give the meal a festive touch, and added the stump of Igor's devotional candle, the bottle of vodka with about two fingers of vodka remaining, and two plates holding the scallop dish. Pablo returned from his flamenco class exhausted and was delighted by this surprise. We ate and drank and then lay down on the narrow hotel bed, where we remained for several days, as it soon became obvious that the scallops I had bought were bad.

"Have you ever suffered from shellfish poisoning, Reverend? Shellfish poisoning is extremely unpleasant, it's accompanied by vomiting, diarrhea, the sweats, chills, and a weak pulse. Our newfound happiness was greatly affected by this shellfish poisoning, and having become rather skeptical because of my previous negative erotic experiences, I asked myself somewhat apprehensively what fate held in store for me this time. But when I looked at his sunken green face I felt only the greatest tenderness and affection for him, and took courage. He had it even worse than I, he was very sensitive when it came to shellfish. We sent for a doctor, and he proscribed the eating of mussels, cockles, oysters, and scallops until further notice. Three days later, still quite weak, we walked down the stairs, gripping the banister, and out of the hotel to go shopping, and as we passed the porter he recognized me and once again banished me from the establishment. Pablo stood up for me and informed the porter in no uncertain terms that he would not remain in any hotel in which a young and defenseless woman was put out onto the street because of some trifle. The hotel porter responded that his departure would not be of any great loss to the hotel, as the other guests had been bothered for five years now by the clacking of his high heels and the sound of loud music coming from his room day and night.

"Totally enervated, we dragged ourselves through the streets. A kind of nostalgia occasionally drew Pablo to the rue St. Jacques, one of the oldest streets in Paris and an early point of departure for those pilgrims traveling to Santiago de Compostela. There we saw a sign on a building that said Concierge Wanted. We passed through a gate into a small, cobblestone inner courtyard and inquired after the building's owner. When we knocked at the door it was opened by a roughly sixty-year-old woman from Montpellier who was holding a pug in her arms and who received us enthusiastically, offering us first a glass of lemon liqueur from the south of France, and soon thereafter the position of concierge. There had been several applicants already, she said, but their faces had said nothing to her. When she saw the two of us standing at her door, however, she had known immediately that we had the right faces for concierges. Pablo, in particular, had the right face for a concierge, she said, and smiled at him. Would he also be available to make small repairs in the building? she then asked. Pablo said that could be arranged, his father, a plumber from Santiago de Compostela, had been a very practical man and had taught him something of this trade, though he had died in an institution for alcoholics, unfortunately. Madame Martel from Montpellier picked up her pug, stroked him, and expressed her sorrow at the regrettable demise of Pablo's father and her joy at Pablo's handyman skills, and said we could move into the concierge's apartment immediately, which, because of the great value she placed on faces, had stood empty for some time now.

"We moved into the small concierge's apartment that very same day, with the help of the Puch sidecar motorcycle. Madame Martel permitted me to park it in the building's courtyard. Pablo, who often was plagued by homesickness for Santiago de Compostela, just as Igor often was overwhelmed by homesickness for Odessa, was happy to live on the rue St. Jacques, as he had the feeling he could set off for his hometown at any moment he wished, just as the pilgrims had done earlier. As an Austrian woman, this kind of homesickness was incomprehensible to me, I was not homesick for Austria, with the exception of a very specific homesickness for Austrian pastry, which wasn't really homesickness in the true sense. Just as Igor had preferred the company of his fellow Ukrainians, Pablo preferred the company of his fellow Galicians; just as Igor had searched for Ukrainian restaurants, Pablo was always searching for Galician restaurants; just as Igor was constantly seeking out Ukrainian music, Pablo was drawn to places where they played Galician music; just as Igor asked at every kiosk for Ukrainian papers, Pablo asked at every newsstand for Galician papers.

"In my case, it was totally different: If I happened to hear an Austrian dialect on the street it immediately put me in a bad mood, and I would give the person speaking this dialect a furious look, for the crude and vulgar sound of most Austrian dialects is irritating to me. I avoided Austrians abroad, and Austrian institutions abroad, like the plague, for the average Austrian, as well as the average Austrian consulate or cultural institution, the average Austrian embassy or trade delegation, generally exhibited a flagrant ignorance and dullness, an astonishing indifference and disinterest. It would never occur to me to ask for an Austrian newspaper at a kiosk, I was happy not to have to see the miserable or unworthy figures, respectively, that rule Austrian public life and not to experience the lamentable or sinister public events, respectively, of Austrian life. In a certain sense I envied people like Igor and Pablo their love of, their pride in, their country, for I had never felt love of or pride in Austria, Austria never succeeded in filling me with love or pride, rather, it often filled me with anger, disappointment, disdain, and sorrow, or at least with shame. So I found Pablo's homesickness incomprehensible in part, and in part touching and worthy of envy. Basically I wished I could be homesick for Austria, but I wasn't.

"The following months of happiness I spent with Pablo in the small concierge's apartment were at first untroubled, then gradually slightly troubled, and finally greatly troubled. At first I was happy to be able to hang my Carmelite's habit in the closet, for we had no money worries at all because of the concierge's salary and the regular income from Pablo's classes. My main responsibilities consisted in keeping the stairways of the building's two corridors clean, as well as the cobblestone inner courtyard, and in distributing the mail each morning by slipping it under the door or ringing the bell if there were something larger. In addition, I had to see that no suspicious characters entered the building and to make myself available for questions. I found this type of work agreeable, and it also gave me the opportunity to improve my knowledge of the French language, through the countless little conversations that developed with tenants on the building's various landings. Pablo gave his dance lessons, and practiced at home, which no one complained about, as the old buildings in Paris had thick walls and the concierge's apartment was on the ground floor, where, at most, the stamping of flamenco shoes might disturb one of the clochards who were always sleeping in the cellar, until I ferreted them out of the house.

"There was also an elderly widower living in the building, who had fled Budapest in 1956 and for decades now had been employed by the Montparnasse Cemetery. I liked talking to him, he was cheerful for a man his age. He would tell me about his day at the cemetery and about the many cats on the cemetery grounds that he couldn't stand. Everyone wanted to see Baudelaire's grave, he told me, everyone wanted to see the tall stone with the relief of a bat. But that wasn't really his grave, he said, it was only a memorial, Baudelaire was laid to rest in the family vault on the other side of the cemetery. Lately, however, more and more people were asking for directions to Sartre's grave, Sartre was now the thing among cemetery visitors. As for himself, he found Baudelaire revolting, if brilliant, whereas he found Sartre merely revolting, even more revolting than the cemetery's cats. You can't imagine what sorts of odd characters visit the cemetery, Monsieur Szabó said to me, you meet the strangest people in cemeteries, cemeteries were catch basins for the greatest diversity of odd characters.

"Among others, there was a young man who frequently visited the grave of a former Russian world champion in chess, he spent hours there talking to the deceased, sometimes he even set up chess pieces on the marble chessboard that adorned the grave, and played a game against himself or against the dead man, respectively. Alekhin always wins, Bela, the young man with the strong Slavic accent, with whom he had a fatherly, almost friendly relationship, would say to him resignedly, I never beat Alekhin. He allowed the eccentric young man, who lived near the cemetery, his way, though his behavior was against the cemetery's rules, said

Monsieur Szabó, and he was happy he had, for a few days
before he had read in a newspaper that the young man had
come to a terrible end. Namely, he had burned to death in his
bed, it had been difficult to identify him. Just imagine, said
Monsieur Szabó, burning alive in bed. Well, he added, he
drank a lot, that was probably the direct or indirect cause of
his death, toward the end he often arrived at the grave of the
world champion with a bottle of vodka, his conversations
with the deceased grew ever louder, and sometimes he even
poured vodka on the grave and began to sing or cry. The
young man didn't answer his questions, exactly, he would
say only that you couldn't trust women, they always had
other men on their minds, and if you gave them a chance
they wouldn't hesitate to go with other men in the coarsest of
fashions. Well, Monsieur Szabó then said, a sad story. But
now I've got to go and give my goldfinch some fresh water.

"I thought of Igor's death only seldom and briefly, for I
had begun a new life with Pablo. If the Frisian distinguished
himself through his tenderness, and Igor through his hot-
bloodedness, it was Pablo's sense of rhythm that made him
such a good lover. Were you familiar with the sexual act,
which is not the case of course, you would agree with me
when I say that rhythmic harmony is central to lovemaking.
As a dancer and, on top of that, a specialist in Spanish and
Latin American dance, Pablo had a strong sense of rhythm,
and as his lover I benefited from his natural gifts. Dance and
the sexual act are closely related, as you will realize even if
you have no practical experience in either area. Just as a
couple enjoys a dance when the rhythm is right, so can a couple enjoy the sexual act when there is rhythm. At first, I
admit, I was a little unskilled, my feel for rhythm was a bit
undeveloped, both in terms of the dance and in terms of the

sexual act. But once Pablo set a metronome beside the bed my sense of rhythm improved at once. The regular ticking of the metronome accompanied us during our nights of love and within a few weeks helped us to reach heights of ecstasy we had never dreamed of before. Normally, Pablo would begin the evening by putting on a CD of Spanish or Latin American dance music, and then bow and invite me to dance. It was wonderful to dance with him, it was as if I were weightless; I soared, I melted. When Pablo felt this foreplay had gone on long enough to get us in the mood he would dance us closer and closer to our French double bed and bend my body so far back that he was almost lying on top of it. It was a pleasure to surrender and sink slowly down onto the bed.

"During the time of this happy beginning I thought nothing of it when the women who took Pablo's dance courses called often. At a dancing school in Marais Pablo taught the rumba, the samba, the paso doble, and the cha-cha-cha, just as they were set down in the international sports program of the 'International Divisions of Dance' of 1963, as opposed to standard dance, but he also occasionally gave private lessons in the tango, bolero, fandango, and flamenco. It was only natural that if a woman went home from his course to practice her dance steps and couldn't remember the next step she would call to ask his advice. Even after one of these callers brusquely asked me who I was, exactly, and I answered that I was Pablo's live-in girlfriend, at which she laughed out loud and hung up, I still didn't catch on.

"Pablo was very busy anyway, when he wasn't dancing he was doing repairs for various tenants, which made us very popular in the building. What a skilled husband I had, said the young fashion designer who always dressed in black, had hair the length of matchsticks, and lived in a small studio on the fourth floor; why, in no time at all he had attached to the ceiling the Art Deco lamp she had bought in an adorable little boutique near the Place Vendôme. Enviable, she added with a mysterious, almost sad expression in her large, dark eyes, it was enviable to have such a husband. Almost none of the men she met in her profession could even drive a nail in the wall, discounting the fact that more than half of them were gay and the rest were bisexual. Perhaps I could tell my husband there was something wrong with her hot water heater, she said, the water was so hot that two days before she had scalded herself. She showed me her left hand, which was wrapped in gauze. Surely it would take him only a few minutes to repair this small problem. It would be wonderful if he had a moment's time that evening, he could come as late as midnight, that would be all right with her. She looked at her hand. She had no idea how she was going to finish the burgundy evening dress in time for the big fashion show with this hand, she said, she really didn't. It was such a big opportunity, this fashion show, such a big opportunity for her career. She then went down the stairs with the words: A wonderful man! I informed Pablo of the fashion designer's request, at which he muttered something about shameless tenants taking advantage of him, but he nevertheless went to her studio around eleven. A short time later I looked out the window to see if there was a full moon. When I accidentally glanced at the fashion designer's window, it was lit up to reveal the shadow of a couple against the curtains, dancing closely together. I quickly turned away from this figment of my imagination.

"Two days later, as I was leaving the apartment to go shopping, I saw Pablo, who was just returning from his dance classes, bending the graceful body of the fashion designer over the landing. When he noticed me he immediately pulled her body upright and I acted as if I had noticed nothing. I assumed he was discussing his work with her, and at her request was showing her a basic step of the tango. But I noticed my jealousy was growing. I told myself this was laughable, I knew from my own experience how one could be tormented by unfounded jealousy, unfounded jealousy was the beginning of the end. But all my worry disappeared that evening when Pablo put on a CD of Argentinean tangos and danced me around the living room, making me feel light as a feather. Our enjoyment of the dance was twice interrupted by telephone calls, which Pablo took and ended after a few sentences I couldn't understand because they were whispered, but that didn't bother me much.

"Several days after that the wife of the traveling salesman who lived in the attic apartment on the seventh floor, a somewhat plump but attractive forty-year-old, asked if my husband could repair her faucet, it was dripping, and the sound of the dripping was very bothersome to her. I communicated this wish to Pablo, who first hissed a few curse words in Galician, but then picked up his blue iron toolbox and climbed the stairs to the attic. Shortly thereafter I began cleaning the stairs, as I did every Thursday, and so, equipped with broom and dustpan, worked my way up to the steps to the seventh floor. As I lifted the doormat in front of the traveling salesman's apartment to sweep under it, I heard music. I knew this music, it was a slow bolero, to the sound of which Pablo and I often danced over to our wide French double bed. The Brazilian probably had the same taste in music as Pablo, they came from countries with similar cultures. She had chosen this bolero to make the repair of her faucet more enjoyable. I returned the doormat to its place and, raising up from my bent over position, my eyes fell on the keyhole.

"Reverend, I don't exactly know why I put my left eye to this keyhole and looked into the apartment, it was a reflex. In the oval frame I saw the bare legs of the Brazilian, from her toes to roughly six inches above her knees. These not exactly slim, but rather stumpy legs were dancing. I put my ear to the keyhole and heard, in addition to the bolero music, the clapping of castanets. Before I went on to the next door to sweep the dust from under the mat, I took one last look through the keyhole, this time with my right eye. Beside the bare and dancing legs of the Brazilian from Belo Horizonte I now saw a second pair of legs, legs in blue work pants, feet in Pablo's shoes and socks. The two pairs of legs, one bare, the other clothed, were moving slowly to the rhythm of the bolero. The clapping of the castanets had stopped. I stood up and went on to the next door, where I mechanically continued with my work.

"The image of the two pairs of legs remained in my mind as I cleared the dust from under all of the doormats, as I swept the steps, one after the other, until I was back on the ground floor. The doubtlessly unfounded jealousy aroused when I accidentally saw Pablo bending the fashion designer's body over the landing was reignited. Reverend, assuming that Catholic priests were not forbidden, but permitted, to marry, and assuming you had a wife: What would you think if you spied through a keyhole and saw roughly six inches of your wife's bare legs dancing closely with the clothed legs of a man? Wouldn't such a sight arouse jealousy in you?"

Magdalena paused to give me time to ponder this question. I tried to put myself in her situation, but try as I might I couldn't imagine being married to a woman. The only woman I could imagine in this connection was my sister, Maria, and though I had always found my sister's legs attractive, find them attractive even today, though after all these years the skin is somewhat marred by varicose veins and her feet are a bit disfigured because of exostosis, this idea strangely enough did not arouse feelings of jealousy in me. At this moment Magdalena, her long, slim legs clad in her tight leather jumpsuit, sat down cross-legged, and suddenly I could better comprehend the situation she had just depicted and the feelings of jealousy that accompanied it. If I had a wife and saw the legs of my wife in such tight black leather pants dancing in step with two men's legs, it would not be unthinkable that I would be overcome by the feeling, dangerously close to that of a deadly sin, of jealousy.

"I can see from your expression that you're making an effort to put yourself in my situation," Magdalena continued. "I appreciate that effort, Reverend, I appreciate your empathy, even if such empathy is part of a Catholic priest's daily obligations. By the time I had finished my sweeping and reached the ground floor again, my attack of jealousy had subsided, not least because once again I was reminded of the unhappy consequences that Igor's jealousy had to our relationship. I would not repeat his fatal mistakes, rather, I would learn from the difficulties fate was presenting me. Having arrived at the bottom step it was clear to me that my suspicions were unfounded. Even the Brazilian's bare legs were not proof of misconduct of any sort. She probably went barefoot at home for reasons of comfort and therefore didn't have on stockings, and her knees probably were uncovered because she was wearing a short, loose-fitting housedress. Pablo and the Brazilian weren't guilty of anything, it was my own far-fetched, near-hallucinatory notions that led me to such ideas. No, Pablo was above such suspicion. Hadn't he stood by me in my troubles with Igor? Didn't he rumba with me every evening, samba and tango me over to our broad double bed? I truly had no grounds for complaint.

"Sweeping the cellar steps, I scolded myself for being so distrustful. Completely lost in thought as I was, I got a sudden shock when my broom brushed up against something soft in the semidark. It was the thigh of the clochard who was rolled up in a ball asleep on the lower landing. Rudely awakened by my broom, he sat bolt upright and let loose a stream of language that was largely unintelligible to me. I had already ordered this clochard out of the cellar twice now, and each time he had obeyed me, if unwillingly. The second time I had threatened to go to my husband, who would not be satisfied merely with driving him off the premises, I said, but would give him a sound thrashing as well. Now the clochard had returned, and to retain my credibility I had to make good my threat. But I didn't want to go back up to the Brazilian's attic apartment to get my husband, not because I wished to avoid an encounter, but because it would have meant climbing 139 steps again, 139 steps that I had just gone up and down. Somewhat undecided, I turned on the cellar light and leaned on my broomstick to get my first good look at the clochard, who continued to curse me in a language unknown to me, but which sounded something like English.

"I hadn't noticed before that the clochard was young, younger than I; the first two times I had seen him his long, straight black hair had been hanging in his face, partially concealing it. But this time he had it tied back and I could see his narrow, oval, very pale visage only too clearly in the harsh cellar light. It was a handsome face with regular features, completely dominated by his large dark eyes. His sharp cheekbones stood out and his lovely thin lips were so red that he seemed to be wearing makeup. I couldn't tell what his body looked like, it was covered in several layers of worn and tattered clothing that was too big for him. Suddenly the clochard broke off his stream of profanity.

"'Why are you staring at me like that,' he asked in intelligible English, 'why are you staring at me as if you've never seen me before?'

"Then he began complaining that his rest was often disturbed in this cellar, about which he otherwise had no complaints at all, by noise coming from the ceiling above, noise that sounded like the rhythmical stomping of one or maybe two dancers. Paris in general was an unbearably loud place to his ears, he said, accustomed to quiet as they had been from birth; Parisian noise was one everlasting insult. He often regretted leaving the Outer Hebrides, the Outer Hebrides was paradise, a paradise he unhappily had recognized as such only after leaving it. If you were born in paradise you didn't consider it paradise, of course, you believed that paradise was elsewhere. This mistake had led him to leave the place of his birth, the Butt of Lewis, northernmost point on the Isle of Lewis, northernmost island of the Outer Hebrides, and go to Canada.

"Once he broached the topic of paradise I began listening attentively, for the subject of paradise has always interested me, Reverend, just as, doubtlessly, it has interested you, for after all, as a Catholic priest you must deal with it, interested or not. The handsome clochard apparently was speaking of an island paradise from which he had driven himself. When I replied softly that I understood quite well what he was talking about, he stuck out his right hand, which was clad in a violet wool glove.

"'Allow me to introduce myself, Jonathan Alistair Abercrombie,' he said smiling, and I noticed that his upper eyeteeth were unusually long and sharp. I realized that the young clochard was beginning to interest me, and in order to repress this interest I ordered him out of the building on the spot. At this he reverted to his initial behavior, threatening me in a flood of words I now believed to be a dialect of the Outer Hebrides, as he rolled up the straw mat he had been lying on, donned his narrow-fitting, brightly colored wool cap and very dark sunglasses, gathered up his large number of plastic bags, and ascended the cellar stairs. He opened the cellar door and then turned and said: 'You won't be rid of me so quickly, Madame.' And with that he closed the door behind him.

"'You won't be rid of me so quickly,' said Jonathan Alistair Abercrombie. Isn't it strange, the significance that certain sentences take on in retrospect? 'You won't be rid of me so quickly, Madame.'

"When I returned to our apartment with my broom and dustpan Pablo was sitting at the kitchen table, reading a letter. As I came in he laid the letter aside, picked out a CD of Brazilian sambas, and then pulled me to him and danced me over to the double bed, in which we soon succeeded in attaining rhythmic harmony. After a while we went to sleep, and when I awoke it was dark. Pablo was lying beside me, snoring softly. When I went into the kitchen to get a glass of water, my eyes accidentally fell on the pale lavender letter still lying on the kitchen table. Reverend, it is not my habit to read letters addressed to others, but you must agree that the temptation to this doubtlessly venial sin is great.

"I glanced fleetingly at the handwriting, which slanted strongly to the right, and against my will read the words:

Pablo, my dearest, *mon chou*, when will we dance together again? I bent over the sheet of paper and read one more sentence, then a paragraph, then the whole letter, which made mention, among other things, of a pug that was still limping on its left hind paw after Pablo had stepped on it in the heat of the dance, and of strings that no one had plucked before he, Pablo, had plucked them. The letter was signed: Your Spanish Hibiscus Blossom. P.S. Don't forget the castanets.

"Shaken by the contents of this letter, I walked over to the window. At that moment Madame Martel, widow from Montpellier, was crossing the inner courtyard and behind her, its left rear paw wrapped in a white bandage, limped her pug.

"Reverend, the hateful feeling of jealousy that I had overcome only hours before raged anew. Once again I told myself there was not the slightest cause for distrust, Pablo probably had felt sorry for the lonely sixty-year-old—who was aware, of course, that he was a dance teacher—and under the influence of her lemon liqueur from the south of France had allowed himself to be talked into giving a short performance after he had finished hooking up her television set to the building's antenna. The reclusive widow undoubtedly had read much more into this neighborly gesture than was intended, and vague widowly desires had gained the upper hand over the common sense of this older, yet still charming woman. Driven by the unseasonably warm temperatures for this time of year her fantasy, with no basis in reality, had gotten the best of her, making Pablo the focus of her widowly desires, customarily suppressed as they were, but not to be contained in this unseasonable heat, and she had summoned him to her apartment on the pretense of hooking up her television set to the building's antenna.

"At this moment Madame Martel glanced up in my direction and we smiled at each other through the window glass.

"In the weeks that followed my misreading of this doubtlessly harmless letter, I saw less and less of Pablo, as he had taken on additional professional obligations. During his absence calls continued to come in from his dance students, which I dutifully recorded for him. When I explained to one of these students that Pablo was often out of the house, because of his added responsibilities, she said that my naiveté was touching, but surpassed healthy bounds, and didn't I know what kind of reputation my life's companion enjoyed and why he was so desired as a dance teacher? I said he enjoyed the reputation of being an unusually gifted dancer and was desired because no other teacher of Latin American dance in Paris had been given the gift of such a developed sense of rhythm. At this the dance student cryptically commented that I was beyond help, and hung up. I refused to be affected by her ominous innuendoes and conscientiously went about my concierge chores.

"Late one afternoon, having taken care of my shopping in Marais, I happened to pass by the dancing school where Pablo was employed, and saw him walking out the front door, on his arm a young woman with short blond hair. Reverend, it is not in my nature to spy on, secretly watch, lie in wait for, observe, or shadow anyone. It wasn't I who took the initiative, it was my feet. As Pablo turned the corner with the young woman, my feet took over and began to follow. They followed them from the rue des Mauvais Garçons, where Pablo's dancing school was located, through the rue du Roi de Sicile and the rue des Ecouffes to the rue des Rosiers, where the two of them disappeared into a building. My feet stopped there. They stood on the asphalt in my new

Salamander doeskin shoes for an hour and a half. They stood on the side of the street opposite the entryway until dusk. And as they were standing on the dirty sidewalk, my eyes were looking into the building's second story window, which was open. The window framed the heads and upper bodies of Pablo and the young blond woman. These heads and upper bodies were turning in a dance, looking suddenly in one direction and then in the other.

"No doubt about it, it was a tango the two were dancing. The soft sound of Astor Piazzolla's accordion music was wafting through the open window. For one and a half hours I watched the two heads and upper bodies lost in the dance, and could imagine what their lower bodies were doing, their legs skillfully executing the complex cross- and congé steps of the tango. When, after one and a half hours, the two heads inclined toward each other and their profiles in the window merged in a long kiss, my feet slowly set themselves in motion. Without my willing it so, they set off for the rue Pavée, crossed the rue de Rivoli, continued on to the Pont Marie, crossed the bridge and the Ile St. Louis, traversed the Pont de la Tournelle to the quay of the same name, and then found their way down the rue des Bernardins and across the Place Maubert to the rue St. Jacques. As my feet were moving, my thoughts were on what my eyes had seen in the window of the rue des Rosiers during the last hour and a half. And by the time my feet entered the concierge's apartment on the rue St. Jacques my head had constructed a peripeteia worthy of Aristotle's *Poetics*.

"What I recently had registered as an illusion—the shadow of Pablo and the black-clad fashion designer on the curtains—had been no illusion at all, any more than the dancing couple in the window on the rue des Rosiers had been an illusion.

The curtain suddenly had been drawn open to reveal what I stubbornly had long refused to believe. I sat on the living room sofa of the concierge's apartment and looked at the feet that had led me there from the rue des Rosiers without any conscious participation on my part. Then I took off my new shoes, stretched out on the sofa, and considered that, though this peripeteia was not particularly pleasant to me at the moment, it nevertheless represented an unavoidably necessary element in the progression of the tragedy. And the tragedy had begun long since. The exposition had taken place when I confided to Pablo my unhappy relationship with Igor, actually even before that, when Pablo opened his door in the Hôtel d'Avenir to complain about the noise when Igor and I were fighting over the pickpocket incident.

"One falls from one tragedy into the next, Reverend. You think the tragedy is over, you think you've finally found yourself at the beginning of a comedy, you're convinced that it's a romantic comedy, but naturally it's a new tragedy following its set course. We deceive ourselves without cease, we're constantly imagining ourselves at the beginning of a romantic comedy, or at the very least at the beginning of a lark, a farce, a musical, a light opera, when of course it's really a new tragedy that is commencing. We deceive ourselves into believing that life has presented us with tickets to romantic comedies. Life has merely presented us with complimentary passes to tragedies, the performance schedule of life holds only tragedies, even if sometimes they're romantic tragedies. Lying on the living room sofa of the concierge's apartment I greeted the event that had opened my eyes, this peripeteia that guarantees that the tragedy has taken its natural course and its laws can now proceed to their logical end. If a tragedy is without a peripeteia, you might, under the circumstances, not even be aware that it's a tragedy you're in. And not to know that you're in a tragedy is the greatest tragedy of all and leads to absolute chaos. If you find yourself in a tragedy—and you will inevitably find yourself in a tragedy—you must see to it that this tragedy develops according to the rules, that the rules proceed accordingly, that the rules accordingly run their course to their customary tragic end. There's a time and a place for everything, Reverend, everything must take its lawful course, surely you will agree with me in this. Just as my tragic worldview is subject to certain rules, so your Catholic worldview is subject to certain rules, just as I speak of the Aristotelian formula for tragedy, so you speak from your pulpit of the formula for divine salvation. Whereas the radical Aristotelian about-face occurs in the acknowledgment of the absolute baseness of the tragedy's villains, your divine peripeteia consists in the acknowledgment of the absolute love and goodness of God and Jesus Christ.

"On the way from the rue des Rosiers to the rue St. Jacques the scales fell from my eyes: Pablo wasn't dancing with me alone, he was dancing with any woman who was willing. It wasn't just the black-clad fashion designer he was spinning in the animated two-thirds or three-quarter time of the paso doble, a Latin American ballroom dance of elementary moves derived from a Spanish folk dance; it was not only the Brazilian from Belo Horizonte with whom he danced the bolero, accompanying himself on castanets, or enjoyed a measured cha-cha, its even beat underscored by various percussion instruments such as maracas, cabazas, and guiros; it was not only Madame Martel with whom he gave himself up to one of three styles of flamenco—Arabic-Indian, Jewish synogogal, and gypsy—with its hand-clapping, foot-stomping quick rhythmic changes; nor was it only the blond dance student with whom he enjoyed the abbreviated steps of the tango—its promenades in two-quarter time interrupted by abrupt standstills—which was developed from elements of the habanera in the area around Buenos Aires. There were others, there were many others with whom he glided across the floor in the short steps of the quick tempo, the even beat and strongly syncopated rhythm of the samba, with whom he surrendered to the exaggerated hip movements of the rumba or danced across the floor to the music of Manuel de Falla's fandango, 'El sombrero de tres picos,' a bed always in the near vicinity.

"Reverend, as someone beholden to the Christian principle of charity you probably would say, if you could say anything at all, that one of the most laudable qualities of man, and above all of woman, is the inclusion of others, and women above all, in that which you yourself enjoy, instead of egocentrically wishing to keep everything for yourself. You probably would say that it numbers among a woman's most pleasant duties not only to tolerate the varied activities of a man, his intense encounters with his surroundings, but to encourage him in these activities, to counsel him in them and, following his encounters, his advances into his near and not so near environs, exciting to be sure, but exhausting as well, to welcome him back gladly, tend to him, and lovingly prepare him for the next such expedition. Surely you are correct in expressing, as you would if you could, such altruistic views, which help women to attain that most lovely of Catholic vocations, along with that of motherhood.

"As I lay on the sofa, my new shoes by Salamander beside me on the floor, I was faced with an inner struggle, which immediately followed on the heels of the moment of dramatic peripeteia, namely, the acknowledgment of Pablo's frequent change of dance partners. Should I support his passion for the dance, which—even if, to my great sorrow, it involved an indiscriminate variety of partners—represented an art form, an art form that, as any art form, should be supported and encouraged, should I view it as a useful way in which to keep Pablo in shape for our boudoir performances? Or should I selfishly insist on being the only partner Pablo danced into bed?

"To express it in your Catholic vocabulary: It was a struggle between the heavenly hosts and the forces of darkness, carried out on the jousting fields of my weak and mortal soul. As you can just imagine, Reverend, egotism, cupidity, and petty self-interest triumphed over selflessness and generosity of spirit, over womanly devotion and empathy for one's fellow man. I did not pass the test presented to me. When Pablo came home and asked me to move from the sofa so he could lie down, adding that he was dog-tired, his professional responsibilities were slowly sapping his strength, I decided to confront him. At first he stubbornly denied any relationship that extended beyond a purely platonic dance connection, and accused me of a pathological possessiveness that probably could be traced back to my difficult relationship with my parents, of an unnatural distrust, even of an abnormal jealousy of his success as a dance teacher. After I revealed to him what my eyes had seen and my ears had heard he spoke of a disorientation of the senses due to the unseasonably high temperatures we were having for that time of year, of hallucinations caused by my highly imaginative yet underused brain, of delusions brought on by previous and unsatisfactory erotic experiences, which had confirmed my initial take on these sad events. Somewhat uncertainly I mentioned the letter I had found on the kitchen table and read. He reacted with surprising fury.

"How dare I spy on him, keep tabs on him, violate his privacy of correspondence, he cried indignantly. I timorously interjected that it had nothing to do with the privacy of correspondence in the true sense of the word, the letter had been lying on the kitchen table, begging to be read. At this Pablo became even more incensed, screaming that I had destroyed his trust in me, how could he continue to live with me under these circumstances, how could he still believe in a woman who did not recoil from such a violation of personal freedom? Without mentioning the contents of the letter he stormed out of the apartment, not to return until four that morning, a habit he held to in the period that followed. We still lived together, true, but we almost never danced over to our French double bed, for by the time he came home I already had been lying in it for hours."

Magdalena picked up the marmalade glass with the praying mantis inside and mechanically turned it in her hands, attentively watching the insect as she continued to speak.

"What a soft green, what a delicate creature. Reverend, in retrospect I began to get a better understanding of Igor's jealousy. Though his was unfounded and mine was founded, the feeling was the same. Each night I lay on the big double bed, sleepless and alone with my thoughts. I saw Pablo dancing with beautiful women everywhere, in the streets and squares, in the parks of Paris, under a starlit sky. He glided across the deserted Place Vendôme and past the gleaming jewelry shop display cases there with an elegant woman dressed in a black evening gown, on the empty Place de Catalogne he danced a barefoot girl in white around the oval basin of the overflowing fountain; in the abandoned Jardin du Luxembourg he spun an exotic beauty with long, shiny black hair, dressed in a sari that glittered with all the colors of the rainbow, around the raised stone floor of the pavilion. Such thoughts plagued me more than those images closer to reality, more tangible—Pablo and Madame Martel, Pablo and the black-clad fashion designer, Pablo and the somewhat busty Brazilian from Belo Horizonte, none of whom, incidentally, had ceased to remind him of his responsibilities as concierge and were constantly requesting little repairs and favors, chores that he always took care of, though not without complaint. Had he continued to allow me to participate in his gift for the dance, had he not neglected me for long and moonless nights, perhaps I could have accepted the fact that I was not his only dance partner. As it was, in his absence I passed my nights in tormenting fantasy, and began to detest him as I had the Frisian.

"Not that I consciously planned his demise from the beginning, not that his liquidation was premeditated. It was just that I kept thinking about the shellfish poisoning that so ominously had marked the onset of our happiness. And I surprised myself occasionally in one of the many bookstores in our quarter by leafing through a work on toxicology, checking, for instance, the tables in which the names, components, and effects of the major indigenous poisonous mushrooms were listed, as well as the edible mushrooms they were easily mistaken for, or I would find myself perusing a botany book at home, examining the color charts of such plants as naked lady, monkshood, hemlock, henbane, jimsonweed, arum, and deadly nightshade. When I asked the pharmacist in the apothecary next door for effervescent tablets of vitamin C, I also asked to his—and my—surprise if he knew which poisons were the strongest, to which he answered hesitantly that, as far as he knew, aconitin, usually taken for the pain of neuralgia; coniine; colchicine, a remedy for gout; and strychnine, used for killing rats, were the most toxic. I thanked him for this information, and when he called after me to ask why I wanted to know this, I acted as if I hadn't heard him and quickly closed the glass door behind me.

"Reverend, I assure you despite everything that Pablo would still be dancing today had I not discovered what the Brazilian from Belo Horizonte was up to. I don't mean the relatively harmless discovery I made spying through her keyhole, I mean the disgraceful way she tried to destroy me personally.

"One day a nice young man knocked on the door of the concierge's apartment and said that he was from the Leconte company and that Madame Martel had enlisted him to install a dish antenna on the roof, and would I be so kind as to show him the way up there? I took him up the stairs to the seventh floor and pointed to the ladder leading to the skylight and through it to the roof. He leaned the ladder against the skylight, climbed up, and pushed open the glass pane to step out onto the roof. Curious, I followed. I had seen a number of films in which the police had chased crooks across the rooftops of Paris, and I had been fascinated by the broad and varied vistas and the wonderful views of the city. The tin roof of our building slanted in part and was flat in part, so that one could walk there. While the nice man from Leconte put up the antenna, I walked up and down the roof, the wind blowing through my hair, and enjoyed the view of the Seine, the Pantheon, the Sorbonne, Notre Dame, the Institute du Monde Arabe, and all the gray rooftops with their rust-red chimneys that looked like the clay targets I used to fire away at in the carnival booths of my childhood, hoping to win a red crêpe-paper rose or a white plastic skeleton.

"My eyes accidentally wandered over to the skylight of the Brazilian, whose husband was often away on business. On some vague impulse I braved a few not undangerous steps over to the edge of the roof, which elicited a soft cry of warning from the man from Leconte, in order to stand next to the skylight. I looked in. The Brazilian was kneeling on her living room floor directly below me. At first I couldn't figure out what she was doing exactly, but then, as I bent down, I saw that in one hand she was holding the severed foot of a chicken and in the other its severed head, and was making broad, sweeping motions with them. On the floor in front of her lay a large, blank sheet of paper. She waved the chicken's foot and the chicken's head over the sheet of paper and began to smear it with blood from the neck. I lowered my head to the opening of the skylight to better see what she was doing. It was my name, Magdalena Leitner, that she was writing in blood.

"I almost plunged through the window in shock. At the last second I regained my balance and wove my way up the slope of the roof until the man from Leconte could take my hand. I closed my eyes and murmured something about having been overcome by a sudden spell of dizziness. The man carefully sat me down on a small flat area of tin roof next to the dish antenna he had attached in the interim, and then lowered himself down beside me and put his arm around my shoulders. We sat like that for a while. In the distance the domes of Sacré Coeur gleamed pink in the light of the setting sun.

"There was no doubt about it: The Brazilian from Belo Horizonte was using voodoo to destroy me, so that she could have Pablo as her permanent dance partner for all those times her husband was away on business."

Magdalena fell silent, shaken by the memory of the outrageous underhandedness of her former rival. I must admit that her report of this heathen's insidious behavior enraged me even if it didn't surprise me, for the writings of pious and well-intentioned men had sufficiently forewarned me of the fundamental perfidy of the female sex. At the same time, I was moved by Magdalena's innocence. I saw her sitting on the tin roof in Paris, downcast and deeply disappointed by the lack of solidarity shown by her fellow woman, and I was overcome by sympathy for her. If only I had been able to free myself of my bonds and sit down in the grass beside her, to put my arm around her shoulders as had the young man from Leconte and at least assure her of a man's support following this betrayal by her own sex. Was it really possible that one could use such diabolical practices to counter God's commandments?

"Surely you're familiar with the cult of voodoo, Reverend," Magdalena continued, "for it includes elements of Catholicism. Initially a secret cult, it spread from nineteenth-century Haiti to other parts of the Caribbean, to the United States, and also to Brazil."

I would have liked to say a few words at this point, for I wasn't pleased that Magdalena mentioned such sinister practices in the same breath that she did Christianity, going so far as to imply they were connected. What did this primitive, heathen, sacrificial cult have to do with the much higher ethical and moral niveau of the Catholic religion, elevated as it was far above such occult machinations? Magdalena had definitely gone too far this time.

"You look as if you would like to say something, Reverend. Before your escape attempt perhaps I would have allowed you your say, but after your escape attempt we unfortunately must do without any expression of opinion on your part, as surely you will understand. Following this event my general condition greatly worsened. Worried by what I had observed I constantly believed I was manifesting the physical signs of a curse. I suffered from migraines, from shooting pains in my chest and bouts of dizziness, all of which I traced back to the evil practices of the Brazilian. My suspicion extended to the widow Martel and the black-clad fashion designer. When I encountered Madame Martel on the stairs her glance seemed more penetrating than ever, and I did not consider it impossible that she knew something of the evil eye, because of Montpellier's proximity to Spain. And I could just imagine that the black-clad fashion designer—whom I often saw staring down at me from her fourth-floor window—belonged to that group of young people who, as Monsieur Szabó had informed me, gathered at the Denfert-Rochereau catacombs to practice their satanic rites. A woman with a man on her mind is capable of anything, even of an alliance with evil incarnate, don't you agree, Reverend?

"Life on rue St. Jacques became increasingly unpleasant. My health complaints were multiplying and Pablo was almost never at home. Other than Monsieur Szabó there was no one in the building I trusted. It was during this time that I again encountered Jonathan Alistair Abercrombie in the cellar. Weakened by all my troubles, I didn't have the heart to chase him away, on the contrary, I was glad to see the handsome young man sitting on the steps, surrounded by his plastic bags. From then on he showed up more often, and it happened that I would lean my broom against the cellar wall and sit down to talk with him for a while. While he was telling me about himself he would often eat a sausage quite popular in France, made of fresh pig's blood, which he sliced into thin pieces with an unusually large and gleaming knife he carried in a leather sheath on his belt.

"At seventeen he had left the Outer Hebrides in search of adventure, he said, and had gone to Canada, where he labored in Quebec as a construction worker on an ice palace. Following this the construction of ice and snow palaces became his passion, his profession even. I could not imagine, he said, how many wonderful kinds of buildings one could create of ice and snow, fortresses sixty feet high, with towers, oriels, merlons, and embrasures; castles with archways, vaults, and ornate columns. There were various methods for building such structures, all of which derived from the principle of igloo construction. At the beginning of ice palace construction there was the igloo principle. Just as Eskimos used large knives and wood saws to cut wind-packed blocks of snow, long, specially made pieces of metal were employed to carve out huge blocks of ice from rivers and lakes. With the help of horse-drawn tackle blocks these massive pieces of ice were raised as walls, set in place with huge forceps, then fitted by so-called ice masons.

"When Jonathan Alistair Abercrombie spoke of his ice palaces his pale face took on a little color and his otherwise somewhat rigid features became animated.

"He had been to Quebec's Winter Carnival many times, he said. The ice and snow palaces were built for these winter carnivals, which were quite extraordinary. Unfortunately, because of the high cost, they had stopped building ice palaces in 1980 and now built only snow palaces, which were impressive, to be sure, but didn't have the wonderfully transparent effect of ice palaces, of course. Today, instead of sawing blocks of ice, they filled huge casts with tons of snow, somewhat similar to pouring concrete, and when these casts were removed, there stood a snow palace.

"As long as the premature heat wave held, I sat on the cellar steps with Jonathan Alistair Abercrombie, who talked about ice and snow palaces, illustrating his story through gestures of his violet-wool gloved hands. To my question of why he dressed so warmly he replied that the Outer Hebrides and, later, Canada, often were very cold and one had to protect oneself against wind and cold. It was a habit he had retained, and in the interim his warm clothing had become natural to him, he froze even in warm weather if he dressed like the average Middle European or Western European.

"I couldn't get enough of Jonathan Alistair Abercrombie's descriptions of the northern winter, the structures of ice and snow. They seemed to correspond to an ice and snow landscape within me, a region of broad and glittering snowy expanses, an area of transparent, frozen waterfalls I never before had encountered.

"To the degree to which my psychosomatic complaints — which I was firmly convinced derived from the black magic with which the Brazilian, and perhaps Madame Martel and the fashion designer as well, were trying to do me harm — worsened, my aversion to Pablo, whom I had to thank for all of this, grew. As I trusted Monsieur Szabó completely and surmised, furthermore, that because of his work as a cemetery guard he would understand my metaphysical dilemma, I decided to have a talk with him when I delivered his quarterly subscription of the *Journal for Amateur Ornithologists*. In his experience as a cemetery guard, I asked in a roundabout way when he appeared at the door with Charles, his goldfinch, perched on his left index finger, did he consider it possible that one person could be negatively influenced by another, who was using black magic? He gave me a long look and then invited me into his living room, where he offered me a chair beneath a portrait of Lajos Kossuth, the Hungarian freedom fighter.

"Without a doubt, he answered, extending the index finger with the goldfinch, without a doubt one could transfer one's will onto another with the aid of various tricks. His blessed mother, a farmer's daughter born near Székesfehérvár and strictly raised in the Catholic faith, had understood such things. I asked if he knew how one could free oneself from such a spell, such a curse. He moved his head back and forth in thought and said his mother had performed exorcisms on occasion, strictly according to the rules set forth in the exorcism catalogue of the Catholic Church, of course, and had enjoyed some success. Strictly speaking, she didn't have the right to do this, strictly speaking, the *exorcismus solemnis* could be performed only by a priest who had been granted special episcopal permission, but as a deeply religious person she had considered it her duty to use her God-given talents to help those of her fellow human beings who were afflicted with various demons. As a young boy he sometimes had attended these rituals, and could still recall a good part of the partly Hungarian, partly Latin phrases his mother had uttered.

"With Charles the goldfinch on his index finger Monsieur Szabó leaned forward slightly and whispered that if I wanted, he would perform an exorcism on me right then in his living room, he only had to put Charles back in his cage and get a fresh hen's egg from the refrigerator. Hens' eggs had played an important role in the exorcisms performed by his mother, he said, the person being exorcised had to hold a fresh hen's egg in his or her hands during the ritual. It was unfortunate that it wasn't an egg from a free-range Hungarian chicken, but rather one bought at the corner supermarket, but in view of the enormous changes in the political and economic situation one simply had to accept this minor drawback. I thanked Monsieur Szabó for his willingness to help. He then put Charles back in his roomy wicker cage, covered it with a cloth, went and got the hen's egg, drew the heavy, dark blue velour curtains closed, and lit a black candle. Then he said I should turn my chair around so that during the ritual I could keep my eyes on Lajos Kossuth, the freedom fighter. I did as I was told and Monsieur Szabó handed me the hen's egg, then stood behind me, placed his hands on my shoulders, and proceeded to murmur prayers and incantations I didn't understand. I stared directly into Lajos Kossuth's fearless eyes, and in my hands the hen's egg grew warmer and warmer.

"After what seemed to me a very long time, Monsieur Szabó completed his ritual service, which, he said, he had performed to the best of his knowledge and conscience and in honor of his blessed mother, nee Rákosi, and though he had been a little distracted by an occasional peep from Charles, which he could hear through the cloth that covered his cage, he believed that the demon that had me in its clutches was now exorcised. He took the hen's egg from my hands and checked its temperature. He said that the evil spirit was now in the egg, that even though it was not an egg from a free-range Hungarian chicken but a small, thin-shelled, white egg dropped by a skinny laying hen, it nevertheless had attained the force, through the relatively high temperature, necessary to draw the evil spirit into it. He would keep the egg for two months and then burn it, as ritual dictated. I could rise and go now, I was healed. I wanted to thank him and ask how I could show my appreciation in some way, but he waved me off saying it was not he who should be thanked, but his dear mother, who for decades now had lain at rest in a simple family vault in a cemetery located on a hillside near Székesfehérvár, where he, incidentally, would much prefer to serve as guard than in the huge necropolis of Montparnasse."

I was somewhat stunned that Magdalena had been exorcised by someone who was not a priest. Even if the profession of cemetery guard had some slight connection to a priest's calling, this vague affinity was in no way sufficient to allow the practice of such a delicate procedure. As far as I could judge he had done a botched job of it, with no way of testing whether Magdalena had, in fact, been possessed by one or several demons. Nor could it be ascertained whether he had precisely followed the set formula for exorcism. His careless and superficial method could have resulted in the demon, or demons, respectively, not being banished but attaching itself, or themselves, more strongly to Magdalena's soul.

"Reverend, strange as it may sound, after this exorcism performed by Monsieur Szabó I felt much, much better," Magdalena said. "I ran up and down the stairs effortlessly, and no longer needed to consult the many doctors I had used, none of whom had ever found a physiological basis for my complaints. If I saw the Brazilian or Madame Martel or the black-clad fashion designer, I would give her a furious look and say not a word. At the same time I was healing physically and spiritually, my increasing estrangement from Pablo was deepening my new understanding with Jonathan

Alistair Abercrombie, who was much less irritable in Pablo's absence, now that he was no longer disturbed by the constant stamping of dancing shoes on the floor above him. I sometimes took him a plate of rice Trauttmansdorff, and he was always happy to see me descending the stairs with the flambé dish, which gave the semidark cellar a blue cast. He continued to tell me about his constructions of ice and snow.

"When he could no longer find work in Quebec as an ice and snow mason, he said, he entered an international snow-sculpting contest, in order to continue working to at least some degree with his favorite material, frozen water. Once, he carved—he used the word carved—a sculpture of Polydoros and Athenodoros based on an art book illustration of the *Laocoon*, a sculpture by Agesandrus of the School of Rhodes, which is in the Vatican's collection. As Jonathan Alistair talked, I stared at his profile, silhouetted by the blue light of the rice Trauttmansdorff flambé; at his high forehead; his noble, straight nose; his strong but not stubborn chin. Without a doubt I was dealing with an artist, an artist in the guise of a clochard. I respected him for the sculptures he had created, which included not only the Laocoon group, but copies in snow of Rodin's *John the Baptist* and Michelangelo's *David*, which he glazed—he used the word glazed—in water to give them a patina of ice. It made me sad to think that these wonderful sculptures long since had melted, and that I would never be able to see them.

"After Jonathan Alistair had shared the story of his past life with me, I slowly opened my heart to him and told him what a bad hand fate had dealt me and how unhappy I was because of Pablo's uncontrollable passion for the dance. He seemed touched by my troubles and said that in the Outer Hebrides such behavior by a man would not be tolerated, in the Outer Hebrides, on the Isle of Lewis, and in particular on the Butt of Lewis, men were raised to be steadfast and true. Pablo's behavior was typical of inhabitants of warm climates, inhabitants of cold climates were different people altogether.

"One day I steered our conversation toward poisons, beginning cautiously with my recipe for rice Trauttmansdorff before going on to the various spices used in cooking, then proceeding to the plants that produced these spices, ending with a general discussion of healing and poisonous plants and the amazing connection between the art of cooking and chemistry. Jonathan Alistair said that sometimes poison could be a blessing, namely in those cases when it helped bring to an end a life totally misspent. He then fumbled at his throat, and from the neck of his tattered sweater pulled out a chain with a little capsule attached. This, for example, he said, was a capsule of cyanide, potassium cyanide, the potassium salt of hydrogen cyanide, a highly toxic white powder that dissolved easily in water and the poisonous quality of which involved blocking the iron of the respiratory enzyme through the CN group. His English uncle had taken this capsule from the corpse of a Nazi officer in World War II, and years later, as he was lying on his deathbed, had given it to him, his favorite nephew, telling him to guard it well, that life could confront one with highly unpleasant situations and that with such a capsule one would be prepared for the worst. He hoped that Jonathan Alistair would never have occasion to use it, but he would be armed in case of an emergency, a thought that comforted him on the threshold of death as he was, for Jonathan Alistair was his favorite nephew. He accepted the capsule, Jonathan said, and five minutes later his English uncle, whose favorite nephew he was, but who in turn was not his favorite uncle, closed his eyes forever.

"I let the chain with the capsule slide through my fingers and then put it back around Jonathan's neck. Reverend, in this instant something unforeseen occurred: We slowly leaned toward each other and kissed, sitting on the next-to-last step of the cellar, in the fading blue light of the rice Trauttmansdorff. The kiss made me feel strangely lifeless, and my head sank to his shoulder.

"Later, I often questioned what the impulse for this first kiss had been. Perhaps it was the intuitive realization that we shared something essential; for Jonathan, perhaps, it was a last chance to start a new life, not to bite the cyanide capsule, and for me, perhaps, an opportunity to end the dissatisfaction of life with Pablo. If we reach the end of our strength, Reverend, and have just one tiny spark of energy left, then we will choose life. Those qualities so dear to your heart and to the hearts of your flock, qualities that St. Paul set down in Corinthians as faith, hope, and charity, are to me and those like me skepticism, rage, and revenge. A good Catholic is unfamiliar with revenge, isn't that so, Reverend? The need for retaliation is alien to a good Catholic. To a sinner like me, I'm afraid, the feeling of revenge is not unfamiliar at all, a sinner like me, I'm afraid, is even capable of wallowing in revenge, just as you and your flock wallow in feelings of faith, hope, and charity.

"I had hoped to merge with Pablo in a dance that would go on forever, I hadn't reckoned with a roundelay, in the course of which one continually releases the arm of one partner to rush into the outstretched arms of another. Pablo had destroyed the most beautiful of my dreams, the dream of a permanent paso doble, an infinite fandango, a thousand-year tango. And for destroying this dream he would pay with his life.

"Once Jonathan showed me the cyanide capsule my plan was set. I wouldn't poison Pablo with henbane or extract of hemlock or a brew of bittersweet nightshade. I wouldn't add thin slices of death-cup to the mushroom stew he so loved, or substitute early mitre mushrooms for the morels in the Chinese rice dish I sometimes prepared. No, it would be the easily dissolvable cyanide capsule that would satisfy my thirst for revenge.

"One evening when Pablo was not at home and I knew that Jonathan was spending the night on the cellar landing I snuck down the stairs and removed the chain with the capsule from Jonathan's neck—he was dead asleep—an act which, following my intense if truncated training with Sergei, the White Russian, and my subsequent practice in the métro, the movie theater, and libraries, proved not at all difficult. I threw away the chain and hid the capsule in a place where Pablo, because of the cessation of any kind of sexual relationship between us, would never find. Then I slipped into the double bed and soon fell asleep. When Pablo returned home around four that morning I awoke briefly to see his familiar silhouette in the cold light of the full moon. The next morning I got up before he did and went into the kitchen to make coffee, humming. I took the capsule from its hiding place, shook out the powder into one of the two cups of café au lait, set the cups on a tray, and carried it, still humming, into the bedroom, placed it on the bed where Pablo, who had awakened in the meantime, was sitting, took the cup intended for me, drank a sip and, smiling, wished Pablo good morning. Pablo looked at me a bit distrustfully, picked up the other cup, and drank. The poison acted quickly. The distrustful look remained in his eyes, even after the light in them was extinguished.

"I turned and left the apartment and went to the cellar where Jonathan was shaving himself with the aid of a broken mirror. I took the mirror from his hands and looked into it. The face of a three-fold murderess looked back at me. I kissed Jonathan's unusually red lips and stroked his lovely straight nose with my finger. Had I found his chain while sweeping the steps? he asked. He had lost the chain given him by his English uncle, a fact that bothered him. I said, no, I hadn't seen the chain. He then said he was sorry, but he had to say good-bye, he had decided to return to the Outer Hebrides, more precisely, to the Isle of Butt, most precisely, to the Butt of Lewis, in an attempt to regain paradise lost. He wanted to start a new life and initiate on the Butt of Lewis an annual snow-sculpting festival, based on the one held in Quebec. I asked him how he would get there, and he said he would hitchhike, it was his only choice. Inspired by the thought of paradise regained, I quickly thought it over and offered to take him there in my sidecar. At first he looked at me in surprise and then, after considering it for a moment, said it sounded like a good idea. I stood up and told him to wait for me, I would be ready to leave in an hour. I then went back up to the concierge's apartment and placed next to Pablo the farewell letter I had prepared.

"Reverend, at the risk of your thinking that what I did was in violation of the Ten Commandments, I must admit that I had been practicing Pablo's signature for some time toward the goal of penning the farewell letter of a suicide who took poison because of his unresolvable psychological problems. I assumed that the intellectual niveau of the French police was superior to that of the Italian, but not such that this slight advantage would suffice to enable them to see through my plan, as in the interim my forgery of Pablo's signature could not be detected even by a handwriting expert. After I laid the letter on the bed beside Pablo's body and took one last look at his distrustful features, I quickly packed a few things and left the apartment, walking with Jonathan over to my Puch sidecar motorcycle parked in the courtyard of our building."

Magdalena stopped talking and leaned back on her elbows to gaze into the sun, like a cat with eyes half-closed. When one considered what this woman had been through, it was almost a miracle that she had retained her beauty and her youthful glow. In contrast, I thought, my sister had aged relatively quickly, in view of the fact that she had led a quiet life at the parsonage, thanks to which she, unlike Magdalena, had not been exposed to a series of male monsters.

Magdalena stood and looked about her in the grass. "Unfortunately, there is no male praying mantis in sight," she said. "We'll have to wait. Telling you all of this has made me thirsty," she said then, and ran the tip of her pink tongue over her lips. She went over to the Puch 800 and began searching through the tool pockets. Finally she held up a transparent glass bottle without a label.

"Austrian apple cider from the Lesach Valley. When I bought the pound of Good Luisas from the farmer's boy I also took a liter of fermented cider. Unfortunately there's almost nothing left."

She came closer, put the bottle to her lips, drank, and shuddered. "Very sour. And much too warm, of course. A barren region, the Lesach Valley. Barren land and sour apples." She looked at the empty bottle and then at me. I was very thirsty.

"Your lips look very dry. Hopefully, after your failed

escape attempt, you didn't expect me to give you any of the sour cider."

She went back to her tool pockets.

"Nothing else to drink and only two Lesach Valley pears left to eat. We need to replenish our rations, Reverend."

She took a map from one of the pockets and unfolded it. "The next town isn't far," she said. "Less than two miles, I'd say. That would be almost four miles on foot in the heavy nun's habit. Tortuous, Reverend, but we've lived through worse, right?"

She returned the map to the tool pocket and took out a plastic bag from which she removed several items of the nun's habit, which she then spread out in the grass. Then she took off her motorcycle boots, unzipped the long zipper of her leather jumpsuit, quickly removed it, and stood naked in the daisy-filled meadow, before a background of light green hazel bushes covered in yellow pussy willows.

Although I knew what a naked female body looked like, from my sister, Maria, and paintings of various representations of the Fall and a few other diverse scenes from the Old Testament, it took my breath away, and the dangerous signs of sexuality that my body had betrayed when Magdalena had laid her head on my groin revealed themselves anew. When I suddenly and unwittingly perceived her curvaceous contours; the swelling convex and shy concave lines; the perfect and implied hyperbolas, parabolas, ellipses, and circles; the soft cones, slender cylinders, and even flanks, I felt dizzy and tried to focus on a tiny ladybug or coccinellid that was crawling across my dalmatic. I concentrated on counting its black spots and though there were only six, I silently thanked our Maker that the world He created for us to perceive with our senses held such variety.

"Why are you lowering your eyes, Reverend, why are you blushing?" I heard the sinner saying, as if from far away. "Look at me."

I slowly raised my eyes from the microcosmic miracle of the coccinellid and looked at Magdalena across the stretch of meadow that divided us. There she stood, blindingly beautiful in the white mantle of the Shoeless Carmelites, and involuntarily I thought of the enchanting face of her unfortunate namesake, Maria Magdalena, in a painting in which that sinner had withdrawn to a grotto to do penance, resplendent in a red mantle, her right shoulder bared. No, Magdalena Leitner was more beautiful, more beautiful even than the wooden statue of Maria Magdalena, the one where she stands with her hands folded, her head bent, and her eyes downcast, with only her long hair to cover her; more beautiful even than the Maria Magdalena of the painting by an Italian artist, in which her right hand and her hair barely conceal her left breast; even more beautiful than the image of her as Jesus' friend, seated in an imaginary mountainous landscape, a pot of ointment in her lap; and much more beautiful than the Maria Magdalena, aware of her own beauty and wearing an ornate dress and precious jewels, of a painting from the Middle Ages, which my dear sister, Maria, and I had seen in a German museum; and much more beautiful than the representation of her standing and looking up at the risen Christ, her hair loose and flowing, accompanied by two angels. I couldn't turn my gaze away from her, I had to go over every fold of her garment with my eyes, take in the play of light on the lines and planes of her white nun's dress. Framed by the nun's veil, her face looked completely different, it had lost its coarse sensuality and taken on an innocence, a spiritual, almost transfigured seriousness that brought tears to my eyes.

"What's wrong, Reverend?" Magdalena asked, and her question brought me back from my contemplative state. "Are your eyes bothering you? No wonder, in this bright light. I'll put the Ray-Bans back on you, though after your escape attempt you don't deserve such consideration."

She glided over to pick up the sunglasses from the ground and set them on my nose. I would have liked to protest, for the miraculous white lost some of its effect through the dark tint of the glass, but regrettably, given my situation, I was unable to voice my objections. Magdalena walked back and forth in front of me, the material of the Carmelite habit swaying as if it were an elegant evening dress being modeled at a fashion show.

"Not a bad fit, don't you agree? White, black, and red are my colors. So, I'm going now," she said then. "But I'll be back." Then she gave an evil little smile and added, "But I can't say when. It might be a long time, longer than I anticipate, at any rate. One never knows what one will encounter, isn't that right? Who or what will cross the path of the pilgrimage of our life, as you probably would express it."

And with that the beautiful Carmelite disappeared into the thick foliage of an elderberry bush. The last I saw of her was the fluttering white tip of her cowl.

I sat there tied to the tree and in the direct path of the hot, early summer sun, and was glad that Magdalena at least had put the sunglasses on me. Though the place she had chosen to tie me up was a lovely natural setting—a clearing with trees that had new leaves and were still partially blooming, covered in soft grass and bright flowers, at the edge of which was a little brook—my situation nevertheless was considerably uncomfortable. I was hungry and thirsty, the rope was cutting into my flesh, and there was little hope I would be able to free myself from these unpleasant circumstances in the near future. I asked myself why God, in His boundless love and goodness, had chosen to test me in this way. Had I neglected my spiritual responsibilities? I was not aware of any fault on my part. I sank into a bottomless pit of despair so deep that I couldn't even pray, nor did I want to. Would I die of thirst, tied to this acacia tree? Would I starve to death before Magdalena returned? The sidecar motorcycle stood in the shadows of the spruce trees, Magdalena would scarcely leave it behind, though there was the danger she could be recognized on it. It was a conspicuous vehicle and the congregation that had rushed to the church portal after she kidnapped me, to stare at us as we departed, had surely seen us drive away on it.

Was Magdalena perhaps planning not to return, but to make it through dressed in the Carmelite habit, as she had done before? Though this thought included the possibility that I would die a miserable death of hunger, thirst, and loss of circulation if no one found me, which was entirely possible, as the clearing was secluded and I was unable to draw attention to myself by calling out, though I might, under the circumstances, be looking martyrdom in the face, a martyrdom not unlike that of our saints, and though all of this was due, of course, to Magdalena and her dangerous, not to mention insane, ideas, I was already beginning to miss her and I would have given anything to see her walk out of the bushes, sit down before me, and open her lovely mouth with its even rows of teeth to continue her tale, for she was a long way from the end of her confession. Of course, as unpredictable as she was, she could at any time seek out a new father confessor, a new listener.

So I sat there, dangling in the deep abyss between hope

and despair, and struggling in my heart with the conflicting emotions there. To divert myself a bit I tried to concentrate on God's wondrous creation, on the virginal nature that surrounded me, and to find comfort there. A large butterfly with beautiful markings landed on my right knee, slowly spread its wings, and then folded them again. These wings were patterned in black and white, with a little blue and orange mixed in at the tips. I watched the insect until it flew away. On the hazel bush in front of which Magdalena only a short while before had stood in all her beauty, first naked and then clothed in the Carmelite habit, before disappearing without a trace, sat a plump bird with a short, powerful beak, black wings, black tail, and red breast, singing its song. I remembered that my sister, Maria, had pointed out such a bird to me, sitting on a lilac bush in the parsonage garden, and had told me it was a bullfinch. A long chain of ants was marching across my alb. A bumblebee buzzed over my head before lighting on a white, desiccated nettle next to me, which sank under the weight of the furry, fat, yellow-black insect. A light breeze passed through the trees and grass with a slight rustling sound. The pussy willows swung back and forth, dropping their yellowish-gold pollen.

Suddenly I heard voices in the distance. Perhaps it was lumberjacks, perhaps hikers. They could be my salvation. Despite the gag I tried to make sounds, but could only produce a soft groan. I tried to lift my feet, tied together as they were, and let them drop on the forest floor, but the dull sound wasn't enough to draw attention to myself. All-powerful and benevolent Father, I prayed, for suddenly I could pray again, you who led the Israelites unharmed through the Red Sea, lead these people, whoever they may be, to me. The voices did, in fact, come nearer, I heard a laugh, a cry, leaves rustled and underbrush splintered. A young couple appeared among the spruce trees roughly seventy feet away. I continued my desperate attempts to get their attention, but in vain. They stopped, kissed, and walked on. Neither even glanced in my direction. They disappeared again behind the tall trees and soon I heard nothing at all. Exhausted from my efforts I closed my eyes and, my head filled with images between sleeping and waking, nodded off. It was a troubled sleep, interrupted by fragments of dreams and periods when I was half-awake, and finally I awoke to the familiar sound of Magdalena's voice.

"Just look, Reverend, at what all I've brought with me."

I groggily opened my eyes and saw Magdalena standing before me in her leather jumpsuit, and it seemed to me that the sight of her, first naked and then dressed in her nun's costume, had merely been a vision floating like a thin white cirrus cloud through my dreams. She set down a large brown paper bag in the grass and took out her purchases one by one to lay them out before me. I was very glad she hadn't abandoned me, and would have taken her in my arms had that been possible. Her face was flushed from the long walk, and a few drops of perspiration stood on her flawless, slightly rounded forehead, with the vein that ran vertically down it clearly visible.

"There was hardly anywhere in the village to shop, of course, only a small store at the gas station."

She held a large portion of smoked ham in front of my nose.

"East Tyrolean smoked ham, lightly marbled."

Then she took out a loaf of bread, creased down its center, and put it down in the grass.

"Peasant bread from Oberkärnten."

Next she removed two large bottles from the bag.

"Mineral water."

And finally she took out a little basket and set it on the ground.

"And cherries. The first of the season. If you behave yourself from now on, Reverend, perhaps I'll feed you some ham and bread, give you a sip of mineral water, and then shove some lovely red cherries into your mouth. The gas station attendant, who also served as the store clerk, was very friendly by the way. Very accommodating. There was a television in the gas station and guess who I saw on the screen?" Magdalena looked at me expectantly. "You'll never guess. Your sister, Reverend. I didn't know you had a sister. Before the kidnapping, when I was watching you, I saw this woman in the parsonage, but I thought she was the cook. At any rate your sister didn't look well. She's very worried about you. Perhaps the television's color was off, but her face was very pale, slightly green. She was constantly using a white handkerchief to wipe tears from the corners of her eyes, which looked sunken and were ringed with dark circles. And her voice trembled as she begged the kidnapper to treat her brother well, he was the dearest thing in the world to her."

As much as my sister's solidarity heartened me and gave me strength, I was a little embarrassed by the somewhat melodramatic tone in which she apparently was seeking my release. Maria did not look her best when she cried, which she did often and at the slightest provocation, and I perceived it as a lack of self-discipline that she would appear before the public on Austrian television in such a state.

Magdalena giggled. "The kidnapper! They still haven't caught on that I'm a woman. Your sister is having a hard time of it, Reverend. She said in a choking voice that she didn't have much money, that running the parsonage wasn't a lucrative affair, but that she was prepared to turn over to the esteemed kidnapper everything she and her brother had saved, and to throw in the silver case with the family jewels. And then she put a very pretty engraved case down on the table in front of her, an unexpected act, by the look of surprise on the face of the newscaster sitting next to her. Your sister opened the case and removed one piece of jewelry after another to hold before the camera so that they were clearly visible. There was a diamond brooch, a gift, as she said, that her — and of course your — mother, who was from the Zillertal, had received at your birth from her — and of course your — father, the eldest son of a respected family of notaries from Lienz. On taking out an oval-shaped, monogrammed gold medallion she commented that it held a photo and a lock of hair from her former fiancé, a promising clerk from Ausservillgraten, who had died tragically during a rock slide while hiking in the mountains.

"At this sad revelation she burst into tears, but before the astounded newscaster could switch over to something else she pulled herself together and produced a very valuable — she claimed — pea-sized, not quite round tie tack of pale pink pearl from the Marianas, in a white gold setting, which your grandfather on your father's side, a highly ethical and moral person who for decades had been a notary in Lienz, had worn to church every Sunday. When the newscaster, who by this time had turned totally pale, tried to interrupt your sister, she became even more determined and stated loudly that the platinum ring with the faceted aquamarine in the square, beveled setting was a bequest of your great-aunt on your mother's side, one of seven sisters from Mayrhofen in the Zillertal.

"As the newscaster, completely beside himself by now, gri-maced at the off-camera cameraman, trying to get him to break off the broadcast, your sister gave a sad smile and revealed the pride of the family jewels to the television audi-ence, a long chain necklace with an old silver clasp in the shape of an edelweiss, with garnets of an unusually intense color from the Gross Glockner in the Hohe Tauern range. The man who had found the garnets, she related, was a mountain guide from Matrei, a sympathetic and God-fearing man who later emigrated to New Zealand and died shortly thereafter of an insidious bacterium that had never been identified. To round out the picture of the family jewels that she was offering the esteemed kidnapper, your sister said in closing, holding up a large, plain crucifix of a massive amount of gold, she offered this treasure, created in the early nineteenth century by a goldsmith in the area of Udine, that a second cousin of her—and of course your—father had pur-chased on a trip to Friaul. Before she could further elaborate on this second cousin, who later had gone to Venice to serve as a housemaid, the *Midday Journal* abruptly ended its pro-gramming."

So my dear sister, Maria, for whose efforts I basically was very grateful, of course, had given the Austrian viewing audience a sample of her typical and tortuously circuitous rhetorical style.

Magdalena took two particularly large pairs of cherries out of the basket, walked over to me, and hung them from my ears. Then she picked up the marmalade jar next to me and looked at the praying mantis.

"She looks a little weak. Too little oxygen. We'll have to change that." From the pocket of her jumpsuit she took out a fat red knife and bore a hole in the jar's lid with a little steel bit. "Very useful, a Swiss army knife, truly very useful. So, now she can get some air. We must see to it that she's in good physical condition when she receives the male, who surely will come along any minute now."

I thought about how laughable I looked, a priest in his Pentecostal robes, tied to an acacia tree and wearing sunglasses, with two pairs of cherries hanging from his ears, and was glad my congregation couldn't see me in this humiliating condition.

"It's time to continue with my confession," Magdalena said. "I get the feeling we must hurry, even though there's no basis for this feeling. Anyway, I'm no longer so sure it will be necessary for me to receive absolution. The longer I talk, the more unnecessary your absolution seems, though I can't exactly explain why. You will recall that Jonathan told me he wouldn't be so easy to get rid of. How often it is, Reverend, that we pronounce some truth concerning the future without realizing its true significance. Had I comprehended the significance of what Jonathan said at the cellar door I would have nipped our relationship in the bud. Out of the frying pan into the fire, Reverend, you're barely out of the frying pan before you're in the fire. At great personal risk I had rid myself of Pablo, that unreliable denizen of a warm climate, hoping that I would be happier with Jonathan, the reliable denizen of a cold climate, a hope that proved as baseless as any other hope. As bad as things are there is no guarantee that things can't get worse. And things get worse, in general, much worse, in fact.

"So Jonathan settled into my sidecar and we drove off in the direction of Calais, not before stopping at a butcher shop he frequented near the Opéra Bastille to pick up a couple of the blood sausages he was so fond of. He said it was possible to find such sausages in northern France, but as he wasn't entirely sure of this he would prefer to visit the butcher he knew, and in whom he had the utmost trust when it came to meat quality, and take along a small supply.

"At the top of the Beauvais the weather changed, it became windy and cool, which put Jonathan, who felt at his best in unpleasant atmospheric conditions because of his Hebridean heritage and his years in Canada, in a great mood and caused him to break into song in the sidecar, singing, as he told me, of passions tied to the heaths and moors of the north country, to a life of fishing and raising sheep. I was surprised that even in this cloudy weather Jonathan wore his very dark sunglasses, and when I asked him why, he replied that his eyes were extremely sensitive to light, probably because during his childhood in the Outer Hebrides the sun seldom shone. We made good time, and after a few hours on the road we decided to stop for the night at a small inn not far from Longpré-les-Corps-Saints on the Somme.

"After we took a meal in our room of thin slices of cold blood sausage, bread, and a bottle of heavy St. Emilion, I stepped under the shower. What can I tell you, Reverend, as soon as I began lathering myself from head to toe with the perfumed soap I had brought with me from Paris, Jonathan, having taken off his heavy clothing, including the violet-colored wool gloves and cap, entered the tiny bathroom, pulled the plastic shower curtain with the blue fleur-de-lis design slowly to one side, and joined me in the shower, taking the lavender soap from my hand and continuing what I had begun.

"The following half-hour will be stamped forever in my memory. We didn't notice that the shower began to overflow. Only when someone banged at the door to our room did we come to ourselves and see that the tiles of the bathroom were flooded and the rug in our room, of a generous floral design, was soaked through. The hotel staff had been alerted to the situation after the water had run out under our door and covered the ugly gray-green linoleum of the corridor, then gurgled down the stairs into the dining room, and as Jonathan and I got out of the shower, wet and naked, and walked hand-in-hand into our room, which was unlocked, there stood the dumbfounded owner of the inn. We immediately covered ourselves with the white terry-cloth towels supplied to all of the inn's guests, and assured the pudgy blond owner in her mid-fifties that, of course, we would cover the damages, and with that we were allowed to change rooms. I was so enervated by the half-hour under the shower that I was barely able to lift my bag, which wasn't at all heavy, and carry it to the new room. We slept excellently.

"The next morning we continued on our journey, having received a rough estimate of the water damages and paying it. It was I, of course, who paid the bill, for like the Frisian, Jonathan had no money. Happily, before leaving Paris I had the presence of mind to withdraw all the money from the account at the Banque Nationale de Paris, Maubert-Mutualité branch, that Pablo and I had saved from his dance lessons and our mutual work as concierge, respectively, and stash it in one of the many pockets of my leather jumpsuit.

"We drove through a light rain to Abbéville in the Somme *département*, stopping briefly to view St. Wulfram, the late Gothic church there, before heading north to Calais. We rested and had some slices of blood sausage in a small poplar woods near Namport-St.-Martin, where Jonathan, laughingly reminding me of the previous evening, bent over me and gently pressed me into the damp grass under the poplars. Reverend, at the danger of embarrassing you, who surely keep your distance from the profane side of this world, I must nevertheless relate the feelings that Jonathan's nearness unleashed in me from the very beginning, as they are an integral part of my confession. Just as it was the Frisian's tenderness, Igor's fire, and Pablo's sense of rhythm that attracted me to them, in Jonathan's case it was the erotic attention he lavished on my neck, and in particular on my throat.

"You look at me somewhat baffled, Reverend—and no wonder, for your throat is constantly concealed by the stand-up collar of the priest. It is not possible to set a priest's throat aquiver with one of the many nuances on the rich scale of emotions with which Jonathan's caresses set my throat aquiver, taking into consideration, of course, that a priest's throat is not fated for such quivering. The destiny of a priest's throat is to provide a protective shell, a kind of pipeline for the transport—through the artful interplay of the various organs of articulation—of the pious admonitions and eternal truths expressed in a priest's words. A priest's throat is not fated to be kissed by the red lips of a handsome young man, to blush under the little nips of his white teeth. Have you ever heard of a priest's throat experiencing such a thing? An absurd idea, not least because a priest's throat never sees the light of day, because of the stand-up collar, and if it does, then in the privacy of the priest's bedroom. As my throat is not subject to such a charge and therefore much more accessible, it could happen that the caresses of Jonathan's lips and teeth, in particular his two well-formed upper eyeteeth, caused it not only to flush, but even to swell a little.

"Much in the same way that I temporarily fell for the

Frisian, the Ukrainian, and the Spaniard, because of the individual talents of each, I also fell for Jonathan, precisely because of the virtuosity he demonstrated in the region of my neck. Just as a talented flutist puts puckered lips to the reed to set columns of air in motion with his breath and charm from it the sweetest sounds, so Jonathan charmed all sorts of sounds from my throat through the skillful use of his lips and teeth. So I looked up into the silver shimmering poplar leaves and abandoned myself to Jonathan's skills. After these caresses I always felt strangely depleted, but didn't pay much attention to this fact.

"Having arrived in Calais we found a small hotel to spend the last night before journeying over to England. The next morning Jonathan arose rested and fresh, whereas I needed to sleep a little longer. After what we knew would be our last continental breakfast we took the sidecar motorcycle on the ferry to Dover. The weather had improved and on the other side of the English Channel we saw the white cliffs of the southern English coast. We stood on deck, our elbows on the railing, and as I looked at Jonathan from the side I thought of the Frisian, with whom I had stood on the deck of a ferry not long before and traveled to an island, though in his case it had been a much smaller island. I asked myself whether Great Britain could be included in my list of much-desired places, of island paradises, or whether, because of its size, it did not fit this category, but I wasn't able to come to a decision. Jonathan was in good spirits and full of energy, if somewhat anxious, indicated by his right foot, which was tapping rapidly on the iron deck. When I asked him why he was so nervous he said that, because of the Parisian climate, he had been unable to practice his ice-sculpting activities for so long that he was beginning to miss them. If an artist is unable to practice his art for long periods of time the artist at first becomes nervous, then irritable, and finally crazy. It was time to continue his work, he just didn't know how. I consoled him and told him we would find the ways and means.

"After we landed at Dover Jonathan said we should spend the next few weeks in London, where he had lived for a few months following his years in Canada and before his years in Paris. The London tramps, he said, were almost without exception very pleasant and civilized people, much more pleasant than the clochards of Paris, even if this wasn't obvious at first glance. The Parisian clochards passed themselves off as intellectuals, as philosophers and poets, but if you scratched the surface of this intellectual, philosophical, and poetic façade it turned out that underneath there was barely one verse by Rimbaud, barely one aphorism by Montaigne, barely one line of Pascal's *Pensées* to be found, that basically they didn't think about anything but how to get their hands on a bottle of—if not excellent, then at least full-bodied—red wine, on a cheese that, if not splendid, was at least palatable. In truth, the majority of the, for the most part, extroverted clochards of Paris were not in the least interested in anything mental, much less spiritual, they spent their time complaining that life had kept them from drinking the best red wine and eating the best cheese. Clochard intellectuality was façade intellectuality, just as clochard poetry was façade poetry, the Parisian clochards were hedonists, epicures, materialists, and positivists of the worst sort, who could stand for hours in front of the display windows of the elegant fashion shops in the rue du Faubourg St.-Honoré, the elegant jewelry shops on the Place Vendôme, and bemoan the fact that fate had kept them from sporting suits by Versace, ties by Cardin, and watches by Cartier. A hedonistic,

Epicurean, materialistic, positivist pack, Jonathan said with-
eringly. In contrast, he often had encountered tramps
beneath the bridges of the Thames who could declaim by
heart not merely one but several of Shakespeare's great solil-
oquies, whole pages of Bertrand Russell's *Religion and Science*,
and long passages from Byron's *Childe Harold's Pilgrimage*.

"He dared say that the tramps of London were among the
most cultured, most sensitive vagrants of the world, and
miles above the crass self-indulgence, the insatiable gluttony,
and the arrogant superficiality of the clochards of Paris. A
mere look at their faces often revealed a mark of spirituality,
even asceticism, that was very sympathetic. He wished to see
again a few of London's intellectually and spiritually superior
tramps, whom he had never forgotten. His years in Paris had
not numbered among his most happy, he had never felt at
home among the clochards of Paris, the shallowness and lack
of substance hiding under the ostensible profundity of the
clochards of Paris had offended him from the beginning. The
only ones he had been able to develop a somewhat certain, if
not friendly, contact with were the female clochards of Paris,
perhaps because women's shallowness and lack of substance
were easier to bear than that of men.

"So spake Jonathan, as we pushed the sidecar motorcycle
off the ferry and started off for London. We stopped briefly
in Canterbury to look at the cathedral there, which was built
in the perpendicular style. There was a small statue of Mary
in one of the wall niches that I liked very much. Her features
revealed no signs of humility at all, but rather alertness and
self-confidence, and she was neither inclining her head as
usual to look adoringly at her son, whom she carried on her
arm, nor looking at the viewer. Her head, as that of her son,
was turned away from the potential viewer and her eyes

were looking off to one side at something nearby, insignificant and yet apparently of great interest to her.

"We then proceeded to London. Crossing the city in our sidecar motorcycle, which raised not a small stir among pedestrians, we traveled in the direction of Hampstead Heath, where one of the most cultured tramps Jonathan had met during his months in London lived in an abandoned garage. This friend, a former milling machine operator from Kingston-upon-Hull, with fiery red curly hair and a fiery red beard, was engrossed in a copy of Freud's *Totem and Taboo* when we arrived. He said that since visiting the Freud Museum located not far from his garage and getting a look at Freud's couch there, the person and work of Freud had occupied him totally. He had read all of Freud's works that had been translated into English and had decided to take German lessons from a tramp he knew from Braunschweig — who lived on the grate over a heating duct of the underground near the Royal Academy of Arts — in order to be able to read the books in the original. He offered us biscuits and tea, which he prepared on a little Bunsen burner, and at Jonathan's request said that during our stay in London we of course could park our sidecar motorcycle in his garage, there was plenty of room. As far as he was concerned we could stay with him, there was plenty of sleeping space — he pointed to several dirty mattresses piled up in one corner — but it might be a good idea, he said, if we looked for something in the center of the city, for I — and he smiled at me politely at this — surely would want to use our limited time there to visit the major sights of London. He knew a former professional boxer, quite interested in the theater, who lived in an abandoned, architecturally outstanding little textile mill from the former century, located near the Aldwych Theatre.

If we wished he would prepare a letter of introduction, he was sure that the native Liverpudlian would give us a place to stay.

"After he had written a few sentences on the reverse side of a scrap of paper that was covered with scribbled comments on *Totem and Taboo*, we made our way to the textile mill, climbed the dilapidated steps with no railing to the second floor, and there indeed found the former professional boxer and three other tramps, who were in the middle of a small colloquium on the theater productions of Peter Brooks. Four sets of eyes stared at us in astonishment as we entered, and we apologized for our unannounced arrival and delivered the letter of introduction, at which we were warmly received and encouraged to join the discussion on Brooks's 1963 epoch-making production of *King Lear* at the Aldwych Theatre, located just around the corner.

"We spent the next several days visiting Jonathan's friends in the various sections of London, and talking with them about aesthetic, ethical, and moral issues. I remember this time very well; Jonathan's depiction of London's tramps had in no way been exaggerated. We spent, for instance, many stimulating hours in the company of a former computer programmer from Worcestershire, who resided in an empty shipyard shed in the docklands and who, as it turned out, was an expert on English portrait painting. His critical opinions concerning the portrait of Lady Jane Grey hanging in the National Portrait Gallery on St. Martin's Place were unforgettable, as was the equally sharp and sensitive interpretation of Milton's *Paradise Regained* we were enthralled by one rainy Sunday afternoon, as delivered in a corner of the Hammersmith underground station by a Welshman who formerly had served in the office of the British War Ministry.

We spent our nights on a ripped, dark-red chaise longue in the abandoned textile mill not far from the Aldwych Theatre with our friend, the former professional boxer from Liverpool, who, to be sure, took his comfort in gin, and having overindulged in the enjoyment of this drink occasionally spent entire nights holding forth in monologues from the blood-and-revenge-soaked tragedies of the English Renaissance, with a partiality for those by John Webster, but who otherwise was a kind soul. We lay on the chaise longue in a large empty room with the wind—not to mention a great many pigeons—blowing through the broken window-panes while Jonathan enthusiastically turned his attention to my throat.

"One morning when I looked into the somewhat clouded mirror I had fastened to the bare brick wall, in order to comb my hair, I noticed two strange little holes in my neck, which scared me at first, before I calmed down and told myself that the room, and the chaise longue, doubtless were crawling with various insects and that one of the larger of them had probably bitten me in my sleep. At the same time I noticed that my face was very pale, which I attributed to London's unhealthy climate. I decided to jog half a mile every day in St. James's Park.

"Jonathan apparently felt quite at home in London with his old friends, he looked strong and healthy and was enter-prising and energetic, which I attributed to the protein-packed diet he chose once we had finished off the blood sausages from Paris. From his former months in London he knew a butcher's shop in Soho that was run by a stocky Cockney and his red-cheeked daughter, and once a week he went shopping there, with his own money, incidentally, as he had begun work for an hourly wage in the icehouse next to the shipyard shed of the former computer programmer from Worcestershire, work that obviously satisfied him.

"He always returned from the butcher's shop in Soho with a rich array of various raw meats, generous portions of roast sirloin, fricandeau, roast buck, ribs, haunches of wild game, tail and marrowbone, juicy cutlets, and bloody steaks. I must admit that the first time I saw him biting into a raw beef tip I was disgusted. In the beginning I also found it distasteful that he would suck the marrow from a bone while smacking his lips, or polish off a steak with such gusto that the blood would run down the corners of his mouth. When he ate, his eyes glowed, or rather gleamed, in a way that I found a bit frightening. When I asked if it was customary in the Outer Hebrides to eat meat raw, he responded that his origins had nothing to do with this preference, it was a quite personal choice, or, to put it more precisely, necessity, for if he didn't eat raw meat he lost his strength and felt tired and enervated all the time.

"Reverend, as I looked at him sitting there on the ripped chaise longue in the empty room of the textile mill, his lips and chin bloody from gobbling down a raw oxtail, a pork cutlet dripping pinkly in his hand, my passion for him cooled considerably. For without a doubt it was passion that tied me to him and his lovely mouth, the mouth he used to excite me so irresistibly in the region of my throat. I suddenly was repulsed by the thought that the same white teeth with which he now was tearing into a boiled fillet of beef would a few hours later gently work their way into the white flesh of my neck. I felt dizzy, and sank down onto the old wing chair covered with a plaid hole-ridden blanket that stood near the chaise longue.

"Ah, passion." Magdalena sighed. "Isn't it strange how

such passion can disappear from one day to the next? A purely rhetorical question, for as a man of God you are of course unfamiliar with passion, disregarding the passion of Christ, which is quite different from the kind of passion I'm talking about, namely, the intoxicated state summoned up solely by sensual stimuli, condemned by you and yours as the deadly sin of *luxuria*. Do you understand what I'm talking about?"

With that she stood, walked over to me, put her full lips next to my right ear, and began to nibble at the cherries hanging there. This necessitated contact with my auricle, my earlobe, even with the highly sensitive skin behind my ear, contact that, strangely, was extremely unpleasant and greatly pleasurable at the same time, and that raised conflicting feelings in me, setting my emotions in an uproar never before experienced. This time even the attempt to divert my eyes to the branches of the acacia, and find distraction in the harmony of colors and forms that divine nature provided there, failed utterly. It was as if the blood in my veins were flowing faster than usual, as if it were coursing through my pulmonary artery like a swollen mountain stream, as if it were shooting through my subclavicle vein like some menacing whirlpool, as if it were surging against the walls of my heart like a storm tide, as if it were tearing through my aorta like a river gone wild.

And when she had finished with the first pair of cherries and turned to the second, and with that to my left ear, my body's thermoregulator went completely crazy. The enormous increase in blood to the skin made my body exude an unusual amount of heat, and I felt the hairs stand up on my neck and drops of sweat gather on my forehead. As Magdalena remained at my ear for a long while I abandoned my attempt to regulate my physiological equilibrium, closed my eyes, and surrendered to her labial proximity. But once I had given up any attempt to resist, deciding to let myself be carried along by the wave that had me in its swell, Magdalena suddenly ceased the mechanical irritation of my left ear and continued with her tale.

"Once again the inexorable decline had begun. It wasn't only Jonathan's eating habits that began to disgust me, I was irritated as well by the fact that he took my sidecar motor-cycle from his friend's garage to the icehouse he worked in and loaded it with blocks of ice, which he then brought to our room in the abandoned textile mill, crisscrossed by pigeons as it was, and went to work on it with his large gleaming knife and metal saw, a project doomed from the start by the moderate English climate. He asked me to model for him, a request I carried out only begrudgingly, for Great Britain's oceanic climate was, on the one hand, too warm for the execution and, above all, the conservation of ice sculptures and, on the other hand, too cold for a woman whose resistance was already weakened to stand around naked for hours at a time, what with the draft coming through the broken windowpanes. And we're talking about hours at a time, for once he had finally captured my upper body in ice and started on a thigh, the head began to drip and then to change form, until all that was left was an irregular lump of ice. If he finished the left arm and started on the right, the left would slowly begin to melt, until there was nothing left but a dripping stump.

"Soon the floor was constantly filled with big puddles from which the pigeons drank. I stood shivering in the mid-dle of the great empty room, one arm outstretched or at an angle, one leg in front of the other or raised, my head up or bent to one side, asking myself if it had been the right thing to do to abruptly end Pablo's life with a cyanide capsule, if perhaps it wouldn't have been more sensible to simply tolerate his mania for the dance.

"I began to consider escape, especially as my body's increasingly weakened state and its mysterious connection to Jonathan's increasingly dynamic activity gradually began to seem suspicious. I lay on the chaise longue each morning with less and less energy, and each morning he jumped up more energetically than the day before. I thought I was suffering from iron-poor blood and bought some iron tablets, but my condition didn't change, any more than it did when I tried various vitamins and minerals. It couldn't be due to a lack of fresh air, as the wind was constantly blowing through the cracks in the walls and the broken windows. One morning, as I was looking at my pale face in the shard of mirror, I noticed barely dried dots of blood on my neck, and my suspicions mounted. After brief consideration I then went to the library of the British Museum on Great Russell Street, which seemed a great distance to me, as because of my weakened condition I had to stop at every street corner and rest a bit. Once in the library I ordered a copy of Bram Stoker's 1897 novel, *Dracula*, and sat down to study it not far from the seat Karl Marx had always occupied.

"Reverend, in less than half an hour I was certain: I was in the spell of a vampire, one of the undead, a bloodsucker who was living on my blood. The attention Jonathan was lavishing on my neck essentially had nothing at all to do with passion, but with feeding himself. The two small holes in my throat weren't insect bites, they were the tracks of Jonathan's well-formed upper eyeteeth, they were his entryway to the fluid that kept him alive. Now I also understood his excessive ingestion of meat. He had to supplement my diminishing supply of blood and, lacking fresh human blood, he was filling the gap with raw pork, beef, and ox. I had to act immediately if I didn't want to become a drained and empty shell lying in our huge room.

"I closed the book and dragged myself back to our textile mill. The discovery that I was serving as a vampire's chief source of nourishment had shaken me, as you can imagine. I went up the steps, stopping on each to rest. The building was empty, the former professional boxer and his friends were off to a theater festival in Scotland, where they planned to meet with tramps from Glasgow and discuss if and how the political theater of the sixties could be revived, and Jonathan was still working at the icehouse. I quickly packed my few belongings in two plastic bags, went down the steps, and opened the front door. There stood Jonathan, somewhat earlier than I had expected. Obviously the late-afternoon traffic hadn't been as slow-moving as usual. He immediately saw that I suspected him, but gave no sign of it, smiling at me and giving me a hug, devoting himself tenderly to my neck, slowly forcing me back into the vestibule and closing the door without turning around. Then he pushed me up the stairs and into our room, and by the time we reached the chaise longue I was so weak I couldn't stop him from taking the plastic bags from me, laying me down on the chaise longue, and softly sinking his teeth into my neck.

"The next morning after he had bathed, whistling as he showered in the stall that the former professional boxer from Liverpool had put in, and had eaten a bit of steak tartar for breakfast, he set off for the icehouse, and I raised myself with effort from the chaise longue. A deathly pale, sunken, and hollow-eyed face stared back at me from the mirror. I took my plastic bags and again descended the stairs, only to find that the front door was locked. Jonathan had realized that I had discovered who he was, and as it would be quite unpleasant for him if I got away, he was trying to prevent it. What could I do? There was no telephone in the building, of course; my only chance was to climb out the window, but I was too weak for that.

"Reverend, I was at the end of my strength. I returned to our room, lay down on the chaise longue, and tried desperately to think of a way out. I lay there for hours, my hands folded in my lap, without coming to a decision. Finally I got up and paced back and forth a few steps in each direction, and in doing so I bumped into the rickety old wooden table where the steak tartar from the butcher's shop in Soho that Jonathan had eaten for breakfast lay on a piece of waxed paper. Out of sheer curiosity I took a bite. It was raw, yes, but finely ground and mixed with other ingredients, so that it wasn't like the clumps of bloody meat he usually gobbled down. I discovered that this popular dish didn't taste bad at all and ate a little more of it, noting how hungry I was. My appetite had greatly diminished of late, more than likely due to my increasing state of exhaustion. I pulled a wobbly chair over to the table, sat down, and ate greedily. As I did so I felt my strength returning, and after half of the steak tartar was gone I felt newborn. A look in the mirror revealed a pretty woman with a fresh complexion, bright eyes, red cheeks, and full lips.

"I went over to one of the high windows to see how best to climb down. At that moment I heard footsteps on the stairs, and had just enough time to hide the rest of the steak tartar behind the chaise longue before Jonathan entered the room. He greeted me amiably and then his eyes fell on the empty

table, at which he immediately became suspicious. At his
question of where the steak tartar was that he had bought
the day before, I answered nonchalantly that I had felt like
having some meat and had eaten it, it had been excellent, I
said, the butcher's shop in Soho was truly excellent.
Otherwise, I had not left the building all day but had read *Ice
Palaces* instead. I found the book informative and instructive,
I said, particularly the chapter on a new procedure in ice
architecture, namely, the use of the shell structure. Jonathan
was overjoyed at my interest in this innovative method of
construction and willingly answered my many questions concerning the paper-thin arches and domes that this method
made possible. The outer surface of a huge balloon was
sprayed with water, he said, and the water was allowed to
freeze, after which the balloon was removed and a beautiful,
transparent ice dome remained. It was possible to create
domes of an eighty- to ninety-five-foot diameter in this way.
An ice palace resembling the Hagia Sophia in Istanbul had
been constructed on a mountain in Vermont using this
method, with its main dome open to the sky.

"We spoke for a long time about this new process, so long
that Jonathan was too tired that evening to devote himself to
my neck as intensively as usual, and he fell asleep before he
succeeded in paralyzing me totally. Once he had sunk into a
deep slumber beside me I carefully reached behind the chaise
longue and quickly finished off the steak tartar to regain my
strength. Then I gently slid from our bed, took the key to the
sidecar motorcycle from the table where Jonathan had left it,
and, carrying a plastic bag in which I had packed those
belongings most dear to me, namely, the pink Sony Walkman
with the two Bach cassettes, my Swiss army knife, the habit
of the Shoeless Carmelites, and copies of G.C. Sansoni's edi-

tion of the *Divina Commedia* and Artemidor's *Interpretation of Dreams*, I snuck on tiptoe to the window farthest from the chaise longue. I was sorry to have to leave behind the Lingen *Atlas*, but it was too heavy. When I climbed onto the window-sill Jonathan turned on the chaise longue, sighing, which caused me to freeze in fear. At no further signs of movement from him I slung the plastic bag, which was tied with a string, over my shoulder, grabbed the gutter pipe with both hands, and climbed slowly down it, cutting my right hand in the process and causing it to bleed.

"Once on the sidewalk I ran around the corner of the building to where the sidecar motorcycle was parked. Reverend, you won't believe it—at the moment I started the machine Jonathan appeared in the sidecar grinning at me, his eyeteeth gleaming. Above him, visible among the television antennas, hung a huge and pale full moon. I was so astonished that it was easy for him to take the key from my hand and give me a shove, at which I stumbled into the middle of the street and fell down. Before he could run me over I jumped up, grabbed my plastic bag, and began to run for my life. He chased me in the motorcycle and would have caught up with me had I not turned a corner at the last minute and run up a tall and narrow flight of stairs between two build-ings. Jonathan parked the sidecar motorcycle and ran after me. At the upper landing there was nowhere else to go, and I turned to see his long eyeteeth coming nearer. I thought I was lost until I spotted a small wooden door in a wall next to me. I rattled the door handle and the door opened onto a dark room. I stumbled across the threshold, slammed the door shut, and fumbled at the lock, finding a key there and turning it. At the same moment the light of a naked bulb was turned on and I saw that I was in a shabby, sparsely furnished room. Sitting straight up on one of the mattresses on the floor was a middle-aged man, who stared at me in astonishment. Outside, Jonathan began pounding his fists on the door, which wasn't very sturdy.

"'Help me,' I begged the man, who sat there as if frozen to the spot. 'Someone is after me. Help me, we've got to barricade the door!'

"I began shoving furniture in front of it—a small table, a bookcase, two armchairs, and finally the man, who was wearing a white, knee-length nightshirt, threw off his blanket, got up from the mattress, and began to help. When in Jonathan's fury the door began to splinter, the man in the nightshirt began piling against the door bundles that were tied with string and stacked against one wall. I helped him, and finally the entire door disappeared behind these bundles, which held brochures of some sort, apparently. Jonathan was still hammering away at the door, and we stood there holding our breath, our arms hanging at our sides. The sparse hair of the slender, rather small man was mussed from sleep, and his dark mustache was a little unkempt. After a while the noise stopped. Apparently Jonathan had given up trying to force his way in. Relieved, we sat down on the mattress in the middle of the room, which was covered with a white linen sheet.

"Only then did I have an opportunity to apologize for my unpardonable nocturnal entrance, introduce myself, and thank him for helping me. He said there was no cause to thank him and anyway, the Battle of Armageddon, in which all the forces of Satan would be destroyed, was at hand. When I looked a bit baffled at this he added that Jehovah was great, and pressed a book in my hands, its title, *The Purpose and Nature of the Second Advent of Christ*, printed in large black letters, and said that this book of the pastor already had sold in the millions of copies. When I still didn't get it he explained that the bundles that had been stacked against the wall and were now piled against the door were copies of *The Watchtower*, the purpose of which was to announce the Kingdom of Jehovah, and his job, in turn, was to distribute it.

"Reverend, the man who offered me shelter was a Jehovah's Witness by the name of Michael Minulescu, whose father was from Puini in Transylvania and whose mother was from Reading. After he offered me a glass of milk and a cheddar cheese sandwich, cleaned the blood from my right hand, bandaged it, and told me a bit about himself, I felt I could trust him, and as I had a strong need to talk about the incredible things that had happened to me because of Jonathan Alistair Abercrombie, and as his father, as coincidence would have it, was from Transylvania—home to the notorious Wallachian count and vampire, Vlad Tepes, called Dracula—I began to pour my heart out, a fatal mistake on my part as it later turned out. I talked until the sun came up over the roofs of London, which I could see from the room's small, barred window, drinking one glass of whole milk after another and eating two more cheddar cheese sandwiches. Then I sank exhausted onto the mattress, noticing only that Michael covered me gently with a highland sheep's wool blanket and put a pillow under my head before I fell asleep."

Magdalena paused for a moment and stared straight ahead, remembering. A fine early-summer rain had set in, which caused her strawberry blond hair to curl even more. I myself was protected by the thick crown of the acacia tree. She didn't seem to notice the rain at all, so lost was she in the memory of the, on the one hand exciting, and on the other, sorrowful events of her past. My respect for this woman, who obviously had landed in the most difficult situations through no fault of her own, grew from moment to moment, and I very much hoped that Michael Minulescu, whom she had met under such dramatic circumstances, would bring a little peace to her tumultuous life. He seemed to possess the positive qualities of helpfulness, concern, and moderation, and given the critical situation, I felt it advisable to simply ignore the fact that, as a Jehovah's Witness, he was seriously misguided.

"When I awoke the next morning," Magdalena continued, interrupting my reflections on her future, "Michael had already returned the furniture and the bundles of magazines to their original places, and served me a cup of tea in bed. He sat down next to me and said he had thought a great deal about my situation during the night. Then he looked at me intently and said that, having escaped the undead by a hair, I had a responsibility to rid the world of this monster. He was particularly repulsed by the phenomenon of vampirism, for to a Jehovah's Witness both the consumption of blood and blood transfusions were strictly prohibited. Through his Transylvanian relatives, whom he visited periodically, he knew a bit about vampires. I was surely aware, he said, that unless they were rendered harmless they would continue their dastardly deeds for all eternity. And they could be made harmless only if a wooden stake was driven through their hearts. With these words he went over to a corner of the room and from a large black brass-bound trunk removed a wooden plug, which, as he said, an uncle of his on his father's side had carved from the wood of a Transylvanian alder, which had stood next to a pond in which a child had drowned.

"'Go and kill the monster!' he said. 'You will be doing a great service to mankind.'

"Reverend, I must admit that I had not the slightest desire to answer Michael's fervent call. As soon as anyone reminds me of my apparent responsibility to the so-called general public, as soon as anyone requires of me so-called altruism, so-called sacrifice, so-called compassion, I get stubborn. I know that this demonstration of my apparently total autism, a quality particularly suspect in a woman, will cause you to condemn me most severely, but I have all too often experienced that people who continually talk about the general good of mankind, and who to all appearances also meet the demands made by the general good they are always talking about, generally count among the greatest of all hypocrites. And naturally it is the good Christians, the good Catholics, who are always talking about the so-called general good, the so-called love of one's fellow man. Believe me, Reverend, a nomadic, capricious lifestyle such as my own offers plenty of opportunity to come into contact with a great variety of human experience and in this way to gain, first, an overview of the breadth, and second, an insight into the depth, of it. The overview I gained, and the insight, clearly demonstrated that one had to protect oneself from those who were always talking about 'sense of community' and 'love of your fellow man' and 'selflessness,' and who also seemed concerned with putting these abstract principles into practice.

"Far be it from me, Reverend, to attack you personally—it can happen, though seldom, that practicing Christians are also good people as well—but to a large, though not total, extent it is difficult to encounter good people among practicing Catholics; I personally have never experienced such malice, such duplicity, such deceitfulness as I have among good Christians, good Catholics. The good people are bad, the bad people are good, that's the way it is, Reverend, and not otherwise. It will not suffice to speak merely of a *coincidentia oppositorum*, a coincidence of opposites, as posited by Nikolaus von Kues, the great German mystic, as you doubtlessly are aware, it has to do with the discovery that truth is not that side of the coin that's obvious for all to see, but the flip side, its opposite. The only conclusion to be drawn from this is that one should distrust those people who appear to be good, and turn to those who appear to be bad. Ever since I began acting on this knowledge, gained through bitter experience, I am seldom deceived and hardly ever disappointed.

"If during my excursus, Reverend, elucidating my reluctance to fulfill the task assigned to me by Michael Minulescu when he handed me the alder stake, your face has taken on a somewhat incredulous, somewhat offended expression, this excursus was nevertheless unavoidably necessary and was interjected for the purpose of instructing you, as a member of the opposition, on the knowledge obtained by me over the course of some very difficult years, and perhaps to move you to a radical reversal, a radical change in course.

"So I looked at the alder stake that Michael Minulescu had pressed into my hand and felt no particular desire to drive it into Jonathan Alistair Abercrombie's bloodthirsty heart, at least not in the service of humankind, as suggested by Michael. It was solely the fear of having to escape from him again, of being chased by him, of fearing for my life—a motivation that you, as a representative of Christian charity, undoubtedly will find extremely egocentric—that, after long consideration on the mattress covered by the white linen sheet, made the monster's swift destruction appear desirable.

"What didn't please me was the instrument of destruction, the alder stake. I asked Michael if Jonathan necessarily had to be killed with this stake, to which he replied that this tool was the only truly appropriate one. As he was explaining why, an idea came to me, an idea I wisely kept to myself, suspecting that he would immediately reject it. I stood up and told him that I would fulfill the task I had been given.

"As I descended the narrow stairs, the alder stake in my bandaged right hand, Michael called after me to bring him back a sign that the monster had been destroyed, something unmistakably connected to him, something, if possible, that was evidence of Jonathan's sinister power. He considered one of the vampire's eyeteeth to be appropriate. I called back that I would try, and set off for the textile mill.

"It was a bright Saturday morning, people were hurrying through the streets going about their business, couples were kissing in the sun, sparrows were twittering in the gutters. Jonathan would be at home, he slept late on the weekends as a rule. I hurried along, as I had nothing else in mind but getting rid of him quickly so that I could lead a normal life again. And the weapon I would use would not be the wooden stake but Jonathan's large and gleaming knife. First, because the blade was very sharp, and second, I could handle it more easily than I could a sharpened piece of wood, as I had often used it in cooking or to cut a thread when darning or to carve a toothpick, in short, for all sorts of common everyday tasks, and third, in my life up until this point it has always proved advantageous to destroy an enemy with his own weapon. And if in the beginning Jonathan Alistair Abercrombie was anything but an enemy, if he had been helpful to me in taking care of my faithless dancer and his spellbinding partners, it nevertheless was undeniable that he had become one in the interim, one who was out for my life.

"The sidecar motorcycle was parked in front of the building. I opened the door and went in. Silently I moved up the stairs and pressed my ear to the door of our room, where I heard the faint sound of running water. As I correctly guessed, Jonathan was under the shower. On Saturdays and Sundays he took long showers in the small stall the former professional boxer had put in, in a corner of the room near the door. I had come at a good time and had to act immediately. I carefully opened the door, pulled the knife out of its leather sheath attached to the belt loop of the raggedy pants carelessly tossed on the wing chair, put the wooden stake down on the chair, and snuck over to the shower stall past a dripping, barely recognizable copy in ice of Rodin's *Thinker*, gripping the knife handle in my bandaged right hand. Jonathan couldn't hear me, as the sound of splashing water covered my light step, he couldn't see me because the walls of the shower stall were clouded with steam. I paused and then quickly shoved the sliding door to one side.

"There stood Jonathan, wet and beautiful, and for a second I hesitated as the memory of our first night together in the inn near Longpré-les-Corps-Saints on the Somme shot through my head. But I quickly came to, raised my arm, and struck with all my might. Jonathan's eyes widened, and he gave a strange smile that revealed his eyeteeth as he sank to the floor of the shower and lay with his face pressed against the tiles. My aim had been true, he was dead on the spot. I stood there with the bloody knife in my hand and watched as blood and water swirled in bizarre shapes around him. I thought of the proof of death that Michael Minulescu had requested, but recoiled from the idea of breaking off one of Jonathan's eyeteeth. I cut off a strand of his long black hair, cleaned the knife, and put it on the table. A large, recent, dark red bloodstain could be seen next to the dried brown one on the white gauze bandage Michael had wrapped around my right hand. I took the alder stake, smeared it with Jonathan's blood, turned off the water, and closed the sliding door. I looked in the pockets of his tattered pants and found the key to the sidecar motorcycle. Then, on an inexplicable impulse, I picked up the Ray-Bans lying on the table and found a little plastic bag in which I put the stake, the strand of hair, the key, and the sunglasses, and left first the room and then the former textile mill."

Magdalena fell silent. She sat before me in the rainy mist, her hair getting wetter. I would have liked to tell her that I admired her courage, her intelligence, and the decisiveness with which she had dispatched the monster. Her act made me think of St. George slaying the dragon. She had crossed the line, of course, drawn for a Christian, a Catholic woman, but one had to take into consideration that in doing so she had saved others from sure death, just as St. George had saved many others from a terrible end by slaying the dragon. I found that Michael Minulescu, though he possessed the positive qualities of helpfulness, concern, and moderation, had not exactly distinguished himself through courage in this affair. He, who as a man should have assumed this difficult task, had simply delegated it to Magdalena, in giving her the wooden stake. And Magdalena had accepted the challenge. What a woman!

"Oh, it's raining," Magdalena said, looking up at the sky. "I didn't notice. I'll sit down here next to you under the tree, Reverend, the tree will protect us from the rain."

She got up, and then sat down next to me, having first removed my sunglasses. Though this woman was holding me by force, though I was totally at her mercy, though she was capable of killing me at any minute just as she had done the melancholy Frisian, the jealous Ukrainian, the faithless

Galician, and Jonathan the bloodsucker, I felt good having her so close. I didn't understand myself anymore. I had to try to distance myself from this dangerous person, who not only had tied me up with green clothesline, but was also binding me ever tighter with the threads of her yarn.

Magdalena put her head on my shoulder.

"It's nice, this rain," she said. "We're sitting under the tree and looking out into the warm rain. We'll be quiet for a little while, Reverend, all right? We'll be quiet and concentrate on the sound of the falling rain."

I felt the sinner's head gradually become heavier on my shoulder. I couldn't see her eyes, perhaps she had fallen asleep. The rain fell softly, making the blades of grass glisten. The monotonous sound put me in a state between waking and slumber, and I had the feeling that I was gliding out of myself and lighting on the outstretched branch of the acacia, like the bullfinch I had seen earlier. Looking down from the branch I saw the odd couple that leaned so peacefully against the trunk of the tree.

I don't know how long I remained in this strange interim state. Suddenly, from above, I saw the sinner twist her beautiful mouth into a horrible grin, saw her reach her slender left hand into the early-summer grass beside her, take out the long gleaming knife, and point its blade at the chest of the priest, whose eyes were closed. I must have jerked upright at that point, for the next thing I heard was Magdalena's calm voice.

"What's the matter, Reverend? Why are you looking at me with that horrified expression? Did you have a bad dream?"

I saw Magdalena's face before me, her blue eyes wide with surprise, her long lashes, the round mole, a few freckles scattered across her light complexion. The Magdalena I had just seen armed with the gleaming knife must have been a dream.

"Now that you've waked me, now that I'm awake, I can continue with my story," she said. "Though I would have liked to sleep a while longer on your priestly shoulder," she added, and rubbed her head against my shoulder like a cat, a motion that electrified me. I was convinced that at the place where her hair met my shoulder there was a crackling sound, even though I hadn't heard anything, and that sparks flew, even though I hadn't seen them.

"So I drove my sidecar motorcycle back to Michael Minulescu, who was busy getting ready for his duties as a Jehovah's Witness, namely, to distribute copies of *The Watchtower* in the underground. He was no longer wearing the knee-length white nightshirt, but a dark brown suit, which looked quite worn and threadbare, but which made him appear quite trustworthy. He wore black shoes buffed to a high shine, a plain, slightly yellowed white shirt, and a dark brown tie that matched his suit. He noted my surprised expression. When one pursued an activity such as his, he said, an activity designed to convert the unenlightened and set them upon the right path, it was of utmost importance to make an honest and upright impression, or, better said, to convey an outward appearance that reflected the honesty and uprightness that naturally resided within each Jehovah's Witness. Honesty, dependability, and moral maturity were absolute prerequisites for belonging to the chosen who were called to spread the word of the kingdom of Jehovah.

"Before he could go into the duties of the Jehovah's Witnesses in detail I interrupted him and pulled the bloody wooden stake and the black strand of hair out of the plastic bag, proof that I had fulfilled his behest. When Michael asked where the eyetooth was and I told him that I hadn't had the heart to break off one of the vampire's eyeteeth, he became irritated and said that one would have to be satisfied with a strand of hair, but that he was surprised, even a little disappointed, at the lackadaisical way in which I had carried out my task. He had assigned it to me, among other reasons, with the idea of testing my suitability in terms of becoming a member of the Jehovah's Witnesses. Membership in the Jehovah's Witnesses required strict discipline, of course, and absolute submission to the will of Jehovah and to those who represented him on earth. Though I had passed the test posed by him with only a modicum of success, he would give me another chance.

"With these words he opened the large black brass-bound trunk and removed from it a woman's plain suit of gray flannel and a dark blue long-sleeved cotton blouse. He gave my black leather jumpsuit and motorcycle boots a disapproving look and said that if I wanted to join the community of the chosen the first thing I would have to do was change my wardrobe. I was immediately to take off my clothing, which blatantly violated the dress code of the Jehovah's Witnesses, and don the unobtrusive clothing left behind by his mother, who, regrettably, had died of a stroke the previous April, having served for years as a pillar to Jehovah's Witnesses in and around Reading. He pressed the suit and the blouse into my hands and returned to the black trunk for a pair of light brown tie shoes with crepe soles and sturdy medium heels, a pair of dark brown wool stockings, and a black capot. He set the last on my head and then stepped back to look at me, remarking that the color and condition of my hair would make it difficult for me to conform to the principles, aims, and general values of the Jehovah's Witnesses. The capot, which covered only part of my hair, was a provisional solution, sooner or later we would have to think about changing my hairstyle. Under the circumstances, a large square kerchief in an appropriate color was a possibility. Then Michael pointed to a small door, saying it was the bathroom and that I should change there, we had to be at work in the Piccadilly Circus underground stop in half an hour. When I didn't react, he pushed me toward the bathroom door, opened it, and shoved me in.

"I stood there in Michael's bathroom, caught totally unawares, suit, blouse, and wool stockings draped over my arm, shoes in hand, the capot on my head. I slowly sank down onto the toilet seat. Reverend, oftentimes we do things we later can only marvel at. In retrospect, my decision to adapt to what Michael and fate had in store for me, namely, an active participation in the edifying work of the international Watch Tower Bible and Tract Society, founded by American Charles Taze Russell, was absurd, but you have to understand that because of my previous erotic experiences I was a little sidetracked, had lost a little of my orientation and control over my life. My diurnal loss of blood had left me quite weak, my resistance was down, my stamina depleted, I felt sucked dry and defenseless and was greatly in need of someone to lean on. When we find ourselves in such a hopeless state someone always comes along who immediately recognizes our condition and uses it to his own purpose.

"So I was sitting on the toilet thinking about what I should do. When Michael knocked at the door and said we had to leave in five minutes, I stood up, took off my motorcycle jumpsuit and boots, and slipped into the clothes of Michael's deceased mother. At least Michael would treat me well, at least he wouldn't be violent like Igor, I thought as I pulled on the brown stockings. He won't lie to me and deceive me like

Pablo, I told myself as I buttoned up the cotton blouse. Michael had his idiosyncrasies, ideologically speaking, but disregarding these he seemed a decent and companionable man, a shy man largely free of destructive tendencies, who appeared to respect women. I would give him a try.

"I opened the bathroom door and stood at its threshold, dressed in the gray flannel suit. Michael looked at me in silence for a moment, then in a soft and emotion-laden voice said it was amazing how much I resembled his blessed mother in those clothes. Would I put my hair up in a bun before we left? he asked. I satisfied this request, which in my almost boundless naiveté I found harmless, and armed with two bundles of *The Watchtower* we made our way to the underground station at Piccadilly Circus. There we were impatiently met by Gabriel Rothenburg, a converted Jew of German heritage whom Michael introduced as his colleague and best friend. Gabriel, a tall and strong young man with blond hair and a slight speech impediment, told me that before he converted he had worked as a clerk in a Jewish deli-cum-bookshop, and that he rented a room from a nice lady on Tottenham Court Road, not far from where Michael lived.

"Michael gave Gabriel roughly thirty copies of *The Watchtower*, which he was to take by underground to Hyde Park Corner to spread the word of Jesus' return and the coming millennium. When Michael explained that Gabriel was by far the most gifted orator of all of London's Jehovah's Witnesses, and that London's Jehovah's Witnesses felt themselves fortunate in having such a persuasive and stirring speaker in their midst, Gabriel gave a shy smile and replied that this talent, as in the case of Demosthenes, Attican rhetorician and statesman, was simply a typical example of overcompensation, that were he not burdened with a slight speech impediment that made him stutter a little, he never would have had the determination needed to develop his gift of eloquence. Our defects often prove our good fortune, he said in leaving, the disadvantages that an apparently adverse fate burdens us with not seldom turn out to be advantages.

"As soon as this nice young man had disappeared, Michael pointed me to a spot in one of the subway corridors, having chased away a blind harmonica player, and said he expected of me a demure and at the same time dignified performance. I should speak only when spoken to and should restrict myself to silently distributing the magazine. Before taking up his position on a nearby corner he gave me a quick lesson in the major tenets of his faith. That would have to suffice for now, he said, I would have the opportunity later to gain a more profound understanding through a thorough study of the Bible, as well as the seven volumes of the scriptures of the pastor.

"Unfortunately, in the two hours I stood there I sold only three magazines, one to an old man who thought *The Watchtower* dealt with the First World War, and the second to a young street musician pulling her harp behind her on a little wagon, who said that we women working in the public sphere demonstrated a lack of solidarity and that she would buy my paper if I would give her a little support the next time I saw her performing at her usual spot on Leicester Square. She stood there for a few minutes talking to me, which caused Michael, who was watching me from his corner, to glower at us. Was I familiar with the function of a harp, the young musician asked, and when I mutely shook my head she told me that a harp was a chordophone, the strings of which ran vertically to the top of the sound board.

The strings, stretched between sound board and neck, were plucked with the fingertips of both hands. The ancient Egyptians used the six-stringed bow harp, so named for its shape; the angle harp; and the frame harp. But only the diatonic Tyrolean hook harp enabled a relatively quick strumming with the fingers, which enlarged the repertory. The harp used today was usually the forty-six to forty-eight string double harp, which was what she had. The double harp was tuned in C-flat major. Using the seven pedals, each note of the C-flat major scale could be raised by a semitone or a tone, so that all the tones of tempered tuning could be created. The range of the harp, therefore, covered almost seven octaves. She had inherited her harp from her foster mother, who had taken her in as an orphan, though she already had seven children. Those were women, she said.

"To demonstrate how her harp worked the young woman began with a simple English folk tune, at which Michael came running over to say she was disturbing business and should clear out. At this the musician left, pulling her little wagon with her harp behind her, but not before whispering that I should come see her the following Saturday at her usual place on Leicester Square. With a woman friend who played flute she was performing Mozart's Concerto for Flute and Harp, Köchel catalogue number 299, or 279 c, respectively, which was more than likely composed in April of 1778 for the daughter of the Duke of Guines, herself a gifted flutist. The duke took his time in paying for it, however. I would have to imagine the two violins, the viola and the bass, the two oboes and horns. Anyway, on Leicester Square we would have the opportunity to talk undisturbed about women's solidarity.

"I sold the third *Watchtower* to a man roughly thirty years old, with a three-day beard and wearing a suit that was a bit too big for him and his hair in a ponytail. Based on his hair and beard I at first took him for one of the better-dressed tramps, and readied myself for a little discussion on some literary theme. But after an introductory exchange, which Michael watched sullenly, it turned out that the man was in advertising. He apologized for his unsolicited interference, but he had observed several different *Watchtower* hawkers at this corner and each time had been astonished at their hair-raising sales strategy. Dressed in the outmoded suit I was wearing I could not possibly hope to get anyone interested in buying anything from me, he said, tugging at the collar of my blouse. One had to dress in a way that appealed to the unconscious desires of the potential consumer. Why didn't I sell my publication in a chic bodysuit; after all, I was an attractive woman. An orange bodysuit would be just the thing, orange was a very effective color, advertising-wise, though a fresh, optimistic pink had recently performed better in market research. The outfit I was wearing aroused absolutely no desire to buy anything at all, just the opposite, and my shoes nipped any buying impulses in the bud. Apologizing once again he loosened my bun, at which Michael rushed over furiously, only to be incorporated into the conversation. Such hair as mine, he said, was an invaluable natural advertising tool that must be exploited and not hidden away. And *The Watchtower*'s layout was completely outdated, we should hire a good graphic artist, there were plenty enough of them around. We could present our message in comic-book form, he said, nothing obscene, of course, perhaps a little erotic, that always upped the consumer ante. As Michael stared at him in amazement he said that the lessons of the Bible in comic-book form would look great on

T-shirts, would sell like hotcakes—Adam and Eve under the Tree of Knowledge, or Maria Magdalena in her various stages of wickedness, he wasn't so familiar with all of them but surely that was a possibility. It was difficult today, he said, to rise above the competition in any area, even in the sphere of sects.

"When Michael stepped in to explain to the advertising man that Jehovah's Witnesses was not a sect but a religion, the former responded by saying he was not in the least interested in such subtle distinctions, he had just wanted to give us a few tips, gratis, which others—in case we hadn't caught on—would pay plenty for. We also might consider a few video clips, he continued, to project onto the white-tiled walls of the underground station. But we shouldn't hire amateurs, there were enough out-of-work actors who would do that kind of work for very little money. And music, music was extremely effective as an advertising tool, why not set our beliefs to some simple musical form or other, get a good rock musician to record it at a decent studio and a good stereo system to play it in the underground corridors. The rock musician could perform live, of course, that would be even better. We should excuse him for saying so, but we obviously had not the slightest notion of advertising, of its conscious and deliberate influence on decision-making and opinion as related to economic, ideological, that is to say, political, cultural, and, yes, religious goals. But he had to go now, he said, he had an important meeting. He hoped, at any rate, that he had started us thinking, had given us a few ideas that would make our work more productive. At that he handed us his card and hurried off.

"On the one hand Michael was intrigued by the advertising man's ideas, and on the other, irritated by the fact that people were always talking to me who didn't show any signs of wanting to convert, but only wanted to keep me from my responsibilities. He grabbed the magazine bundles and said that was enough for today, in terms of my further education he would suggest that we go to Hyde Park Corner and listen to Gabriel speak.

"Gabriel was standing on an overturned mineral water crate, speaking to an audience of two—a young girl in a nurse's uniform guiding the wheelchair of an elderly lady with both legs in casts. Standing on a beer crate next to him, and surrounded by several hundred people, was a representative of an extreme right-wing group who, constantly interrupted by applause, was calling for the revival of English alliterative poetry, as well as the tried-and-true method of carefully integrating foreign minorities through the use of ghettoes.

"Gabriel was having a hard time making himself audible to the lady in the wheelchair and her attendant in communicating his vision of paradise on earth, which would become reality once the forces of Satan were destroyed in the bloody battle to be waged at Armageddon. I pricked up my ears at the mention of this future paradise for, as you know, I have always been intrigued by the idea of paradise. Unfortunately, Gabriel all too quickly turned away from his description of this greatly coveted thousand-year arcadia in order to belittle state and nation at the same moment the right-wing speaker on the beer crate began his glorification of the nation-state. In the midst of Gabriel's criticism of compulsory military duty, lucid as it was sharp, the elderly lady instructed her young attendant to push the wheelchair over closer to the extreme right-wing speaker, as his simultaneous call for a general draft appeared of greater interest to her. Robbed of his audience Gabriel stepped down from his mineral water crate and the three of us went to an inexpensive vegetarian restaurant located not far from Harrod's.

"I was impressed by the warm understanding that Gabriel and Michael shared with each other, they seemed to value each other not only as Jehovah's Witnesses but as friends. Over spelt soup, stuffed cabbage rolls, and yogurt with millet seed and huckleberries, the two of them enlightened me further on the responsibilities of a Jehovah's Witness, informing me, furthermore, that members were obligated to pledge a certain financial contribution. When I indicated that the savings I had brought with me from Paris were slowly dissipating, and that after paying room and board I would have hardly anything left over, their faces darkened.

"After a whispered consultation, Michael informed me that I could live with him if I wished, and donate the rent money I would save to the organization. Under normal circumstances I would not have accepted his offer, but the events of my recent past had left me feeling greatly insecure and with a strong desire for friendship, for the feeling that I belonged, a desire for community. We humans are full of contradictions, isn't that so? On the one hand we distrust community deeply and run from it, and on the other hand we long for it. Reverend, I fell into the community of believers trap, just as you fell into the community of believers trap, just as, sooner or later, we all fall into the community of believers trap. It wasn't the goals of the community of believers that interested me, or the ideals of the community of believers, it was the warmth and shelter of the community of believers that interested me.

"The abrupt end to Jonathan's life not only had complicated my connection to his group of London's tramps—in which I had felt quite comfortable because of the exciting intellectual climate—it had made it impossible. They would find Jonathan's body, at the latest, when the former professional boxer returned from the theater festival in Scotland and, as I had disappeared, would suspect me of having killed him. I therefore had to avoid at all costs the tramps with whom Jonathan had been friends during his months in London, an undertaking that wouldn't be easy, as the paths of London's tramps and Jehovah's Witnesses often crossed—both preferred the London underground system and both frequented public streets and squares. I would have to be careful.

"In retrospect, of course, the most rational thing would have been to leave London immediately, but we humans are just as irrational as we are contradictory, don't you agree, Reverend? The longing for a community of believers, this absurd feeling, kept me in London, and after the pleasant evening meal in the vegetarian restaurant, I followed Michael back up the narrow set of stairs to his room with the barred window, to stay with him for an undetermined period of time. Lacking a second bed we shared the large mattress in the middle of the room, covered with the white linen sheet, and our relationship was as pure as the white linen.

"It turned out that Michael was an extremely reserved person, a quality I appreciated, my relationship with Jonathan having sapped all of my strength. Each evening as we lay next to each other on the mattress following a long day of meeting our responsibilities to Jehovah's Witnesses, he in his white knee-length linen nightshirt, me in one of the two long nightgowns with the pastel floral pattern and high collars that his blessed mother had left behind, Michael would put his arm around me in a brotherly fashion and say how glad he was that I had accepted one of the principles of the community, according to which one had to keep oneself from being defiled by the world. It was difficult enough, he said, having constantly to deal with the immoral advertising in the tube and on the street. Nor did it help to simply look away, there was so much of it that your eyes naturally fell on the next ad. Women's naked arms and legs everywhere, everywhere women's eyes, women's mouths, women's hair.

"And what was even worse, he said, absentmindedly stroking my upper arm bedecked in the pastel flowers of his mother's gown, as a Jehovah's Witness one naturally dealt with precisely those people most in need of Christ's message, those hard-boiled sinners of the red-light districts, who earned their living performing unspeakable acts, or who spent their living procuring them.

"Shortly after he became a Jehovah's Witness, he said, the London office had sent him and two experienced Witnesses across the Channel to the Amsterdam office, to distribute the Dutch edition of *The Watchtower* in the red-light district there, one of the most notorious in Europe, a Sodom and Gomorrah on the dark waters of the *grachts*, a kind of trial by fire, so to speak. It had been awful—in the back canals there were all sorts of instruments of animal behavior, the purpose of which he wasn't familiar with but could sometimes guess, and scantily or undressed white, yellow, brown, and black women everywhere, shamelessly offering themselves in display windows. Even today he shuddered, thinking back on this initiation he had undergone as a guileless young man. He, who had inherited from his mother a tendency to headaches, had returned from Amsterdam with a terrible migraine, which had kept him from carrying out his responsibilities in the field for two whole weeks.

"Incidentally, he said—taking from the wood floor next to

the mattress the framed black-and-white photo that always stood there and that showed his mother in a plain black dress, standing next to a large man of solemn mien—even though his mother, shown here during a trip to the United States beside a high-ranking Jehovah's Witness from central headquarters in Brooklyn, had fallen victim to a cerebral stroke, he was convinced that she—a sensitive woman who abhorred the animalistic obscenities of life—had had her spirit broken long before, through her constant confrontation with a wicked world. This destruction of spirit always manifested itself in the form of violent migraine attacks, which were helped only slightly by taking ergot alkaloids and which, in his opinion, an opinion based not on medicine but on intuition, led to her final fatal cerebral hemorrhage.

"Reverend, through Michael Minulescu my life took a different turn, a turn I would never have considered possible. We rose early, went to bed early, ate well, abstained from alcohol, and fervently devoted ourselves to spreading the message of Christ's second coming, which—having been anticipated in 1914 and failing to materialize, as was also the case in 1918 and 1925, both dates based on absolutely solid calculations—now was at hand. Gabriel was not the only other Jehovah's Witness I met. In the course of the various obligatory meetings, the Bible studies, the gatherings centered around preaching and lecturing and analyzing *The Watchtower*, I met a large number of unassuming yet resolute people from all levels of society, who had placed their lives in the service of witnessing. Together with a sympathetic single librarian in her mid-fifties, by the name of Frances Flint, I soon was instructed to pay visits to the homes of the unconverted to shed a little light on their existence, unenlightened as it was up until then. Every Wednesday afternoon we would have tea on Regent Street with a retired Anglican priest, a free-spirited and loquacious man. His homey living room, furnished with dark and massive pieces of Victorian furniture, became a sort of oasis for us, where we fled a reality in which doors often were slammed in our faces, curses heaped upon our heads, and English greyhounds or Irish setters set on our heels.

"And it wasn't only our stuffy fellow citizens, uninterested as they were in any kind of higher spiritual development, who made our lives hard. Even worse was the hostility shown us by the other confessions. After two young male members of the New Apostles, a strongly Bible-oriented group, lay in wait for us one day in Parson Bond's building and pushed us down the stairs, calling out as they ran away that we had better not show our faces again on their missionary turf—an event that so upset the parson, who rushed to our aid, that his blood pressure soared to a dangerous degree—and, a short while later, after we managed to escape a group of the Holy Grail movement that was stalking us, saved at the last minute when a grade-crossing gate was lowered between us, Frances and I had to split up and make our house calls in the company of male Jehovah's Witnesses. And that, as it turned out, was no guarantee that we wouldn't be molested. One evening as Gabriel and I were returning from a long visit with a family of Pakistani immigrants in Brixton, both windows of the room he rented on the ground floor of a building on Tottenham Court Road had been smashed, and the words FUCK THE WITNESSES spray-painted in black letters on the faded pink house wall, an event that placed a serious strain on the warm relationship Gabriel enjoyed with his landlady. The next day a former Ufology sect member, who had managed only with effort to disassociate himself from his fellow believers, got word to us that the perpetrators of this act had been two exceptionally rabid Ufologists. I gradually began to ask myself whether the fact that Michael had saved me from Jonathan the undead had been a particularly fortunate occurrence."

I looked up at Magdalena's profile, damp with rain, as she sat beside me. I would liked to have said that I didn't find it surprising that she had landed in such a difficult situation. In my opinion her problems stemmed solely from the fact that, instead of seeking her certain salvation on the broad path of the one true holy apostolic Catholic Church, she instead had chosen the twisting side alley of one of countless sects, all of which were nothing more than dead ends. It was clear that this was not the path to finding her way out of the jungle of compulsions and afflictions, conflicts, and complications that mark us as poor mortals, but one on which she would simply sink deeper into them. The rain was still falling, splattering softly against the thick foliage, which was beginning to divide here and there and even open a little in spots to let the large raindrops through.

"At the tube station at Piccadilly Circus, however, it was still relatively peaceful," Magdalena continued with her tale. "Occasionally a tramp whose face seemed familiar to me would sit down to beg not far away. He often would glance in my direction, and after long consideration I recognized him as one of the three people in the textile mill who had taken part in the discussion on Peter Brooks's theater productions led by the former professional boxer. I noticed the man shortly after I saw a headline on a London evening paper at a kiosk in a passage of the underground that read: DEATH UNDER THE SHOWER: MYSTERIOUS MURDER AMONG LONDON'S STREET VAGRANTS. Had Jonathan's friends become suspicious and begun to follow me? I tried to dismiss this disquieting thought and to ignore the man and concentrate on selling *The Watchtower*. Every once in a while the young harpist would turn up and distract me with talk of women's solidarity and music composed especially for the harp, in particular the various adaptations of the Orpheus saga, as set to music by Monteverdi, Gluck, and Händel. At that time, as she revealed to me, she was trying to find six other female harpists, or male if it came to that, on the streets and in the underground passageways of London, in order to perform on Leicester Square a simplified version of Richard Wagner's opera, *Rheingold*, which called for seven harps, as I was surely aware. It was quite difficult, of course, if not impossible to drum up such a relatively large number of harpists, female or male, but she wouldn't give up so easily. She had already found one male harpist, a Croatian and former orchestra member from Zagreb, who at present was living under the Waterloo Bridge and with whom she got along well, despite the fact that he was a man, as he, too, was an orphan. I, as a nonorphan, was of course unfamiliar with the fact that nothing was so binding as the connection between orphans, for how could nonorphans possibly conceive of being orphans?

"Before the young woman walked on, pulling her wagon with the double harp behind her, she wished me luck in my endeavors, especially those concerning women. And once in a while the blind harmonica player found his way to me, whom Michael had chased off the first time I had sold *The Watchtower*, but whom he now begrudgingly tolerated, after I appealed to his social conscience. I found the presence of this silent, gentle young man, who had not been born blind and who lived in a home in Stepney Green, quite pleasant.

"One day, several weeks after I began selling papers in the Piccadilly Circus tube station, a man loaded down with various utensils appeared in my section of the passageway. He stopped across from me, opened a folding wooden chair, set up an easel, and began to paint. Reverend, it was I he had chosen as his model, just as Jonathan had chosen me as a model for his sculptures, though the circumstances under which I now was being painted were totally different from those under which Jonathan created his sculptures. The man, who after three days of intensive work crossed the subway corridor to shake my hand and introduce himself, was none other than the respected sociologist and amateur painter Richard Thorneycroft, who felt a deep empathy for those less favored by fate, for society's outsiders, and was compelled to capture a number of these socially disadvantaged on canvas. The photographs of these paintings gave visual credibility to his publications, which sold in numbers that would make your head swim. To the same degree that the advertising man found my outfit lacking, Richard, as he insisted I call him, found it authentic, touching even. Michael, of course, immediately tried to drive him off as well, but was placated when he heard that a picture of a Jehovah's Witness at work, reprinted in a bestseller by the sociologist, would be of considerable promotional value. Richard said my face and strawberry blond curls reminded him of the type of femme fatale that the Pre-Raphaelites portrayed in their paintings. Once Michael was gone, Richard asked me to take down my hair, in order to reinforce my resemblance to this female type. Sometimes he would walk over and lift my chin slightly or rearrange a strand of hair, or tell me to hold the magazines in my other hand, his tone always amiable and respectful. Once he politely asked the blind harmonica player to stand next to me, and two days later he had finished a picture that he wanted to use as the cover illustration for his new book on marginal social groups, *The Outcasts*.

"One day he asked the harpist to lift her instrument from her little wagon and loan it to us briefly—in order that I might sit down at it with my hair down, so that he could finally capture an image that had been floating around in his head for some time, namely, a watercolor of a harp-playing red-haired angel, in the manner of the Pre-Raphaelites, which he wanted to call *Subway Angel*—but she objected, saying her harp wasn't there for someone to just sit down beside and pretend to play, her harp was a splendid double harp she inherited from her foster mother and not a toy, and anyway, she had to go, in half an hour she was rehearsing the *Rheingold* in an empty furniture warehouse not far from Leicester Square with the two male harpists and two female harpists she had assembled to perform it.

"Days passed, and I ignored the glances of the acquaintance of the former professional boxer as long as I could. But one day, when the former programmer and expert on English portrait painting from the shed in the Docklands showed up and sat down with him, I became seriously worried. The attentive way in which he was watching Richard and me could have been due to his basic interest in painting, of course, but I found his presence somewhat strange, as he didn't speak to me but only watched me from a distance. One evening after work I was walking alone from the Piccadilly Circus tube stop back to Michael's room. The street was deserted and, feeling exposed because of the unpleasant experiences I had had with the members of diverse sects, I jumped when I heard footsteps behind me. When someone put his hand over my mouth from behind I was sure it was a member of the Mun sect who wanted to frighten me. But before whoever it was let go of me and ducked around the next corner, he hissed in my ear: What happened to Jonathan Alistair Abercrombie?

"Reverend, you will understand that this was the last straw in terms of my peace of mind. Not only were members of the various religious sects after me, now I was also being threatened by Jonathan's friends, the tramps. I felt I would never be safe, whether making house calls or selling the magazine in the underground. I grew jumpier, more nervous, and this didn't exactly impact positively on potential customers, as a result of which I sold even fewer copies of *The Watchtower* than usual. I was always looking around me, would flinch at the slightest sound, and was tormented by nightmares in which tramps and sect members chased me deep into the tunnels of the underground system, up onto television towers, and across broad stretches of tracks, before finally cornering me against a fire wall, at which I would wake up and Michael would amicably take me in his arms and comfort me.

"During this period the shabby room with the barred window at the top of the high narrow stairs was a place of refuge and renewal for me. Michael treated me with consideration and tenderness. Evenings, we often lay on the mattress in the middle of the room and talked about the conflict-ridden, aggressive, and disharmonious situations we had encountered during the course of the day because of our work carried out in the public sphere. Michael would nestle his sparsely covered head against the ruffles of one of the two nightgowns his mother had left behind, which now were worn by me, sigh in contentment, and remark how pleasant it was to be able to relax with a woman in a relationship untainted by any sexual inclinations and gather his strength for the coming day. Think of all the couples, he said, whose private life together consisted of nothing more than a continuation of the struggle for existence they waged in the outside world, their nights filled with excesses, dissipation, and outrages of all sorts, who could find no peace, because of their uncontrolled passions. He was fortunate in having found a kindred soul in me, he said then, and put his arm around my hips covered in the pastel-colored natural fibers of the former nightgown of his mother, a twin to whom concepts like chastity, shame, and moral virtue were not merely empty words, but a living reality.

"When Michael lay beside me talking so convincingly about the unsullied character of our relationship I had to agree with him, though his innocent touches sometimes called up tiny little physical reactions in me, which of course I didn't call attention to, as even the most tender demonstration of a sensual nature would have offended him and knocked him off-balance. He appeared to be such a sensitive, almost ethereal creature that I often felt my own robust nature to be coarse in comparison to his fragility. I grew accustomed to our evenings of close talks on the mattress, and when Michael came home later than usual, which could happen, of course, after long sessions at Tottenham Court Road going over the accounting books with Gabriel, I would wait impatiently for the sound of his key in the lock.

"To the same degree I felt secure in my harmonious private life with Michael, I felt exposed and endangered whenever I moved about the city alone. One day, on my way to the Theocratic Pastoral School, I passed by a gun shop and decided to buy a small handgun for my own peace of mind. I entered the shop and after a long discussion chose a handy

Smith & Wesson. The fact that I didn't have a gun permit
didn't seem to particularly bother the man who sold me the
gun, who also was the shop's owner. After I placed a little
more money on the counter than he had asked for, he handed
me the pistol and said I shouldn't forget to carefully read the
instructions on how to use it. I stuck the Smith & Wesson in
my purse and went on my way, feeling much safer than
before. Telling Michael about my purchase didn't seem necessary. It wasn't long before I had the opportunity to pull out
the gun for the first time: Early one morning, as I was walking through St. James's Park, a habit I had retained from my
time together with Jonathan, a black man with a bowie knife
jumped out from behind an azalea bush and threatened me,
saying I had sold my last *Watchtower* in Catholic Fundamental-
ist territory. I took the lady's pistol from the small holster
strapped to my belt and pointed it at the man, who immediately disappeared behind the azalea bush.

"A few days later Gabriel and Michael asked me during
lunch in our little vegetarian restaurant if I wouldn't like to
take Gabriel's place on the mineral water crate on Hyde Park
Corner and speak on the coming millennium that would
bring paradise to earth, as keeping the organization's books
was taking up more of their time than expected. Reverend,
you, who gave your first sermon as a Catholic priest at some
point, will perhaps understand that I was frightened of public speaking, not least because my English is not exactly
accent-free. But the fact that it was one of my favorite topics,
that of paradise, allowed me to leap over my shadow and
agree. In preparation I did a bit of reading in the works of
Charles Taze Russell, above all his 1877 title, *Three Worlds, or
The Plan for Salvation*.

"When I arrived on Hyde Park Corner the right-wing

extremist was already on his beer crate speaking to a large audience about reverse consciousness in the value system presented in the *Edda*. I stepped up onto the mineral water crate and began to speak. When I realized that no one was paying any attention to the Jehovah's Witnesses' idea of paradise, which didn't seem too exciting to me either, I altered the concept a little and began to weave in other versions of paradise, though not to such a degree that I felt I was betraying the community of Jehovah's Witnesses' believers in any serious fashion. After I portrayed the paradise of Jehovah's Witnesses as being a bit similar to the Greeks' concept of Elysium, throwing in my recollection of a splendid summer I spent in the Greek isles, I had attracted five people. I then proceeded to imbue this paradise with all the attributes of the land of milk and honey, with roast pigeons in the air, delicious fish in the brooks, and fruit that dropped from the trees into the open mouths of those lying beneath them relaxing in the sun. People really liked that. Not only did nine more people join the five already there, at least twenty of the right-wing extremist's audience stepped over to hear me. At this, the right-wing extremist gave me a furious look and began ranting even more loudly against the mixing of the Anglo-Saxon and foreign races, which already had done untold damage to the purity of the English culture and language. I, too, raised my voice, and launched into a colorful depiction of the world to come, which, precisely speaking, resembled the Islamic idea of paradise but which could be carried over to that of Jehovah's Witnesses without much effort. As I was describing in great detail the beautiful girls who would dance around the blessed of Elysium, fifty more of the right-wing extremist's audience came over to listen.

"Reverend, when I became aware of my effect on the public, and as the number of those hanging on my every word grew, I was overcome by a feeling of elation that is difficult to convey. Exhilarated by the apparent attention of so many, I swung into an extremely lively and forceful speech.

"Perhaps my euphoria on that occasion is comparable to the rapture you doubtlessly feel on Sundays and Catholic holidays, when the captivated eyes of the many believers are upon you as you preach from your pulpit on the Fall, on fratricide and the Flood. Unfortunately, my enthusiasm and that of my listeners was brought to an abrupt end when a group of skinheads of the right-wing extremist's inner circle approached my mineral water crate, making gestures that were unmistakably threatening, and appeared ready to push me off it. In view of the escalating situation I felt it would be best to exit the scene immediately. As I was making my way through the crowd I heard my audience murmur their disappointment. Calling out to them: Friends, I shall return! I abandoned the field and ducked into the azalea bushes in the park.

"Now that I was forced to number not only tramps and sect members, but London's skinheads as well among my enemies, I began to contemplate leaving the city. That same evening I informed Michael of my thoughts on the matter. At this he clasped me to him, holding on to his mother's nightgown as a drowning man grasps at straws, and begged me to stay with him, he needed me, not only as a fellow combatant for his religious beliefs, but as a woman offering him a new hold in a world from which his mother had departed the previous April. When I saw that the nightgown's ruffles were wet with his tears I decided to put off my departure. I told him of my decision, and in a display of gratitude he covered me with kisses.

"Reverend, I must admit that the fervor and gratitude of

these kisses had an effect on me that Michael surely did not intend. I was barely able to conceal the excitement that his totally platonic embraces aroused in me through the pastel nightgown.

"In his joy at my decision to stay, Michael continued to shower me with brotherly affection for weeks to come, and I didn't dare confess to him that this put me in exactly the iniquitous state of mind he so condemned in others. I decided simply to accept the situation and try to hide my passionate feelings, which wasn't very difficult as Michael, in his innocence, was totally unaware of the flame he was fanning. You, who as a man of God are familiar with the constant vacillation between good to evil we sinners are subject to, who has encountered the oscillation of the weak and frail between virtue and vice, will surely understand the problematic situation in which I found myself. What was I to do? I couldn't encourage Michael to act in ways that blatantly contradicted his beliefs. I would have risked putting him, sensitive creature that as he was, in a deep existential crisis. But believe me, with each evening Michael's devotion became increasingly tortuous to a young and healthy woman such as myself, whose sensory apparatus was functioning excellently, and who had an immediate reaction to stimulation of all sorts. I didn't know which was better, for him to stay away evenings poring over the books of the Jehovah's Witnesses, or to come home early.

"One evening Richard Thorneycroft appeared at the Piccadilly Circus station with a bottle of Veuve Cliquot, three champagne flutes, and two complimentary copies of his new book, *The Outcasts*. He gave one copy to the blind harmonica player and one copy to me, popped the champagne cork against the white-tiled wall of the underground, and filled three glasses. We were celebrating the publication of his new book, he said, to the success of which the harmonica player and I had contributed in serving as models for the cover illustration. Had Michael been standing on his corner I never would have dared to drink alcohol, of course. But as he was in bed with a migraine I had two glasses of champagne and returned home in high spirits to lie next to him on the mattress, at which he immediately put his arm around me. Reverend, I know that my behavior would be condemned equally from a Catholic point of view and from a Jehovah's Witness point of view, but the effect of the champagne was such that I abandoned my usual reticence. Understand me when I say that I did not deliberately seduce him, it was more an instinctive, spontaneous reaction to his protective gesture. I do admit, though, that I forgot myself and once again overstepped the line drawn for my sex.

"My silent but obvious show of sexual interest had immediate consequences: Michael sat bolt upright in bed and stared at me as he had at our first encounter, though his surprise then had been based on something else entirely. He then picked up the photo next to him, of his mother and the formally dressed man she was with, and held it before my eyes. On his fortieth birthday, he said, his mother had made him promise to refrain from any kind of lustful contact with a woman that would diminish the energy he was to reserve wholeheartedly for Jehovah's Witnesses. Then he gave me a reproachful look and said I was more receptive to temptation than he had thought. He suggested that a cold shower might bring me to my senses. It would not be right to rob our disciplined relationship of its uniqueness because of some sudden irrational desire. Others might give in to such dubious impulses, but we, as people who had overcome our animal qualities through inner strength to attain a higher spiritual plane, were above such impulses. He spoke so forcefully that there was nothing I could say in reply, indeed, I was so ashamed of my open display of desire that I withdrew to the little sink in one corner of the room and began splashing myself with cold water. Then I returned to the mattress, where Michael received me in friendship, soon to fall asleep."

Magdalena fell silent, and the scene she had just described ran through my mind. The ambiance, complete with the little sink, reminded me of the parsonage. My sister and I slept in separate rooms, of course, but the pastel-colored nightgown could have belonged to Maria. It was beginning to get dark, and as my sister retired early it was entirely possible that at this very moment she was standing before the sink, as Magdalena had.

"The next day Gabriel and I made two house visits," Magdalena continued, "and around four that afternoon I went to the tube station with copies of *The Watchtower*. Right after the old man who was interested in the First World War came up to request an issue that would describe in detail the September 1914 Battle of the Marne, the former milling machine operator and current Freud specialist stepped out of the corner shadows and aggressively thumped me on the chest with a paperback edition of *Culture and Its Discontents*. I shouldn't kid myself, he said, Jonathan's friends knew very well who had him on her conscience. Even though the police hadn't caught up with me I wouldn't escape them, Jonathan's friends. Then he grabbed me by the collar of my dark blue blouse, pulled my face right up to his, and breathed on me with his bad breath. There was no hurry, he hissed, Jonathan's friends had plenty of time, and one day they would fish my body out of the Thames, or find me on a garbage dump with a knife in my back, or in the azalea bushes of Hyde Park.

"Before another variety of death could occur to him, Richard appeared around the corner with his easel, his palette, and his folding stool, with the intention of starting work on a half-length portrait of me, tentatively titled *Young Woman in Capot Hat*. When he saw I was being threatened he shoved the tramp in the back with his folded stool, at which the tramp took flight. Simultaneously, two figures in disguise stormed down the steps of the underground, tore the pile of magazines out of my hands, threw me to the ground, and ran off shouting: Pentecost Lives! The young harpist, approaching from the other direction, tried to push the little wagon with her harp in their path, at which they knocked it over and dashed around the corner. The harpist bent down to help me to my feet, but at that very moment three skinheads stomped down the corridor toward me, swinging chains. Had the advertising man not suddenly shown up and had the presence of mind to comprehend the seriousness of the situation, at which he cleverly engaged the skinheads in a little conversation on the form, color, materials, and emblematic significance of popular brands of combat boots, I wouldn't have had time to draw the Smith & Wesson from my handbag, back up the steps holding it in my outstretched hands, and flee the scene. Totally beside myself, I ran in the direction of Tottenham Court Road, intending to seek out Gabriel and Michael, who once again were working on the organization's accounts. Having arrived at the violet-colored house, still marred by the black spray-painted slogans of the Ufologists, I was so upset that I leaped right up onto the eighteen-inch wall, in order to inform them as quickly as possible through the broken windows of Gabriel's ground-floor rented room of what had happened.

"Reverend, what happened in the moments that followed remains in my mind only as a series of disconnected images, as a silent film torn and retaped in places, as a succession of slow-motion movements. I looked into the room through the big hole in the window, expecting to find Gabriel and Michael sitting at the table, their heads bent over the accounts. There was no one seated at the table. My eyes flitted back and forth across the room like a disoriented housefly, glided over the floral wallpaper, an open hearth, and an old cupboard, finally to come to rest on the bed that stood in one corner of the room. Reverend, I know that what I will now say will come as a shock to you, a Catholic priest, but in moving toward the climax of this episode I must relate it to you as it happened.

"The bed was not in a tranquil state. The covers were moving as if during a storm at sea, tossing waves that heaved up one after the other, and as my eyes cautiously approached one end of the bed I spotted two familiar heads, one sparsely covered with hair, the other blond. The two heads could barely be told apart, they twisted and turned in jerky motions. Then a male back rose up like a great winding snake, and though it wasn't covered as usual in a white linen nightshirt, I immediately recognized it as Michael's.

"When I saw this naked back, his skinny neck and the bald spot on the back of his head, my reasoning powers, which normally function relatively well, reached their end. The scene swam before my eyes, and when I could focus again I saw this back suddenly covered in blood, rising up a second time only to sink down onto the second figure in the bed. I looked down at my right hand, still holding the Smith & Wesson with which I had covered my retreat from the Piccadilly Circus tube station. When I comprehended that it was a bullet from this Smith & Wesson that had penetrated Michael's back, I bounded off the wall, ran into the crowd that filed through Tottenham Court Road at this time of day, and turned down a narrow, empty passageway. I stopped there and tried to clear my head, then ran back to our room, zigzagging through the narrow alleys and side streets. I threw my few possessions into a big plastic bag from Harrod's, ran back down the steps, jumped onto my Puch 800 parked in front of the building, and left London heading south, into an unusually red, unusually large and rising full moon.

"It is unclear to me how, in my confusion, I could find the entrance to the highway, how I was in any shape at all to steer the motorcycle. But I soon found myself in Canterbury, and decided to spend the night in this venerable archbishop's seat. Only as I lay in my bed in the modest little hotel could I think clearly again and comprehend what I had done. I had critically wounded Michael, if not killed him, in the heat of the moment, in the intense and relatively brief state of emotional excitement that overtook my psychological functions, my motoricity, and parts of my autonomic nervous system, during which one's powers of judgment are reduced to the point of eliminating one's critical faculties, and control over oneself is lost, the sort of excited state that accelerates the course of actions, the result of which is uncontrolled and without regard to significance or possible consequences. In my case the emotion was fury, blind fury at someone who was always talking about virtue and who rejected a serious offer of love from a healthy, strong woman of child-bearing age on the basis of the necessity of sexual abstinence, yet who, under the false pretense of sitting over the books for nights at a time, was simultaneously carrying on a homosexual relationship. It was this betrayal, this inexcusable violation of human trust, that drove me to my deed.

"Despite all the extraordinary events of this memorable day I slept very well and woke the next morning to the ringing of cathedral bells. I dressed, went down to the dining room, sat down at the breakfast table, and opened the morning paper. On page three, under the headline BRUTAL MURDER OF HOMOSEXUAL IN SECT CIRCLE, there was a long article on what had happened. Apparently I had fired not one but four bullets into Michael, one of which penetrated his heart, one his liver, and two his lungs. Several witnesses had observed a middle-aged woman dressed in a gray suit and black capot hat climb up on the wall under the window of the apartment where the murder occurred, fire shots, and then flee the scene. Information was requested leading to the whereabouts of this woman. The friend of the victim, who had been present at the shooting, was in shock. As of press time no one had gotten more out of him than a few confused words about fanatic members of the Baha'i sect.

"Before I could finish the article I got a chill: I was still wearing the gray suit and the capot hat! I immediately paid my bill, hurried out of the hotel, and went to the public toilet in the park, where I exchanged Michael's mother's clothes for my motorcycle jumpsuit. As I had given all of my money to the Jehovah's Witnesses, I was as good as broke. I went over to the cathedral and entered the same nave, empty at this early hour, that Jonathan Alistair and I had visited on our way to London, went over to the niche with the lovely statue of the Virgin Mary, and concealed the statue. Then I mounted my sidecar motorcycle and rode on to Dover, where I managed to get through passport and customs controls, drive my sidecar motorcycle onto the ferry, and cross the Channel without problem. Nor did I run into trouble with the French border guards in Calais."

Magdalena drew a few deep breaths, stretched her long slender neck, and leaned her head against the trunk of a tree. Not only were her hair and face damp from the soft rain that was still falling, and which the foliage of the acacia couldn't begin to contain, her jumpsuit as well glittered with moisture, and if I looked down and to the left I could see countless little drops of water on the small triangle of skin revealed by her open zipper.

Following her depiction of the outrageous scene she had witnessed through the broken windowpanes it was hard for me to concentrate on her continuing story. What Magdalena had described disturbed me greatly, for it showed that the sects that had split off in futile rebellion against the Mother Church were more deeply entangled in wickedness and disgrace than I had imagined. Was it possible that people who claimed to be doing God's work could sink to such unnatural acts? Could such people become so deeply mired in sin? How happy I was to be secure in the lap of the Holy Apostolic Catholic Church, in which such false paths, such perverse degeneracy, has no place.

In the meantime darkness had fallen and I was beginning to feel a bit tired. Not only did telling a story take a lot of energy, as Magdalena maintained, but listening was tiring as well. Next to me Magdalena moved, and I saw her shadowy outline go over to the sidecar motorcycle and return with something dark in her arms, which, as she came nearer, I identified as her sleeping bag. She put it down on the ground under the tree and then something happened that I hadn't expected. Without a word Magdalena began to untie the green nylon clothesline that bound me to the tree. This accomplished, she then untied my hands from behind my back. My hands, resting at my sides now, were numb. Magdalena took first my right and then my left hand between her palms and rubbed them slowly and gently. Feeling gradually began to return to my fingers. Magdalena let go of my hands and proceeded to my upper body. She stroked the cloth of my dalmatic and her touch called forth a strange sensation in me, as if a thin sheet of ice were cracking. She continued to stroke me, and more and more fine cracks and crevices opened in the sheet of ice, until finally it split into tiny pieces and sank into the black water. Then she lay the sleeping bag down next to me, took my bound feet in her hands, and placed them in the softly padded opening. I slid in and she slipped in beside me. When I went to remove my gag she grabbed my hands and held them tightly.

"Not yet," she said. The rain had stopped, it was very quiet.

The next morning I was awakened by the sun shining in my face. I opened my eyes and saw the back of Magdalena's strawberry blond head next to me. It took a while for the memory of the night before to sink in. My hands were free, I could have untied my feet and run away, though it probably wouldn't have taken long for Magdalena to catch up with me. I could have grabbed the piece of green nylon clothesline and overpowered Magdalena, or at least tried to, even though she was stronger than I. But I didn't even consider it. I enjoyed the close warmth of my abductor, this murderess breathing softly next to me, and squinted into the sun, waiting for her to awake. The birds were singing and the grass was glistening, and the raindrops that had fallen the day before were slowly evaporating in the morning sun. Magdalena turned, murmured something unintelligible, and buried her head in my shoulder. How could I have run away from this woman after a night such as the previous one?

She opened her eyes, smiled, and kissed me on my cheek, which was mostly covered by the gag. Then she slid out of the sleeping bag and went over to the sidecar motorcycle, to return with bread, ham, and cherries, at which she again slid in next to me and began to eat. I removed the gag without any protest from her, so that the black Kashiyama bodysuit hung like a kerchief around my neck, took a pair of cherries from her hand and put them one after the other into my mouth. The taste of the sweet plump fruit on my tongue was wonderful. Magdalena turned to me and put her right index finger to her lips. It wasn't necessary to remind me to remain silent, I had not the slightest inclination to talk at the moment. So we sat in the sleeping bag under the acacia tree and ate breakfast.

"You shall not speak, Reverend," Magdalena said after a while. "Your time to speak has not yet come."

I was prepared to do anything this woman asked, as long as she kept me near her and continued to treat me as she had the previous night.

Magdalena picked up the marmalade jar next to her.

"Oh," she said, "look what's happened."

The jar was filled to the brim with water, and the praying mantis was floating in the midst of it.

"She's dead. I should have thought of that. The rain got through the holes in the lid. The praying mantis has drowned."

Magdalena unscrewed the lid and with a high arching

motion poured the rainwater with the praying mantis over the daisies of the meadow.

"All of us return to the earth in the end," she said. "It's too bad that a male didn't come along in time. It would have been interesting to see the elementary forces of Eros and Thanatos reveal themselves one after the other." Then she nestled up to my stola.

"But to return to my confession: I didn't exactly know where I wanted to go from Calais, I only knew that I had to put the greatest possible distance between me and the island that had failed to fulfill my hope that it would be the place I so desired, an island paradise. I decided to avoid large as well as small islands in the future, and even the shore they could be seen from, and to proceed east into Europe's interior. I took the road to Reims, where I visited the famous thirteenth-century cathedral there in my nun's habit and talked a bit with a Cistercian nun from the south of France about the labyrinth motif, which is often evident in French cathedrals, and after she left I removed from a side niche a gilded chalice, its cup ornamented with lovely leaf work, and proceeded on to Strasbourg, where I also viewed the splendid cathedral there and had an interesting though unfortunately brief discussion on the famous Emperor's Window on the northern side aisle with a woman from Nancy, a secondary school teacher, after which I stuck two delicate silver candelabras into the roomy pockets I had sewn into the lining of my habit.

"Reverend, if you were to ask why, not once but several times, I committed the serious crime of robbing the Church, I wouldn't be able to give you a clear answer. On the one hand, my desperate financial situation led me to such acts, and to the consideration of foisting these treasures off on a fence. On the other hand I felt strangely compelled to com-

mit these thefts, which must be similar to what a kleptoma-
niac feels. As I have noted, sometimes we do things that are
incomprehensible to us afterward."

As I no longer was gagged I could have interjected that
these thefts constituted a grave sacrilege, but that God, in
His boundless goodness and mercy, would forgive her if she
repented. But I refrained from any verbal intervention as she
had indicated when raising her finger to her lips, and nothing
was further from my mind than angering her such that in the
night to come she would withhold the sweet and unspeakable
things she had done to me the night before.

"As I said, at first I thought I would have someone fence
the statue, the chalice, and the candelabra, but after crossing
the Rhine high up in Offenburg I suddenly realized that I
was in a part of the country I was unfamiliar with, where I
had no chance of coming into contact with people who could
carry out such surreptitious requests. Pulling out my map at
an autobahn rest stop I decided to take a short detour north
and use the last of my money to buy chips at the casino in
Baden-Baden and try my luck at roulette.

"At my arrival in the elegant old spa I took a room at a
small pension on the hill where the cathedral stands. I
arrived at the casino at about ten that evening, but the liver-
ied gentleman at the door refused to admit me, as I was not
properly dressed. Though dress codes today are much looser
than they were a few years ago, he explained, he nevertheless
could not admit a woman attired in a motorcycle jumpsuit
and boots to this casino, the most beautiful casino in the
world, built in the nineteenth century by Parisian architects
in the style of French royal palaces, surely I would understand. Somewhat annoyed, I returned to my pension, took
off my jumpsuit, and donned my nun's habit, including the

white mantle, convinced that this formal clothing would satisfy the casino's high standards. My disappointment was therefore all the greater when the man in livery once again raised objections. He was surprised, he said, that in the God-fearing state of Baden, a nun devoted to a life of contemplation would feel the profane desire to visit a casino. He couldn't turn me away, but would find it highly inappropriate to imagine me sitting in my habit at one of the roulette or baccarat or blackjack tables. I was too proud to force the issue. Before I turned to go, the man looked me closely in the face and said that my resemblance to a woman in a motorcycle jumpsuit, whom he had refused admittance a half-hour before, was amazing. I returned to my pension discouraged and was about to go to bed when it occurred to me that I still had Michael's mother's gray outfit. I changed once again and for a third time appeared before the exacting gentleman, who at first didn't notice me at all, probably because of the inconspicuous color of my dress, and then waved me in with an arrogant motion of his white-gloved right hand. I walked by and when I looked back I saw the man, who apparently once again had noticed a similarity, staring at me nonplussed. I quickly mixed with the large number of casino guests, thus removing myself from his field of vision. I purchased chips and walked about the rooms of the casino. Then I sat down at a roulette table between a stout lady in a long, pink satin dress with a plunging neckline and an elegant older man in a black suit. The table was humming with activity, players were crowded around it, and I admired the sovereign way in which the croupiers oversaw the action, not missing a thing.

"At one point in my past I had been interested in numerology, and now decided to use that modest knowledge at the roulette table. I first bet on 10, the numeral of totality in motion, of the universality of creation, a number that seemed to me a winner because of its eminent symbolic significance. After the ball landed on 18 I put my hopes on 36, a highly interesting number connoting cosmic solidarity, the meeting of the elements, and cyclical evolution. Twelve won, and I put two of my five remaining chips on 9, in consideration of its significance as a numeral of abundance, the symbol of the heavenly spheres. It is no coincidence that this number played an enormous role in mythology and in the shamanistic rituals of the Turko-Mongolian peoples, and was viewed by the freemasons as the numeral of immortality. Nine would bring me luck. After the stout lady in the pink satin dress won a bundle on 27 instead, I decided to put my last three chips on 5, with good reason: Wasn't 5 the numeral of unity, the wedding numeral, as the Pythagoreans called it, the numeral of the center, of harmony and balance? Didn't it symbolize to the Chinese the merging of yin and yang, didn't the Mayans consider it the emblem of perfection, a sacred number? The ancient Mexicans saw in it the indelible connection between the light and dark sides of the universe, and the Dogon and Bambara of Mali the chaos of a new beginning, and incomplete creation. Hildegard of Bingen went so far as to develop an entire theory based on the number 5 as the symbol of humankind, and even today Moslems extend the five fingers of the right hand as protection against the evil eye, a gesture that imbues the numeral with magical powers. I would win with 5, 5 would end my financial problems once and for all. It came up 30.

"There I sat, despondent in my gray flannel suit, my dark blue blouse and capot hat, surrounded by the elegant casino guests. I was out of money. Reverend, what I will tell you next will come as no surprise to you as a priest: In the moment that I was forced to admit to myself that I was broke, that my defeat was total, a miracle happened. One of those divine breaches of natural law and perpetual causality occurred in the form of a pile of chips that was shoved in front of my nose from my right. I turned in surprise and stared into the smiling face of an elegant older man in a black suit. Thirty-three, he whispered, put everything on 33! I put everything on 33 and won. I won a lot.

"An hour later, as we were having a light repast of oysters and a white wine from Baden in the restaurant of the casino, Baron Otto confessed that the reason he had suggested 33 was that he had been born on the third of March. Also, Christ was crucified at age thirty-three, and he had always had a very personal connection to Christ's crucifixion. He could have bet on 33 himself, of course, but he always lost when he himself placed the bet, so it was his custom to look carefully at the crowd and choose a guest, male or female, who appeared lucky to him, and to ask that person to bet on the number he chose.

"With roulette, he said, it was not only a matter of the number, but of the hand, and with it the person who placed the chip on the number. It had to be a special hand and therefore a special person, a person born with a lucky hand, so to speak, he said, toasting me with his liver-spotted right hand. He said he owed his intuitive powers to the fact that he had been born under the sign of Pisces, and therefore usually could recognize such types. He not only enjoyed playing roulette himself, he also enjoyed the game of using his intuitive powers to choose players with lucky hands. If a player had such a hand it didn't necessarily mean that he had a lucky head, that is to say, a brain that would intuitively come up with the right number. A combination of lucky hand and lucky brain was extremely difficult to find. He, for example, had been given a lucky head, but he needed someone else's lucky hand to win, he said, as he used his wizened hand to place another oyster in his mouth, full as it was of gleaming false teeth. The amount of the win meant nothing to him, fate had blessed him with wealth enough, he was interested only in the game. He always gave the winnings to the one with the lucky hand, male or female, and this evening it was I.

"Reverend, I could barely believe my good fortune, I was in a state of happy confusion, which, like all baffling good fortune, would later turn out to be an ominously deceptive emotion. Where was I staying, Baron Otto inquired, was it at the Hotel Brenner perhaps? I answered that I had a room at a modest pension on the hill near the cathedral. Holding a sparkling wineglass in his slightly trembling hand, the Baron, whom I judged to be about seventy, bent slightly forward across the small round table with the white tablecloth and, apologizing for his indiscretion, said he would like to know more about my life, for certain reasons of his own. I told him that I was an independent woman who traveled a great deal, at which he asked if I would like to enter his employ as a companion, it was difficult to find a companion of his niveau, in the last year alone he had engaged two companions and had been forced to let them both go within a regrettably brief period of time. As a Pisces he trusted first impressions, and the impression he had of me was overwhelmingly positive. He would require that I live in his house, where I also would take my meals, and for this he would pay me an appropriate wage.

"Though Baron Otto seemed to me a dear and cultivated, if somewhat eccentric, man, I was not especially interested in his offer, as the money I had won would take care of my

financial worries for a long time to come, and I turned him
down. At this the Baron sank back in his chair a little, looked
at me sorrowfully, and said it was too bad I didn't want to
accept his unconventional offer to come to live with him in
paradise. At the word *paradise* I pricked up my ears. I asked
the Baron what he meant by the word paradise, and he said
that, as a stranger to the city, I couldn't know, of course, that
Paradise was the name of that section of Baden-Baden where
his villa was located.

"Reverend, you will probably think I'm a little crazy, but
in this instant I decided to accept the Baron's offer. I took the
opportunity to live in Paradise as a good sign, even if this
Paradise was merely a city district. The Baron was overjoyed, and asked me to explain my sudden change of mind. I
made brief mention of my fundamental interest in paradises
of any sort, and as a Pisces he spontaneously understood my
thought pattern, which might have appeared strange to anyone else.

"The next day I drove my Puch sidecar motorcycle
through the wrought-iron gate, which was opened for me by
the gardener, and proceeded down the white gravel drive to
the huge old villa, which had been in the possession of the
Baron's family for centuries. The housekeeper, a Bohemian
who had been with the family for forty years and was the
daughter of a glassblower, showed me to two lovely and large
rooms in the east wing, which looked out onto a tall plane
tree. Then the Baron himself gave me a tour of the house and
the park, with its stand of old trees, which was surrounded
by a high wall. He then introduced me to rest of the staff,
with whom he lived a secluded life in the villa, namely, the
cook, who came from Basel; the gardener; and the chauffeur,
who was roughly thirty years old and to whom I took an

immediate dislike, as he was from Austria. After this the Baron escorted me to the drawing room, offered me a glass of sherry, and went over a few details concerning my future responsibilities.

"Among other things he asked about my wardrobe, and when I told him in all honesty that, in addition to the gray flannel suit, I owned a leather jumpsuit and boots and a nun's habit, this for some unknown reason seemed to put him in high spirits. He informed me that I was to read to him aloud before his midday nap, a cherished habit he indulged in every day between the hours of two-thirty and four-thirty. The book he pressed into my hands was a leather-bound, richly illustrated edition of a title vaguely familiar to me, an Indian work called the *Kama-sutra*. I was a little surprised by my new employer's taste in literature, but I then turned my concentration to this sensuous work and read as well as I could, until he was tired and nodded off on the sofa on which he had stretched out.

"On the way to my room I encountered the Austrian chauffeur, apparently on his way to his rooms in the west wing, and gave him a dirty look. As I became aware in the days that followed that my sole responsibilities were to take my meals with the Baron, go for long walks with him in the park, and read aloud to him, I was overjoyed at the good fortune that had led me to this man, a joy that soon would turn into its antithesis, just as all joy sooner or later turns into its antithesis, as indeed it must. In the generous leisure time granted me I occupied myself intensely with the *Divina Commedia*, which, thank God, I had been able to rescue from the London textile mill when fleeing Jonathan Alistair Abercrombie, and which I hoped to translate into German during the course of my life. What a pleasure it was to open the mildewed pages of the 1905 G.C. Sansoni edition, published in Florence, to read:

Nel mezzo del cammin di nostra vita
mi ritrovai per una selva oscura
che la diritta via era smarrita.

"When it was time, I closed the book and went to the Baron's drawing room, where he already was impatiently waiting for me to treat him to a new chapter of *Yonosuke, Three-Thousandfold Lover*, a work by Japanese author Ibara Saikaku.

"Except for Clemens, the chauffeur I didn't like because he was Austrian, I found the rest of the staff to be quite pleasant. I often helped the gardener—who, incidentally, had worked for years in the Berlin Botanical Gardens and after that in the park of Potsdam's Sanssouci as an assistant—with weeding, pruning the boxwood hedges, and staking the rosebushes. It was summer, and after the miserable weather of London I enjoyed getting out-of-doors. Every once in a while the Bohemian housekeeper would join us, and when the cook, who was from Basel, had time, which was seldom, the four of us would sit on the stone bench under the pergola, which was framed in deep red roses. Once, the cook asked me how I liked my new position, and when I replied that I liked it quite well, that the Baron was an extraordinarily generous and sweet man, the housekeeper, gardener, and cook all suddenly fell silent and looked at me with something like pity. I didn't understand their silence or their expressions, and quickly added that there were some things, of course, on which we didn't agree, on questions of literary taste, for example, but that didn't harm our amicable relationship. At that moment Clemens the chauffeur walked over, and I stood and excused myself, saying that I had promised to read the Baron three further episodes of the fairy tale *A Thousand and One Nights*.

"One evening I was dining with Baron Otto at the beautifully set table in the dining room. After the Basel cook had served a beef bouillon with a side dish of homemade dumplings, the Baron said he was very satisfied with my work, he had not thought that a young woman would be so well able to understand a seventy-six-year-old man such as he. Then he stood and walked the ten paces from his end of the table to mine to stand behind me and place something cool around my neck. He said I should go take a look in the mirror that hung on the wall between the two tall windows. Reverend, the Baron had given me a gold necklace set with light blue sapphires. Blushing, I told him I couldn't possibly accept such a gift, he was much too generous, to which he replied with a smile that it made him happy to add to a young woman's natural beauty. Then a thought occurred to him: The next time I read aloud to him from *Justine and Juliette* could I do him a favor and put on the leather jumpsuit and boots I had mentioned before? I must forgive him, he said, but he was a little tired of seeing me in the gray suit I always wore. At that moment the Basel cook came in to serve the soup and, paradoxically, when she saw the beautiful necklace the same strange expression of pity came over her face.

"That same summer's day, after I had spent time in my two rooms in the east wing reading the *Divina Commedia*, specifically the fifth canto of the *Inferno*, which deals with carnal sinners, I made the fatal mistake of writing to my family, for the first time since leaving Austria. Reverend, perhaps my motives for writing this letter weren't exactly pure, but I ask you: Could you hold it against a woman who for months has lived in dire, or, relatively speaking, moderate poverty, and who because of this poverty was occasionally forced to steal, would you hold it against her if she wished to communicate to her loved ones that her situation had taken a turn for the better? Can it be held against her that she wanted to express joy about the fact that fate had led her to a millionaire noble-man who spoiled her, and to share this with them? In my fathomless folly and recklessness I mentioned in the letter addressed to my parents and sisters not only that the Baron's family estate was located in so-called Paradise, but also told them about my fantastic luck at the roulette table and about the sapphire necklace. When the heart is full the tongue will speak, isn't that so, Reverend?

"The next day I dressed as the Baron had requested, one result of which, among other things, was that Clemens the chauffeur, whom I met on my way from the east wing, stopped in his tracks and looked me up and down with an expression of deep amazement. Before I continued reading from *Justine and Juliette*, the Baron, to no small surprise on my part, pressed a riding crop into my hand and told me to hold the book in one hand and the crop in the other, that that would look nice. I did as he bade me. After the Basel cook had served and then cleared the evening meal, not without throwing a sympathetic look in my direction, the Baron said he had something to show me. Walking past the Bohemian housekeeper coming up the stairs with a large jar of home-made pickles, and who gave me a worried look, we descended the stairs to the cellar vault. We crossed through the storage rooms and then the Baron opened a small iron door and we entered a dark, high-ceilinged chamber. Baron Otto lit the seven candles of an old silver candelabra, and their flickering light filled the room, empty with the exception of a plank bed in one corner. Could I imagine chaining him to this bed and striking him with the riding crop as I read? he asked shyly. He then pointed to some braces on the wall and said if I preferred, of course, I could chain him to the wall, perhaps it would be easier to use the whip that way. Before I could answer, the Baron took from the floor a number of different whips, among them a cat-o'-nine-tails, some strips of leather, and a dog's collar with leash attached, and said I could choose from among them, all were at my disposal, I could choose the ones that seemed most suited to the task.

"I stood in the middle of the high dark cellar vault and didn't know what I should do. What Baron Otto had asked was highly repugnant to me, of course. On the other hand, I was living a very comfortable life in his house, which I did not intend at the moment to give up. As often had happened before, angel and devil battled within me, to use your terminology, and as often before, heaven's messenger suffered a crushing defeat. When the Baron gave me a pleading, almost shameful, look, signaling that I should take the opportunity to test the elasticity of the riding crop, I fulfilled his wish, at first hesitantly and then, after several minutes, somewhat more emphatically, as his reaction indicated that I was doing it correctly. After ten minutes, however, I dropped the riding crop, ran up the cellar steps and out of the house, hurried past the gardener, who gave me a concerned look, and collapsed on the bench under the arbor. When Clemens the chauffeur strolled by and indicated that he wanted to sit down next to me, I didn't have the strength to get up and go back to my rooms. For the first time the fact that he was a countryman of mine didn't seem a disadvantage. After lengthy remarks on how mild the evening was, the man with the dark curly hair asked me if I felt lonely in the house, I looked so sad sometimes. I said absolutely not, he was wrong, I felt wonderful, and anyway, I had to go, it was getting late. As I stood and headed off through the dew-covered grass he called after me to ask whether I might like to make my way from the east wing to the west to have a cup of coffee with him, his mother had sent him an apricot strudel from Waidhofen on the Ybbs, and as I surely knew, the apricots in and around Waidhofen on the Ybbs were among the best in Austria. I was almost tempted to turn back and accept his invitation, but then I went back into the house without answering him.

"Reverend, once again it was clear that this was one of those steep ascents that would end in a fall, as indeed it must. During the weeks that followed I read to the Baron, dined with him each evening, and then went with him to the cellar vault. Despite the horrid turn our relationship had taken we treated each other with politeness and consideration, and even when the Baron asked me to do things to him in the cellar that I would not dare to even begin to describe to you, he did so with manners that one could only call impeccable. The civility we maintained on the surface was in strange contrast to the depths we simultaneously explored together. I must admit that there were moments when, dressed in the nun's habit he so venerated, I stood before the Baron, strapped to the wall like Christ on the cross, and cracked the whip with a certain pleasure. I would never have believed that such cruelty, explicitly requested though it was, would call up even the tiniest feeling of lust in me. At the moment the Baron and I opened the iron door to the vault something deep inside me opened as well, a secret subterranean vault inhabited by nimble-footed rats and mice, and spiders, a place the existence of which I had never before surmised, a kind of medieval torture chamber with ancient blood sticking to its walls. We shared an understanding for which words were unnecessary, despite the quite submissive yet always precise instructions of the Baron.

"Though he asked for this treatment, indeed desired it and rewarded me for it with gifts and adulation in order that I wouldn't withhold it, I was aware that I was in dangerous territory and this awareness sometimes caused great feelings of guilt in me, so that I would interrupt what I was doing, drop the cat-o'-nine-tails, and run up the cellar steps and outside, to throw my arms around the trunk of a maple or lean against one of the old oaks that gave the park its unique atmosphere. The gardener, cook, and housekeeper would give me silent and knowing looks; only Clemens the chauffeur seemed not to have the slightest idea what was going on, and would walk whistling through the house and repeat his invitation to me for coffee.

"Around this time I became accustomed to paying a visit to the thermal baths. Though the Baron didn't like for me to leave the confines of the estate he reluctantly agreed that the chauffeur could occasionally drive me in the dark brown Bentley with the soft leather seats from Paradise down to the Friedrich Baths or the Caracella thermal springs, where I would immediately throw myself into the heated water. Undoubtedly there was a direct connection between what the Baron and I were doing in the cellar and my strong need to submerge myself in the warm liquid. Reverend, in the healing waters that sprung from the great volcanic depths I hoped to wash away the feelings of guilt occasioned by the brutality the Baron had forced me into, gently but unrelent-

ingly. I held my hands, which the evening before had
grasped the whip handle, and my feet, which had stepped on
the Baron's back in my motorcycle boots, in the strong
stream of the underwater jets and hoped the water would
wash away all the evil it came in contact with. Sometimes I
wished I would just sink down in the water and never come
up again. I believe that you, as a man of the Church for
whom baptism is a sacrament, will understand my attempts
to use the water to cleanse myself of all wrongs, to emerge
after an hour or two in the large round pools as if reborn, will
understand my need for forgiveness and regeneration. When
I rejoined the chauffeur in the Bentley, my hair still damp, he
always remarked how fresh I looked.

"Reverend, when we are at our lowest ebb, when we look
in the mirror and cannot believe that the innocent-appearing
person looking back at us has actually committed the horrible things she has committed, when we have reached that
point, then inevitably something beautiful occurs somewhere
else in our lives. Slowly, slowly the horror subsides to make
room for something new, something beautiful. The more I
was repulsed by what was repulsive between the Baron and
me, the less repulsive became the company of Clemens the
chauffeur. One evening after I had helped the Baron up the
cellar stairs and into his drawing room I felt the need for a
little walk in the park. In the darkness surrounding the circular rose bed I almost ran right into the chauffeur, who had
been working in the garage on the Baron's Bentley and had
lost track of the time. We sat on the bench next to the roses
and their fragrance wafted over to us. Clemens lit a cigarette
and the flame of the match made the contours of his face
appear soft and mysterious. After a long silence he said that
if I still wanted to taste the apricot strudel his mother had

sent I would have to visit him soon. This time I accepted.

"The next day, when the Baron fell asleep after a few pages of Bocaccio's *Decameron*, I got up quietly and went to the west wing. Already from a distance I could smell the aroma of fresh-brewed coffee in the corridors. The chauffeur's rooms were large and bright and looked out onto the arbor and the gravel path leading to the wrought-iron gate. There on his little table were two cups, two saucers, two dessert plates, and a sugar bowl and Gmundner ceramic creamer of a floral pattern, a sight that, as you can imagine, called up ambivalent feelings in me. The apricot strudel was excellent and the long-denied pleasure of Austrian pastry led to my feeling a bit more open to the man from Waidhofen on the Ybbs. He sat quietly on a rattan chair in front of the window, and suddenly his curly locks reminded me of Belvedere's *Apollo*.

"Why hadn't I noticed before how attractive the chauffeur was? He looked at me and then placed one of his large hands, which were shaped like spatulas, on my right knee and said he had the feeling that something was bothering me, couldn't he help? I shook my head vehemently and said no, no, everything was fine, the Baron was a little trying because of his advanced age, but other than that everything was just fine. Before I left, Clemens suggested that someday soon we go to a distant corner of the park and have a little picnic, to take advantage of the good weather. I hesitated, saying the Baron demanded a good deal of me but that perhaps we could meet during his midday nap, between two-thirty and four-thirty. Clemens laughed and said all right, until tomorrow then, he would meet me by the drawing room door with a picnic basket at two-thirty.

"Reverend, though I was not bound to the Baron by any

particular feelings of affection, I nevertheless felt that agreeing to the picnic was a breach of loyalty to him, even a
betrayal. Though Baron Otto was never less than considerate, since the beginning of our excursions into the cellar I
had noticed a stronger devotion on his part, which seemed to
be developing into a kind of possessiveness. I was not at all
sure that he would approve of the new understanding I had
with his chauffeur.

"The following day, when I left the drawing room where
the Baron was taking his midday nap on the sofa, the chauffeur was indeed standing by the door. We went to a corner of
the park, a place not unlike the one in which we now find
ourselves, and Clemens spread out a big blue blanket on the
grass. We ate the rest of the apricot strudel, which improved
my mood and spirit, and drank a dry white wine from the
Wachau region, which Clemens's former employer had sent
him for his birthday and which allowed me to forget the previous evening in the cellar vault. After a while Clemens
raised his glass and said we had to drink to the fact that
today he was thirty-three years old. The glasses made a fine
ringing sound and the autumn sun shone down on me, its
warmth intensifying the effect of the Wachau white wine, so
that the cellar vault became both brighter and further away
in my mind, and I sank down onto the blue blanket. I looked
up into the sun and closed my eyes, and the red field behind
my lids swam with little yellow lights. Right after that I felt a
soft mouth press upon mine.

"During the weeks that followed I led two completely different lives. In one of them, in the cellar, I was at the constant bidding of the Baron, whose demands were becoming
ever more imperious and eccentric. In my second, and new,
life I made my way from the east wing to the west wing as

often as I could without arousing the Baron's suspicions. So the paradise the Baron had enticed me into, which had in fact proven to be the inferno, began in small part to justify its name, namely that part consisting of the chauffeur's two large rooms with the high windows, the curtains of which were drawn with the help of a long rod. We lay on the floor in the semidarkness, looking at each other and at the reflection of light shaped by the leaves of the trees swaying outside the windows, which danced on the closely woven natural white material of the curtains and made them seem transparent. Occasionally a sunbeam would penetrate the narrow slit between the two curtains and pierce some part of our bodies, an elbow, a clavicle, and illuminate it, or we would roll into the bright square of light the sun had projected onto the carpet and lie for a while squinting in its glow, arm on arm, leg on leg, so intertwined that there was no space between us at all. Sometimes we saw the shadow of the gardener or the Bohemian housekeeper or the Basel cook appear on the curtain, pause, and slowly move on. They knew what was going on. Just as my hands healed themselves in the warm jets of the thermal bath's water, they also healed as they glided through the chauffeur's thick hair, soft as underbrush, to seize fistfuls of his curls. And my feet healed when he took them in his hands and pressed the soles against his warm belly, to stroke the instep until I lost all sense of time. Paradise is in the midst of hell, Reverend, it is at its center, and if we wish to reach it we must cross hell to get there.

"One day, having concealed my copy of the *Divina Commedia* under my nun's habit, I went to Baron Otto in the drawing room, who was delighted with my costume, and read to him from Sacher-Masoch's *Venus in Furs* until he fell asleep, before making my way to the west wing to read to the chauffeur from the *Paradiso*. We lay on the soft cloth of the nun's habit and Clemens understood not a word as I read aloud:

> *E come in fiamma favilla si vede*
> *e come in voce voce si discerne,*
> *quando una è ferma a l'altra va e riede,*
> *vid'io in essa luce altre lucerne*
> *moversi in giro più e men correnti,*
> *al modo, credo, di lor viste eterne.*

"But he listened, then kissed my cheek, took the book from my hands, and, stumbling, tried to read it himself:

> *Non fur più tosto dentro a me venute*
> *queste parole brevi, ch'io compresi*
> *me sormontar di sopra a mia virtute;*
> *e di novella vista mi raccesi,*
> *tale che nulla luce è tanto mera*
> *che gli occhi miei non si fosser difesi.*

"That was all we read that day.

"It lasted for three weeks, Reverend, three weeks in the two rooms with the natural white curtains. The more room the narrow cellar vault took up in my soul during this time, the more blinding the brightness became that was emitted from some invisible light source to penetrate even the farthest corners of the cold room, such that the mice, rats, and spiders began to flee the more the walls began to collapse under the chauffeur's soft touch, and the darker the real cellar vault became in which the Baron locked us every evening, and the more strident his commands. I did everything that was required of me as if sleepwalking, it was I and yet not I who beat him, and the woman who later untied him, offered her arm, and led him up the steps was a different woman from the pale-faced, thin-lipped one with the riding crop in her hand, who remained behind in the cellar.

"When behind closed curtains toward the end of the three weeks I bent over the chauffeur, lying on his back with his eyes closed and offering me a view of his lovely neck, I became suddenly aware of his carotid artery and the blue tint of the blood pulsing through it. All at once I was overcome by a strong desire. I wanted to bite into his muscular neck browned by the sun, with its prominent Adam's apple. Just as I was about to surrender to this impulse and had buried my head in his neck, a strange sense of uneasiness held me back, something like a fleeting and unpleasant memory. At that moment the chauffeur opened his gray-green eyes and pulled me to him. He was tired, he said with a smile, I showed him no mercy, sometimes he had the feeling that I was sucking all the strength out of him.

"In the days that followed the desire to sink my teeth into his neck became almost irresistible, and it took all of my willpower to resist. My anxiety surrounding this desire grew stronger and stronger and finally turned into suspicion once I caught a glimpse of myself in the mirror that hung between the windows of the drawing room and saw that my upper eyeteeth looked unusually powerful. The next time Clemens drove me to the Friedrich Baths I asked him to drop me off at the library, where I perhaps could find a German translation of the *Divina Commedia* so that I could read to him in our mother tongue the passages he so liked, but was unable to understand. I went into the library, pulled out the catalogue card drawer that held authors Scha—Sty and flipped through the cards, fingers flying, until I found a reference to Bram Stoker's *Dracula*. I found the book, pulled it from the shelf, and, after producing a piece of identification and filling out a form, was allowed to take the book home with me.

"Reverend, my inexplicable concern proved only too correct. I had read the book so quickly in the library of the British Museum on Great Russell Street that I had missed something very essential: A person from whom a vampire has sucked blood becomes a vampire himself. Michael Minulescu, who knew something about the undead from his father's side of the family, apparently also had been in the dark on this particular detail. Or was a fear of being contaminated the real reason for his reticence to my attempts to get closer to him? I would never know.

"You, as a Catholic priest, of course are not familiar with the feeling that I myself experienced for the first time when I toasted Clemens in the park on the occasion of his thirty-third birthday, you could not, of course, know this feeling. But as you are an empathetic person, as I have long since noticed, you will realize how terrible it was for me to discover that I was a vampire. After all of my wanderings I had finally met someone whom, despite the depressing fact that he was Austrian, I hadn't been able to get enough of for three weeks now, with whom I appeared to be standing at the beginning of a path that truly seemed to promise not to lead to the usual one-way street, the usual dead end. Here was a man who didn't say much, didn't ask a lot of questions, who was neither melancholic nor jealous, neither faithless nor parasitic, and who wasn't infected with ideology, a man who, for the first time in my life, gave me exactly what I needed. And I was going to have to give up this man, give up all the things that had transpired in the fluid light of his two rooms, all the amazing acts we performed together, if I didn't want to turn him into one of the undead, into a living corpse forced to wander restlessly through the night in search of human blood, who would never find peace. Reverend, for the first time in my life I was less concerned about myself than I was about someone else. I wasn't sorry that it was I who had become a monster through Jonathan Alistair Abercrombie's affections, which I had suffered gladly, I was only concerned that Clemens the chauffeur not share the same fate. That must be what you refer to from your pulpit as Christian charity, am I right?

"After I had thought for a long while about how I could tell the chauffeur that our relationship, blossoming like the fragrant roses in the circular rose bed, had to come to an end before it barely had even begun, and considered what excuse I should use to explain to him why my path suddenly no longer took me from the east wing to the west wing, but only to the drawing room, and had come up with nothing, the problem solved itself, because we were discovered.

"One Thursday morning Baron Otto summoned me to the drawing room, which surprised me as he didn't usually require me at that time of the day. When I entered the room he wasn't lying on the sofa as usual, but standing in front of the window with his back to me. As soon as he heard me he turned, wearing an expression I had never seen before, not even during our worst sessions in the cellar vault. His face mirrored anger mixed with pain and disappointment. He had, he began in a restrained voice, taken me into his home and treated me like a daughter, heaped gifts upon me—he need only mention the gold necklace with the sapphires that matched the color of my eyes, which a goldsmith in Freiburg in Breisgau had created for me, the ivory rococo bracelet from Nuremberg, which had cost him a fortune, and the diamond earrings, for which he had dealt with diamond cutters in Antwerp and almost become involved in dubious dealings with the Mafia—nourished me on the choicest dishes, aesthetically presented, placed suitable quarters at my disposal and paid me a handsome wage to carry out duties which, to be sure, required special abilities such as human understanding and certain manual skills, but which had not made unreasonable demands on my time, not to mention that at the beginning of our acquaintance he had helped me win a considerable sum at roulette. In addition, he had never failed to show me the greatest respect and had never molested me in any fashion, be it through touch or through words. In exchange for entrusting a woman without references, but whom he trusted and believed in, with a job that, in his opinion, should be highly ranked, one could expect, in addition to competence and a certain power of performance which, he had to admit, I was not lacking, at least a minimum of integrity and loyalty, did I not agree?

"When I somewhat meekly began to respond, he interrupted me and said that even though I had not proved a trustworthy member of his household, others had proved so and had told him that I had not limited myself to the east wing when resting from, or preparing for, my responsibilities, but in a wanton effort at expansion, in an ill-considered appetite for adventure, had penetrated far beyond the boundaries set for me, into the west wing and there, in the rooms of his chauffeur—of whom such behavior, in view of his being an Austrian and also of his status as a Bentley expert, was equally unexpected—had allowed myself to be carried away to the point of doing things that simply were not in accord with someone in his employ.

"With that he took several black-and-white photos from the pocket of his tweed jacket and with an icy expression held them in front of my face. There was no point in lying, he said, his voice trembling, his loyal vassal had found the ways and means to show him my damnable behavior without his having to lower himself to spying on me. I took the photos from him. Someone—and I could guess that this someone was the gardener or the Bohemian housekeeper, for though the Basel cook was capable of whipping up the most exquisite dishes of haute cuisine and getting them to the table in an amazingly brief period of time, I wouldn't have trusted her with the simplest of cameras—someone had pointed a merciless aperture through the slit in the curtains as the chauffeur and I were in positions that customarily would be referred to as compromising.

"Once again I began a halfhearted apology, and again the Baron interrupted me. He didn't want an answer, he said, any answer would be a mockery, the photos spoke for themselves. In view of the fact that the present lamentable lack of skilled personnel would make it difficult to find a substitute for me, he would keep me in the house. But he would reduce my pay and refrain from presenting me with gifts, and henceforth would be forced to take his meals not with me, but with the Bohemian housekeeper. As far as the chauffeur was concerned, he would be sorry to lose an excellent driver and Bentley expert who had been in his employ for four years now and whom he had intended to offer not only a raise in pay but the intimate second person form of address, but it was obvious that such a breach of trust could only be met with immediate dismissal, as in his case it would be somewhat simpler to find a replacement.

"After this conversation I returned to my two rooms

dejected, to seek comfort in the *Divina Commedia*. And sure enough, I was cheered by the fact that though Dante had lost his Beatrice on earth, he found her again on his mysterious pilgrimage. I would lose Clemens, too, and paradoxically our separation was made easier by the betrayal of the household personnel, for I would not have to take it wholly upon myself, which would have pushed me to the limits of my psychological capabilities: It had been forced on us from the outside. The little paradise we had created in the midst of the inferno was lost, but once I had read further in Dante's *Paradiso*, the idea that at some point and somehow it could be regained did not seem totally absurd.

"I lay down on my bed and sank into a kind of half-slumber, during which the face of the chauffeur appeared with an expression that at first was friendly and loving, but which soon became more harsh and rigid. Then suddenly it was he who was cracking the cat-o'-nine-tails threateningly, and with a soft scream I woke up. At that moment there was a knock at my window. It was Clemens, who wanted to talk. As I opened the window I saw the Bohemian housekeeper round the corner of the building and give us a suspicious look. Clemens embraced me across the windowsill and said that the Baron had just fired him, which had so mortified his chauffeur's honor that he wanted to leave the house that very day, though not without me. He was sure that, though three weeks was not a long time it was long enough for him to come to a decision. And he knew that I, too, would find it a good idea to go with him to Waidhofen on the Ybbs, to get married there in the late Gothic church. His old employer at the auto mechanic's shop would take him back at any time, and he would provide for us in an honest and appropriate manner. His father had died a few years before, but his mother was still alive and would be happy to see him marry, for years now she had been encouraging him to start a family. We would live in his mother's single-family dwelling, he said, he liked working on the house and had plans to expand the attic. He would expect me to prepare three meals a day, see to his clothes and the laundry, keep the expanded attic clean, have some knowledge of cultivating fruits and vegetables and flowers, as well as follow the instructions of his mother, as this would greatly alleviate the cohabitation of two generations in a single-family dwelling. His mother was a good-hearted woman, but her not always harmonious, decades-long marriage to his deceased father, an equally good-hearted but rather weak man, had accustomed her to having others bend to her will, and one could not expect a woman of her advanced years to change essentially in this respect.

"Then he looked at me tenderly, adding that he hoped to have children, of course, and had not the slightest doubt that I, as a strong and healthy woman of child-bearing age, would give him the four sons and two daughters he had always dreamed of. He would leave to me the raising of his six children into suitable Lower Austrians, as he would be fully occupied with his work at the auto mechanic's and with the constant responsibilities in and around a single-family dwelling. After this speech, which was the longest he had delivered in the entire time we had known each other, he fell silent and looked at me expectantly. Before answering I asked him to climb in the window and take a seat for a moment in my comfortable armchair. He swung one leg over the windowsill, and at the moment he pulled his other leg over it the gardener came down the gravel path, looked in our direction in amazement, and disappeared into the toolshed.

"After I had gently pressed the chauffeur into the lime green Art Deco armchair and taken a seat on one of its arms, I told him that his offer was an honor, it was the first marriage proposal I had ever received. It surely had not escaped his notice during the three weeks that we had spent chiefly on the floor of his two rooms that the feelings I had for him exceeded by far those of usual proportion. The picture of the future that he had just portrayed so colorfully seemed to me—with the exception of a few small and basically unimportant details—well worth realizing.

"Then I took a deep breath, gently took hold of his curly locks, and suffused my voice with all the firmness and seriousness I could muster. We could not, however, think solely of our own happiness, I said, for that would be selfish and egotistical to the highest degree. He was still young and had his whole life before him, whereas the Baron was old and fragile and needed me. I had hurt him deeply with my relationship with him, Clemens, begun as it had somewhat impulsively perhaps, and my conscience would not allow me to leave him now. He, Clemens, knew as well as I that the Bohemian housekeeper, the Basel cook, and the gardener were thinking only of the Baron's money, and in this respect I considered these three—on the surface quite nice, but at bottom unconscionable—people capable of anything. What if the Bohemian housekeeper locked him in the cellar and let him starve? What if the cook poisoned him? What if the gardener arranged it so that a sawed-off oak branch fell on him? The Baron was incapable of standing up to this dubious trio alone, he needed my support. I would not deny him this support, even if he had caused me great pain by firing him, Clemens. I knew that I was asking a great deal of him, Clemens, in expecting him to understand me in this. He should be assured, I said, that the separation forced upon us by an adverse fate would hurt me as much as it hurt him, and that I would be able to forget him just as little as he would be able to forget me. But we had to prove ourselves mature adults and do what reason dictated. One never knew, perhaps fate would bring us together at some later date, which wasn't totally out of the question, I had had the most amazing experiences in terms of the delayed fulfillment of fate. But now he must climb back out of my window, for in fifteen minutes the Baron was expecting me to read to him.

"What was I to have done? Every word I said to Clemens the chauffeur cut me to the quick, and the increasingly bewildered expression with which he received my explanations and looked up at me sitting on the lime green arm of the armchair pierced my very soul. I couldn't tell him that he was in mortal danger, that for the last three weeks he had lain in the arms not of a normal young woman but of a vampire, who at any moment had the power to turn him as well into an undead who lived off others.

"I had offended him deeply. His lower lip trembling and his voice shaking, he said he had no other choice but to respect my decision, but my strange and not quite logical reasoning had confused him and he didn't understand any of it at all.

"He rose and said, well then, he would return to Waidhofen on the Ybbs alone, and try to find the girl whom he had asked, on a bench in the main square ten years before, to be his wife, for he didn't wish to, nor could he, give up on realizing the future plans he had just outlined for me in rough. I wished him much happiness, and after he took me in his arms one last time he climbed back out of the window and disappeared from my life.

"I lay down on my bed and let flow the tears that had welled up during our farewell. Then I got hold of myself, donned my nun's habit, and went to the drawing room to read to the Baron for a while from the *Memoirs of Fanny Hill*. As I was reading I glanced occasionally at the rich old man who was lying on the sofa, listening attentively. Reverend, it was on that afternoon that I began to hate him. Not content with merely drawing me into the vicious circle of his depravity and inducing me to perform perverse acts in a dark cellar, he now had kept me forever from making my way to the two large and bright rooms with the natural white curtains in the west wing of the house. With every stolen look my disgust at my supposed patron grew, for in reality he was my enemy and had prevented the happiness that had been within my reach with the chauffeur. My feelings of sadness concerning Clemens's departure were replaced by vague thoughts of retaliation, which in turn were interrupted, though not abandoned, one day by the unexpected appearance of my older sisters.

"One afternoon as I was walking in the park, enjoying the glowing yellow, the deep red, and the warm browns of the autumn foliage, the elder of my two older sisters suddenly stepped out from behind an oak tree. I couldn't believe my eyes at first, I shut them briefly and then opened them again, convinced that this ghostly apparition would have disappeared in the interim. But my elder sister was still standing there smiling, and then she began to talk: She was so glad finally to see me again, it had not been easy to get to me, a man in blue work pants and a white undershirt had turned her away at the wrought-iron gate, answering her inquiry of whether she could speak to Magdalena Leitner by saying that she must be mistaken, there was no one here by that name. After she had pushed the letter I had sent through the bars, pressing it into the hands of the man who probably was the gardener, he took a quick look at the return address and said there must be a mistake, then abruptly excused himself with the words that he had to return to his raking and piling of leaves. But she had not, she said, allowed herself to be discouraged by the man's evasive manner.

"At this moment the younger of my two older sisters stepped out from behind the smooth gray trunk to continue the report: They had walked along the wall surrounding the property and, not finding an open side door, had then climbed over it, which hadn't been easy. The elder of my two older sisters had put her back against the wall and laced her fingers, at which she, the younger of my two older sisters, had used these fingers as a step and, with all her strength, had pulled herself up onto the wall. Then she had stretched out her hand to her sister and helped her to climb up onto the wall herself. Then they had jumped down from the wall to the thick grass and carefully made their way into the park, where, luckily, they soon caught sight of me.

"After this opening, the younger of my two older sisters came over to me and made motions as if to take me in her arms, at which I took a few steps back and, as nicely as possible, asked to what I owed their unexpected appearance.

"My letter, explained the elder of my two older sisters, had made them—my sisters, as well as my parents, and my four nieces and three nephews—very happy, for it was clear that I, wholly in contrast to them, was living well. They wanted to wish me the best in my new and propitious situation, and congratulate me on the fact that fate had been better to me of recent than it had been to them, my parents, my three nephews and four nieces. I knew, of course, they said, that the cost of living in Austria had skyrocketed, and that the education of seven children was devouring large sums of money. On top of which, said the younger of my two sisters, on top of which, she planned to marry, he was a nice man, but because of a series of heavy blows dealt by fate, totally penniless. And, finally, one had to consider the fact that my parents weren't getting any younger and that it was the responsibility of the children to provide a relatively carefree old age for them. As she was talking, both sisters were coming nearer and nearer. In view of the unmistakable fact that the wheel of fortune had turned, continued the younger of my two sisters—who during her novitiate with the Carmelites had had the opportunity to acquire a useful, though incomplete, education—and that it was I who now was at the top, whereas the rest of the family was at the bottom, they considered it only right and fair, in view of the difficult situation in which Austria, and therefore they themselves, found itself or themselves, respectively, at the moment, that I should support them.

"Reverend, after I had made the greatest of efforts to flee from the demands of my family, after I had thwarted their dismal plans for me at the last minute, foiling with my escape their intention to turn me into a crazy person or an aunt or a Carmelite, respectively, after I had asserted my independence at great cost, my family finally had caught up with me. I immediately grasped the seriousness of the situation.

"You, as a member of an interest group that considers natural bonds, the so-called blood bond, unbreakable, will protest, of course, when I say here that family is the most dangerous place one can find oneself, that nowhere is one more outcast and in jeopardy than within the so-called circle of loved ones, and that if your life is dear to you, you will, indeed you must, escape this sphere of disaster, this site of calamity, as early as possible.

"As you must have noticed, my unfettered lifestyle often presents me with situations that undoubtedly are risky, with people who unquestionably are suspect. Such situations, such people, are harmless compared to the situations, the people, one faces every day as the member of an average family. This alleged refuge of safety is in reality a nest of vipers, an execution block, a Mount Golgotha where one mercilessly battles others under the affectation of mutual aid, where one delivers mortal wounds under the pretense of steadfast affection. Nowhere is the lack of freedom, and deprivation and coercion greater than in the so-called lap of the family, nowhere does one hate more vividly, lie and cheat one another more openly, nowhere is rivalry more bitter, envy so all-consuming and the struggle for dominance more tenacious than beneath the surface of harmonious family relations. Only in the rarest of cases is it the autonomous, upright, and independently thinking person, rather than a cowering, crippled, and helpless individual who emerges from this basic unit of the state, which, all evidence to the contrary, is most energetically supported by the overwhelming majority of politicians, preachers, and pedagogues; psychologists, psychiatrists, psychotherapists, and psychoanalysts.

"You, as an Austrian priest to whom the preservation of the Austrian family is, of course, indeed must be, of utmost importance, will, indeed must, vehemently object when I say that of all the family machines of destruction, the Austrian family's machines of destruction are among the most efficient in the Western world, as they take particular aim at the most sensitive, most intelligent, most talented of family members and normally do not take long in destroying this inherent sensitivity, intelligence, and talent. Not for nothing is the family, and in particular the Austrian family, the most common site of acts of violence. I, who in the course of my travels have braved the worst sections of big cities at night, who have climbed into the cabs of strange truck drivers on the most deserted stone streets in East Anatolia, assure you that these places, commonly held to be dangerous, are not where the most horrible crimes take place, it is the nuclear family, and the Austrian nuclear family in particular, that provides the place and the corresponding background for the most terrible of deeds.

"The classic Austrian family tragedy goes like this: One Saturday morning Gustav A., an upright, quiet, industrious nonsmoker and nondrinker who has worked for fifteen years as a plumber in the Upper Styrian town of T., takes a pipe wrench and crushes the skull not only of his thirty-two-year-old wife, Ilse; his ten-year-old son, Thomas; and his fifteen-year-old daughter, Daniela, but also that of his three-year-old dog, Rex, after which, without any show of emotion, he surrenders to the local police. There are occasional variations in this story, for instance, the case of the pretty and universally beloved twenty-seven-year-old wife of renowned ear, eye, nose, and throat specialist, Gernot S. from H., who first threw her younger daughter, Sabine, and then her older daughter, Christine, from the bedroom window of their spacious doctor's apartment on the seventh floor of that county seat's only high-rise building, only to leap after them; or the no less typical incident in which Johann C., a thirty-seven-year-old unmarried vintner from the southern Burgenland village of W., a thoughtful and cheerful man of excellent reputation, takes a Riesling vine and strangles his parents as well as his eighty-year-old great-aunt, all of whom live with him under the same roof.

"Permit me to interrupt this little excursion into the family sphere, in particular the Austrian family sphere, to return to my confession, and listen to what I had to say in response to the request of my two older sisters: It is true, I told them, that Baron Otto, who so generously had taken me in, presented me occasionally with a small piece of jewelry, nothing expensive, a little unset jade pendant on a thin chain of nickel silver, for instance, or a simple narrow gold ring with a tiny rose quartz in the form of a heart, oh, and the pretty little teardrop earrings of dark red glass that he brought me from the flea market at the old train station. When the elder of my two sisters impatiently interrupted me to ask about the sapphire necklace I had mentioned in my letter, I shrewdly avowed that it was only a copy, of course, that Otto had presented to me in friendship, that the original, which had been handed down from the East Prussian branch of the family, was quite a valuable old piece and was kept in a safe. After a brief and somewhat confused silence the younger of my sisters said I could at least hand over to my family a portion of the high stakes I had won at the roulette table, of which I had written, to which I replied that I would gladly do so, but that, first, the winnings hadn't been as high as they might have believed, and, second, I had already invested every last pfennig in a corporation with extensive land holdings in Argentina.

"After yet another pause the elder of my sisters said that, nevertheless, the long journey from Lake Ossiach to Baden-Baden had not been gratis, the least I could do was offset their travel expenses. I asked them to have a little patience, I would be right back, and then I went to my room, took from my closet the chalice and the two silver candelabras I had stolen, and returned with them to my sisters. I gave the younger the gilded chalice and said the Baron had presented it to me, it was from his private chapel, as were the two candelabras. With that I pressed one silver candelabra in the right hand, and one in the left hand of my elder sister. They appeared satisfied with this, and when I said they had to excuse me, the Baron was expecting me for tea, they apparently did not object to my rather vague farewell. I helped them back over the wall with the stolen goods and before they jumped down to the other side, asked them to say hello to my parents and my seven nieces and nephews for me.

"Reverend, after my two older sisters had disappeared, I sank down into a wicker chair under a weeping willow and began to berate myself. What kind of person was I? What kind of woman was it who did not hesitate to break the commandment on bearing false witness, to lie to her sisters only in order not to help her family, which truly might need help, and who, in order not to share with them the good fortune that had come her way, but to selfishly keep it all for herself, had committed the deadly sin of *avaritia* as well? Like a pig wallowing in filth I reveled in my own rottenness. After I had berated myself for a while in this manner I slowly returned to the house, and as I was passing the windows of the drawing room I saw something I surely would not have seen were it not for the gene, inherited from my father's side of the family, that had equipped me with unusually sharp vision, for the soft net curtains somewhat restricted the view.

"You won't believe it, but there in the drawing room stood the Bohemian housekeeper, and behind her the Baron, who was placing around her neck a chain in the form of a flower, the petals of which, even through the curtains, I recognized as emeralds, rubies, and diamonds. I went to my room and threw myself down on my bed. My suspicions were confirmed, it really had been the Bohemian housekeeper who had taken the pictures of me and the chauffeur. I could understand that the Baron no longer gave me gifts and, though it was painful to me, that he was docking my pay, and I could even have accepted that he now took his meals with the Bohemian housekeeper. But that it was she who now stood before the mirror in the drawing room instead of me, and allowed the Baron to drape her with jewelry that properly was mine, I simply could not tolerate. If, as he maintained, I had betrayed the Baron through my relationship with the chauffeur, he had now betrayed me in a way that was equally shameful. The vague notions of revenge that passed through my head when I would steal a look at him while reading aloud from de Sade's *School of Excess* took on concrete form as I lay on my bed and waited for evening, the time we usually went down to the cellar vault.

"The simplest thing would have been to bite him on the neck, which wouldn't have surprised him too much and would appear totally harmless compared to our usual activities. What kept me from this was not the worry that he could then bite the Bohemian housekeeper, nor was I concerned by the fact that this, in turn, could endanger the gardener. But I didn't want the Basel cook turned into a vampire. This woman, highly talented in the art of cooking and whose sense of taste reacted to the finest nuances, deserved better.

"By the time I got up from my bed and dressed in my motorcycle jumpsuit to go down to the Baron, my plan was established. The bizarre amusements the Baron indulged himself in with my help in the cellar were many in number. Among other things, he took pleasure in my tying him with four silk scarves to the rings mounted on the wall and wrapping a fifth scarf around his neck so tightly that he could barely breathe. That evening I suggested this diversion and he found it a splendid idea. So I bound him with the four brightly colored scarves from the Indian boutique in the pedestrian zone in Baden-Baden. Then I took the fifth, a very pretty orange-colored batik scarf of shantung silk with a discreet pattern of blue semicircles, and wrapped it about his thin and withered neck, pulling it more tightly than usual. The Baron, who was hanging from the iron mounts like the Christ on the cross you and your flock so admire, and who was unaccustomed to such ardor on my part concerning this particular pleasure, looked at me in astonishment, having immediately grasped what I was up to. He managed to utter the beginning words of a sentence intended to dissuade me from my plan, the second half of which was reduced to inarticulate groans as the pressure on his vocal cords increased.

"It wasn't hard to strangle the Baron, as his constitution, weakened by his age and the physical punishment he voluntarily had subjected it to over the years, wasn't the most robust. At the same time I strangled him I was killing all of those who over the years had moved me, either through verbal persuasion or through force, to commit acts I basically had not wished to commit. Of the seven men I murdered it was he whom I killed with the greatest determination, the highest degree of cold-bloodedness. I looked at him. He hung there lifeless, his head to one side, his open eyes staring at the wall. He would not rise from the dead like the Christ you and your flock so admire.

"I took him down and removed the orange-colored scarf. Then I climbed up on a chair and threw one of the leather straps over a large iron hook on the ceiling. I took the light body in my arms, climbed up on the chair, tied one end of the strap to his thin neck, and pulled on the other until the Baron appeared to be standing on the chair. Then I knotted the strap, climbed down from the chair, and knocked it over. It would appear as suicide. I took one last look at the Baron, lightly swaying, then turned and closed the iron cellar door behind me forever."

Magdalena fell silent, then reached into the basket next to her and ate two cherries. I looked at her slender hands. The depiction of her sixth murder had engrossed me more than her description of all the horrors that preceded it. I could scarcely believe that these hands—the touch of which the previous night had put me in a state comparable only to the mystical ecstasy experienced by certain Catholic saints, the same hands that, first under the sleeping bag and then under my priest's robes, had devoted themselves so tenderly to my body—had summoned the strength needed to strangle a man. In addition, her candid description of the, in my opinion, highly pathological excesses of the cellar vault had shocked me. How could a woman who possessed such feminine warmth, as I knew from the night before, sink to such perversion? Women, and Magdalena in particular, were truly extremely mysterious and unfathomable creatures.

Yet despite the disgust I had felt during her tale I could barely wait for night to fall. Once again, I might have passed professional judgment on what she had reported, might have pointed out that in the cellar vault she had started down the path to evil but her soul, because of God's unending love and goodness, was not lost for all eternity, and once again I chose to say nothing.

Magdalena handed me a few cherries.

"I fear I must return to the village a second time," she said then. "As we are about to leave this delightful place and travel on, we must see to it than no one recognizes us. I spotted some cans of car paint on a shelf at the gas station. I'll pick out a suitable color and then we'll paint the Puch 800 together."

Magdalena slid out of the sleeping bag, went over to the motorcycle, and returned with her nun's habit. She slipped out of the jumpsuit that covered her like a second skin and the thin leather of which, as my hands had ascertained the previous night, was soft and pliable. This time I felt strong enough to dwell a bit longer on the sight of her pale, flawless body, but before I could concentrate on it she had pulled on the black item of clothing that, until recently, had been used to gag me. She put her hands on her hips and walked back and forth, swinging them in front of me. True, I had seen women in bathing suits before, during summer vacations on the banks of Lake Ossiach, and once, by accident, I had surprised my sister in the bathroom as she was putting on her corset, which had been rather large and shiny pink and bore a remote resemblance to the paper-thin undergarment called a bodysuit, but which basically wasn't comparable at all.

"Do you like it?" Magdalena asked. "An expensive piece. The insert is of Brussels lace."

Then she walked over—I was still in the sleeping bag— and bent down to me.

"Feel it," she said, and it wasn't an invitation but a command.

When her décolleté, which was a bit deeper than the neck of her jumpsuit, suddenly appeared before me, when these dangerous curves and swells were close enough to grab, I was once again overcome by a spell of dizziness, and by the time I had stretched out my right hand she already had stood up and was in the process of donning the habit.

"You stay here, Reverend," she said. Then she looked at me and smiled. "I won't tie you up again. I don't think that will be necessary. Till later, then."

And with that she smoothed the folds of the nun's habit and disappeared into the thick foliage of the elderberry.

Magdalena's appraisal of the situation was correct. Only twenty-four hours ago I had been feverishly trying to figure out how to escape my kidnapper, but in the interim our relationship had changed so radically that I couldn't wait for her to return. It was clear to me, not only from the standpoint of Catholic doctrine, that it was scandalous for a consecrated Catholic priest, a man both respected and popular in his parish and beyond, to be at the point of entering into a relationship of an unambiguously erotic nature with a woman who led a highly disreputable life in comparison to the majority of those of her sex, and who had kidnapped him at gunpoint, but also from the perspective of so-called common sense that it was a sign of imprudence bordering on insanity and could result in excommunication. But I simply put such ideas aside. As it was, the thought of standing in the pulpit of my church and executing my office was not particularly appealing to me at the moment, presupposing as it did the disappearance of Magdalena from my life. I shoved another cherry into my mouth and decided for the first time in my life to wholeheartedly try something new. Even Magdalena's assertion that she had been bitten by a vampire and was now one herself couldn't keep me from my first erotic adventure. A Catholic priest believes in the doctrine of the Church, not in rumors set in motion by ignorant, superstitious Rumanian peasants and transformed by some windy English writer into an overblown, amateurish piece of literature. I occasionally suspected Magdalena of embellishing her confession, of weaving in events that in reality had transpired somewhat differently. Not that I attributed to her the least bit of ill-will, it was more that the wings of her fantasy seemed to carry her at times to spheres that had the loosest of connections to reality. I briefly considered taking a little walk, but then decided to stay in the sleeping bag, the folds of which were redolent of Magdalena, and to dream of her return. I lay down, closed my eyes, and began to imagine the night that was to come. Soon I had sunk so deeply into my imaginary desires that I lost all track of time. When my fantasies of a quite imminent future were interrupted by the sound of Magdalena's voice, it seemed to me that she had only just left. I opened my eyes and saw her standing before me with a green plastic bag.

"The choices were quite limited," she said. "A light red seemed the most appropriate." She took two cans from the bag and placed them on the ground. Then she took out two brushes, several sheets of sandpaper, and finally a license plate.

"There was a motorcycle parked in front of the gas station, a BMW, a good opportunity to get a new license plate. While the attendant was busy helping someone in the store I quickly unscrewed it." She removed the Swiss army knife from a fold of her nun's habit. "My Swiss army knife has a little screwdriver. Very practical, a Swiss army knife." She returned the knife to its place and then removed a newspaper from the plastic bag and opened it.

"We must stay informed, Reverend. I'm curious as to whether they've discovered anything about our hiding place. You see, they're seeking information on a black Puch 800 with a Felber sidecar and plate number K 180.488. One of your flock appears to have good eyes. Excellent, my idea to take the license plate. The cardinal has offered ransom money, incidentally. He appealed for contributions and Austrian Catholics proved themselves quite generous. They donated more money than has ever been raised on that TV show, *Licht ins Dunkel*, the one that supports good causes. What do you say to that? East Tyroleans in particular were quite unstinting. The special mass that was held at St. Stephan's appears to have been a great success. They reported huge crowds of people and the square in front of the cathedral was black with believers. At the express order of the cardinal they rang the big bell for half an hour. Big white banners bearing your likeness were hung from the cathedral's outer walls. A speaking choir intoned: 'The only good kidnapper is a dead kidnapper.' The cardinal spoke from the late Gothic sandstone pulpit created by Pilgram. Stating that he was categorically opposed to the death sentence he added that this special case, in which taboos had been broken that simply should not be allowed to be broken, required, of course, an atonement commensurate with the magnitude of this crime, with this inexcusable breaking of taboos. And if Austrian, and in particular East Tyrolean, believers stuck together in this dark hour they would find the kidnapper, of that he was sure, for God was just. Then he asked the people gathered there to observe a moment of silence, to think of the kidnapped priest and in this way to announce their solidarity with the victim of this brutal act."

Magdalena giggled.

"If only the cardinal knew how we had spent last night. He'd be surprised, the cardinal, wouldn't he?" Then she continued, "At the moment we don't seem to be in any danger. Though the gas station attendant did give me a strange look this time. And as I was leaving the gas station he stared after me for a while, which didn't escape my attention. Perhaps I should have told him a story, given him some plausible explanation for the purchase of two cans of auto paint and two brushes. Why would a Carmelite nun buy two cans of light red auto paint and two brushes? I probably made a mistake in not offering the attendant an explanation. Be that as it may, get up, Reverend, we're going to paint the sidecar."

I stood up and she pressed a can of paint, a brush, and a piece of sandpaper into my hands and pushed me in the direction of the motorcycle. Quickly, so quickly that I caught only a brief glimpse of the black lace maillot—sufficient enough, however, to cause a chill to run down my spine that probably was comparable only to St. Teresa's sensation at seeing a vision of Christ—she removed the nun's habit and put on her jumpsuit before turning to the machine. She unscrewed the license plate and began sanding the front fender while I concentrated on the sidecar. We worked in silence. Above us a bullfinch twittered on a lightly bobbing branch of the spruce tree under which the motorcycle was parked.

"Where was I?" Magdalena asked after a while. "Oh yes, at the point where I left the cellar vault in Baron Otto's villa for good. I went up the steps, hurried to my room, and packed my things. It must have been midnight. It was quiet in the house, the Bohemian housekeeper, the gardener, and the Basel cook were asleep. I got my Puch sidecar motorcycle from the garage, pushed it down the white gravel path to the wrought-iron gate, opened the gate, behind which hung a big white full moon, pushed the machine through the gate, closed it, and stepped on the starter. It was night and I didn't know where to go. I randomly chose to drive down

Sophienstrasse into the center of Baden-Baden, and when I took a right to the Alte Bahnhof I saw in the distance the casino in which the Baron had shoved a pile of chips over to me, and in so doing had unwittingly hastened his own end. The city lay in slumber and I passed the old train station and went on to the new train station and finally to the autobahn to Karlsruhe. From Karlsruhe I turned east toward Stuttgart and when I felt tired I parked at a rest stop on the autobahn, climbed into the sidecar, made myself as comfortable as possible, and went to sleep.

"I awoke to a bright morning, with trucks thundering by. I pulled out my map and decided to head for the heart of Central Europe, to Prague, a city located at a comfortable distance from those larger and less large islands that appeared from afar to be paradise, but which up close were disappointing. I had a bite to eat at a restaurant in Stuttgart, then missed the exit to Nuremberg and without knowing it headed in a southeasterly direction to Ulm. In Ulm I decided to make a detour to Regensburg, and from there to go on to Prague, but once again I drove in the wrong direction, namely toward Munich. I comforted myself with the thought that from Munich it would still be possible to reach Prague, but by then I began to wonder if some mysterious force were drawing me back to Austria, the land where the cultured educated, in particular the psychologists, psychiatrists, psychoanalysts, and psychotherapists, as well as my parents, my two older sisters, and my total of seven nephews and nieces lay in wait for me, and where the people on the street either look right through me or view me as an abnormality, a curiosity, a monstrosity. What was it that was drawing my Puch 800 to Munich, and from there on to the Austrian border in a manner verging on witchcraft? This mysterious pull to the southeast began to occupy my thought so totally that roughly twenty kilometers outside Augsburg I veered so far to the left that I almost collided with a Toyota that was passing me, bearing an Ingolstadt license tag. Right before Munich, and after a few additional near-fatal misses, I had probed my subconscious to the point that I was forced to admit that it was Austrian pastry exerting this magnetic pull, and not just any pastry, but an apricot strudel prepared with apricots from the region around Waidhofen on the Ybbs, like the strudel on the floral dessert plate of Gmunder pottery that Clemens the chauffeur had extended to me with his spatula-shaped hand.

"This insight overwhelmed and confused me so much that I soon found myself in the middle of Munich, which I had wanted to avoid at all costs. It was early evening, and as I was already in the city I parked my motorcycle in a side alley and went to find a café where I could get something to drink, and perhaps a little something to eat. Roughly thirty feet in front of me I saw a not particularly inviting façade with a light green neon sign that said Hansi's Café. The H in Hansi was flickering. I didn't feel like looking any further and so decided on this somewhat dubious establishment. Once I had chosen a corner table and ordered a beer and a slice of warm meat loaf from the sullen white-blond waitress, I continued to brood on what my desire for a piece of apricot strudel served to me by Clemens the chauffeur could possibly mean, and came to the conclusion that it must have to do with a state of mind commonly referred to as love. Belated and crystal-clear as this knowledge was, it shocked me to such a degree that I immediately ordered a second glass of beer, which I quickly downed.

"I stared into the tall and empty glass. The chauffeur had

probably reached Waidhofen on the Ybbs long before and proposed marriage to the girl he had asked to become his wife ten years ago, whom he surely had located by now. This thought made me so sad that I ordered a third glass of beer to cheer myself up a little. Paradoxically, it only made things worse. To divert myself from the frightening fact that for the first time in my life I was actually experiencing what commonly is referred to as love, something I never before had considered possible, I looked around me. Three more people had entered the café in the meantime, a middle-aged couple who were holding hands, and a brunet of rather muscular build, from what I could tell at that distance. Then a kind of master of ceremonies dressed in a light gray suit got up on the small stage at the back of the café on which was standing a video camera and monitor, picked up a microphone, and announced that it was karaoke time. At the same time the sullen waitress handed each guest a list of songs. The MC cheerfully exhorted those present to step outside themselves for once in their lives and be a star. He seemed disappointed that neither the middle-aged couple nor the brunet were interested in trying their luck as singers. I threw a fleeting glance at the list of music videos at our disposal and saw among them Rod Stewart's 'The First Cut Is the Deepest.'

"Reverend, do not ask what made me decide to step up onto that stage—more than likely it was the pain at parting from Clemens the chauffeur, which was hitting me slowly and for that reason all the more hard, and the subsequent but, for all that, clearer understanding that what is commonly referred to as love is quick-won and quick-lost, mixed with a fleeting memory, called up by the title of this song, of the vampire Jonathan Alistair Abercrombie, who had made this thing commonly referred to as love impossible from the beginning. At any rate, to the joy of the MC I took the microphone in hand and sang the song, and I put all the feeling, all the fervor I was capable of into my performance. Even the MC appeared moved, for when the song was over he fell silent for a moment before he cleared his throat and said it was too bad that only three other people besides the waitress and himself had had the good fortune to listen to such a voice as one seldom heard, a voice that had pierced him to the heart. The couple and the brunet man applauded loudly and I bowed and sat down again at my table, at which the waitress brought over another glass of beer, saying this one was on the man at the bar, by whom she obviously meant the brunet. I looked in his direction and he nodded a greeting. When I smiled back at him, he came over with his glass and asked politely if he could share my company. As he seemed totally nice I scooted my chair a little to one side to make room for him.

"He set his glass on the table and then sat down, leaning his elbows on the Formica, to say that he couldn't tell me how much my performance had affected him. The strange excitement he felt at my singing had to do neither with the words, moving though they were, nor with the melody, pleasant though the melody was. It was the timbre of my voice, the special tone, the color, so to speak, that had awakened in him painful memories he had thought he had control of, memories of his first days with his second wife, Erika, who for years had sung in the Wetterstein mixed choir, as she, in fact, still did today. My timbre was exactly the same as his second wife, Erika's, and he hoped it wouldn't seem brazen of him to request the chance to encounter my gift again. He then stuck out his right hand across the Formica tabletop and introduced himself as Karl Danzinger, swim instructor at the large public pool in Garmisch-Partenkirchen. Reverend, I wasn't exactly thrilled by his comparison of my voice, which, if not excellent, perhaps, does seem unique to me, with that of his second wife, Erika. Who likes to be compared to a second wife Erika? But his handshake appealed to me. His hand was dry and warm, rather smooth, and finlike, the skin elastic and firm, while at the same time pliant and soft; in short, a hand I was not disinclined to get to know better, though it was perhaps not terribly wise to trust my perception after four glasses of beer.

"At any rate, we began talking, and in my boundlessly casual and careless way I told him I was an independent woman who traveled around a great deal and was on my way to Prague, an intention that was proving somewhat difficult to realize, it seemed, as for some time now something was mysteriously and against my will pulling me away from Prague and toward the Austrian border. At this he commented that it was perhaps unwise to dictate a certain direction rather than simply to give in to this unknown force. Then he glanced at his digital watch, saying that my presence had made him totally forget the time, he hoped he could still catch the last train to Garmisch-Partenkirchen. What was my means of travel? he asked. When I truthfully answered that I was driving a black Puch sidecar motorcycle parked only a few steps away, he reacted with enthusiasm. That was a Styrian make, he said, a true rarity, something of a collector's item, would I be willing to show it to him?

"He paid the bill and we left the café and walked over to the Puch 800. He circled it curiously a few times, examining it closely, and then asked what I would think about driving him in the sidecar to Garmisch-Partenkirchen and staying as a guest at his home for a few days. As I doubtlessly knew, Garmisch-Partenkirchen was a charming part of the country and he would consider himself fortunate to be able to reveal to me some of its physical charm. Garmisch-Partenkirchen's location at the northern foot of the Wetterstein Mountains made it an ideal point of departure for mountain tours and as in addition to his chief occupation as swim instructor he occasionally served as a mountain guide, it would be a good time to take advantage of the unusually mild fall weather to go on a few short hikes. Then he smiled and added that this wouldn't interfere in the least with whatever was drawing me to the southeast instead of the northeast. As he had already stated, he personally didn't think much of reacting stubbornly and insensitively to what obviously was a sign from fate.

"Having said this, Karl Danzinger swung himself into the sidecar. His life, which had not always been easy, he continued, had taught him that it was foolish to struggle against forces stronger than we, it made much more sense to cautiously accommodate oneself to them, if not to give oneself over to them entirely. With that Karl Danzinger pulled out from under him the motorcycle goggles and leather helmet I had inherited from my uncle—who strangely enough had the same first name—which I always carried with me but seldom wore and which he accidentally had sat down on. While he continued trying to explain that my obstinate insistence on going on to Prague would, in all probability, impact disastrously on my fate, at the same time remarking that it was no coincidence that he lived in the very direction my vehicle wished to travel, he donned the goggles and the leather helmet. He fastened the helmet under his chin, adjusted the goggles, and said that coincidence as such didn't exist for him, there existed only phenomena that resembled coincidence, but which on closer inspection were anything but.

"Reverend, in my fragile state of mind brought on by the equally belated and momentous knowledge of the irrevocable loss of my only experience in what commonly is referred to as love, I did not have the strength to withstand Karl Danzinger's tempestuous temperament. While he proceeded to differentiate between absolute coincidence, which is neither essentially inevitable nor clearly determined by cause and effect, and relative coincidence, which is an unintentional, unforeseen, indeterminable, unplanned, and unregulated encounter or occurrence, respectively, of things and events that might be causally determined but that did not necessarily have to follow and could just as well have happened otherwise and at some other time, I wordlessly mounted my motorcycle and drove to Garmisch-Partenkirchen, toward a temporary idyll that, like every idyll, was to prove extremely fragile.

"Karl Danzinger lived in a lovely private home at the edge of the forest. We arrived late that evening and parked the Puch 800 on his well-tended front lawn. My host showed me to a lovely upstairs room that was furnished in larch wood, and invited me to come down to the living room before I retired for a glass of Zirbengeist, that wonderfully pine-scented schnapps, and to sing a little something for him. I hung my gray flannel suit and nun's habit in the ornate carved-wood armoire, walked out onto the sturdy balcony with its equally lovely woodwork trim, looked out over the lights of the city, and took a deep breath of fragrant mountain air.

"In my totally groundless and naive optimism—which more than once has landed me in complicated situations from which I was able to extricate myself only with the greatest difficulty—in this absolutely unfounded optimistic naiveté, which repeatedly has brought me to the edge of ruin, I looked out over the quiet nocturnal landscape and thought that perhaps Karl Danzinger was right, perhaps it really was best to give oneself over to life's natural rhythm and not to swim against the current, which was too strong for my well-but not overly-developed upper arms and my long, if not truly powerful, legs to handle.

"I heard an owl cry in the distance. At the hour in which my pain at the loss of the chauffeur was at its greatest an apparently propitious twist of fate had led me to a stranger who wished to take care of me. After all the ups and downs of my unsettled life I was grateful to my protector for his hospitality, for the possibility of resting for a few days in the healthy mountain air.

"I went down the wooden stairs, the landing of which also was adorned with lovely woodwork, to the living room where Karl Danzinger was impatiently waiting for me with a bottle of Zirbengeist. We talked for a while and after enjoying three small glasses of Zirbengeist I let him talk me into a rendition of the Beatles' song 'Let It Be.' He listened attentively and then tenderly touched my elbow with one of his gentle, finlike hands, which contrasted so strangely with his muscular arms, calling forth in me a tiny electric current that shot all the way down to my fingertips. Once again I tried for the greatest possible lyrical interpretation, and in doing so created an emotional mood that unfortunately was destroyed by the shrill ring of the telephone. It appeared to be important, and when Karl Danzinger still hadn't hung up a half-hour later I stood and quietly mounted the larch wood stairs to my larch wood bed with its lovely grooved slots. I slept excellently, which on waking the next morning I ascribed to the spa's healthy air. The sun was shining into the room and, as far as I could ascertain from the bed, the sky was clear.

There was a knock at the door and Karl Danzinger entered the room with my breakfast on a small round tray. He placed it in front of me and then sat down on the edge of the bed. I must forgive him, he said, last night's interloper had been his first wife, Susanne.

"This marriage with his first wife, Susanne, he elucidated, had gotten off to a good start, but over the course of time had become quite unhappy because of the drinking problem of his wife, a trained druggist, and had ended in divorce over ten years before, following a long and mutually painful process. Though he personally was not in the least interested in maintaining contact with his first wife, she had called him regularly since their divorce. These calls, which usually lasted longer than the average telephone conversation, revolved around problems either having to do with her drinking, which had not improved since their split-up at all, but in fact had gotten worse, or having to do with the uncommonly turbulent childhood and adolescence of Martin, their son. The conversation of the night before, for example, concerned who would pay for putting a new coat of paint on an external wall of the public swimming pool, his place of work, on which their fifteen-year-old son had spray-painted in black letters, FATHER, WHERE ARE YOU?, a somewhat ill-considered act during which he had been surprised by a security guard. Susanne, incidentally, had phoned from the private clinic she periodically checked into in order to better control her drinking, the cost of which he in part bore.

"As I drank the delicious coffee and ate the croissant that Karl Danzinger obligingly had spread with butter, I slowly began to realize why the day before he briefly had referred to the fact that his life had not been an easy one. After he then told me some more about Susanne's drinking, he said he had to go to work at the swimming pool, and left me a set of keys, telling me to make myself comfortable. At the door to my room he turned and said he would be happy, on coming home at five that evening, to have a hot meal, but he didn't want to put me under any obligation. Nevertheless, if I felt disposed to cook, I would find everything I needed in the refrigerator.

"Having said this, he left the house. I was a little surprised by his request, though he had expressed it politely. But when I considered the fact that for years this man had martyred himself to a marriage with a serious alcoholic, a marriage which still affected his life, on top of being the father of an obviously difficult half-grown son who went so far as to break the law to let him know what a bad father he considered him to be, I decided to do him the small favor of cooking dinner for him. Besides, I had plenty of time till evening, so I burrowed down into the thick feather bed and went back to sleep for a few hours. Once I was fully rested I got up and opened the door to the balcony. The view was breathtaking: Below me lay the extraordinarily pretty little town with its red and green roofs and church with the onion-shaped dome so typical of Bavaria, behind which stretched green meadows dotted with little haystacks and dark green forests, and in the background, the towering and sheer inclines of the Wetterstein Mountains.

"This time fortune had smiled upon me, I thought, here I would recover from the burdens, the unpleasantries of the past, which for the most part were the result of the unusual characters of the men I had known; here I would finally find peace and quiet and perhaps be able to transfer this new-found quiet, this newfound inner peace to another human being, who also appeared to have behind him difficult years of his own. I decided to take a little walk through town to get my bearings and take a look at the public swimming pool where Karl Danzinger worked.

"After I had strolled through the town for a while it occurred to me that people were looking at me with an expression of displeasure, the kind of umbrage that vaguely reminded me of the expressions on the faces of the citizens of my homeland. I looked down at myself but didn't find anything unusual, unless it was my black leather jumpsuit and boots that were dismaying the townspeople. After some brief but intensive deliberation I asked myself whether the distrustful looks of the citizenry could have something to do with the geographical and religious landscape, whether the similarity shared by the expressions of Austrians and southern Bavarians perhaps had something to do with the connection of both to Catholic Alpine foothills and stretches of Alpine countryside. Before I could pursue this interesting line of thought, however, I found myself in front of the swimming pool, looking at Karl Danzinger knocking excitedly on the huge piece of glass that permitted a view of the indoor pool, apparently trying to signal to me.

"I entered the building and he hurried toward me in his bathing trunks. He was very happy I was visiting him, he said somewhat breathlessly, but at the moment, in addition to keeping his eye on the swimmers, he was also busy with the elder of his two daughters from his second marriage with Erika, of which he had already spoken. This daughter was a dear and sweet girl, who unfortunately had suffered from birth from a spinal deformity, which was why he gave her special instruction in swimming whenever her mother would allow. Before returning to his duties as swim instructor and to his obligation to his daughter, he asked if I had already begun preparations for the evening meal that he was looking so forward to.

"So I went back to his home, built partly of stone and partly of dark wood and situated behind a green wooden fence, to begin dinner. As I didn't find much in the refrigerator I decided to prepare a simple dish that would suit the mountainous landscape, namely, a consommé of Tyrolean dumplings. Just at the moment that the dumplings were rising one after another to the water's surface, Karl Danzinger returned from the pool and sat down at the kitchen table. He ate the dumplings with visible enjoyment, but at the end of the meal remarked that they needed a little more salt and that I could have used a tad more flour, they had been too soft. Susanne, though an alcoholic, it was true, was a wonderful cook and her Tyrolean dumplings had been incomparable. Her secret, more than likely, was the smoked pork she bought exclusively from a farmer who lived high up on the mountain not far from the Zugspitze, meat that came from free-range pigs. He would ask Susanne for the recipe so that next time I would know how to prepare the dish.

"I swallowed the small disappointment I felt at this criticism and considered that Karl, as I now called him, merited understanding because of the spinal deformation of his daughter. It turned out to be a very nice evening, not least because of the plentiful supply of Zirbengeist, and around midnight we ascended the larch wood stairs and shared the larch wood bed. The swim instructor's soft finlike hands were incredibly skillful as they moved over my skin. I had not been wrong. Shortly before falling into an exhausted slumber I thought I heard Karl softly murmur the words Norma Jean, but before I had time to ponder this I was asleep.

"Karl had the next day off, and to my great delight glided his gentle hands over the landscape of my body for the larger part of the morning, much like a pianist gliding his fingers over the ivory keys, after which he suggested a little trip to the mountains, an idea I welcomed. Our departure was delayed, not insignificantly, by another telephone call. While we were taking Karl's jeep up a narrow mountain road he asked me to forgive this slight delay, this time it had been his second wife, Erika, and once again it concerned an irksome financial matter. As I knew, for years now Erika, as one of the few true sopranos—most presumed sopranos were in reality mezzo-sopranos—had been an indispensable member of the Wetterstein mixed choir, a fact that more than six years before had indirectly and calamitously led to the breakup of what until that time had been a harmonious marriage. A short time after joining the choir Erika had felt herself increasingly drawn to another choir member, a baritone seven years her junior and from the other side of the border, namely, from Seefeld in the Tyrol. I should understand, Karl said, skillfully avoiding a small pothole, that membership in a choir carried with it a certain danger to long-standing relationships. The Wetterstein mixed choir, namely, often went on tour for shorter or longer periods of time. Actually, it was understandable that the strongly emotional act of singing often elicited feelings one would not even be conscious of in more subdued surroundings, the shared work setting of a factory, say, or a laboratory.

"In Erika's case a performance of Verdi's *Requiem* had been the trigger. Karl turned briefly to look at me, which considering the winding road we were taking was not without its own dangers. I should know, he said, that Erika had never lied to him, she had admitted her feelings from the very first signs of her inclination toward the baritone seven years her junior, had described to him in detail the torment these unexpected feelings had plunged her into. Erika was not without reproach, he said, cutting a blind curve a bit too sharp for my taste, Erika had her faults, as did everyone, but she had always been honest with him. At any rate, the choir had traveled to Kempten, in the Allgäu region of Bavaria, to perform Verdi's *Requiem* at the Sankt Lorenz church there. After Erika returned from this two-day journey he immediately noticed that she had changed. She told him right off that because of a summer storm—which during the performance had unleashed a lightning streak that lit up the semidark nave of the church and with it the young face of the baritone from Seefeld—and the powerful music, she suddenly had known that she loved the man.

"After Karl parked his jeep on the side of the road and we had walked a short distance along the well-marked path, he tried to explain to me the pain caused him by the loss of his second wife's love as she turned it at the same time to the man from the other side of the Wetterstein Mountains. After an hour and a half of vigorous hiking during which he succeeded in arousing my sympathy, we spent the first half of our stop at a pretty forest clearing, eating bacon sandwiches and drinking glasses of Zirbengeist while Karl continued with a detailed description of the initial period of separation requested by his second wife, Erika, following the fateful performance of the *Requiem* in Kempten in the Allgäu, so that she might enter into a new relationship with the baritone.

"During the second half of our stop Karl was silent and, to my great satisfaction, let his hands do the talking, which went a long way toward alleviating the somewhat irritating fact that all the way back to the jeep he did not cease discussing his failed marriage with Erika and the divorce, which apparently wasn't quite as painful as that from Susanne, but which nevertheless had left its mark. We got into the jeep and as he steered the vehicle down to the valley at breakneck speed, probably because of his imbibing the Zirbengeist, Karl complained that Erika had denied him the right, expressly established in their divorce decree, to see their two daughters—the elder of which, as he had already told me, suffered from a deformity of the spine, and the younger of which, with the exception of a not too disturbing though noticeable cross-eyed condition she had been born with, was healthy, thank God—every other weekend, saying it would only confuse them to have two fathers, namely, their biological father and their stepfather, and it would be much more beneficial to their psychological development if they were to totally break off their contact with him, Karl, their biological father. After we arrived back at his house we sat down in his living room, where Karl began talking somewhat more generally about the problems of children from split homes, until he noticed that I was no longer listening with the same attention I had at the beginning of our little outing, and stopped.

"In truth I was a little tired, a tiredness that nevertheless dissipated once we entered the room with the larch wood bed. Before we fell asleep Karl asked how well I knew Verdi's *Requiem* and if I could possibly sing something from it. Though I have no particular knowledge of Verdi's work I am familiar with the *Dies Irae* from the *Requiem*. To repay Karl for the great pleasure he had bestowed upon me through the conscious employment of his finlike hands, I sat up in bed and began to intone this powerful section of the mass for the dead. Karl remained silent when I finished, and after a few minutes said that my rendition had impressed him beyond measure, but this time it had occurred to him that although the timbre of my voice was similar to that of Erika, in his opinion I was not a pure soprano but a mezzo-soprano at best, if not an upper register alto. But this had not, or only slightly, diminished his listening pleasure.

"Around three that morning I awoke with a shock as Karl, apparently dreaming, sat straight up in bed and cried: Don't go, Norma Jean, I need you and the twins! Then he lay down again and after murmuring something unintelligible went back to sleep. I bent down to the man whose past seemed to pursue him even into his dreams—for it was to be assumed that Norma Jean, whom he already had mentioned twice, was also an important chapter in his life—and pitied him. But this pity, without my willing it so, was mixed with a familiar desire at the sight of his muscular and vulnerable neck. I had to repress my longing to sink my teeth into this solid flesh, an impulse that frightened me, though not as much as it had with Clemens the chauffeur.

"The next morning when Karl brought me breakfast in bed I told him what he had said in his sleep. He sighed, remarking that it was an ultimately unhappy story, which at the moment he didn't have the time to relate to me, as he had to go to the swimming pool. He suggested I come by a bit later for a swim, he could get me a free pass. Perhaps then he would have an opportunity to tell me about that part of his life, as unforgettable as it was sad. Then he left. I slept a little longer and then went to the public pool, where Karl indeed did present me with a book of ten free passes. I got into the water and swam a few lengths. As had happened during the walk I had taken the day before in Garmisch-Partenkirchen I felt that the other swimmers were giving me strange looks, as if there were something odd about me. At first I couldn't imagine what it was, but then I noticed that apparently it was the Kashiyama bodysuit, which, lacking a presentable bathing suit, I had put on and which truly was somewhat tight, on top of which the lace appliqué allowed a few square inches of skin to show through here and there, which attracted some attention.

"Soon Karl jumped into the water and swam next to me for a while in order to tell me about Norma Jean, his third and thus far last wife, a high diver from California whom he had met on the occasion of an international high diving competition that had taken place at this very pool, which was equipped with a high diving board. I could not imagine, he said, swimming a few strokes on his back, how elegant Norma Jean's dives had been. She hadn't emerged victorious from the competition, but nevertheless had earned a well-deserved second place. After the competition he had gone up to her and in his relatively fluent English told her that he hadn't agreed with the jury's decision, her jackknife had been impeccable and her full gainer had taken his breath away. Her takeoff on the backward double somersault hadn't been 100 percent, perhaps, but in his opinion it was she who had deserved first place and not the ugly Czech diver, whose running corkscrew was open to debate.

"Yes, that's how the story with Norma Jean had begun, he said, and abandoned me briefly to put a Band-Aid on a little boy who had slipped on the wet tiles and cut open his knee. Then he returned and said that Norma Jean had been very attractive in a typically Californian sort of way, with strong white teeth, healthy tanned skin, a radiant smile, and sun-bleached blond hair, and he had fallen in love with her immediately, based on her sensational performance, even if the jury hadn't agreed, a feeling that was reciprocated, for

Norma Jean had flown back to the States later than planned, having spent a few magical days and nights with him in the home that Erika had vacated only a short time before, after which she called him almost every day from Eureka, the town where she had been born and now lived. In the end she returned with three suitcases, and they had married a few weeks later at a civil ceremony in Garmisch-Partenkirchen, a marriage resented by both Susanne and Erika, for reasons not altogether clear to him, perhaps because Norma Jean was a foreigner.

"Karl swam a few yards of the crawl and then said that fifteen months after their marriage the twins were born, fraternal twins, a boy and a girl, who had turned four in the meantime. The problem, he said, quickly dipping his head under water, the problem was that Norma Jean, with her California mentality, her typically West Coast mentality, couldn't adjust to the landlocked state of Bavaria. She was used to the Pacific, to surfing and high waves, and the nearby Eibensee, even though it was a natural lake and not a swimming pool, just wasn't adequate in the long run. Karl paused in his story, which gave me the opportunity to draw his attention to an elderly gentleman in black trunks and a tight-fitting red swimming cap at the other end of the pool, who apparently had swallowed too much water, I said to him, couldn't he see that the man was coughing and turning more and more pale, Karl should go and help him, I felt refreshed enough now and would return home.

"Karl came home from the pool early that evening and immediately sat down to the dinner I had prepared for him, braised sweetbreads with vegetables and stewed apples. To my relief he liked it, though he did say that although braised calves' sweetbreads was an excellent dish he personally preferred his sweetbreads baked. Had I forgotten to put the sweetbreads in boiling salt water, he asked, it seemed to him that they tasted a bit different from those that Susanne prepared occasionally. When I assured him that of course I had put the sweetbreads in boiling salt water, he said perhaps the water hadn't reached the boiling point, or perhaps I had added a tad too little salt. Susanne had always maintained that the correct preparation of calves' sweetbreads was a very delicate operation. I was happy that Karl, for the most part, liked the stewed apples, though he was sorry that I had not added cinnamon sticks along with the cloves. When I said I had added a little ground cinnamon, as I had not found any cinnamon sticks on his spice rack, he said that it was a cook's responsibility to see to it that she had all the right ingredients and that I should have taken the footpath down to the nearest grocery store, a mere twenty minutes away.

"I started to counter this and then stopped at the last minute, which was the right thing to do, for in the tender hours in the larch wood bed following the meal the undivided attention of his hands far outweighed his harsh judgment of my cooking. That night Karl again talked in his sleep, this time it seemed to concern his difficult son, Martin, with whom he was conversing and whom he begged for forgiveness for not paying more attention to him.

"So the days passed. Karl pursued his work as a swim instructor, I cooked for him and sang something for him once in a while, went swimming regularly, and on his days off we went to the mountains. It was a quiet and healthy life— though Karl's past intruded on us quite frequently—and it seemed to be doing me good, judging from my rosy complexion, my slight weight gain, and my generally strong physical condition.

"When Karl suggested one day that, since I wasn't using my motorcycle, I should fill the sidecar with soil and plant flowers in it, that would look quite nice, he said, I was somewhat skeptical at first, but agreed when he put his arm around me and added with a smile that his jeep was car enough for us both, and surely I didn't intend to leave him as his three wives had done. So one sunny morning I filled the sidecar with gardening soil and planted a few pink hydrangeas in it. He was right, they looked quite nice.

"The only thing that worried me during this initial peaceful time with Karl Danzinger was my lust for his neck, a lust that increased with each passing evening. He talked in his sleep every night, waking me in the process, and I simply had too much time in the darkness, which actually was only a faint semidarkness because of the pure air that allowed starlight through the curtainless windows, to observe his powerful neck. I felt a certain affection for Karl, but this feeling was not at all comparable to the intense feeling I felt for the chauffeur, which is commonly referred to as love. And for this reason there had been several occasions on which I had been tempted to bite it. But coincidence intervened to free me from the worry that I would be overpowered by this urge and turn Karl, who basically was a decent fellow, into one of the undead: One day when I was in the public swimming pool and not far from the starting blocks—in order better to hear Karl, who was sitting at the edge of the pool telling me about his separation from Norma Jean, who after three years of futilely trying to fit in to Garmisch-Partenkirchen had decided to return to Eureka with the twins, a decision that had plunged him into despair— a thirteen-year-old boy, well-developed for his age, jumped off starting block one right onto my head.

"Reverend, during the course of my confession I am not

sure if I have mentioned that because of the valvulitis I suffered at eighteen, which unfortunately never quite healed, I have valvular disease, which in turn has caused a so-called left incompetence, that is, the left chamber of my heart does not pump as it should, and because of this incompetence my heart is very susceptible to strain of any kind. The minor shock caused when the thirteen-year-old landed rather ungently on my head knocked the wind out of me, and I fainted. Karl summoned a doctor right away, who gave me a shot in the heart, and I recovered rather quickly.

"This incident ended once and for all my desire to bite any man's neck. I assume the penetration of the needle had an effect similar to that of a wooden stake driven into a vampire's heart. You can imagine how happy I was to no longer represent a danger to the men in my life."

I looked at Magdalena, kneeling in the grass beside the motorcycle as she painted the sidecar red. She looked a little overheated, perhaps from the combined effort of talking and painting, and this rise in temperature made her even more fetching than usual. Her cheeks were red and she was licking little droplets of perspiration from her swollen upper lip.

I hadn't really believed her vampire story, but I wasn't entirely sure that it had all been a figment of Magdalena's imagination. What if she was telling the truth? What sort of tragic twist of fate was it that had her send away the man in her life with some sort of excuse or other in order not to turn him into a walking dead, only then to be freed from her terrible vampire nature not long thereafter through an unexpected circumstance, but too late to find happiness with the chauffeur! At any rate, in the case of Magdalena, who had not exactly been pampered by love, I considered it entirely possible that her weak heart was not the result of valvular disease but the lamentable, though not irrational, result of having had her heart broken over and over again by inconsiderate and egotistical men.

Yet even as I sympathized with this woman who had endured the unspeakable, it was clear to me that the possibility that the chauffeur had married his childhood sweetheart could only prove advantageous to me and my relationship with Magdalena, which was only just beginning. The chauffeur was lost, but perhaps in the course of the night to follow, which I greatly anticipated, she would experience things that would put in the shadows everything that had come before. I refrained from uttering a word about my secret hopes, however, as I didn't want to counter her request for silence on my part until she finished her confession.

"This strange and doubtlessly positive occurrence, which signaled the end of my time as a vampire," Magdalena continued after she had clamped the rosy tip of her tongue between her lips in an effort to apply the paint evenly, "this injection given to me by the doctor also signaled, however, a change in Karl's and my relationship. At any rate it was exactly at this time, though at first unnoticeably, that the inexorable decline began. The idyll with the hydrangea in the sidecar began to develop fine cracks.

"Our first difference of opinion was the result of Karl's request that I join the Wetterstein mixed choir. He felt I had a voice that shouldn't be kept from the public, that I should share with the community. And there was always the justifiable hope that with constant training and practice my mezzo-soprano perhaps would develop into a true soprano, a goal he felt every woman should strive for. Reverend, I recall that in the course of my confession I have already spoken of the fact that any appeal to my so-called duties as a so-called member of society inevitably results in recalcitrance on my part. In this case as well my first impulse was to refuse Karl's request. But I didn't want to risk his punishing me by taking away the gift of his gentle hands, so I declared myself willing to attend a choir practice.

"One Tuesday evening I found myself in the auditorium of the local girls' school where practices were held. I wore my motorcycle jumpsuit, having given the gray suit to the Red Cross of Garmisch-Partenkirchen a short time before, as it reminded me too much of Michael Minulescu and his betrayal. The jumpsuit aroused the visible displeasure of the elderly ladies of the choir, who had lent their voices—which had begun to vibrate strongly in the interim—to the choir for decades now. I had to put on a long black robe like everyone else, said the eldest of these imposing, almost frightening elderly choir ladies sternly, there would be no exceptions. She brushed aside my timid remark that I would be willing to stand in the back row; in the back row my jumpsuit, which was, after all, as black as the robes, wouldn't be noticed. The eldest choir lady pressed the score of the *Johannespassion* in my hand and I tried to sing along as best I could. Next to me stood a small woman with piercing eyes and a hook nose, who stamped on my foot during a fugue and hissed in my ear that I would regret having nested down in the house she had lived in for years, leading me to deduce that this was Karl's second wife, Erika. Apparently word of Karl Danzinger's new relationship had made the rounds in Garmisch-Partenkirchen.

"During the break a woman came up to me and introduced herself as the employee of a drying-out clinic for alcoholics and said I should give some thought as to whether I wished to continue living with Karl Danzinger; his first wife, Susanne, had been destroyed physically and psychologically by this outwardly sweet, but in reality very dangerous man. Finally, the local civil magistrate, also a choir member for many years, turned to me and asked if I knew that Karl Danzinger was still married to a high diver from California. I found all of this so unpleasant that I left the auditorium of the girls' school before the break was over and returned to Karl's home, where he accused me of wanting to escape my social obligations and of having as little wish to fit into a small-town community as had Norma Jean.

"Since he brought up Norma Jean I asked him if it was true that he was still married to her, at which he became furious and asked which busybody had whispered that in my ear, without directly answering my question. Then he said that, by the way, the pork stew I had prepared for him ahead of time and that he had warmed up was terrible, what had possessed me to choose loin instead of shoulder, on top of which I should have used sweet instead of hot paprika, the roof of his mouth was still on fire. He picked up his coat and said he was going to Susanne's, she had just come home from the clinic. In the telephone conversation he had had with her fifteen minutes before, concerning their son Martin's ability to spell, he had mentioned my pork stew, at which Susanne agreeably had offered to fix him something, she had a lamb ragout heating on the stove.

"Though Karl was conciliatory two days later—when from three to five in the morning I patiently listened to a nightmare he had had in which his son Martin was threatening him with a machine gun, and during which he told me about his son's legasthenia that had been brought on by the divorce of his parents, as well as about Norma Jean's constant demands for money by telephone and letter—our relationship, following my refusal to join the Wetterstein mixed choir, was never the same. While it was true that we spent as much time as before in the larch wood bed, Karl was more and more often interrupted in the manual attention he devoted to my body and which called for a great deal of concentration, by calls from Susanne or Erika or Norma Jean.

"But even more difficult to take than his increasing criticism of my voice and my cooking was a comment he made one evening in the larch wood bed. The control that Norma Jean had over her body after years of practice as a high diver, he said, bordered on the miraculous, and not only in the water had she moved like a beautiful sea animal, a mysterious octopus, a smooth sea snake. You could turn and twist and bend her like a rubber doll, he said. He appreciated that I swam in his pool regularly, but not enough, apparently, to keep me in shape, in the admittedly extraordinary shape that Norma Jean had been. He advised me to supplement my regular swimming with a gymnastics class at the school of continuing education. Short of the high dive, gymnastics was an excellent way for a woman to retain her flexibility.

"Reverend, I didn't like that comment. Up until then Karl had restricted himself to criticizing the quality of the meals I prepared and my voice, and I had accepted his objections because of my inborn good-naturedness. But his criticism was beginning to extend to an area in which I am very sensitive, and that hurt and infuriated me. I controlled myself, however, and swallowed my anger. Karl's suggestion, though an insult to my femininity, perhaps was worth pursuing. It was in my own best self-interest to stay in good shape physically. I bit the bullet and registered at the school of continuing education for the gymnastics class, which had just begun, and the following Wednesday proceeded to the girls' school gym, where it was held. I hadn't thought to buy a special leotard and appeared in my black bodysuit, which seemed to me elastic enough for gymnastics.

"The housewives of Garmisch-Partenkirchen who made up the majority of the class apparently didn't find my choice of clothing suitable, judging from their looks of outrage. I tried to be friendly and to concentrate on the exercises, but the housewives themselves didn't prove particularly friendly. It was customary for one of the experienced gymnasts to stand beside the rigging to assist those who were less practiced. I counted on this help, but when I took a few fearful steps on the totally unfamiliar balance beam, lost my balance, and reached out for the hand of the pharmacist's wife standing next to the beam, she simply turned away as if she hadn't seen anything and I landed hard on the floor, resulting in a hematoma on my left thigh. And when my arms proved too weak to side vault the horse, the notary's girlfriend pulled away at the last minute the hand she had stretched out to me, so that when I hit the rubber mat I twisted my left shoulder. Not to be discouraged, I picked up a leather ball from the floor, smiled at the wife of the owner of the largest sporting goods store in Garmisch-Partenkirchen, and asked if she wanted to play. I was quite delighted when she agreed, for it was evidence that not all of the gymnasts were as ill-disposed as I was beginning to assume. But five minutes later when my eye swelled shut after the sporting goods store's owner's wife hit me as hard as she could with the ball, I again began to question the goodwill of the housewives and sank down, somewhat defeated, onto the wooden bench against the wall of the gym until class was over.

"When I arrived disheartened back at the house Karl led me over to the sofa and obligingly placed an ice bag on my eye, saying I shouldn't give up, not everyone had at her disposal the natural self-assurance of movement that Norma Jean had excelled in, and next time it surely would go better. That evening as we were lying in the larch wood bed he said he would refrain from touching me, because of the minor though surely sensitive injury to my shoulder. On top of which it was possible that he might unintentionally brush against the hematoma on my thigh, and he couldn't bear to cause me the least little bit of pain.

"I stayed home the next day to recuperate a bit from my injuries. Around five that afternoon the telephone rang. It was Erika, who wanted to speak to her ex-husband. I said he would be back from the pool a little later than usual and asked if I could give him a message. At this she burst into tears, saying she cursed the day she had met her present husband, and when I asked if she meant the day that Verdi's *Requiem* was performed in Kempten im Allgäu she seemed somewhat surprised at my knowledge of her personal life, but then immediately proceeded to relate her difficulties with the baritone.

"It was unthinkable, she said, but sensitive, impulsive, and gifted singer that he was, he had fallen in love with her thirteen-year-old daughter. I quickly inquired whether it was the daughter with the spinal deformity, a question that astounded Erika anew and to which she answered, yes, exactly, it was that daughter, she didn't know what to do and needed to speak to Karl, but Karl wasn't there. I told her she could talk to me, that I didn't know her very well, of course, but that over the course of my active life I had gained a certain knowledge of people and perhaps would be able to advise her in some small way. So we talked about Erika's problem until Karl came home and I told her he had arrived and would hand the phone over to him. She said that before I did she wanted to thank me for my understanding and apologize for stomping my foot during choir practice. I replied that it wasn't so bad, I had been wearing my motorcycle boots, and then handed the receiver over to Karl, who was standing by impatiently.

"The next day Erika called at two-thirty, and when I asked if she wasn't aware that Karl was always at the swimming pool at this time of day, she replied, yes, she knew that, but yesterday's phone call had done her such good woman-to-woman that she felt the need to talk with me a little more. She was totally confused, she said, three hours ago her present husband had appeared with her daughter and said they, he and the daughter, could no longer conceal their admittedly uncommon love from a hypocritical society and intended to go to the pedestrian zone of Garmisch-Partenkirchen, there to walk hand-in-hand in an effort to break through the social ostracism they would encounter as a couple.

"Just imagine, Erika cried on the telephone, the pedestrian zone! She had been born in Garmisch-Partenkirchen, the consequences of such a scandal were unforeseeable, her father, a respected citizen and Catholic, had been so upset at her divorce that he was now wearing a pacemaker. I tried to calm the distressed woman as best I could, and finally she said she felt better, thanks to me, and that she would no longer burden me and go help her second daughter with her homework instead.

"Though my injuries were almost healed I still wasn't receiving the attention of Karl's gentle hands, as we now spent our evenings in the larch wood bed discussing Erika's serious problem in the hope of helping her resolve it. I could understand that a former spouse might feel a responsibility after a separation, on top of which I myself was getting more and more involved in Erika's difficulties, as it was now her habit to call every day around noon and tell me how the situation was developing. I advised her as well as I could, dipping into the store of experience I had gathered in the course of my nomadic existence. In exchange, Erika taught me a few melodies that meant a lot to Karl, but this happened only two or three times, as she understandably was seldom in the mood to sing.

"I tried to revive my relationship with Karl, which had suffered since my refusal to join the choir, and even went back to the gymnastics class, which in view of the way it had gone the first time represented no small sacrifice on my part. The second and third classes didn't go any better than the first. Among other things I hit my nose when the wife and the sister-in-law of a reputable hotelier deliberately tripped me with a jump rope, and my attempt at a free circle on the uneven bars came to a bad end after the daughter of the owner of the T-bar lift pretended to show me how to hold on to the bar, but then in a flash yanked my left hand away as I was in the midst of the exercise. The fall resulted in a bruise to my coccyx bone, at which Karl said I had to have total rest and didn't touch me with his finlike hands for four days afterward. And even if he had there would have been little time for the kind of attention Karl usually lavished on me, as he was now having frequent overseas conversations with Norma Jean, for the fraternal twins, who had been quite small at the time of the separation, were beginning to suffer from the absence of their father, evidenced by their nightly bedwetting.

"The only thing that truly made us both happy was our nature hikes, though we had to hike at a lower altitude than before because of the snow that was already falling in the higher regions. In the mountains we were far away from

Erika and Susanne and their difficulties, in which we were increasingly involved, and even Norma Jean seemed farther away than usual the farther we got from the phone. Once as we were sitting at our favorite spot high above Garmisch-Partenkirchen on the cliff they call Virgin's Leap, Karl put his arm around my shoulders and said that while it was true that he had five children, all five were strangers to him because of his separation from their mothers, a fact that often depressed him, which perhaps I had noticed. Could I imagine, he asked, giving me a solemn look, was it conceivable that I would agree to become the mother of his sixth child?

"Reverend, I remember that autumn day well. High above us cirrus clouds sailed through the sky, and from the valley we could hear the faint echo of the Sunday bells of St. Martin's. The bottle of Zirbengeist had passed between us several times and I was in such a life-affirming mood that I was close to giving this long-suffering man a positive answer to his question. There was even a brief moment when it occurred to me that we could remove the hydrangea and the potting soil from the Felber sidecar and use it for our future child's cradle. This child would grow up in a healthy environment, in a private home with a garden and in secure circumstances that, with the exception of the Baron, who couldn't have come into question as a father because of his advanced age, none of the men in my past could ever have offered, ignoring the fact that, up until Clemens, no one had approached me with such an offer and had they done so their desire for children would have appeared highly inappropriate to me.

"I don't know, Reverend, why I evaded Karl's question. Perhaps it was the sharpsightedness I inherited from my father's side of the family, which enabled me to recognize the impossibility of realizing such a wish. In the days and weeks that followed, however, my hesitation proved to have been instinctively correct.

"One evening in the larch wood bed Karl announced that it had been decided that his first wife Susanne and his son Martin were moving into the house with us. When I looked at him in astonishment he said I shouldn't look at him in astonishment, he was the last person to decide something like this. But ten years before, during the course of his divorce proceedings and in his youthful inexperience and haste, he had agreed to a clause in the divorce agreement suggested by the opposing lawyer, according to which he would take responsibility for caring for his former wife should she be unable to work because of physical or psychological reasons. Susanne, who because of her constantly worsening drinking problem was no longer capable of practicing her profession as pharmacist, was now putting this clause into effect and he had no choice but to take in her and their son, as he could not afford the expense of finding them their own apartment. After all, he was also paying child support for the two daughters from his marriage with Erika, and for the California twins, he had been on the brink of financial ruin for some time now and were it not for the additional income he brought in as a mountain guide and the small sum his parents sent now and then he would have had to sell his home long ago.

"After this revelation I fell silent for a while and then said that, under the circumstances, I couldn't really imagine our relationship continuing and that I must be on my way, to resume my former unencumbered lifestyle even though I found many aspects of a sedentary life quite acceptable.

"Karl's reaction to my news was totally identical to that of

Michael Minulescu, except that I wasn't wearing a pastel nightgown that Karl could cling to. I couldn't abandon him in this situation, he sobbed, without me he wouldn't be able to endure Susanne, the alcoholic, and his difficult son and would become an alcoholic himself, during the final stage of his marriage to Susanne he had come perilously close to it. On top of which he had become so accustomed to my voice, even if it wasn't a pure soprano, and to my cooking, even if my ability to coordinate the various nuances of culinary taste left something to be desired. He knew that of late he had not devoted the attention to the landscape of my body that it deserved, but he promised to improve this in the future.

"What can I say, Reverend, the pity, the understanding that, unfortunately, I had felt for this man from the beginning conquered my reservations and I remained. A short time thereafter the devastating consequences of this understanding, this pity, were revealed, and since that time I no longer subscribe to pity and understanding but to pitilessness and nonunderstanding. Once one begins to exhibit pity and understanding the end is near. Those with pity and understanding only set the worst things in motion with their pity and understanding. Instead of being merciless and unrelenting, and in this way helping the weak—who are always appealing to understanding and pity—to become stronger and more self-sufficient, they make the weak even weaker, with their pity and their understanding they drive the weak to their ruin. You have to protect yourself from the helpers, as soon as a helper approaches with the intention to help it is advisable to disappear, as the least bit of help from a helper creates a little more need of help, whereas the helpers become stronger, an irrefutable fact known to the majority of helpers, which is a logical explanation for why they are so keen to help. The so-called helpers, the so-called benevolent are the ones who make others so truly weak in the first place, so truly bad, that's just the way it is."

Magdalena had talked herself into a frenzy, a condition that made her irresistible. Her eyes darkened dangerously, emitting sparks, and her right hand, still gripping the paint-brush, stretched out in accusation. I was happy to see that the sun was setting and that nightfall was not far away.

"A few weeks later Susanne and Martin moved into the house. Susanne occupied the pine-paneled room on the second floor, and Martin the spruce-paneled room between the pine-paneled room and my larch wood room. Martin did not prove to be particularly sociable. When he was home he usually locked himself in his room and at meals, which at Karl's request were no longer prepared by me but by Susanne, he was totally silent. As long as Susanne cooked, the symptoms of her alcoholism all but disappeared, except that she usually used a large amount of alcohol in the dishes she prepared. When she cooked she became another person altogether, and she cooked well. But the rest of the time she drank, and she drank without moderation.

"One evening when I returned from the gymnastics class she was lying at the foot of the stairs, and when I asked what had happened I took from her murmuring that she had fallen down them. She had sustained only a scratch, but I was somewhat limited in my movement because the wife of the dentist, pretending to assist me, had pushed me off the tram-poline and when I crashed to the floor I had sprained my ankle, making it difficult to help Susanne up the stairs and into the pine-paneled room. Ignoring the minor injuries she sustained in and around the house when she was drunk to the gills our life together was relatively problem-free. She couldn't stand Erika and Norma Jean, but liked me. Her enmity toward Erika was based on the fact that Erika had delivered the fatal blow to a marriage already shattered by Susanne's drinking.

"The depth of this animosity became apparent when Erika paid me a visit one day, not knowing that Susanne was living at the house again. Erika had called and said she was in the neighborhood, couldn't she drop by, it would be nice after all our telephone calls if we could meet in person; after all, our brief encounter at choir rehearsal didn't count. Out of politeness I agreed, and five minutes later Erika appeared at the green wooden fence with two pieces of cheesecake. Over coffee and cake we excitedly discussed the fact that Erika's second husband and her older daughter had left her to move together to Seefeld in the Tyrol, so excitedly that Erika's lovely voice penetrated the pine-paneled room on the second floor and must have startled Susanne out of her alcoholic stupor. At any rate she suddenly appeared at the top of the stairs, her hair disheveled.

"I cannot remember verbatim the exchange that followed, but Susanne, quite unwilling to let bygones be bygones, accused Erika of destroying her marriage and maliciously trying to wreck her happiness, which—and at this she lifted her head and smiled in triumph—was indestructible by her, Erika, proven by the fact that Karl had taken both her and their son back into the home the two of them had built with their own hands. At this Erika got up, walked the few steps over to the larch wood stairs, and scoffingly said that the only reason Karl would have taken this step was that he could no longer afford to pay her clinic bills and that for years she, Susanne, had been the laughingstock of all of Garmisch-Partenkirchen, and as far as her useless son, the wall-besmudging felon, was concerned, it was already obvious that he would end up homeless.

"At this Susanne walked down three steps and screamed that it was she, Erika, who had her, Susanne, and her son on her conscience. For years she, Erika, had lay in wait for Karl at every street corner in Garmisch-Partenkirchen, had thrown herself at him at every possible opportunity, and even the most faithful of husbands—and Karl, at least when he had been married to her, had been one of the most faithful—couldn't in the long run withstand a woman who out of sheer malice had set her mind on destroying a marriage. Yes, it had been sheer malice, she said, drowning out Erika, who was trying to defend herself, sheer malice, for she, Erika, had never loved Karl, in contrast to her, Susanne, the whole town knew from the beginning that it was the house that she, Susanne, and Karl had built with their own hands that she, Erika, had in mind, the house and Karl's salary as a swim instructor, love had never entered into it.

"Erika, with an ominous expression, took the four bottom steps two at a time, put her hands on her hips, and said softly but forcefully that it was monstrous to accuse her of never having loved Karl, she had loved him a great deal, to the point of madness, namely, and only out of love had she decided to free Karl from the stranglehold of a hysteric, a drinker who had converted the greater part of his hard-earned swim instructor's salary into Zirbengeist and had almost succeeded in transferring her own self-destructive urge to Karl, the good man.

"Holding on to the banister Susanne descended three more steps, balled her free hand into a fist, and cried: Free, don't make me laugh, in her greed she, Erika, had taken Karl's every last cent, it served her right that she was left with one cross-eyed and one crippled daughter, though her daughter's spinal deformity clearly didn't keep her from walking hand-in-hand in the pedestrian zone with the rube that she, Erika, had taken as her second husband, it was being shouted from the rooftops that the spinally deformed daughter was involved with her mother's husband.

"After Erika had come five steps closer to Susanne and the two were separated by only three steps more she said that did it, she had had enough, she would no longer listen to her, Susanne's, vulgar aspersions, after all—and with this she turned briefly to me—after all, she had a witness who would testify to what a slanderer her husband's first wife was. She, Susanne, could consider herself lucky that she, Erika, had no desire to lay hands on a pitiful alcoholic, otherwise she would have scratched her drunken eyes out, which from an aesthetic point of view, at any rate, would not have made a great deal of difference.

"At this Susanne took the three steps remaining between them and with a cry of rage fell upon Erika and began pulling her hair. I stood up and was about to cry out when the telephone rang, and as I picked up the receiver the two spitfires stopped their altercation, assuming the caller was Karl. But it wasn't Karl, it was Norma Jean calling from Eureka, asking me to tell Karl that she finally had found a therapist for the children whom she felt could cure them of their bedwetting, but he didn't come cheap. When I answered Susanne and Erika's impatient questions by truthfully saying that it was Norma Jean from Eureka I was speaking to and not Karl, Erika ran down the stairs, grabbed the receiver from my hand, and began yelling at the Californian, saying what was she thinking, bothering Karl about her brats long-distance after all these years, brats who already as babies were so ugly that the people of Garmisch-Partenkirchen who happened to glance into their baby carriage crossed themselves in shock at the sight.

"Susanne, who in the meantime had staggered down the last few steps and across the rustic rug to the telephone to stand next to Erika and nod vehemently, now grabbed the receiver and said that though she and Erika differed on many things, on this point they were in total agreement—she, Norma Jean, who had bewitched Karl with her high diving, should leave him in peace once and for all and find a Californian dumb enough to take on her, Norma Jean, and the two brats. As far as she, Susanne, and Erika were concerned, she, Norma Jean, shouldn't dare return to Garmisch-Partenkirchen, for she, Susanne, and Erika would use all their influence on Karl and all the respect they enjoyed in Garmisch-Partenkirchen to see to it that she, Norma Jean, and her brood were driven out of town posthaste.

"Before I could tell Norma Jean when she could reach Karl again at home, Susanne hung up the phone. Far from continuing their dispute the two ladies sat down at the coffee table and Susanne ate the rest of my piece of cheesecake and then turned to tell Erika it was delicious and ask whether she had baked it herself. Erika, mentioning her busy professional and musical activities, said no, she hadn't, adding that Karl had always praised her, Susanne's, cooking, she must truly have spoiled him in this area, she said, quite in contrast to his third wife, Norma Jean, who, as Karl had once admitted to her, couldn't soft-boil an egg, just imagine, couldn't even soft-boil an egg. Yes, she had heard that, too, Susanne confirmed, taking a sip of my coffee, Karl had spent untold sums of money in restaurants for the simple reason that Norma Jean's cooking was inedible. While the two of them entertained themselves with a lively discussion of Norma Jean's character I stood and went up the stairs to the larch wood room, took the statue of the Virgin Mary from Canterbury out of the closet in which I had stored it, set it on the chest of drawers, knelt before it, and wept."

Magdalena fell silent. In the meantime both the motorcycle and the sidecar had received a first coat of red paint. I stood up, took a step back, and looked at our work, but it was already too dark to give it a thorough check, and in the late dusk the bright red looked burgundy. Magdalena got up as well, blew a lock of hair out of her face, and wiped her forehead with her arm.

"Not bad, Reverend, not half-bad our mutual effort," she said. "Tomorrow we'll apply a second coat. You've earned your supper at any rate." And then she smiled slightly, adding, "And perhaps a good night's sleep as well."

Her casual comment catapulted me into a state of blissful anticipation. This woman offering me the most exquisite of hopes—was she the same woman who had knelt weeping in a rustically furnished room before a stolen statue of the Virgin Mary?

From the tool kit Magdalena took out smoked bacon, bread, and mineral water, and we sat down on the sleeping bag under the acacia to eat in silence. Her description of the little scene in the larch wood room had proven that she was not the hard-boiled sinner her actions indicated, which relieved me greatly. I could understand that she couldn't deal with Karl Danzinger's quite active past and found it amazing that she was so patient and understanding of people she didn't know, and that she took the time to listen to all the trials and tribulations and problems that of necessity accompany our lives in this world. Beside me in the darkness she cut thin slices of East Tyrolean bacon with her Swiss army knife, put them on a piece of bread, and handed it to me. I held the bread in my right hand and put my left around her shoulders. I felt her warm skin under the tight thin leather. She gave me a quick kiss on the chin and continued with her tale.

"I wept for a long time. They were frustrated, hysterical tears. Suddenly I felt totally out of place in this town, in this house, with these people who unmercifully were involving me more and more in their lives. After Erika had gone and Susanne had opened a new bottle in her pine-paneled room, I sat down on the sofa with the intention of thinking about my situation, but at that moment Karl walked into the living room and asked what was for dinner. Reverend, at this moment it became clear to me that my understanding and my sympathy were at an end. Nevertheless, if anyone had told me at that moment that I would kill Karl the following Sunday I would have said that person was crazy."

Magdalena put the bacon and bread down in the grass, drank a sip of mineral water, and handed me the bottle. Then she yawned and stretched out beside me on the sleeping bag. It had gotten so dark in the meantime that her face appeared to me only as a dark oval shape. I leaned my head against the trunk of the acacia and enjoyed the quiet, the darkness, and Magdalena's proximity. The water in the little brook trickled softly, and a cricket chirped. The sky filled with stars. Suddenly I felt a hand pulling at the sleeve of my dalmatic. When I didn't react the hand pulled harder, and I understood that she wanted me to lie down. I must have obeyed this wish, though I can't exactly remember what followed, or to put it more precisely, the memory of what followed is not of an intellectual but a solely sensory nature. My sensory nerves, my sensory nerve cells, were in full swing in their effort to transform Magdalena's plentiful supply of charms into stimuli and only my visual faculty appeared to be more or less uninvolved, as I soon closed my eyes. In terms of my aural impressions I remember the cooing, murmuring, gurgling, whispering, and humming sounds coming from Magdalena's mouth, a sweet music that swelled and subsided, a lovely melody that ebbed and flowed, crescendos of moans, decrescendos of sighs. At the same time my sense of smell registered fruity and floral aromas, and a fine odor of musk and vanilla penetrated my olfactory nerves as Magdalena snuggled up against me. My gustatory receptors classified the taste of her mouth as both sweet and bitter, and the taste buds buried in the side wall tissue of the papillae of my tongue perceived her skin as preponderantly salty.

But what knocked me almost unconscious was the intensity with which my touch receptors received the many tactile stimuli that Magdalena transmitted to me. As opposed to the night before, when I had felt Magdalena's caresses through stola, dalmatic, and alb, this time she slowly, slowly removed one layer of my clothing after another, until nothing else remained between her fingers and my skin. It was as if a hundred hands were caressing my epidermis, and my fingertips traveled over soft, warm, pliable planes, hills, hollows, and valleys, through small and yielding forests until they could no longer tell whether it was my own skin or Magdalena's. For her body was no longer covered by the second skin of her jumpsuit, and I no longer recall whether it was my hands or her hands that opened the long zipper, any more than I know how the bodysuit ended up in a small, delicate ball between us. So we lay there on the sleeping bag under the acacia on a warm summer night.

It was the Fall that followed the eating of the cherries, and while we sinned and sinned it kept passing through my head that I wasn't being expelled from any Garden of Eden with this *felix culpa*, this happy transgression, but rather I was being led into a little garden of paradise. At some point I fell asleep on Magdalena's breast.

The next morning I awoke to a soft touch on my forearm. I opened my eyes and saw that a small blue butterfly had landed on my right arm, which was draped across Magdalena's waist. I watched it until it rose up into the air to light again on Magdalena's cheek. She sighed softly and reached toward her face, causing the butterfly to fly away. Then she opened her eyes. I looked at her and thought, Today we'll put on a second coat of paint and soon we'll set off together, away from East Tyrol, away from Austria, to a warmer climate. They would find a successor for my parish.

"Good morning," said Magdalena. She stretched and stroked my forehead and squinted into the sun. She seemed to wake up immediately mornings. "Good morning, Reverend." She then once again put her finger to her lips. "Don't speak, Reverend. Don't speak before I tell my seventh story to its end. And I will tell it to you now." She sat up and then put my head in her lap.

"The following Sunday Karl and I took his jeep for an outing to our favorite place, Virgin's Leap. It was a sunny day in late autumn and the wind that was blowing was just as cool as the mood between us the last few days, a mood that could be traced back to Karl asking me in the larch wood bed exactly what it was we were doing in gymnastics class. Were it not for the fact that my body was covered with bruises, he said, he would never have believed my assertion that I was still attending it every Wednesday, for my agility still left a great deal to be desired and was nowhere near Norma Jean's flexibility and suppleness. On top of this I had slept badly, for a blue full moon had lit up the larch wood room in a ghostly fashion.

"Karl parked the jeep near Virgin's Leap and we spread out a blanket in the grass and ate the sandwiches I had prepared. My mood was not improved when Karl opened his sandwich and asked where the sliced pickles were, didn't I know that he only liked liver sausage with sliced pickles, and why hadn't I let Susanne make the sandwiches, Susanne had known what he liked for well over a decade now. In order not to start screaming at Karl I began to sing a song, an Alpine folk song that relates the story of a lovelorn girl and seemed appropriate for Virgin's Leap. Even before I finished the first verse Karl brusquely interrupted my song to say that I was totally out of practice, my mezzo-soprano was degenerating into an alto instead of lifting to soprano heights, a voice had to be trained just like a body, but I had been too much of a coward to join the Wetterstein mixed choir.

"Reverend, Karl wouldn't stop talking and I felt something dangerous, something uncontrollable, rising up in me, a kind of heat emitting from the center of my body. In order not to do something foolish I stood up and performed a few deep knee bends and walked around a bit on the hard tufts of grass at the edge of the cliff. Not long thereafter Karl was standing beside me, and put a hand on my shoulder to point with his other hand to a body of water shimmering greenly in the distance. That was the Eibensee, he said, the lake he and Norma Jean often raced in. He was a good swimmer, but Norma Jean had beat him by several lengths every time. It had thrilled him each time he watched her slender body cut through the clear water like a predatory fish, he said.

"Reverend, I swear to you that I didn't intentionally push Karl into the abyss. It must have involved some unconditioned reflex, some arbitrary automatic response of the organism to external or internal stimulus. With Norma Jean's name on his lips Karl stumbled over the grass-tufted edge of Virgin's Leap. He didn't catch any trees on the way down.

"I drove the jeep back to his house, went into the front yard, and under sidelong glances from Susanne, who was slumped against the green wooden fence, began removing first the hydrangea and then the potting soil from the sidecar. I then went up to the larch wood room and packed my few belongings in the gray rucksack I had bought in Garmisch-Partenkirchen. As I drove away Susanne leaned swaying over the wooden fence and gave me a shaky wave."

Magdalena stopped speaking and stroked my stomach pensively. At this moment we heard a crashing through the underbrush and, startled, I grabbed for Magdalena's hand. The time has come, was the thought that shot through my head, the heavily armed antiterrorist unit from Vienna has arrived. While Magdalena was telling me the disastrous denouement of the seventh episode they had surrounded the clearing and now were pointing their machine guns at us. At any moment a sharp voice speaking through a megaphone would urge Magdalena to give herself up.

The hazel bushes parted, causing yellow pollen to fly in all directions, but what stepped through the bushes was not Austrian antiterrorist troops, but two East Tyrolean gendarmes discreetly attired in gray, who were visibly taken aback by the sight of the naked kidnapper sitting under a

tree with the equally naked Catholic priest she had kidnapped lying in her lap. And behind the two upholders of the
law appeared, to my great surprise, the face of my sister,
Maria. This face, familiar to me down to its last detail, mirrored in rapid succession the most conflicting of emotions,
until it settled on an expression of profound amazement.
Then the small, thin mouth in this face opened and a single
word escaped it.

"Christian!"

What happened next took place very quickly. Shocked
out of a prompt reaction through sheer confusion, the gendarmes were incapable of drawing their pistols before
Magdalena could push me away, jump to her feet, and in a
single motion pull on the nun's habit lying in the grass, then
run over to the sidecar motorcycle gleaming redly in the sun,
swing onto the saddle, and take off past the elderberry bush
and down the bumpy path. The bullets the two astounded
East Tyrolean gendarmes fired after some initial hesitation
managed only to stir up a few clumps of earth and rocks of
the forest path down which Magdalena had long since vanished.

I turned my head and saw my sister, Maria, approaching.
All at once I understood what I had lost. I jumped up and
ran over to the path, looking in the direction in which the
motorcycle had disappeared. Not the least little bit of the
hem of the nun's habit, not even a small cloud of dust could
be seen.

"Magdalena!" I cried.

But then my sister was beside me, leading me carefully
back to the acacia tree and helping me into my clerical gar-
ments that were scattered about on the grass, one piece at a

time. Then she put her arm around me and slowly led me to the gendarmes' white Golf, which was parked some distance away. I took one last look back at the point on the horizon where the forest path disappeared over a hill.

Magdalena. She would be able to take care of herself. And I would keep the seal of confession, and not betray her.